# DROSSELMEYER:
# CURSE OF THE
# RAT KING

D1496193

PAUL THOMPSON

**DROSSELMEYER**
**Curse of the Rat King**

ISBN: 978-1-7372498-0-1

211 E. Louisiana St. Suite B
McKinney, TX 75069

This book is a work of fiction. Names, characters, and incidents are a product of the author's imagination or used fictitiously. Any resemblance to persons, living or dead, is entirely coincidental.

Printed in the United States of America

Design by Transcendent Publishing
Editing by DragonflyWings.Ink

# DEDICATION

For my best friend, Andrew.

# TABLE OF CONTENTS

# CHAPTER I

*"There will always be weak people. There will always be powerful people. There will always be tyrants until someone stands up and says, 'No.'"*

—Othar, First Wizard of The Order

Fritz awoke with a start.

He blinked and stretched, causing dollops of snow to fall over the edge of the roof and plummet three stories to the cobbled driveway below. The muffled plops echoed off the old, stone front of the orphanage.

The afternoon patch of sun was now gone, replaced by the blue-gray hues of evening.

Several floors below him, Dolph shouted his name, mingled with epithets and curses. His voice reverberated through each crumbling floor of the orphanage.

As Fritz scrambled to his feet, a small, gold pendant hanging from a leather strap fell from under his shirt. He tucked it against his chest, closed the threadbare layers over it, and cinched his coat tighter.

The residents of Ivanov's Home for Orphaned Boys were not permitted to own jewelry. If anyone arrived with anything remotely valuable, it was immediately confiscated and either sold or added to Ivanov's personal collection.

Ten years ago, when Fritz first arrived at the orphanage, he had hidden the coin-sized piece of gold in his mouth, fearful that his only family heirloom would be taken from him.

Nurse Galina had paid no attention to him then, choosing instead to coo over his infant brother, Franz. Her only words to him had been, "Not a talker, are we? Probably for the best."

Fritz couldn't make out the threats Dolph was currently hurling at him in absentia, but he knew the habitually drunk foreman would try to make good on all of them.

Headmaster Ivanov seemed uninterested in Dolph's treatment of the boys. As long as his coffers remained full from the orphanage laundry business, he stayed in his office high above the main workroom. From time to time, though, he would exit his lair, pace the balcony, and choose an unsuspecting boy. After climbing the twisting iron stairs for a meeting in Ivanov's office, the boy would return to his post a short time later with no explanation for his fresh bruises.

Fritz squeezed through the small window that led from the roof into the attic and picked up the sack of soiled linens that he should have delivered to the wash station hours ago. He raced down the stairs, around the corner, and plopped the sack down by the giant wash cauldron.

A gaunt-faced boy pushed the stewing clothes around a basin with a long stick in slow, repetitive circles. He jutted his chin toward the sound of the yelling.

Fritz sighed heavily and rounded the doorway into the large central room where stations of boys folded, ironed, and sewed articles of clothing for the wealthy citizens of the Central Kingdom.

"Here, sir," Fritz said.

Dolph squinted. The veins in his jaundiced eyes stood out against his leathered skin.

"Where've you been?" he slurred. Fritz made out the profile of a flask in Dolph's coat pocket. The large man teetered unsteadily.

"I'm sorry, sir," Fritz mumbled. "There was a problem in the washroom."

"A problem in the washroom," Dolph repeated, mocking him. The large foreman slapped Fritz with the back of his hand. The boy stumbled back, clutching the reddening patch on his face. "I don't have use for boys who don't work."

Dolph lumbered over to Fritz, his short, squat body more than double the size of the younger boy's emaciated frame. He leaned in and whispered, his alcohol-soaked breath making Fritz recoil, "Can your brother do that memorizing thing? Ivanov only needs one of you to keep records. Maybe we should send Franz up to Ivanov's to find out." Fritz stiffened. He reflexively looked over to where his younger brother stood at the end of a table, folding clothes.

Dolph followed his glance and then pulled Fritz in closer—his large, fleshy chest pushed up snug against Fritz's shoulder. "You got privileges because you're useful. Once you're not useful, you got no privileges." The large man stepped back and barked, "Franz! Get over here."

The ten-year-old looked up, frozen with terror.

Fritz felt his heart pounding. His breathing quickened.

Dolph screamed again, saliva flecking his lips. "Hey! I said get over here."

Franz inched toward him. He stopped just outside of the drunk man's reach.

"Your brother is slacking off on his duties," Dolph shouted to Franz. The room went quiet; all eyes shifted to the unfolding scene. "That means that every boy in this room …" Dolph turned in a clumsy circle, "has to do extra to cover for him."

Franz fought back tears. Fritz continued to look at his brother, trying to comfort him from several feet away.

"He disrespected you all," Dolph bellowed. "He disrespected me. And you know how my Da used to deal with us boys when we disrespected him?"

No one answered. He reared his fist back and swung. Fritz toppled sideways, cracking his head on a nearby table. He curled into a ball on the floor, clutching his wound. Warm blood oozed from the gash, covering his fingers in a slick, red film.

"My Da taught us boys right!" Dolph yelled and kicked Fritz's curled body. "We didn't disrespect our elders." He grabbed a nearby table for leverage and kicked again. Fritz cried out in pain as the boot connected with the lower half of his back.

"And you think because you got some kind of smarts that you're something special. Well, you're not." Dolph's crazed eyes went wide.

Fritz shielded his head and face with his arm.

"You're nothing!" Dolph yelled. He punctuated his speech with unsteady kicks. "And *you* … don't get … to disrespect … *ME*."

He lifted his leg, preparing to stomp on the prostrate boy, when a raspy female voice stopped him. "That's enough, Dolph." All heads turned toward the commanding tone. Nurse Galina descended the back stairwell, her wrinkled eyes, cheeks, and lips set in a pursed scowl.

Dolph inched closer to Fritz's prone body like a dog protecting his bone. "He started it."

"And it looks like you finished it," Nurse Galina barked back. She was nearly two feet shorter than the large man, but he backed up when she approached. "Are you satisfied with your victory over a sixteen-year-old boy?"

The two stared intensely at each other, locked in a silent power struggle. Dolph glowered, made a vulgar gesture, then plowed through a huddled group of boys as he stormed out the door.

Nurse Galina knelt by Fritz and patted his cheek until he came to. "Take him to the stacks, and let him rest 'til the end of shift," she directed three tall boys. "The rest of you get back to work!" she yelled to the room and the boys complied, scooting tables back into place, righting fallen piles of laundry, and continuing with their tasks as if they had never been interrupted.

The sharp staccato of her shoes punctuated the somber atmosphere as she ascended the stairs in the back and disappeared through the door that led to Ivanov's office.

Later that night, Fritz lay in bed trying not to move. His left eye, cheek, and lips were swollen. The bruising had settled into dark shades of purple and red. His head still pounded, and a high-pitched ring droned in his ears.

"Are you feeling better?" Franz inched closer to him on their shared bed.

"A little." He lied.

"A lot of boys got adopted today after shift," Franz said. He forced a meager grin but his own green eyes clouded over as he struggled to hold back his emotion.

"That's exciting." Fritz tried to encourage his brother. "We should be happy for them."

"Why didn't we get adopted? Will we ever get to leave?" Franz asked, now disconsolate.

"I don't know," said Fritz. "But it doesn't matter because we'll always have each other, and that's more than most people have."

Franz sniffed and wiped his nose with his wrist. "When I get big, I'm going to break Dolph's arm."

"You do that, Franz." Fritz winced and scooted farther under the blanket.

"Fritz, can you tell me a story?"

"I'm not really in a storytelling mood."

"Just a short one? The one Mom used to tell you about the knight and the dragon?" A single tear streaked down Franz's dirty face, and Fritz raised his hand to wipe it away. A jolt of pain shot through his arm.

"Ok. A short story. But you have to close your eyes and keep them closed."

Franz obeyed. Fritz closed his own eyes as he replayed a scene from his childhood in his mind. He was in a nursery. Franz was lying nearby in a white bassinet, and he was sitting on his mother's lap. Her dress was soft and warm from the sunlight beaming in through the window. The gauzy curtains swished gently in the breeze, and Fritz rubbed a curly strand of his own hair between his fingers as his mother read his favorite book. He could still see every line and color on the page, the shape of every letter still vivid in his memory. Even now, he imagined her soothing, tranquil voice reading to him as he told Franz the familiar story.

*A knight charged into a cave to battle a dragon living there. His shield melted in the dragon's flame, but he kept on fighting. His sword snapped against the dragon's hide, but he pushed on. He was too weak to wear his armor, so he shed it.*

*The sight of the knight in his underclothing caused the dragon to laugh. He laughed so hard that tears started falling from his eyes. The knight began to laugh with him, and they soon became fast friends. Once a week, the knight visited the dragon for dinner, and they lived happily as friends for the rest of their lives.*

Franz yawned. "Is the cave warm?"

"Yes," said Fritz.

"Does the knight get to eat until he's full?"

"Yes."

"I wish I was the knight."

Franz's breathing steadied, and he drifted to sleep. Fritz closed his eyes and saw his mom lean over and kiss him on his forehead. And then he, too, fell asleep.

Days later, Fritz sat folding a pile of sheets at one of the tables in the main hall. The swelling in his face had subsided, and the fuzzy shapes in his left eye were sharpening into clear images.

From his balcony high above the workers, Ivanov watched the boys with darting eyes. He flicked his tongue over his wrinkled lips, his spindly fingers wrapped tightly around the rail.

"Adrian, I would like to see you in my office." The sound of Ivanov's raspy voice made everyone freeze.

Adrian fixed his stare at the shirt he was folding and began to tremble. Dolph slapped the back of his head. "Headmaster wants to see you."

Adrian stood up slowly and reluctantly made his way to the back stairs. Ivanov walked into his office, and Adrian followed silently. When he closed the office door behind him, the workroom, already quiet, hushed to an unsettling silence.

A few moments later, they heard Adrian scream. There was a loud *thump* on the floor, and Adrian cried out again—this time, muffled. Fritz choked back the bile rising in his throat.

"Hey," Dolph yelled, cuffing a nearby worker. "Get back to work." The boys complied, wary of catching the larger man's ire.

A few moments later, Adrian descended the stairs and returned to work, his face streaked with tears. His right eye was already darkening with a bruise. Fritz rose from his chair and limped over to the young boy.

"Sit down!" Dolph yelled from across the room, but Fritz ignored him.

He knelt down next to Adrian and put his hand around his shoulder. Adrian flinched at the touch but calmed after seeing Fritz. "Are you ok?" Fritz asked him.

Tears rolled down Adrian's cheeks—a silent answer to Fritz's question.

"I. Said. Sit. Down." Dolph cast a warning glance then crossed the floor to Fritz.

Adrian buried his face in his hands and began sobbing.

Dolph grabbed the back of Fritz's shirt and started to shake him. "I said ..." Dolph began, but never finished.

Fritz dropped out of his overcoat, leaving Dolph with an empty piece of clothing and a shocked expression on his face. Before the lumbering man could react, Fritz turned and kneed him between the legs. Dolph grunted and dropped to the floor.

Fritz leaned over to Adrian. "I want you to go see Nurse Galina, ok? She will protect you."

Adrian moved from his seat, stepping over a pile of laundry.

"Franz!" Fritz called out. Franz ran over to him, giving Dolph a wide berth. "Take Adrian up to Nurse Galina. Tell her he needs help."

Without question, Franz obeyed and hurried to Adrian's side.

"Watch out!" Adrian screamed.

Fritz ducked instinctively, and Dolph's fist narrowly missed his head. Franz turned to run, but Dolph grabbed him by the arm. Fritz struck Dolph's face, but the blow barely stunned the large man.

Dolph grabbed Fritz with his free hand, raised him up, and slammed him down on a table. Fritz wheezed as the breath was knocked out of him. He searched nearby for anything to defend himself with, grabbed a hot iron, and held it against Dolph's head. The man recoiled, clutching his seared scalp, and swore.

Ivanov, alerted by the shouts and screams, exited his office to witness the melee from above. His tongue darted over his lips, leaving a wet slick over the cracked skin.

Dolph overturned a large table in front of Fritz and Franz, blocking their path. Fritz tugged his brother away from Dolph, but he was too slow, and the enraged drunk grabbed Franz's arm and twisted it until the boy shrieked in pain.

Fritz swung his fist at the large foreman to no avail. Dolph easily caught him by the wrist, twisting it until Fritz had to stand on his toes to keep the bones from snapping.

Ivanov paced from one corner of his loft to the other, his thinning hair falling in wispy strands over his face. "Dolph, bring them both up here."

Dolph dragged the boys up the stairs with little difficulty.

"Take Fritz to the box," Ivanov said, rubbing his hands together. His wanton gaze fell on Franz as he licked his lips. "Leave the young one with me."

"No!" Fritz screamed in protest and kicked as hard as he could. Dolph drove his fist into Fritz's gut and yanked him out of the office. As the door closed, Fritz saw Ivanov run his spindly fingers over the collar of Franz's shirt.

Helpless, Fritz cried, "Please, don't do this."

Dolph dragged him toward a small, upright cabinet at the end of the hallway. He opened the door and shoved Fritz into it. Fritz tried to jump out before the large man could shut him in, but Dolph punched him in the chest, and Fritz crumpled backward.

Dolph recoiled with a yelp and looked at the red welt forming on his knuckles. "What are you hiding under there?" He ripped open Fritz's shirt and fingered the gold pendant hanging from the boy's neck. "What's this?"

Dolph ripped the medallion free and scrutinized the small, gold charm. Fritz reached for the heirloom, but Dolph closed the thick wooden doors on him and dropped the lock in place.

The tiny prison, barely big enough to stand in, allowed no extra space for leveraging any kicks. Even if it had, Fritz wasn't strong enough to do any damage to the old, hardened wood. Fritz ran his fingertips over the surface of the door, knocking and crying out at intervals.

Dolph's taunting whisper could be heard just outside the door. "You know what's going on with your brother in there? Can't be very pleasant. Too bad you're locked in the box."

Fritz yelled in primal rage. As his anger grew, so did the volume of his scream. The sound soon turned into a rumble that shook the entire cabinet. His mind filled with a blazing white light. A small point of pressure began to build behind his eyelids. His fists began to burn as his feeble pounding on the side of the wooden cabinet deepened into quick, methodical thuds.

Dolph rapped on the door with his fleshy fists. "Shut up. I can barely hear what's going on in the office." He snorted at his own taunt.

Fritz stopped yelling. His vision blurred white and then snapped into crystalline focus. A force erupted from his body, pinning him hard to the back of the box.

The locked door exploded outward, hurling Dolph backward from the blast. Thousands of splinters pelted the walls on all sides of the cabinet.

Fritz bolted from the cabinet, his breath coming in ragged gasps as he raced down the hallway toward the sound of Franz's screams. He threw the office door open and Ivanov looked up, frightened by the sudden interruption. Franz lay helpless, his hair caught in Ivanov's spidery clasp. The young boy's face was red and his lip bloodied.

"Fritz, help!" Franz cried.

Fritz reached for Ivanov but before he could grab hold of the headmaster, another blast of energy shot out from his hands. The force knocked Fritz backward. Ivanov crumpled like a limp rope into a bookshelf and fell to the floor with a sickening thud.

Fritz's head felt fuzzy from exhaustion. His knees buckled, but he caught himself on a nearby chair. Franz rushed to his brother's side.

"We need to go," said Fritz as he fell forward, his strength nearly drained. Franz supported him with his shoulder, and they crossed unsteadily toward the back stairs.

Seconds later, Dolph crashed into the office, splinters embedded in his body. He stumbled over to Ivanov's desk and pulled out a pistol. Only the wealthiest families had guns and, even though Fritz had never seen one used, he was fully aware of what they did. Dolph aimed it shakily at Fritz and pulled the trigger.

The bullet struck Fritz in the arm, inches away from Franz's head. Fritz cried out and fell to the floor. An oozing stain of blood turned his shirt dark red. He struggled to stand. Franz pulled him to his feet, his eyes wide with terror.

Nurse Galina rushed into the office with Adrian close behind her. "What is going on?" She saw the growing bloodstain on Fritz's shirt and gasped. "Dolph! What have you done?"

Dolph ignored her. He pulled back the hammer, raised his pistol, and aimed it at Fritz's head. Nurse Galina jumped in front of Fritz just as the gun fired a second time. The acrid smell of gunpowder filled the room. Nurse Galina spun around, an arc of blood spewing from a gaping wound in her chest. She fell against a table, then toppled to the floor.

Fritz froze. The world was fading into a hazy gray, and the room began to spin.

Franz began to scream in short, loud shrieks.

"Stop screaming!" Dolph shouted. His crazed yellow eyes bulged and flecks of saliva pooled at the corners of his mouth.

Franz continued to scream.

Dolph gripped his head with both hands, then stumbled toward the distraught boy. As he advanced, he pulled out his knife.

Fritz groaned, unable to move in front of his brother.

Dolph moved closer, but a swirl of black and red smoke blocked his path, causing him to stop and gawk in confusion at the anomaly. The smoke materialized into a cape, and a figure rose up from beneath the mantle, tall and imposing. He had broad shoulders, salt and pepper hair, and a neatly trimmed beard. His face was stern and and his gaze intense.

He stepped toward Fritz and Franz, unfazed by the large man pointing a knife at his back. He closed the gap between them in a single stride and threw his cape around the two boys.

The office disappeared in a whirl of black and was instantaneously replaced by a wood-paneled room warmed by a crackling fire. The dingy interior of Ivanov's office had transformed into a spacious quarter with windows and a large, soft rug.

Franz stopped screaming, and his eyes glazed over. The copper tinge on his tongue from his bloody wound mingled with the earthy smell of burning wood.

The mysterious man shoved Franz to the side and tore the tattered pieces of cloth away from Fritz's arm. "Let's have a look at that." He studied the protruding skin.

Fritz's eyes rolled back into his head, and he slipped into unconsciousness.

# CHAPTER 2

"Fritz, are you awake?"

Fritz opened his eyes. His brother's "gentle" nudges felt like a bell clapper on his head. His mouth was dry, and his eyelids blinked slowly open. He squinted at the sunlight streaming through a large window next to his bed. Clocks of various sizes and styles decorated the room, all ticking in perfect synchronicity.

"Where are we?" he asked, rubbing his eyes. He noticed his brother's new clothes. "Where did you get those?"

"Boroda gave them to me," said Franz. "He also gave me this." He pulled a knife from the sheath on his waistband and grinned. "He's teaching me how to carve figurines."

"Boroda?" Fritz tried to shake the fuzz from his mind.

"Yes. He owns this house. He's been taking care of you for the last three days."

"Three days?" Fritz started.

"Yep." Franz helped Fritz stand up, then ran to the window and pulled both curtains wide open.

Fritz grimaced at the sudden explosion of light. When his eyes had adjusted, he joined his brother and peered out over a sprawling field covered in snow. A large forest lay beyond the field. Behind the forest, or

17

perhaps in the middle of it (Fritz couldn't tell), a purple mountain range blended into the brilliant blue sky.

"Where are we?" Fritz asked.

"Beautiful, isn't it?" a bass voice rumbled behind them. Fritz and Franz whirled around.

Boroda joined them at the window. "Let me check your arm." He pulled up Fritz's sleeve. "Healing very nicely. Bullet wounds are tricky to mend. You'll have a nice scar, but you should be ok." He pulled the sleeve down, but Fritz immediately pulled it back up and looked at his skin in bewilderment.

The gaping wound had closed, and a fully formed scar had taken its place.

"I never heal scars. They're good reminders of what we should have done differently." He pulled a pipe from his pocket, walked over to a chair, and sat down. "How are you feeling?"

"I'm confused, sir," Fritz said, rubbing his hair.

"As am I." He studied Fritz carefully and lit his pipe. "At least about a few things, but there's a little time for that. And please, call me Boroda."

Fritz sat on the bed, leaning against one of the posts. "Well, for starters, sir—Boroda—how did we get here? … And where is *here*?"

"You are on my estate; *where* is not important. *How* you got here is supremely so." Boroda straightened. "I transported you here by magic."

"Magic?" Fritz stared at the man to see if he was joking.

"Yes." He swept his hand and a tea cart appeared, full of sandwiches and cakes and a steaming pot of tea. He motioned again, and a chair materialized, catching Fritz in its path as it slid toward the table. Franz, unfazed by the display, darted forward and snatched several cakes, which he shoved into his mouth.

"Tell me about yourself, Fritz."

Fritz shook his head. "Magic, sir?"

"Yes, magic." He poured the hot tea into two mugs and added a block of sugar to one. "Who are your parents?" Boroda picked up the teacup with sugar and handed it to Fritz.

"Uh ... I don't quite know how to answer that," Fritz said, still processing. "They died when I was young. My brother was just an infant."

"How did they die?"

"In a house fire," Fritz said. "At least, that's what Headmaster Ivanov told me."

"Did he?" Boroda muttered to himself.

Fritz shifted in his bed. "Are you a magician?"

"I am a wizard, as are you."

"Me?!" Fritz guffawed. "I think you may have made a mistake. I can't do magic."

Boroda studied Fritz over the rim of his teacup. "I beg to differ."

He set the mug on its saucer and crossed a leg. "Tell me what happened the day you were shot. Spare no details."

Fritz started at the beginning of the day and ended with the appearance of Boroda. "And then I woke up here, very confused," he said.

Franz held two small sandwiches in his hands. His mouth was still full of cake. Boroda looked at the small boy and a slight smirk played at the corner of his mouth. "Franz, would you please give your brother and me a moment to talk?"

"Can I go skate on the pond?" Franz asked and then turned to Fritz. "Boroda has real skates that you clip to your shoes! I can skate all the way across without falling down!"

"Of course." Boroda moved two fingers with a casual flick. "Your coat and scarf will be on a hook near the back door."

Franz snatched two more sandwiches and skipped out of the room.

Boroda cleared the tea caddy with a wave of his hand. "Every wizard has a moment when their magic manifests, and they cast their first spell," he began. "We call this *the snapping*. Most wizards snap as a young child. They usually move a small item like a stick or a cup. An especially powerful wizard may cause a chair to slide across a floor. But because magic requires a lot of energy, a new wizard will experience extreme exhaustion. Some have tried to do too much too soon and died of overexertion. Magic is equal parts skill and restraint."

Boroda leaned forward. "You reduced a cupboard to splinters, sent a very large man tumbling down a hallway, and threw another grown man several feet into a bookcase with enough force to knock him unconscious." Boroda pointed at Fritz's arm. "All that, combined with the nasty gash on your arm, makes me wonder how you are even still alive."

"I don't know," Fritz offered apologetically.

Boroda shook his head. "I don't expect you to. But still, your ignorance doesn't change the requirements of magic." He trailed off, lost in thought, before returning to the conversation at present. "Have you ever been in contact with a magic item before?"

"I wouldn't know, sir," Fritz said.

"Have you ever worn any jewelry? Rings, pendants?"

"My parents gave me a charm when I was a boy. It was a small gold piece."

"Gold? Are you sure?" Boroda asked.

Fritz nodded.

"Then that wouldn't be it. Gold is not a magic metal. It cannot be enchanted."

"That's the only thing I've ever worn."

Boroda stood and motioned to a nearby wardrobe. He waved his hand and the doors opened, revealing a solitary outfit hanging on the rack. "Walk with me out-side. I need some fresh air."

Fritz put on the clothes and followed Boroda down the stairs and out the front door. The fresh snowfall crunched under their feet. They made their way beyond the front lawn to the side garden and walked through a small opening in a stone wall that led them to a wooded path.

"What do you know of the history of the Five Kingdoms?" Boroda asked.

"Almost nothing," said Fritz.

Boroda walked down the path at a leisurely pace as Fritz kept stride beside him.

"Many centuries ago, before the Five Kingdoms existed, the world was ruled by hundreds of smaller kingdoms. Some were good and served their people. Most were tyrannical and lusted for more power.

"These rulers were constantly engaged in war, killing whomever they needed to gain control. Over time, the kingdoms joined together in treaties and began to rise up against each other. These coalitions eventually became the Five Kingdoms: Northern, Southern, Eastern, Western, and Central.

"It was customary for a ruler to employ a wizard to advise them and help their armies in times of war. The rulers of the Five Kingdoms each retained a powerful wizard for this very reason.

"After years of mindless bloodshed, the five wizards met together in a secret enclave. There they formed The Order, with the express purpose of ending the wars and promoting peace among the nations. It was successful, and soon the nations engaged in commerce rather than battle.

"This group of wizards eventually voted in a sixth wizard to lead the group and act as an impartial judge and arbiter for the remaining five. From that moment on, The Order has consisted of six wizards: five to advise the rulers of the Five Kingdoms and one to rule The Order.

"The Order created six medallions from the rarest, most pure metals known to man. Each one has unparalleled ability to store enchantments and spells. The wizards who wear these medallions have access to unfathomable power.

"But it wasn't long before wizards started engaging in their own battles to vie for the vacant positions when wizards in The Order died. Some even murdered sitting members to take their medallion and seat in The Order.

"In an attempt to discourage this, the head wizard decreed that all sitting wizards must train an apprentice to succeed their master. To ensure that no apprentice would kill their master, apprentices were bound with a powerful spell called a Life Bond. While under its enchantment, no apprentice can harm their master.

"For centuries, this line of power has remained unbroken from master to apprentice. Each master, save the head of The Order, advises a ruler of one of the Five Kingdoms, and the apprentice trains under that master to take his place when the time comes."

Boroda stopped walking and faced Fritz. "I would like you to be my apprentice."

Fritz gaped.

"I will warn you, though: It's not an easy life. Wizards, like men, are prone to greed, envy, and lust. The main difference is that they have the aid of magic to pursue their desires.

"For this reason, we must rid ourselves of anything or anyone that can be used as leverage against us. We take on a new name, hide any trace of our true identity, and leave our friends and families behind."

Fritz stopped walking. "So, if I were your apprentice, I would have to leave Franz?"

Boroda didn't answer. He walked ahead slowly, and Fritz followed. "Do you want to learn how to use your magic?" Boroda asked him.

"Maybe," Fritz stammered. "I mean, yes. I don't know. I'm not even sure what all this is."

"But it does interest you?"

"Of course," Fritz said.

"Good," said Boroda, growing impatient. "Now, will you join me as my apprentice?" He held out his hand, but Fritz ignored it.

"Join you? As quickly as that?" Fritz winced. "I need some time to think this through."

"We don't have time, Fritz," Boroda said. "The meeting of The Order is tomorrow night and, for reasons I won't go into right now, they have given me an ultimatum: I must have an apprentice by then or risk removal. I'm afraid I can't wait long for your answer."

"If it means leaving Franz, then, no. I'm sorry; I can't do it," Fritz said, his shoulders drooping.

Boroda sighed. "Very well. I will take you and Franz back to the orphanage."

Fritz's breath caught in his chest. "We can't go back there. Dolph will kill me and Ivanov will … please, sir."

"You can't stay here. I'm sorry," Boroda said without expression.

"Please, there has to be another option," Fritz begged, stepping in front of Boroda. "I want to be your apprentice. I want to learn magic. I do, but I can't do it if my brother isn't safe."

Boroda's eyes glazed over, making him appear deep in thought. "I may have another option for Franz."

After a pause, he said, "I know of a family unable to have children of their own. He is a general in the Central Kingdom who reports directly to the Czar. They are a good family, and I can assure you Franz would be well taken care of.

"Be my apprentice, and I will see to it that they adopt him, but no one—and I mean NO ONE—can ever know of your relationship to him."

"Will I get to see him?" Fritz asked.

"For this to work, I would have to erase his memory. He won't remember you or the orphanage."

Fritz fidgeted. After a short time, he stopped. "You can promise me he'll be safe?"

"I don't make promises," Boroda said. "But I believe the family will protect him as their own. They are very wealthy. Franz would want for nothing."

Fritz fought back a lump in his throat.

Boroda spoke in a low voice. "Left untrained, your magic could kill you and those around you, but under my guidance, I will help you develop your power. With your abilities sharpened, you will be able to protect your brother from a thousand men like Ivanov."

Fritz met his gaze. His chest burned with renewed anger at the mention of the headmaster's name. "I'll do it. I'll be your apprentice."

Boroda breathed a sigh of relief. "Very good." He held out his hand, and Fritz shook it.

"There is much to do," Boroda said, after pulling his hand back. "I wish I could give you more time, but The Order meets tomorrow."

Fritz waited for his first instructions.

"I will go speak to the General and his wife about Franz." Boroda set off for the house and Fritz followed. "You will find your brother at the pond, skating. Say your goodbyes."

They stopped outside the gate in the stone wall.

"I will leave you here. The pond is that way, just beyond the garden." Boroda spun and vanished in a cloud of smoke.

Fritz stuck his hands in his pockets and walked toward the pond. Franz was skating slowly, wobbling back and forth, arms flapping for balance. He waved when he saw Fritz and nearly toppled on the ice.

Fritz called him over to the shoreline.

"Do you want to skate with me?" Franz yelled. "I think there are more skates in the shack."

He pointed to a small, wooden structure on the end of a dock close to where Fritz stood.

"No. Not right now." Fritz walked across the frozen surface to the shack and waited for Franz to join him.

"What's wrong?" Franz asked. "Do we have to go?"

Fritz held his hand out and helped Franz walk over to a bench. "I have to tell you something. I hope you can understand it, and I hope you won't be angry."

Franz removed his skates slowly.

"I've decided to stay and study with Boroda," Fritz said.

"Are you going to study magic?" Franz asked excitedly.

"Yes. But there's more. Boroda said there are bad men who will try to stop me by hurting the people I love. So, I need to leave you for a while, somewhere you'll be safe."

"How long?" Franz asked.

"I don't know," Fritz said. "It may be a long time."

"Where will you be?"

"Here. With Boroda."

"Then where will I be?" Franz clutched his skates close to his chest.

"Boroda knows a family who wants to adopt you. Just like when some of the boys leave the orphanage to be with new families. Franz, you're going to get a new family." Fritz tried to sound happy, but his voice caught.

"But you won't be coming with me?" Franz asked.

Fritz shook his head.

Franz sniffed and stepped back. "But you said we would always have each other."

Fritz hugged him tightly. "I will still be your brother. Nothing can change that. But this is a chance for you to have a mom and dad—and our mom and dad would have wanted that. They'll love you and take care of you. Can you do this? For me?"

Franz stared at Fritz, his green eyes glistening with tears. He nodded and wiped his nose on his scarf. "Promise you will come and see me?"

Fritz glanced down at his feet. "Whenever I can."

They walked back to the house in silence but once seated by the large fire in the kitchen, they began to imagine what life would be like living with rich parents. Fritz made up stories about furniture made of cake and fountains of hot chocolate that Franz's new family probably owned. Franz laughed and pantomimed jumping in and swimming in such a pool.

Boroda returned in a hiss of mist, interrupting their levity, and strode over to the fire. "The General and his wife are very eager to meet their new son."

Franz held on to Fritz in a tight hug.

Fritz pulled away and looked him in the eyes. "Goodbye, Franz. I love you."

Franz lifted his chin bravely and stepped back from Fritz. "I love you, too."

Franz took Boroda's outstretched hand and in a flash of smoke, they were gone.

# CHAPTER 3

While Fritz waited for Boroda to return, he wandered around the house poking his head into each of the many rooms, opening closets and drawers, and running his fingers over the clothes and trinkets he found there. From thick fur coats twice the size of Fritz to delicate silk gowns speckled with semiprecious jewels, each room held treasures more glorious and exquisite than he had ever seen.

Every room also had multiple clocks, either on the walls or standing tall in a corner. Some were ornate, some plain, but each one clicked in perfect unison. Even the greenhouse had clocks with vines and flowers carved out of exotic wood. When the hour struck, several clocks chimed and little figurines popped out to mark the time.

Fritz discovered the kitchen and helped himself to a board laden with cheese, cured meats, and sandwiches. A wooden clock with crooked hands and poorly painted numbers hung above the counter. Every other clock spun with exactitude, but this one ticked asymmetrically.

With bread in hand, Fritz climbed on the counter to get a better look at the crude gouges carved into the wood. They looked as though they were made from a carving knife. Although he had never learned to read, he recognized the gashes as letters, something he'd seen on tags labeling sacks of laundry at the orphanage.

He traced the letters with his hands and committed them to memory. Fritz hopped down and cut a piece of meat from the charcuterie and retraced the shapes from the clock into the bread crumbs on the board.

His ability to memorize shapes, colors, and details had made him an invaluable asset at the orphanage. Even though he couldn't read words on tags, he could remember the shapes of the letters and which clothes belonged with which name.

On long winter nights, the boys in his bunk room enjoyed his unique ability of describing, in vivid detail, pictures he had seen and stories his mom had told him years ago.

He had stuffed another bread and cheese sandwich in his mouth when Boroda's voice made him gasp. He coughed until the food dislodged from his windpipe.

"Fritz, time for your first lesson." Boroda motioned to a chair at the kitchen table.

Fritz swallowed. "Yes, sir. Um, did Franz seem ok?"

Boroda ignored the question and folded his hands loosely on the table. "There are several types of magic to learn about: magic of the will, spells, enchantments, and potions."

Boroda dug in his pocket and handed him a small charm. Simple, twisting strands of silver hung on a thin, silver chain.

"Before I forget, this is your apprentice charm."

Fritz took it.

"I will teach you to store spells later, but for now ..." He stood up. "Let's learn to travel."

"To where?" Fritz asked.

Again, Boroda ignored him and continued his lesson, glancing at Fritz intermittently. "Traveling is a magic of the will. To travel, you need only picture where you want to go and then will your body to be there."

"Can I go anywhere?" Fritz asked.

"If you've been there before, yes."

Fritz frowned. "I've only been to the orphanage, and I'd rather not go back."

"Then go to your room."

Fritz shrugged, closed his eyes, and pictured the room. Nothing happened.

"Do I have to say something?" he asked, opening his eyes.

"No. You have to will yourself to be there," Boroda said. "What you do is often preceded by what you want, so, if you WANT to go to your room, then you WILL go to your room."

Fritz closed his eyes again.

He tried to envision his room but could only picture Franz opening up the curtains. His breath quickened, and a lump rose in his throat.

"Open your eyes," Boroda commanded. He was holding a small box in his hand. "Your brother gave me something to give to you—to remember him by."

The box vanished as Fritz reached for it.

"It's on your bed now," Boroda told him, holding out his empty palms.

Fritz felt a pang of loneliness and turned to race up the stairs but, instead, ran headlong into his bedpost. He fell back on the floor, clutching his eye as smoke drifted away from him and faded into nothing. Ignoring the excitement of his magical accomplishment, he scrambled to the bed and tore open the box.

It was empty.

"Congratulations. You traveled." Boroda stepped from his own plume of mist.

Fritz held out the box. "There's nothing in here."

"No," Boroda said. "But you traveled to it because you wanted it. What did it feel like?"

Fritz scowled. "It felt like a tug. My whole body sort of lurched."

Rubbing a bump over his eye, he said, "I also hit my head on the bedpost."

"Because you were running when you traveled," said Boroda. "If you're running when you travel, you'll be running when you arrive. That's important to remember—especially if you're traveling anywhere near a cliff."

Fritz looked confused.

"Magic of the will does not expend much energy," Boroda explained. "You could travel or use telepathy all day and be fine. It does, however, require knowledge. Take shape-shifting, for instance."

Excited, Fritz interrupted. "I can shape-shift?"

"Yes," Boroda said. "But it requires a lot of knowl-edge or else you end up as a fox with unusable leg joints or a fish that doesn't have the correct lungs to breathe underwater."

"Oh … ok." Fritz hesitated.

"You must first know how tendons and sockets work before you can shape-shift into something that uses them."

Boroda reached out toward a chair and pulled his hand back. The chair slid across the floor and stopped behind Fritz. "Kinesis is also a magic of the will, but it's a power you need to be smart about."

He made another motion. A chair materialized a few feet behind him and slid to his position. He sat. "Moving things requires lifting their weight. Lifting will drain your energy quickly if you try to muscle your way through the lift—sort of like what you did with Ivanov. When you destroyed your prison box, threw Dolph across the room, and rag-tossed Ivanov, your magic required the same energy as if you'd done all of that physically. That's why you passed out and nearly died from the energy drain."

Fritz sickened at the memory. "What's the point of moving something by magic if it takes the same energy to do it naturally?"

Boroda cocked his head. "Mostly for convenience." He pulled out a thick, silver medallion. "But, if you find yourself in a situation where you need to move heavier objects, we can store energy in these."

Fritz held up his minuscule charm.

"Yes, even in that," Boroda told him. "You'd be surprised at how much can fit in an apprentice charm."

Fritz turned it over in his hands.

"It is a very pure silver—much different from the sort that women use for jewelry. It acts as a sort of purse you can put …"

The clocks chimed in unison, and Boroda stared at the wall in disbelief. He clapped his hands and rose up from his chair.

"I'm afraid that is all for your training today. We have to get your clothing before the shops close," he said.

"At a real shop?" Fritz brightened.

"As opposed to?" Boroda questioned him.

Fritz wiggled his fingers. "Why wouldn't you just …"

"I can't create something out of nothing," Boroda answered. "Wizards have to buy stuff just like everybody else."

He swirled his cloak around them both. They vanished, then instantly reappeared in a darkly lit stone courtyard. Boroda walked out of the enclosure and down a small alley.

Fritz followed, small tendrils of mist trailing behind.

"Where are we?" Fritz puffed, trying to match Boroda's stride.

"Anadorn Market." Boroda walked to the end of the lane and turned up another street with a set of steep, uneven stairs. "There are shops here that are used to dealing with our kind." He motioned to a clothing shop, and Fritz walked up the cracked steps to the aged, oak door.

They entered the clothier's shop, and a short man with an unusually long salt-and-pepper mustache greeted them. "Welcome to Worthington's. How may I assist you?" he asked in a slow, nasal tone.

Boroda addressed the short tailor. "I'd like five outfits, general-purpose; one dress, with hat and cape; and five uniforms, two winter and three summer."

The man nodded and waddled over to Fritz. "The uniforms will be for St. Michael's, yes?"

"Yes," Boroda replied. "And top priority on the dress outfit."

The tiny man nodded again and motioned for Fritz to hold his arms out by his sides, then directly above his head. Fritz mimicked his movements, expecting him to pull out a tape like the boys who sewed garments at the orphanage.

The short man squatted, and Fritz followed suit. For the next several minutes, they stood in various poses, moving their arms and legs in all directions. Finally, the short man twiddled his mustache and announced he was finished.

Boroda handed him some coins. "Deliver them to the market on Anadorn Square."

"Is he not going to take my measurements?" Fritz asked as they hurried down the alley.

"He did," Boroda replied curtly.

"But he didn't have a tape. How is he going to get accurate measurements without a tape?"

Boroda didn't respond.

"And what is St. Michael's?" Fritz was breathing hard, caught between a walk and a jog.

"It's the school you will be attending at the start of this next term."

"School?" Fritz said. "I've never been to school. I don't even know how to read."

Boroda stopped and turned toward Fritz with a slow, grinding turn on his heels. "You never learned how to read?"

Fritz shook his head. "They didn't think it was important at the orphanage. None of us learned how to read."

Boroda rubbed his eyebrows and groaned. "This certainly complicates things."

"I'm a fast learner," Fritz assured him.

"We'll worry about that later," Boroda sighed. "For now, let's concentrate on getting ready for the Life Bond ceremony tomorrow."

He stopped outside a shoe shop. "In here."

A large sign decorated in colorful swirls and scrolling letters read: Pemberton's Shoe Shop.

The door chimed, and a shopgirl poked her head out from behind a stack of boxes on the counter. "Can I help you?"

Her eyes widened in recognition. She jumped up and bowed to Boroda. "Pardon me. I didn't know it was you. Are your shoes in need of repair?"

"No," Boroda said and motioned to Fritz. "He needs shoes. Dress, general-purpose, and school."

The girl bowed and faced Fritz. "I'm Sadie."

"I'm …" Fritz began but was cut off by a sharp cough from Boroda. "Happy to make your acquaintance."

Her eyes twinkled. "Let's get you some shoes."

Sadie measured his feet and rambled aimlessly from one topic to another while fitting him. Fritz enjoyed hearing her speak. He hadn't met many girls and the high, tinkling laughter in her voice made him smile.

When she was satisfied with the fit and styles, Sadie packaged up the pairs of shoes and smiled broadly at Boroda and Fritz. "That should do it!"

Boroda paid her.

"Anadorn Market?" Sadie asked.

Boroda nodded, put his hat back on, and exited the shop without a word.

Fritz smiled and waved timidly at Sadie. She returned the gesture with a bright grin and brisk shake of her hand.

Boroda stopped for an early supper in a nearby pub. The air smelled heavily of cooked meats and beer, and the strains of an ill-tuned instrument wafted from a far corner.

Behind the bar, an enormously large woman with darkened stubble on her chin stopped wiping the counter when they entered. Her bulbous nose covered much of her face, and her lips, painted bright red, were half hidden by it. She motioned to a table in the back.

Boroda sat down at the dimly lit table.

Fritz collapsed in the seat opposite him. "I am worn out."

"Yes," Boroda said. "We will need to work on your fitness. All in due time, though."

The large woman approached with two beers and two bowls of stew, then turned and left.

Fritz devoured the food and guzzled the beer. Boroda took a few bites, then slid the bowl away. Fritz eyed the stew.

"Tomorrow, when we meet with The Order to perform the Life Bond ceremony, I need you to follow a few instructions."

Fritz nodded slowly, keeping his eye on the neglected bowl of stew. Noticing the distraction, Boroda sighed and shoved his uneaten bowl to Fritz. The boy snatched it and began to eat the second bowl in wolfish bites.

"I need you to follow a few instructions," he reiterated. "Do not talk unless you are asked a question ..." Boroda paused. "And even then, I will let you know if you can answer. In the world of magic, knowledge is the most powerful tool you have. The wizards of The Order and their apprentices will try to get as much information from you as they can. Your job is to give them as little as possible."

"Don't you trust each other?" Fritz scraped the bottom of the second bowl and looked at the bar, wondering if he could get another.

"Yes and no," Boroda answered. "The Order is unified in the purpose of keeping the Five Kingdoms from entering war.

"We are, however, less unified about how The Order should be run. Like any other institution, there can be ... power struggles."

Fritz noticed Boroda was particularly careful choosing his words.

He continued, "Secondly, do not trust the other apprentices. You may tell them your name and only that."

"My real name or my fake name that I don't have yet?" Fritz reminded him.

Boroda drank the last of his beer and set the mug down. "Your fake name. I will assign you one. Later, though."

Boroda stood, left a coin on the table, and they both walked down the labyrinth of alleyways back to the courtyard where they had arrived in a puff of smoke.

"See you at the house," Boroda said and disappeared.

Fritz was about to follow Boroda when someone spoke.

"Hello."

Fritz jumped.

A small boy sat atop the crumbling fountain wall, dipping his feet in the icy water. He was covered in a thick layer of soot, and his bright blue eyes sparkled like two small sapphires set on black velvet.

"Are you a wizard?" he asked with wonderment.

Fritz stood, stunned, unsure of what to do. "Who are you?" he finally demanded.

"I'm Toby," the boy said and held out his hand.

Fritz shook it warily. "Nice to meet you, Toby."

"Are you a wizard, like your friend?" he asked again with a smile.

Fritz didn't know how to dodge the question. "No. Not yet. But I'm not really supposed to talk about it."

"That's ok," Toby said as he swung his feet around, sliding them into a pair of shoes barely attached to their soles. "I won't tell anybody. Where did the other man go?"

Fritz furrowed his brow. "I honestly don't know."

Toby stood to his feet gingerly and grimaced.

"Why are you putting your feet in the water, anyway? It's freezing," Fritz said. He held out his arm so Toby could use it to balance while he slid his other foot into the shoe.

"I deliver coal for Mr. Nickleson, but my shoes aren't very comfortable. After I finish all my deliveries, I like to soak them here for a little while. It's more comfortable in summer."

"It may be time to buy some new shoes."

"I don't have enough money yet." Toby brightened. "If you need anyone to deliver anything, you can find me at Mr. Nickleson's. I'm really cheap."

Feeling awkward, Fritz stiffened. "Ok. Sure. I'll do that."

Toby shook Fritz's hand again, then he raced out of the fountain plaza, singing a bouncy folk tune.

Fritz closed his eyes and stepped forward. He felt a tug and when he opened his eyes, he was looking in the mirror perched atop his dresser. The fog thinned out around him and melted away.

Boroda knocked on the door, causing Fritz to jump a second time, then entered the room unbidden. He crossed to the closet, opened it, and waved his hand. An outfit appeared. It looked similar to Boroda's except the vest was gold instead of crimson.

"Wow." Fritz marveled at the fabric.

"This is your apprentice's outfit," said Boroda. "Wear this tomorrow for the ceremony. The rest should be here in time for school."

Fritz rubbed the fabric of the cape between his fingers. The thick, silky texture slid smoothly back and forth with a satisfying *swish swish*. A moth darted from the folds. Fritz slapped at it, but it evaded his hand and flapped up to the light.

"Watcher, curse the bugs," Boroda swore under his breath. "One of the downsides of living in the country, I'm afraid."

"It's ok," Fritz said. "We had way worse than that at the orphanage." He held up his clothes. "Thank you!"

"You're welcome," Boroda replied warmly. He turned to leave. "I sent word to The Order earlier today. They are eager to meet you. I have some other items to take care of, so I'll be gone the rest of the evening. Get some sleep. We have a full day tomorrow."

Fritz watched Boroda leave. He waited a few minutes, then checked the hallway to see that the wizard was gone. He closed the door quietly behind him and padded down the stairs.

In the kitchen, he pocketed some cheese and a large chunk of bread and let himself out the back door to the garden. The full moon bathed the snow-covered fields in a creamy light.

While eating his snack, Fritz meandered a bit and ended up near the old shack on the dock. Light leaked through the decrepit ceiling and illuminated messy piles of fishing equipment, boat paddles, and several pairs of ice skates. He swallowed back the lump in his throat and picked up the skates Franz had worn the day he left.

He hoped his brother was happy. He ran his hands over the tired leather. A tag sewn into the tongue interrupted the otherwise smooth surface, and Fritz squinted to look at it. There were shapes drawn in faded ink.

Fritz leaned in closer.

The marks were the same as on the clock in the kitchen. Not as jagged since they'd been drawn rather than carved, but definitely the same shapes.

He wondered if the clock had belonged to the same person who owned the skates. He set the skates down, closed the door, and walked back toward the house.

In the distance, the windows shone golden. Fritz breathed in deeply, then took a large, deliberate step. He saw the field and garden blur, and his room materialized in front of him. He laughed out loud, his voice bouncing off the wooden walls of his bedroom.

He climbed into bed, reveling in the excitement of the day.

He was a wizard now.

# CHAPTER 4

Fritz jolted awake early the next morning.

Boroda's voice boomed through his room. "Time to get started. Breakfast is in the kitchen."

Fritz fell out of his bed in a tangle of sheets. He twisted around, looking for Boroda.

"Are you up?" the wizard asked again. Fritz followed the voice and saw Boroda's head floating in his mirror in a hazy greenish specter.

"I am now," Fritz stammered.

Boroda's face vanished, and Fritz flopped backward on his bed. He yawned and stretched, slowly tracing the outline of his room with his eyes.

"Now, Fritz!" Boroda's voice cut through the air like a cannon firing. Fritz scrambled out of bed, grabbed his clothes, and rushed to get dressed.

Over breakfast, Boroda said, "I have some work to attend to this afternoon, so we need to address your training this morning. During the week, it will be after school—in the afternoon and evening."

Fritz listened as he spooned large piles of scrambled eggs into his mouth.

"Merciful Watcher, Fritz. Stop eating your food like a starving dog." Boroda looked away.

Fritz lowered his fork, unsure of how to proceed. He looked at his plate of food and then back to Boroda.

Boroda sighed, picked up his fork, and held it out for Fritz to see.

Fritz switched his grip to match Boroda's.

Boroda scooped up a small piece of egg and brought it to his mouth.

Fritz shoved his fork under a large pile of egg and began lifting it, but it slammed back onto his plate as if driven down by a large hammer.

Boroda shook his head and demonstrated again.

Fritz stiffened his posture and copied Boroda's movements. He watched Boroda's face for expressions of approval.

"I want you to eat a piece of human-sized food," Boroda told him.

Fritz picked up the fork and lifted a small amount of food to his mouth.

"Very good," Boroda muttered. "Now do that every time you eat."

After several more bites, Fritz set down the fork and announced that he was full.

Boroda stood up. "We need to train. Follow me."

They walked through the house and into a large, empty room. Boroda waved his hand, and a table with two chairs appeared.

"Some of the most necessary skills for a wizard to have are pushing, pulling, lifting, and traveling," Boroda began.

"You've taught me to travel already," Fritz reminded him.

Boroda shot him a look of annoyance. Fritz closed his mouth and gave Boroda his full attention.

Boroda waved his hand, and a teacup filled with hot water appeared on the table. "Traveling is not just something you do with your body. You can travel objects to and from places as long as you know where they are and where they're going. If two objects try to take the same space, then the preexisting laws of physics take over."

Fritz nodded, although he was confused.

"As a wizard in The Order, I have access to an infinity room, as will you," Boroda continued. "In it, you can store any number of objects to be traveled for your use."

He pointed to the teacup.

"I have water that is in a perpetual state of boiling, and I have a teacup, and when I traveled them here, I combined them."

Fritz leaned in to study the cup carefully.

Boroda eyed him. "It's a normal cup, Fritz. There is nothing magical about it—only the manner by which it was brought here."

"Can I do that?" Fritz asked, pointing to the cup.

"Yes. Later."

Boroda continued explaining the technique of grabbing objects and pulling them, pushing them away, or lifting them. He had Fritz practice the same moves on the teacup with his hands behind his back. Fritz became frustrated each time the water sloshed out, but Boroda refilled it.

Fritz tried using the pushing spell to hold the water still when he moved it, but Boroda snapped his fingers.

"Smart," said Boroda, "but that's cheating. Move the glass so that no water spills out."

They worked for a few more hours until Boroda was confident Fritz could move the teacup in any direction without spilling the water.

Boroda stood up. "On your own time, I want you to practice that until moving something smoothly is second nature."

Fritz sighed. "Yes, sir."

Boroda whisked the table, chairs, and cup out of sight. "To Anadorn Market," he announced, then disappeared in a puff of smoke.

Fritz followed. The fountain was blanketed in a fresh layer of snow. A gust of wind whipped around him. Fritz rubbed his arms, trying to warm his goose-pimpled flesh.

Standing beneath the stone arch leading out of the plaza, Boroda asked, "Where is your coat?"

"In ... my ... closet," Fritz said in halted bursts.

"Travel it, and let's go." He turned and left the plaza.

Fritz envisioned his room, his closet, and then his coat. He reached out to take it from the hanger, and he felt the woolen garment in his hands. A moment later, he threw it around his shivering shoulders. Face beaming, he glanced up at Boroda, but the man had already turned away.

Fritz sighed, then followed Boroda down the alley to an open plaza. Empty carts were arranged in neat rows in the center, and shops lined the perimeter of the market square.

Boroda walked into a large corner shop.

The shop owner, a squat man with dark hair around the sides of his head, nodded to Boroda but said nothing.

Boroda walked to the back of the shop and opened a door. He led Fritz up a steep stairway to a long hallway spanning the entire length of the shop below.

The hallway was empty, save for six doors set at equal intervals. Boroda walked to the second from the last one and whispered something. The doorknob turned with a click. He held it open for Fritz.

The room had a wooden floor like the rest of the shop, but the walls and ceiling looked like an open sky at night. It wasn't just dark; it had a spaciousness that conveyed the absence of light. Fritz felt his head begin to spin.

"What is this?" Fritz asked with breathless wonder.

"It's an infinity room," Boroda said. "There are only six in existence. One for each member of The Order."

Fritz walked around staring at the unending rows of objects. "Where did all of this come from?"

"These objects were collected by the first wizard who occupied my position in The Order, and every subsequent wizard has added to the collection." Boroda bowed slightly.

"How far back does it go?" Fritz asked and ran his hands over a wall full of axes and spears.

"As far as you need it to," said Boroda.

"You can travel any of this when you want it?"

"Yes. If I can remember where it is, anyway," Boroda confessed. "As an apprentice, I tried to memorize all the contents in here but there are centuries worth of accumulation."

Fritz wandered around, gasping at each new find. He threw open the lid of an old trunk and yelped.

Boroda looked in his direction. "Ah, yes. That is one of many trunks of gold collected by an especially greedy predecessor of mine. Called himself Palan. Squirreled these trunks all over this place because he didn't want anyone to find all his wealth."

"Is he dead?" Fritz asked, running his hands through the treasure.

"Yes," Boroda said and motioned to the trunk of gold. "But his greed and selfishness are still evident."

"So why did he hide all this treasure if he can't use it?" Fritz asked.

"It's not enough for selfish people to have something. It must be theirs—and theirs alone—to use." Boroda glanced at his watch. "We don't have much time. I want to show you some important sections of the infinity room."

Fritz followed him past mounds of items to a newer-looking section.

"Here are my weapons," Boroda said. "You will be learning to use them."

Fritz picked up a sword and swished the thin blade back and forth.

"You will need to memorize that section." Boroda pointed to another area of the room. "Here are my food and provisions. I have meals delivered regularly and preserved so that the food never spoils and always remains at the correct temperature. You will also need to memorize this region."

He walked over to another area. "Furniture. You will need to memorize this zone as well."

Fritz glanced away from the food and took in the furniture.

"And finally, here." Boroda pointed to an empty spot on the floor lit with a muted, yellow glow. "This spot is a special space. Anything that is touched by this light can travel to us without us needing to see what's there. It is used mostly for mail and special deliveries."

"Like my clothes and shoes?" Fritz asked.

"Exactly," Boroda said. "Whether you know what they look like or not, you can travel them."

"Who puts them here?" Fritz asked.

"The only person allowed in here, outside of the wizards of The Order and their apprentices, is the shop owner. All deliveries go through him."

"Aren't you afraid the other wizards will steal your stuff?" Fritz asked.

Boroda looked away. "Each door is locked and can only be opened with a secret word."

"What's the word for your room?" Fritz asked.

Boroda answered flatly, "If you need to come in here, I will let you in."

Fritz blushed and silently purveyed the objects around him. Boroda glanced at his watch and hastily exited the room.

As they made their way back to the fountain plaza, Boroda pointed out important shops and stores to Fritz. Anadorn was a sprawling network of alleys, courtyards, and squares. Each section had a distinct personality and Fritz, who had never been outside Ivanov's, consumed the sights and smells with a voracious appetite.

"See you back at the house," Boroda said once they had stepped into the fountain plaza and disappeared. Seconds later, Fritz joined him in the kitchen.

"I want you to travel as many objects from the weapons section as you can remember and put them in the training room," Boroda said. "I have some work I need to attend to."

Fritz asked, "Is there enough space in the training room?"

Boroda raised an eyebrow. "If you can fill the training room, I'll give you one of Palan's chests of gold."

Fritz dropped his jaw. "Really? Ok. Deal."

"When I get back, it will be time to go to the Life Bond ceremony."

"What about my fake name?"

Boroda cursed under his breath, then waved Fritz off. "I'll figure that out." He vanished, and Fritz made his way to the training room.

Fritz closed his eyes and pictured the racks of weapons in vivid detail. Swords, shields, axes, and spears appeared in the room, filling an entire wall. He waved his hand and stacks of arrows, bows, whips, and clubs clattered to the floor in piles in front of him. Weapons rained down until there was no space left.

There were still racks of weapons left in the infinity room, but Fritz figured this would satisfy Boroda and win him the chest of gold.

He traveled back to his room, took off his coat, climbed into bed and dozed until Boroda called him through the mirror. Fritz jogged down the stairs and met him in the den.

"A few things before we go to the ceremony." He motioned for Fritz to sit down in a nearby chair. "Tonight, The Order will ask you to do some things that may sound ... strange." He took out his pipe and lit it. "I need you to obey without question."

Fritz agreed.

"After the Life Bond ceremony, you and the other apprentices will travel to the garden until The Order finishes some business at hand. The other wizards will have tasked the apprentices with gaining any information about both you and me." Boroda lowered his voice. "I cannot stress the importance of telling them nothing."

"Yes, sir," Fritz answered.

Boroda leaned forward and punctuated each word. "Tell. Them. Nothing."

Fritz nodded, and Boroda dismissed him. He returned to his room, dressed, and waited to be called. He passed the time pushing, pulling, and lifting a mug of water he'd traveled into his room.

Boroda appeared in the mirror, and Fritz slung the mug into the wall in shock.

"Meet me in the foyer," was his only command.

Fritz descended the stairs to find Boroda pacing impatiently.

"Is this ok?" Fritz asked, adjusting his cape.

"What?" Boroda glanced at Fritz. "Oh, yes. You look fine. Let's go."

He wrapped his arm around Fritz, and they melted into a misty portal. They emerged in a small, circular glen in a dark forest. There was no moon present, but a pale light bathed everything in a soft, blue glow. The outer ring of the glen had six concave openings with one large chair per space. Each chair nearly filled the opening, though each was shaped in a wildly different fashion.

"Go to the center of the ring," Boroda commanded Fritz. "Do not speak unless spoken to."

Fritz obeyed, and no sooner had he planted himself in the center of the field than he heard a rush of wind. He turned and saw a tall, thin man standing in front of an oak tree, dressed in coal black clothes that glinted in the faint light. His sharp nose matched the contour of his cheekbones.

He sat down on an ornate divan covered in purple cushions with golden tassels and gilded iron legs. He studied Fritz but said nothing. He raised his eyebrows, as if surprised or amused by something he saw.

From another cloud of mist, an olive-complexioned boy about Fritz's age appeared near the oak and stepped to the side of the purple couch, standing at the ready. He had jet black hair and a lean, muscular build. His outfit and robes were gold and purple, like the cushions. He stared resolutely forward except when he caught Fritz's gaze—then he gave the slightest wink.

A clump of ash trees to Fritz's right fluttered, and he saw a slender, elegant lady in a long, shimmering blue dress take a seat in a gleaming silver chair. Its tall spires jutted out in sharp spikes. Her hair was pulled up loosely atop her head, only a few shades whiter than her pale skin. Her lips, in stark contrast to her ghostly pallor, shone dark red.

From behind the lady, a young girl, also roughly the same age as Fritz, stepped beside her master. Her dress was the same color blue, save a line of silver trim along the bottom. Her hair was blonde, but Fritz could see a streak of white running down the outside edges.

Behind him, a girl giggled. He spun around to see who had made the noise. A plump lady with auburn hair, glowing pink skin, and a dress made of hundreds of ribbons sat in a throne of woven tree roots and vines. The vines snaked through the roots, and flowers were beginning to sprout.

She smiled warmly at Fritz, and he heard the girlish giggle again. Next to the woman, in a flowered dress, stood a girl with a large, peach-colored flower held firmly on her head by a network of small vines, pinning her hair into a wild braid.

Fritz blinked and switched his focus from the girl with flowers to the girl in blue. The latter returned his look with a steeled glare.

They were identical.

The one girl sniffed a flower on her lapel and nodded as if to confirm his suspicions.

Two shrouds of mist wafted from the remaining alcoves as the last two wizards arrived with their apprentices.

One was a large man with a long, red beard. His biceps were the size of most men's heads and covered in runic tattoos. He had an axe in one hand and a shield slung over his back. His protégé was only slightly shorter, a little smaller, and had no facial hair. His bright red hair hung in a series of knots and matted patches around his head. The younger boy brandished a large hammer.

The large wizard plopped into a throne made of hewn wood riveted together with bronze straps.

The final wizard wore a close-fitting kimono with an embroidered dragon, the head at her shoulder and the scaly body wrapped around her midriff, ending at her waist. Her hair was pulled neatly into a bun, and two black sticks held it in place. She sat in a chair made of sharp, black wood, polished brightly and padded with red material. She made no attempt to catch Fritz's attention but stared at the first wizard seated on the purple couch.

Her apprentice stepped out from behind her. She was dressed in a half robe and silk pants with similar colors but no dragon. Her hair hung loosely around her face.

Fritz caught his breath. She was beautiful. He looked away hurriedly when she met his gaze. His face flushed red.

The first man by the oak tree stood to speak. He raised his hands and intoned, "This meeting of The Order is convened. We meet to add a new wizard to our ranks and bind him to Boroda." He stretched out his right hand. "Let us cast the spell of Life Bond and commence the apprenticeship of …"

The head wizard stopped and looked at Fritz. "What is your name?"

Fritz turned to look at Boroda.

Boroda grimaced, then stepped forward quickly. "His name is Drosselmeyer."

The older wizard hesitated but continued. "Let us cast the spell of Life Bond and commence the apprenticeship of Drosselmeyer to Boroda."

On cue, each of the six wizards approached Fritz, chanting words to a spell. They formed a ring and began walking clockwise around him, hands working in synchronized movements. After a full rotation, Boroda joined Fritz in the center and took his forearms.

As the wizards circled, a slight wind whipped the leaves on the forest floor. It grew stronger, kicking up dust, the tree tops swaying in the gusts. An unseen energy pulsated through Fritz's chest, washing over him in a cold wave.

Boroda released his grasp.

Fritz wiped his palms.

The older wizard held his hand up, and a scimitar appeared. The sword floated to Fritz and hung motionless at his shoulder. "Take the sword, young Drosselmeyer, and strike your master."

Fritz took the sword and searched Boroda's face for affirmation.

Boroda didn't move.

He swallowed, raised the sword above his head, and swung. The sword hit something hard but didn't make a sound. He opened his eyes, slowly at first, then widened them. The sword was not lodged in Boroda's skull as he was expecting. It was inches from Boroda's face, suspended with a haze of purple light along the edge.

Boroda breathed out a long sigh of relief.

Fritz continued to hold the sword in his hands, mouth open, breathing hard.

Boroda took the sword and handed it back to the older wizard.

The older wizard vanished the sword and addressed the other wizards, still circled around Boroda and Fritz. "It is complete. The Life Bond spell is cast."

The older wizard turned to Fritz. "Welcome to The Order, young Drosselmeyer. I am Borya, Chief Wizard of The Order. This is my apprentice, Faruk."

Faruk waved and smiled openly.

"I am Glacinda, wizard of the Northern Nation. This is Gelé," the lady in blue said and bowed slightly.

"I'm Eric, wizard of the Western Nation." The giant man stepped forward and shook Fritz's hand with a crushing grip. "This is Andor. He's deaf. If you want to talk to him, he can read your lips, or he does know a spell he can put on you to help with the hand signs. Or you can ignore him. Your choice."

Fritz extended his hand to Andor who shook it, grunted, and stepped back.

"Welcome," the flowered lady said excitedly and wrapped her arms around Fritz in a warm embrace. "We weren't sure if Boroda was ever going to pick a new apprentice," she cackled. "I'm Sylvia, wizard of the Southern Nation, and this is Vivienne."

Vivienne cut in. "You guessed it right earlier. She's my twin sister," she said, pointing at Gelé.

Fritz listened as Vivienne continued in rapid, rambling fashion.

"Yes, we are identical. She's older by two-and-a-half minutes. No, we don't feel it when the other one gets hurt. And yes, we have switched places with each other but only at school." She giggled. "We always get those questions, so it's just easier to answer them all at the beginning."

"Isn't she precious?" Sylvia cut in. "I am so glad Boroda finally got someone. After the last one ..."

Boroda cleared his throat loudly.

Sylvia gasped. "Oops. Oh, I always talk too much. Watcher, help!" She leaned in closer and whispered loudly in Fritz's ear, "I hope you can loosen him up a bit. He is so uptight." She winked at Boroda who remained stone-faced.

"I am Hanja, wizard of the Eastern Nation." The wizard in the kimono stepped forward, interrupting Sylvia. "This is my apprentice, Marzi."

Marzi put her right fist over her heart. "I am honored to meet you."

Fritz felt his face warm. Instinctively, he glanced down at his feet.

"The Order has business to attend to," Borya announced. "Faruk, please take Drosselmeyer to the garden and make him feel welcome."

Without a word, Faruk crossed next to Fritz and hooked his arm around him. A moment later, they were standing under a wooden arbor under a bright, sunny sky. Around them, stretching as far as Fritz could see, hedges grew in shapely mazes, disappearing into the blue horizon.

Several couches, sofas, and loveseats formed a circle around a stone table. Faruk plopped unceremoniously onto a couch and motioned to a nearby chair.

"Have a seat," Faruk said in a much brighter, more relaxed manner. "We all hang out here while The Order discusses business."

"Where is here?" Fritz turned in a circle to view the terrain.

"No one knows," Vivienne said and skipped next to him. "We've all explored this place, but none of us has ever made it through the maze."

"I got the farthest," Gelé bragged. She tossed her braid back and sat down opposite Fritz.

"She had the idea of leaving a marker, then traveling to it each time we visit here," Vivienne said. "Brilliant, right? She's the smart one."

Gelé blew her sister a kiss.

"Why not just cut straight through the shrubs?" Fritz asked after taking a seat.

"Ask Andor about that," Vivienne said and skipped over to where he was sitting cross-legged on a circular, flat pad. Andor made some movements with his hand, face full of expression.

Marzi spoke up, eyes on Andor. "He says, 'I broke my axe on the first swing. The enchantments are very strong.'"

"Andor is deaf," Vivienne chimed in.

"Eric said that," Fritz responded. "Do you all sign?"

"Only Marzi." Vivienne tucked her legs up under her and pulled a flower from her belt. "Sylvia would feed me to her plants if I let anyone put a spell on me."

The others expressed their agreement.

"Did Hanja not mind?" Fritz asked.

Marzi's eyes narrowed. "It is none of your business what my master thinks."

"Sorry," Fritz apologized. "I didn't know."

There was a brief lull in the conversation.

"Watcher, this is awkward," Vivienne said. "There are a few things you need to know about being an apprentice."

"Vivienne!" Gelé warned.

"What?" Vivienne asked pointedly. "He's obviously new at this, and it's best he's prepared."

"Stop talking, Vivienne," Marzi said, head bowed.

"Prepared for what?" Fritz asked.

"You're an apprentice," Vivienne said heatedly. "That means you belong to your master."

Gelé twisted uncomfortably. "Faruk, tell her to stop."

Faruk shrugged but didn't say anything.

Vivienne continued, "They can do whatever they want to you because you belong to them."

Fritz looked around the group. Each person nodded in agreement, Marzi the last to add her assent.

"Like, they hit you?" Fritz asked. He was used to being hit at the orphanage, but he didn't see Boroda as the hitting type.

Faruk snickered and began to toss a ball up in the air and catch it. "Yeah. Hitting is one thing."

Vivienne's flower began to sprout and small thorns poked out from the stem. "Has Boroda told you what happened to his last apprentice?"

The group grew tense.

"I didn't know he had one," Fritz said uneasily. "What happened to him?"

Vivienne shrugged. "I don't know. Only Faruk was around then."

"I was six years old," Faruk said and began tossing his ball in the air again. "I don't even remember his name."

"I heard Boroda killed him," Vivienne said casually.

"Vivienne!" Gelé cautioned.

"Killed him? Why would he do that? They're not allowed to do that, right?" Fritz looked around the group.

No one spoke. Faruk continued to toss the ball and the pat-pat-pat of the toy striking his palms only accentuated the quiet.

Gelé was forming a cube of ice in her hand, and Vivienne stretched tendrils from a vine along the table. Even Marzi shifted uncomfortably behind a book she had begun reading.

"They can't kill us … right?" Fritz asked with more desperation.

"I'm afraid they can if they want to," Faruk said and held the ball.

"But why would they want to?" Fritz pulled his arms close to his body, hoping none of the others saw his hands trembling.

"If they find another apprentice they think is more powerful than you," Gelé said.

Fritz stared down at the table as if in a trance.

"The longer you last, the less likely it is, though," Faruk added. "It's not worth their time to train someone from the beginning after investing years of time in you."

"Being an apprentice is hard work," Vivienne added. "Don't screw up, and you'll be fine."

"Stop talking, Vivienne," Marzi warned from behind her book.

"They're more likely to just injure you," Vivienne said, ignoring Marzi.

"That's enough, Vivienne," Marzi said again, more forcefully.

"Hanja broke Marzi's fingers for letting Andor put the sign language spell on her," Vivienne burst out.

Marzi stood up quickly, her hand glowing red with magic. "I said: Stop. Talking."

The other apprentices all shot to their feet, hands full of glowing magic at the ready.

Fritz backed away slowly.

Marzi and Vivienne locked eyes.

"Everyone, calm down," Faruk said, and his hands returned to their normal color. "Drop your spells," he coaxed.

The girls didn't move.

"Vivienne, you should stop talking," Faruk told her.

Vivienne pouted, then dropped her hands and sat down. "Fine. But I think it's only fair that Drosselmeyer knows what he's getting into."

The others sat down, but the air was tense for several minutes.

"Who's ready for school?" Gelé broke the silence.

She was creating a little ice sculpture in her hand. It was a curvy spiral that branched off like a tree but ended in spikes.

"Can't wait!" Vivienne jumped in.

"What is it like?" Fritz asked.

"Great," Faruk offered. "You should try out for the rugby team or water polo. Do you swim?"

Fritz shook his head.

"Did Boroda tell you about the rules for us?" Vivienne asked. She was cheerful again, and her flower was twisting itself into a small carriage and sprouting decorative buds.

"He hasn't told me anything," said Fritz.

"No magic whatsoever allowed," Gelé said.

"Not like you could, even if you wanted to," Vivienne added.

She looked at Fritz and mouthed, "There's a spell."

Fritz didn't understand but nodded his head.

"The school grounds are protected by some very powerful enchantments," Faruk said and tossed the ball to Fritz.

Fritz tossed it back.

"No one can perform magic on school property, and if you try …" He threw the ball to Fritz. "You will get called before The Order and probably removed."

"What is 'removed'?" Fritz asked.

"Kicked out of The Order. Expelled," said Vivienne.

"How would anyone know?" Fritz asked, amazed.

Vivienne pointed to Faruk.

"Borya has a Celestine," Faruk said. "It's a device that registers every time someone uses magic. It's how all of us were found when we snapped."

The twins looked at each other and put their hands over their hearts. "Twins snap together." They spoke in perfect unison.

"But we use magic all the time," Fritz wondered aloud. "How could anyone keep track of it?"

Faruk switched sides on his couch. "There are certain alarms for different types of magic, I guess. Borya says it alerts him differently when a child snaps versus when someone attempts to use magic at St. Michael's."

Fritz nodded slightly. "Ok."

"It's confusing," Faruk said glibly, "but it's one of the many responsibilities of the Chief Wizard."

"What was your snap?" Vivienne asked excitedly.

Fritz stammered, "I, um. It was nothing huge."

"You don't have to answer," Marzi said bluntly from her chair.

Vivienne rolled her eyes. "Drosselmeyer is really long and awkward to say."

Andor signed to Fritz.

"He says it's hard to spell," Marzi translated. "He's giving you a sign name."

Andor held up his hand, fourth and fifth fingers creating a circle on his thumb, with the first and second finger wrapped together in a twist.

"I'm calling you Drossie," Vivienne said with her signature giggle.

"Ok. That's fine, I guess." Fritz hoped nicknames weren't against the rules.

"Where are you from?" Vivienne pressed.

Fritz tensed up.

"Leave him alone, Viv," Gelé said. "Can't you see he's scared of you?"

"Ugh! I am so bored. We should play a game or something." Vivienne swung her feet over the arms of her chair and made her flower roll forward a few inches on twisting, viny wheels.

Faruk leaned backward and plucked a flower bud from a nearby plant. "Hey Viv, catch!"

He tossed the bud in her direction, and she stopped it midair and twirled it around her fingers. The bud opened up and grew a stem, followed by leaves.

Gelé dropped her ice sculpture and waved her own magic over the flower. A static-charged cloud grew, then turned into a block of ice.

Faruk waved his hands and a tiny ball of flame hovered over the block of ice, causing drops of water to dribble off the top in a miniature rain shower. The drops collected on the flower petal and showered on the stone table below.

"Marzi!" Faruk called out.

Marzi caught the drops in midair and started floating them in various patterns around the flower. Each droplet began to pulse with light—first white, then changing to blues and reds and yellows.

"Your turn, Drossie," Vivienne said, concentrating.

Fritz glanced around. All he had ever moved was a teacup. He didn't know anything else. In a panic, he reached out with his magic and felt something coarse and light. He clapped his hands together, unsure of what would come with it.

Dirt flew through the air, pelting everyone and glomming onto the floating topiary. It doused the fire, turning the cube to mud and coating the flower in a layer of filth.

Everyone yelled out in surprise, except Andor. He brought his hands together in a thunderous clap and crushed the flower, then let it drop, limply, to the table. He laughed and applauded, then signed to Marzi.

"No," she said aloud and signed. "We're not doing it again."

The apprentices complained loudly as they brushed dirt from their clothing.

"Drossie! What exactly were you trying to do?" Faruk asked, rubbing his eyes.

"Point of the game is to beautify the collaboration," Gelé scowled. Her dress was caked with mud and every brush of her hand left a long streak of smeared dirt.

Andor smiled and gave him the thumbs-up, then hit his head a few times to knock the larger chunks of mud from his red hair.

"In his defense, you didn't tell him the rules," Vivienne pointed out to Faruk.

"I'm really sorry," Fritz managed to stammer.

"No worries, buddy." Faruk smiled at him. "We're just giving you a hard time."

Gelé huffed.

Fritz was about to apologize again when a bell tone sounded inside his head. It vibrated his skull.

Everyone else jerked their heads up.

"The master calls," Faruk mumbled. He waved and vanished with a puff.

Marzi and Andor disappeared as well.

The twins blew each other kisses and dematerialized.

Fritz took a brief moment to enjoy the fresh garden air before traveling back to his bedroom. Standing at the foot, he fell backwards, arms outstretched on his bed, and wrapped the luxurious coverings around himself like a linen cocoon.

"Please meet me in the kitchen," Boroda requested from his mirror.

"Yes, sir," Fritz said half-heartedly. He rolled out of bed and walked downstairs, where Boroda had a tray of sandwiches waiting on the table. Boroda sipped out of a mug, then pushed the tray toward Fritz and looked at him expectantly.

Fritz shoved a sandwich in his mouth and tried not to make eye contact.

Boroda tapped a finger on the table. "Tell me how it went with the other apprentices."

Fritz told him about the garden, the school, and then the muddy end to the game. He left out the part about the apprentices' abuse. He wasn't sure how much he trusted Boroda yet.

"Don't worry too much about the mud," Boroda reassured Fritz. "They were just trying to test how powerful you are. It's good to play it close to the chest."

Fritz put his unfinished sandwich on his plate. "Where did the name 'Drosselmeyer' come from?"

Boroda set his mug down. "I was unprepared for your name. I am sorry." His voice trembled. "In time, I hope to tell you, but for now, I'm afraid you'll have to be fine with the mystery."

"Ok," Fritz agreed. Then he added, "Don't forget, I don't know how to read, and school starts …"

A loud thud interrupted him. The house shook, and a few clocks twisted on the wall.

Boroda's eyes narrowed.

"What was …" Fritz began to ask but was immediately shushed.

Boroda closed his eyes and held out his hands. He vanished.

Ten seconds later, he appeared again, eyes wide and teeth bared.

"Run, Fritz. Get out of here!" he yelled. A broadsword appeared in his right hand, and his left glowed silver with heat.

"What's wrong?" Fritz's voice quivered as he stood up. The house shook, and the ceiling timbers buckled. Pieces of plaster sprinkled onto his head but before he could brush them off, the kitchen wall ripped from its foundation.

A large ape raised the section of wall above its head and roared, exposing a row of sharp teeth.

Boroda sidestepped a falling chunk of plaster as he shot a beam of silver light at the creature's chest.

The long gash bubbled, leaking foamy streaks of blood, then healed itself, leaving a knobby scar in its trace. The animal wailed in pain and threw the wall at Boroda.

Boroda launched forward with blazing speed and sliced the monster's leg with his broadsword.

The ape swung at Boroda, missed, and shattered the wall behind him. The wall crumbled, and the floor above sagged.

Boroda hit the ape in the chest with another beam of light, and it screamed a loud, piercing wail.

Fritz cupped his ears. He reached out to a heavy pan on the far wall and flung it with all of his might at the giant creature. The pan struck the animal in the head, but it barely registered the attack.

Boroda flew around the ape, vanishing and reappearing, striking and burning, but the wounds closed almost as fast as he inflicted them.

The ape flailed its arms wildly, roaring with a deafening howl. Boroda miscalculated the trajectory of the swinging arms and traveled directly in the path of the creature's meaty fists. The ape struck him, and he flew across the room like a discarded piece of rubble.

Boroda slammed into a wall, and his sword clattered to the ground. He struggled to his feet.

The lumbering creature hopped toward Boroda with knuckles dragging the ground. Bloody foam collected near its mouth as it reached out to grab the stunned wizard.

Fritz focused on Boroda's sword across the floor. He reached out for the sword and pulled it to him. The blade shot toward him, and he ducked just in time to dodge the pointed tip. It stuck into a wooden beam inches above his head.

The animal followed the sword's path and fixed its red eyes on Fritz. With trepidation, it inched toward him, its head snapping back and forth. In a shrieking tirade, the ape smashed through the ceiling, creating space to stand at full height.

Fritz pulled the sword from the wall and ran at the beast.

The ape cocked its right hand for a blow.

Fritz rolled under the swing, leapt up from the floor, and plunged the sword into the ape's calf. The animal's flesh closed around it, and Fritz tumbled away, swordless, but out of the creature's reach.

Boroda righted himself and pushed on the sword with a burst of energy, driving it deeper into the muscle.

Fritz searched the room for something he could use to protect himself and remembered the piles of weapons in the training room. He reached out, traveled in a crossbow, and fired it at the ape.

The animal whimpered and grabbed for the arrow, but another arrow, loosed from a crossbow in Boroda's left hand, stuck tight in the other calf.

The ape recoiled and snapped the arrow, but in that time, Boroda had traveled to the exposed second floor and, spell in hand, delivered a long, burning gash down its neck.

The creature screamed and pounded frantically, ripping flooring, timbers, and rock from their foundation.

Fritz looked up and saw his bed upend and splinter on the first floor as the animal smashed at the walls and floors separating the now demolished interior.

He traveled in a pile of daggers and sent them hurling at the ape in rapid succession.

The ape turned and charged him, grabbing a clock and throwing it at Fritz.

Fritz tried to stop the oncoming clock with a push of magic and felt the energy drain from his body. The clock fell short and crashed to the floor.

The ape charged at Fritz, but another flash of silver heat dug into its calf. Boroda traveled inches away from the animal, stabbed the exposed flesh with a dagger before it healed, and then traveled to a broken joist hanging from the second floor.

The knife detonated, and the leg exploded in a shower of flesh and bone. The beast fell and took the remaining west wall with it. The cold night air rushed in.

Boroda continued to fire short bursts of magic at the downed animal. It swatted at him with quick strikes. One landed, and Boroda spun in the air and hit a post.

Fritz traveled in a longsword and ran, screaming, at the monster. He dodged its right arm and gave himself a push from the floor. He sailed up toward the second floor and planted his feet sideways on a bent wall.

His vision started to get fuzzy.

With the last bit of his energy, he shoved off the wall toward the monster's head. He twisted midair and struck the ape just over the right eye, digging the sword in with as much force as he could muster.

The monster let out a guttural roar and threw Fritz away. A force stopped him from impaling on a cracked wooden beam, then dropped him to the floor. He glanced up just in time to see Boroda look away and charge the downed ape.

Boroda appeared directly over the creature's head, blood running in rivulets down his face. His medallion was glowing through his shirt. With an enraged scream, he shot a bolt of electricity at the ape's exposed leg, eliciting a full-throated howl, and using both hands, sent a red hot stream of magic down the ape's throat.

The molten shaft seared the fur surrounding the mouth, and the acrid smell of burnt flesh and hair filled the room. Fritz stumbled back from the intense heat and shielded himself behind the overturned kitchen table.

The ape stopped roaring, and its sides glowed red. The flesh on its stomach bubbled, then melted open as its bowels, now red hot, oozed to the floor.

Boroda slowly descended to the ground, watching it cautiously. His medallion faded to a muted orange.

"What was that?" Fritz gasped.

He tried to stand but his strength gave out, so he leaned back against a shattered beam.

Boroda studied it more closely. "An enchanted creature of some kind." He wiped the blood from his face. "Looks to be an ape."

"Did it come from the woods?" Fritz asked. He swallowed hard, trying to stop the bile rising in his throat from escaping.

"No. This creature didn't come from any woods." Boroda examined the ape's hands.

Fritz tried to breathe through his mouth and tasted the liquified intestines. "So how'd it get here? Are there more?"

Boroda stepped away from the animal, whispered a few words, and the corpse began to fold in on itself. Smoke billowed until all that remained of the animal was a small pile of dust on the floor. Then he answered, "I don't know how it got here. Until now, I thought you were the only one who knew where I lived."

"I didn't send it," Fritz said, folding his arms.

"I know." Boroda turned in a circle and surveyed the damage. "That means someone else has figured out where I live."

"Do we need to keep watch or something?" Fritz struggled to keep his eyes open. His breath came in labored gasps.

"We can't stay here." Boroda looked around. "Travel to the courtyard in Anadorn Market. Wait for me there."

Fritz gave a weak thumbs-up, then passed out.

# CHAPTER 5

The first thing Fritz noticed when he woke up was the pounding in his head. He kept his eyes shut to mitigate the pain. The smell of musty bedding didn't help the already tenuous situation in his stomach, and nausea waved over him.

Fritz heard Boroda in the room, talking softly with someone. He couldn't see them. Their voices were deep and cavernous, as if they were speaking in a large, empty room.

"We're safe for now," Boroda said. "Just keep your eyes open and warn the others."

"Do you think the attack was intentional?" the other voice asked.

"I'm almost positive," said Boroda.

"Did the Black Wizard show up?" asked the other person.

"No. It was only the ape, but that was bad enough," Boroda said. "Had my apprentice not been there, it might have ended differently."

"How is he?" the other voice asked.

"He will sleep many hours more," Boroda said, turning to look at the bed.

Fritz breathed steadily.

"Something is different about this one," Boroda said. "A normal wizard, this newly snapped, would have died or fallen into a coma after using that much magic."

"Will he help our cause?" the man asked.

"Perhaps," said Boroda. "I may tell him in due time, but he has a lot of training ahead of him."

The other person grunted.

"Tell the others to be on guard," Boroda said. "I will be working on protective charms as quickly as I can, but in the meantime, watch your back."

The other party promised to spread the message as Boroda placed a small hand mirror on a nearby table.

Fritz closed his eyes the rest of the way; his exhaustion overtook him, and he slept again.

Boroda shook Fritz awake. The curtains were open and the sun glowed with afternoon warmth. He handed Fritz a cup. "Drink this."

Fritz sat up and took the mug of warm tea.

"It's best not to breathe in through your nose when you drink it, but it will help you heal," Boroda said.

Fritz drank the liquid, even hazarded a taste, but didn't think it was any worse than the food at the orphanage.

Boroda helped him up, traveled in some clothes, and sat in a chair while Fritz dressed.

"It's time to train," he said.

"Already?" Fritz gaped. The contents of his drink began to warm his muscles, and his headache dulled to a mild throb. "Is it safe to start again so soon after that attack?"

Boroda shifted in his seat. "After that attack, your training is more important than ever. I have taken all necessary precautions and believe we will be safe going forward." He moved his hand, and their current room melted away. They both stood in a large empty room with racks of weapons along the wall.

Fritz felt his energy return. His muscles loosened, and he stretched out his arms while turning and looking in amazement at the new room. "Where are we?"

"One of my other houses," Boroda said.

"How many houses do you have?" Fritz asked, eyes wide.

"Too many."

He led Fritz through a series of calisthenics, weights, and basic gymnastics. The wizard demonstrated each move and ran through the routines with grace and ease. When Fritz needed to rest, Boroda pumped out a few more reps on his own.

Fritz was sweating profusely when Boroda finally called an end to the session. He clutched his sides and bent over, trying to catch his breath.

"A wizard's magic is, in many ways, connected to his own fitness levels," Boroda warned. "Being fit is the best advantage you can have in a battle." He wiped a small mist of sweat from his head with a rag and dropped the cloth. It vanished before it hit the floor. "Powerful wizards have lost to lesser people because they weren't physically fit."

Fritz nodded that he understood; sweat flung from his nose with the movement.

"Let's see how good your memory is." Boroda motioned to the empty table. "Travel in some tea."

Fritz closed his eyes and walked the long corridors of the infinity room in his mind. He saw a shiny teapot, steam curling out. He looked around until he found a tray with sandwiches and cakes as well. Then he picked some mugs from a shelf.

He motioned to the table and the pot, cups, tray, and food appeared in a heap.

Boroda steadied a teetering cup. "You have to arrange them on the table."

Fritz grabbed the pot, but Boroda stopped him and pointed to his own forehead. Fritz concentrated on the pile before him and began to rearrange them using only his mind. Once satisfied, he looked up and smiled at Boroda.

Boroda twitched his face, and all the ingredients snapped into a formal setting. Napkins, plates, and a small tray with sugar and milk appeared beside the tea.

Fritz sighed and grabbed a sandwich.

Boroda laid a napkin in his lap. "Magic is art in motion. It is manipulating the very fiber of existence and shaping it to your will. But to learn magic properly, you must first be able to see it."

He sipped his tea and continued teaching. "Wizards have the ability to see magic and construct spells and enchantments with them. We call this *magic vision*. When activated, you can study the shapes of every magic spell and enchantment around you."

Fritz blinked and then gasped. Thousands of swirling lights and shapes filled his vision. Some moved quickly, undulating, while others turned slowly, almost imperceptibly.

"What is this? It's beautiful." Fritz ran his fingers through the sparkling points of light.

"It's magic," Boroda explained. "Each shape and movement is part of a spell or enchantment and has a different function." He drew in the air and a line of magic followed his finger. It popped and sparked with energy.

Fritz's mouth dropped open. Excited, he started drawing in the air, too. A stream of magic followed his fingertip as he traced a circle. "What does this do?" He pointed at the pulsing ring of magic hovering in the air.

"Absolutely nothing, I'm afraid," Boroda said.

Fritz scowled.

"The circle is a useless shape. It has no application in magic," Boroda said and brushed away the magic runes in front of him. "Much like its metallic counterpart, gold. It's no coincidence that the ancient symbol for gold is a circle."

Fritz brushed away the shape in the air and folded his hands.

"Now I will draw a spell, and I want you to copy it." Boroda traced a shape in the air.

Fritz followed suit, and soon they had a small network of shapes twisting in various directions.

"No spell will be enacted until you cast it," Boroda went on. He gathered the shapes in his hand and threw them at his mug of tea. The water boiled and vaporized. "That was the spell for heat."

Fritz threw his spell at the cup in front of him. The cup began to shake, then shattered. He yelled and covered his face.

"You have to focus on the liquid," Boroda said, picking up his napkin and dabbing his face. "Once you have a spell committed to memory, you can attach an associated word. This word will conjure up the shape without having to redraw it."

He poured some more water in his mug, pointed his finger, and whispered, "Solis." The water vaporized.

Fritz pointed his finger but Boroda waved him off with an outburst. "Not yet!"

Fritz jerked his hand back.

"You have to memorize the shape," Boroda admonished.

Fritz extended his finger and drew the shape.

Boroda studied the spell. "You memorized that quickly. I'm impressed."

Fritz swelled with pride. He cast the spell, and the water hissed and turned to steam. He smiled with satisfaction but felt a draw on his energy.

For the next several hours, Boroda drew and Fritz copied. The wizard drew increasingly difficult shapes, and Fritz retraced them perfectly after a few moments of study.

When sweat ran down Fritz's forehead and his lines of magic turned to squiggles, Boroda stopped for a break.

"All the spinning shapes are making me dizzy," Fritz confessed with a glazed look on his face.

"You can turn the vision off," Boroda instructed. "Eventually, you will learn to focus only on the shapes you want to see."

The swirls vanished and once again the air was as clear as it had always been. Fritz leaned back in his chair and closed his eyes until Boroda announced the end of the break.

Boroda pushed on with his lesson until dinner. He traveled them both to a café in a small village in the Southern Kingdom.

The owner greeted Boroda warmly, delivered their food without a word, then left.

Mounds of fresh cheese topped a tomato base with poultry, grilled vegetables, and tangy capers. Fritz consciously cut his food into smaller bites and chewed slowly. It was only through a conscious force of will that Fritz didn't inhale his food.

After a few bites, Boroda said, "Your fellow apprentices have already had the benefit of several years' training. As a future member of The Order, you will need to prove you have the skills and power to keep up. You don't want to be the weak link.

"Each member of The Order has a specialty, and they are passing on that knowledge to their apprentice. Borya with flame, Sylvia with plants, and so on." Boroda paused as the owner refilled his wine glass.

"Each apprentice has been studying magic since they were very young. They've mastered the basics and have begun to study their focus magic.

"When the apprentices meet in the garden, not only are they trying to ferret information about each other to tell their masters, but they are also demonstrating ability level. To some degree, they are learning to work with each other, although that is probably the least of their concerns."

Fritz shifted his weight and kept his gaze low. "How long do you think it will take me to learn the basics?"

"At your current rate, not long," he said. "However, it would behoove you to do some studying on your own."

"How do I do that?"

"I have an extensive library at the mansion," Boroda began, then stopped. "And when you learn to read, you can start there."

"What is your specialty?" Fritz asked.

Boroda set down his fork and wiped his mouth with his napkin. "Time."

"Time?" Fritz said and then brightened. "Can you travel back in time?"

"Watcher, no!" Boroda burst out. "Time is an unbreakable barrier." Then he mumbled, "Unfortunately."

"So what does your power do?"

"Close your eyes and tell me what you hear."

Fritz closed his eyes. The owner was sweeping a small pile of dust into a tray, and his wife was chopping vegetables for the evening's meal. The "click click click" of her knife rang through the air in an even tick. The broom swished in a lilting manner against the stone floor.

Then the noise stopped.

Fritz opened his eyes and looked around.

The wife stood still. A small chunk of carrot held suspended just off the knife's edge. The owner's broom remained motionless in his grip, a cloud of dust frozen around the straw bristles.

"You froze them?" Fritz gasped.

"I stopped their time," Boroda corrected. "The world outside my spell is continuing on as it always does. When they reanimate, they will be unaware that any time has passed at all—unless I let them stay stopped until the sun goes down or they happen to be conscious of their clock at this very moment."

Fritz walked around the café, looking first at the owners, then at the magical shapes of the spell, dazzled by the complexity of the shapes and motions.

Boroda cleared his throat. Fritz looked at him and noticed a bead of sweat above his eyebrows.

"Oh!" Fritz said, realizing the incredible energy this spell must require. He ran back to the booth and sat down.

Boroda made a motion, and the lines vanished. The knife clicked away, and the whoosh of the broom picked up mid sweep.

"That's incredible," Fritz said. "Is this why you have so many clocks?"

"I use the clocks to test my ability and build endurance," Boroda explained. "I started by freezing time in one room with two clocks until I could get them to click together. From there, I added more clocks and more rooms. Now, I can stop the entire cottage and set the clocks to the same exact moment."

Fritz snickered. "Except for the little clock in the kitchen. You missed that one."

Boroda's eyes darkened. "Yes. I suppose I did." He stood up and laid several coins on the table. "Let's be off."

"More training?" Fritz winced.

Boroda took a slip of paper from his pocket and wrote on it. He handed it to Fritz.

"Travel to the plaza near Anadorn Square. When you get to the square, find O'Dentry's Bookstore. Tell him you need to purchase *Madame Venetta's Schooling Primer*. Show him this slip and you shouldn't have any trouble gaining access to the back room."

Fritz nodded and took the slip of paper.

He traveled to the plaza and wandered up and down the cobbled streets, pausing to peer into windows. He was happy to be out of training and took his time walking to the market. He rounded a corner, and the tight clump of buildings opened up to a large, red brick establishment with piles of coal out front. Lying on a small pile of burlap sacks next to the coal, rubbing his feet, was Toby.

Fritz whistled.

Toby looked up and brightened. "Hello."

"Hi," Fritz said. "I need your help. I'm looking for O'Dentry's Bookstore."

"In Anadorn Square? I know it."

Fritz held up the coin Boroda had given him. "I have to buy a book, but I'll give you whatever is left over if you take me."

Toby's eyes widened. "Whatever's left of a gold gilder?" He hopped up and led Fritz through a network of buildings until they entered the market square. He walked him down an alley to a store where the front window was completely covered with books.

They stepped inside as an elderly gentleman in a worn tweed jacket looked up from a book and peered over his half spectacles at them. "May I help you?" he asked in a monotone voice and returned his gaze to his book.

He addressed Toby from behind his novel. "If you are just escaping the cold, please leave."

Toby made a move for the door, but Fritz stopped him. "My name is … Drosselmeyer. Boroda sent me. I'm here to buy a book."

The man placed a slip of paper in his opened book and closed it with slow, methodical precision. "Which one?"

"*Madame Venetta's Schooling Primer,*" Fritz said and laid the slip of paper on the desk.

The older man pursed his lips and took out a case from below the counter. He put his glasses in this case and donned another pair of glasses with a purple haze over the lenses. He studied the note Fritz had given him, his top lip moving over his teeth as he read it. Satisfied, he took the glasses off.

Fritz blinked on his magic vision and saw a twisting line of runes sparkling around the purple glasses and Boroda's note. He guessed the glasses allowed non-wizards to view magic.

"This way." The elderly clerk walked down an aisle of books with the two boys following. At the back of the store, he turned and, stepping over large piles of unshelved books, made his way to a large cabinet in the corner. He unlocked the door and when he opened it, the cabinet swung on hinges to reveal a spiraling staircase that descended into darkness.

Holding a lantern high, O'Dentry led them down the stairs, which emptied into a dark, cavernous room. He flicked a switch. Two large chandeliers and several wall sconces illuminated the room. Tables and couches sparsely filled the center area. Tall bookshelves lined the walls.

Fritz and Toby gasped in amazement.

"I've never seen so many books," Toby whispered.

Fritz had to blink off his magic vision to keep his head from swimming. "Same here."

O'Dentry watched as Fritz and Toby wandered around looking at the voluminous shelves.

"What's this say?" Toby asked, holding up a book.

Fritz shook his head. "I don't know."

"I believe you were looking for this?" O'Dentry held out a book for Fritz.

Fritz took it, and O'Dentry pointed to the staircase.

As Fritz and Toby walked up the steps, the lights below blinked out.

Fritz gave O'Dentry the gold coin, which he exchanged for a small pouch stuffed with silver coins.

Once outside in the snow, Fritz handed the bag over to Toby. "Here. This is for helping me."

Toby's eyes bulged. "I can't take all of that."

"Why not?" Fritz asked.

"It's too much for just showing you a bookstore." Toby eyed the leather sack.

"Well … consider it an advance for the times when I'll need a guide."

Toby pondered a moment then held out his hand. "Deal!"

He took the coins and stuffed them in his pocket.

After Toby led him back to the fountain plaza, he reached out to shake Fritz's hand. "Nice doing business with you, Mr. Drosselmeyer."

"And you, Mr. Toby," Fritz responded with a chuckle and shook the boy's hand.

Boroda was waiting for Fritz when he returned to the training room. "I'll show you to your room," he said and led Fritz down several long hallways and up multiple staircases.

Fritz asked, "Did you ever find out how the ape found us?"

Boroda replied, "It was most definitely sent to my country house with specific intent on the part of the sender to do me harm."

"Who would want to harm you?" Fritz pried.

"Who, indeed?" Boroda muttered. "How the sender found my house is the bigger mystery."

"So, the ape wasn't magical?"

"No," Boroda quipped, then added, "I mean, it was physically altered and definitely had some regeneration enchantments, but it was a normal ape otherwise."

Boroda led Fritz down a very richly decorated hallway. They worked through a long maze of corridors and staircases.

"It was under mind control," Boroda said.

"Mind control? That's a thing?" Fritz rushed to keep stride.

"Yes. It's a … thing. It's a very complex thing and highly frowned upon."

"Who do you know that can do it?"

Boroda thought for a moment. "Anyone I know who is skillful enough to do that sort of magic wouldn't dare attack a member of The Order. In the past, other groups of wizards have tried to challenge and even attack The Order, but that hasn't happened in ages. Certainly not in my lifetime."

"There are other wizards that aren't in The Order?" Fritz asked, intrigued.

"Watcher, yes. Many, many other groups. But, The Order is the most powerful and has been for centuries." Boroda opened the door and stood back. "Here's your room."

Fritz surveyed the massive space, complete with a bed and two fireplaces, desks and dressers, wardrobes and couches, chairs and tables.

"This is all mine?" he asked.

"It is. Personally, I prefer the smaller, more cozy accommodations of my country manor, but for now, this will have to do."

Boroda walked to the two fireplaces and set the logs ablaze. "Can I get you anything else?"

"A map?" Fritz replied.

Boroda chuckled. "In the morning, I will show you the kitchen and give you extra time in the afternoon to explore the house." He traveled out of the room, and Fritz closed the door once the mist had settled.

He flopped down on the bed, kicked off his shoes, and took out the book he'd purchased from O'Dentry's. Emblazoned on the first page was a large, bronze seal. The paper-thin metal stuck up from the pages. Above the seal was a picture of a hand with an outstretched finger. As he looked at the hand, it began to move.

Fritz blinked. The picture was moving on the page. It took him a moment to realize the hand was tracing a spell.

He mimicked the path of the finger until it had worked its way around the edges of the page, enclosing the center seal with a series of shapes. "What now?" he asked out loud.

The seal pulsed slightly, then settled back onto the page.

Fritz collected the spell and cast it on the seal. A small beam of light appeared overhead. The light grew brighter until the entire room was awash in its warm glow.

The next thing Fritz knew, Boroda was knocking on his door.

"Get up. It's time to train."

Fritz rubbed his eyes and glanced down at his bed. *Madame Venetta's Schooling Primer* was opened to the last page.

He read, "Congratulations. You can read!" as small streamers glided down the page.

Boroda walked in, noticed the book, then sighed with relief. "Ah. Good, you can read now. Let's go."

Fritz rushed through breakfast then traveled back to the training room.

Boroda took off his coat and began to stretch.

"Boroda," Fritz asked between stretches, "when I finish my training—like, all of it—will I get to see Franz again?"

"Franz will not remember you, as we discussed. His memory was wiped for both his and your protection."

Boroda picked up a long wooden staff and tossed it to Fritz. "Let's begin with combat."

Boroda and Fritz sparred most of the morning then worked on spells, enchantments, and hand-to-hand combat.

Shortly after lunch, Boroda announced the end of training, and Fritz traveled up to his room.

He jumped into his bed and rolled around on the plush duvet. He couldn't help but think of the thin mattress he and his brother had shared less than a week ago. He hoped that Franz was enjoying his new life.

He rolled to his side and wiped a tear from his eye.

*You will see Franz again,* he promised himself. *You just need to find out where he is.*

A clock on the wall chimed eight o'clock.

There were not as many clocks here—only one in his room that he could see. It was a mahogany grandfather clock with gold filigree. It was large enough to see from his bed but not loud enough to hear the tick-tock.

Fritz rolled over on his stomach. He laid his head on his hands and looked at the clock. He thought of the odd clock in the kitchen at the country manor. It was so different from the masterful piece on display here. The tiny clock had been crudely nailed together and the figurines sloppily painted. The letters "PA" carved into the side were sloppy, much like the "PA" scrawled on the skates in the boathouse.

He burst into a loud laugh. "I can read letters!"

He lay back in bed, the fatigue of training washing over him. "I'm going to find the library and read all the books." He stretched and yawned. "Tomorrow."

He rolled over and fell asleep to the crackling sounds from the burning logs emanating warmth from the fireplace.

# CHAPTER 6

Fritz threw himself into training, arduously performing every task and directive. He listened attentively to Boroda's instruction, ever hopeful that the wizard would congratulate him on a job well done.

Even though he excelled in memorizing spells, their execution took a certain finesse which he lacked. His past life was a crude collection of utilitarian chores, and the endless nuances of magic frustrated him. Magic was, as Boroda described it, "part artistry, part force of will, but mostly knowledge."

Enchantments abraded his patience the most. If an enchanted object didn't work as intended, it could only be negated, or "turned off," by drawing it backward—unlike a spell, which he could terminate with the sweep of his hand.

"Different materials hold enchantments differently," Boroda explained. "Metal holds enchantments much longer than porous materials like wood and stone but require more skill to enchant. Wizard-grade metals, like the pendant you wear on your neck, can hold vast amounts of spells but are much harder to obtain."

"Why?" Fritz asked, turning the silver charm in his hand.

"Wizard-grade metal has *only* been found in the Central Mines, and Czar Nicholaus is *only* interested in mining for gold," Boroda said, his voice laced with ire. "On rare occasions, the miners have found a small deposit of a Wizard-grade metal, but it hasn't happened in many years. So, as you might imagine, it's quite difficult and expensive to come by."

"I see," Fritz said.

"To enchant or hold spells in your pendant, you draw the sign for Wizard-grade silver, then you draw the enchantment with the sign for silver worked in at regular intervals." Boroda demonstrated. "See how the magic grows legs and attaches to the pendant? That's how you know the enchantment holds and is successful."

In the evenings, Boroda taught Fritz how to carve. "It calms the mind and steadies the hand," he explained. "It also gives you an object to practice enchantments on."

One night, as Fritz was practicing a simple walking enchantment on a wooden doll he had carved, he grew frustrated at the stationary toy and knocked it over with a huff.

He checked and double-checked the enchantment. It was perfect, but still no movement.

"Why?" Boroda quizzed him.

"I don't know why! If I knew why, I would fix it," Fritz huffed.

Boroda stood Fritz up straight with a flick of his wrist. He made a few more gestures, and Fritz's knees and elbows locked in place.

"What are you doing?" Fritz yelled in protest.

"Walk!"

*They can do whatever they want to you because you belong to them.* Vivienne's words rang back loudly now in his mind.

"I can't!" Fritz said in a panic.

He searched around for something to defend himself against a blow, but his neck wouldn't turn.

"Why not?" Boroda asked.

"My body won't move. Please help, I'm falling!" He began to tip forward, unable to catch himself.

Boroda leaned back in his chair, waved his hand, and Fritz tumbled forward with perfectly functioning limbs.

"If you can't walk without joints, how do you expect your doll to?" Boroda asked.

When he finally understood Boroda's point, his panicked breathing switched to an excited gasp. "I need to make knees for my doll. How do I do that?"

Boroda set a small knife on the table. "You will need to carve them into the wood."

Fritz picked up the knife.

"The closer they resemble the real thing, the more lifelike the doll's walk will be," Boroda said.

"What does a knee look like?" Fritz asked, then added, "On the inside, I mean."

Boroda waved a few fingers, and a book appeared before Fritz. It was a large book on human anatomy. "Here's where you start."

The week progressed, and as Fritz learned Boroda's teaching style, he began to enjoy the training sessions more. All of them except for combat.

Spells and enchantments were getting easier. He could memorize the shapes in seconds and recall them quickly. Once a word was connected with a spell, all he had to do was write it down and it was locked into his memory.

Even his doll was progressing nicely. Fritz continued to work on the anatomy and spent the evenings carving. The legs and arms received ball-and-socket joints, and the fingers and toes got phalanges. He hinged the wooden limbs together with high-quality copper, then used these to hold enchantments.

But combat was the bane of his apprenticeship.

Boroda held nothing back. Every strike was full force and when it landed, which it usually did, the pain made Fritz's vision blur.

"Do not watch my knife! Watch my shoulder!" Boroda yelled, and to prove his point, thrust forward and buried the knife in Fritz's arm.

Fritz fell back, hand clasped over the wound as blood oozed between his fingers.

Boroda knelt down and healed the wound. "Ok. Let's go again."

Fritz tried to use a blocking spell to stop a blow, and Boroda slammed him against the wall with a swift, but powerful, kick.

"Magic is not a crutch! Learn to fight without it," Boroda said over Fritz's prostrate body.

Fritz yelled and lashed out, but Boroda jumped back.

Fritz charged Boroda in a blind rage. He turned his shoulder for a tackle but Boroda stepped aside and, with a strike of his fist, broke Fritz's collarbone.

Fritz collapsed, gasping in agony. Sparks flashed and his voice caught. He barely had time to speak the healing spell before he crumpled, heaving on the floor.

"Never lose your temper," Boroda said. "Even if you are down on the floor, and your opponent is standing over you, ready to plunge the sword into your chest— do not lose your temper. A calm opponent is far more deadly than a frothing lunatic with flailing arms."

Fritz sat quietly and cradled his arm. The bone was mended, but the muscles were still throbbing.

"I think that will be all for today. Your first day of school is tomorrow. You should rest." Boroda pulled his gloves off and traveled them away.

Fritz answered in a disappointed sulk, "Yes, sir."

Boroda disappeared, and Fritz moped to his own room.

It was dark outside, and a heavy blanket of snow whipped through the air in angry torrents. Fritz made his way to the library, picked up a book he had started reading the night before, and settled into the cushioned window seat.

The little alcove jutted out from the library and overlooked the back gardens. The simple, flat panes of glass provided an unobstructed view. Fritz curled up in the blanket and snapped his fingers. A floating ball of light appeared above him, illuminating the pages below.

He lost interest in the book and perused the shelves for another. While searching the vast array of scholarly titles, he came across a thin book called *Pickety Wickett*. He noticed it because it was definitely out of place sitting between two large volumes dealing with chemistry and crockery. The front cover was made of writing paper with colorful scribbles and was sharply creased down the middle from being shoved haphazardly between the surrounding books. The spine was bound with a single piece of yarn strung through several holes and tied in a bow.

Fritz snickered and pulled it down.

On the inside cover, drawn in crayon, was a large heart. There were other pictures drawn in the same infantile manner; the artist was obviously a young child. The dogs, horses, dragons, and unicorns all looked like the same creature save for a horn or pointed wings.

The heart, however, was the central focus. It was the biggest of all the figures and colored in with scrawling red strokes.

The next page had a simple but elegant handwritten message in the blank section.

*To my little Drosselmeyer.*

Pickety Wickett

Fritz sat up.

*Drosselmeyer? Did Boroda really name me after a character in a children's story?*

He shrugged and turned the page.

These illustrations, as opposed to the cover page, were colorful and whimsical. They radiated blissful happiness. The wispy lines and shades seemed to move on the page, pulling him into the story.

Fritz ran his fingers over the page, unconsciously smiling with the cartoons.

*Franz would have loved this!*

Tears welled up in his eyes at the thought of his brother, and he quickly flipped the page.

> *Pickety Wickett sailed over the sea*
> *To find a rare gift for Rosamund Lee.*
> *For she was his true love and he for she*
> *Was Pickety Wickett and Rosamund Lee.*

> *One gift would soothe her;*
> *Just one she preferred:*
> *The magical song of the Drosselmeyer bird.*

> *Pickety Wickett searched forest and tree*
> *But still had no bird for Rosamund Lee.*
> *For she was his true love and he for she*
> *Was Pickety Wickett and Rosamund Lee.*

> *This was her first choice*
> *Not second or third:*
> *The magical song of the Drosselmeyer bird.*

*Pickety Wickett fought lion and flea*
*Still no bird was found for Rosamund Lee.*
*For she was his true love and he for she*
*Was Pickety Wickett and Rosamund Lee.*

*She would soon dance to,*
*He gave her his word,*
*The magical song of the Drosselmeyer bird.*

*Pickety Wickett bowed low on one knee*
*He hadn't a bird for Rosamund Lee.*
*For she was his true love and he for she*
*Was Pickety Wickett and Rosamund Lee.*

*In love, she embraced him*
*Then suddenly heard*
*The magical song of the Drosselmeyer bird.*

*Pickety Wickett was filled with glee*
*To give this rare gift to Rosamund Lee.*
*For she was his true love and he for she*
*Was Pickety Wickett and Rosamund Lee.*

Fritz closed the book and shoved it back in between the two large tomes.

He grinned happily as he made his way back to his room. He skipped to his bed in the lilt of *Pickety Wickett and Rosamund Lee* and hummed a tune with a similar cadence.

He was still smiling when he woke up the next morning. The smile vanished, however, when Boroda called him from the mirror and told him to get ready for school.

# CHAPTER 7

Fritz tugged at his collar and stepped from the secluded gap in the hedges. Up ahead, under an arch, a looming steel gate stood open—a cold, mechanical welcome. The spires and turrets cut jagged shapes into the sky. The wall surrounding the building ran parallel with the street in front and disappeared into a thick forest behind it.

A long line of carriages wrapped around the edge of the school. Students disembarked from the ornate barouches and entered the building, followed by servants carrying bags headed toward the dormitories.

"Once you step into the dome of St. Michael's, magic is strictly forbidden," Boroda reminded Fritz.

Fritz nodded.

"What's your name?" Boroda quizzed.

"Drosselmeyer," Fritz answered and nearly broke into a stanza of *Pickety Wickett*.

"How are we related?" he pushed on.

"You're my uncle," said Fritz.

"How?" asked Boroda.

"My mom is your sister," Fritz answered, then cut in. "Is this really necessary? Is anyone going to ask?"

"It's best to be prepared if they do." Boroda stopped outside the gate. He inspected Fritz's jacket and straightened Fritz's tie. "It's also best to say nothing if you don't know what you're supposed to say."

They were met at the door by a middle-aged man in a tailored suit. He shook Boroda's hand and ushered them inside.

"I'm Headmaster Peabody," he said to Fritz. "It's good to have you. This way, please."

Parents milled around the vestibule, but Peabody stepped past them, acknowledging calls for his attention but ultimately ignoring them.

They stepped into a front office where a lady with thick glasses sat behind a large, mahogany desk.

"Mrs. Fairchild," the headmaster said as he walked past. "Will you bring me the class packet for Mr. Drosselmeyer, please?"

Mrs. Fairchild smiled at him. Her hair was pulled back into a tight bun, and her red-lipped smile revealed brilliant, white teeth. Without a word, she handed him a packet and continued working.

Peabody led them into his private office and closed the door.

Once seated behind his large, oak desk, he addressed Fritz. "I suppose your uncle has explained all the rules here at St. Michael's?"

"Yes, sir." Fritz swallowed and fidgeted, his stiff collar scratching his neck.

"St. Michael's is one of the most exclusive schools in the world, and we pride ourselves on decorum and academic achievement. Your uncle has assured me that you will not disappoint."

"Yes, sir. I mean, no sir, I won't disappoint," Fritz said.

"Good." He stood up.

Boroda and Fritz followed suit.

Peabody addressed Boroda. "I know you are a busy man," he said, "so I have arranged a student to guide Drosselmeyer to his classes."

On cue, Mrs. Fairchild knocked twice, then poked her head in the door. "The guide for Mr. Drosselmeyer is here."

Beside Mrs. Fairchild, dressed in her school uniform, stood Marzi.

Fritz stifled an excited gasp.

"Drosselmeyer," Peabody began. "This is Marzi Pan. She will be your guide. Feel free to ask her any questions."

He looked warmly at Marzi. "Marzi is one of our top students. I am confident she will take good care of you." He clicked his heels. "You are dismissed."

Fritz left without saying anything to Boroda.

"Welcome to St. Michael's," Marzi said once they were outside the office. "Lockers are down the main hall, and you will be in the third to last hallway on the right."

Fritz wove around a clump of people. "I'm kind of nervous."

"You shouldn't be," Marzi replied. "St. Michael's is a great school. It has the best teachers and its own library."

"It has a library?" Fritz exclaimed.

Marzi looked at him quizzically. "Do you like books?"

"Yes!" Fritz replied.

"I love books, too," she said, then lowered her voice. "None of the others do. We never talk about anything interesting."

"Do you have any other friends here? Are the apprentices the only ... you know, special people here?" Fritz looked over his shoulder.

Marzi laughed. "No. I don't have any other friends yet. And yes, the apprentices are the only 'special people' here. We mostly stick together. It's safer that way."

She stopped and pointed. "Here's your locker."

Fritz deposited the contents of his bag, and Marzi showed him which books to grab for first period.

The hallway was sparsely populated, and the few groups of students present were involved in their own conversations and oblivious to the new boy.

"Why does the most powerful group of wizards in the world send their apprentices to a school where they can't do magic?" Fritz asked in a hushed tone.

"Because the most powerful group of leaders send their children to St. Michael's," she replied acerbically. "That means the future rulers attend here now."

"Ah. So we're supposed to cozy up to a family so we can be their ..."

Marzi touched her finger to her lips. "We shouldn't talk about it in the open."

"Ok. Sorry," Fritz said. "It's just that Boroda doesn't talk much."

"Neither does Hanja ... but she is wise, and I trust her." She paused and thought for a moment. "Meet me in the library after school. There is more privacy there."

Fritz grinned. "Ok."

Marzi cocked her head. "Why are you smiling like that?"

Fritz startled. "Like what? I wasn't smiling. I was ..."

"Come on," she interrupted. "First period is science with Ms. Wakimba. You do NOT want to be late for her class."

Ms. Wakimba was a middle-aged woman with ebony skin and sharp eyes that scanned the class in slow, steady sweeps.

After the bell chimed, Ms. Wakimba punctuated her greeting with force. "Good morning class."

"Good morning, Ms. Wakimba," the class replied.

"Welcome back," she said as she scanned the room. "To our new students—or *student*," she said as she made eye contact with Fritz, "welcome to *you,* as well."

"Drossie!" a chipper voice called softly from behind Fritz.

Fritz turned to see Vivienne waving at him. Her face was pink and bright, and her hair was pulled back at the sides with a flowery clip.

Fritz smiled and waved back timidly.

"Now that the formalities are over, get out your textbooks and turn to page 227." Ms. Wakimba turned to write on the chalkboard.

The class obeyed.

Fritz opened his book, and as he was approaching the right page, a folded note fluttered past his hand and nearly dropped into his lap.

He glanced over at the short, heavyset boy who had delivered it. He looked several years younger than everyone else in the class. Without breaking his gaze on Ms. Wakimba, he adjusted his glasses with his left finger and simultaneously motioned with his thumb behind him.

Fritz turned to look and saw Faruk wave at him and point at the note.

Fritz smiled and opened it.

*Don't get caught passing notes.*

Fritz smiled at the note, then froze as Ms. Wakimba addressed him. "Anything you'd like to read to the class, Mr. Drosselmeyer?"

Fritz turned a deep shade of red.

She tapped the chalk in her hand.

"No, ma'am," he said and wadded up the note.

"Perhaps no one has told you about my class yet, but since you are new, I will explain it to you, and let it serve AS A REMINDER TO THE REST OF THE CLASS that there will be no note-passing, unauthorized talking, or outside work while in my classroom. Do you understand?"

"Yes, Ms. Wakimba," Fritz said.

"Class?"

"Yes, Ms. Wakimba," they chanted in unison.

A tall, muscular boy in the front corner of the class caught Fritz's eye. He studied Fritz closely.

"Mr. Nicholaus," Ms. Wakimba called out again, and the boy turned lethargically to face her. "I want you to read the first paragraph. You can meet the new student on your own time."

Nicholaus sighed and began reading in a bored, monotonous tone.

Fritz kept his gaze down or forward until the bell rang.

"Homework is due before the first bell tomorrow," Ms. Wakimba reminded them. No one lost any time closing their books or leaving the room.

"Come on," Marzi said, pulling him from his chair. "We have to get to literature."

Fritz followed Marzi from class to class, swept along in the current of bodies all rushing to the next class period. He joined the apprentices for lunch but said little.

"Looks like Nicholaus has his eye on you," Vivienne said when she sat down at the table. "He was sizing you up during first period, and I saw him staring at you in the hallway."

Fritz shrugged.

Faruk laughed. "Viv is just jealous. She wants him."

"Ew. No I don't," Vivienne said playfully.

Gelé played with the food on her tray. "Drossie's already got dibs on him, Vivienne."

Fritz looked up. "What? I don't even know him."

Gelé looked at him incredulously. "How can you not know who Nicholaus is? Hasn't Boroda told you?"

"What has he got to do with any of this?" Fritz dodged.

"Um … Nicholaus's father is Czar of the Central Kingdom. He's Boroda's boss. Nicholaus is next in line to rule, and you're next in line to advise," Vivienne explained.

"Oh. I see," Fritz stammered.

Andor sat down and signed to Marzi.

"Andor says, 'Hi, and welcome,'" Marzi said to Fritz.

Fritz waved back at Andor.

Gelé ignored Andor and stood up as soon as the large apprentice sat down. "I have to get ready for my next class," she said, then turned to Vivienne. "You coming?"

Vivienne stood up and waved goodbye, pausing by Andor long enough to recoil slightly in disgust as he shoveled food in his mouth.

Andor, with a large smile plastered across his face, continued to eat. He signed to Marzi.

She slid her tray across the table. "I'm not going to finish. It's yours."

She took a book from her bag and began reading.

"What's wrong with them?" Fritz asked Marzi.

Marzi looked at him sullenly. "They don't like Andor."

"Why?"

"Gelé and Vivienne are used to more, shall we say, posh company?" Faruk cut in.

Andor wiped some food from his chin with his hand and reached for his glass. He smiled at Fritz and signed.

"He wants to know if you're going to eat your roll," Marzi said over her book.

Fritz tossed the bread to Andor, who stabbed it midair with his fork.

He held the roll up for the rest of the table to see. Fritz laughed and gave him a thumbs-up.

They finished lunch and continued through their afternoon classes.

The last class of the day was gym. Fritz stood awkwardly in his tight-fitting gym clothes while Mr. McGregor, a bearded, barrel-chested man, led them through calisthenics.

"Give me fifty push-ups!" he roared.

"Yes, sir," the class chimed and dropped to the ground with a smattering of grumbles and complaints.

"At the end of the semester, you'll be put through the trials!" McGregor bellowed to the grunts of the students.

"Running through the woods, building forts, fighting a war, trying to defeat the other team: the trials aren't for weaklings. The trials are for fighters!" He tapped a boy's arm with his foot and the boy corrected his posture and continued the push-ups. "Look at you! You aren't fighters—you're a bunch of weaklings."

The class answered his insult with agonizing moans.

"The trials show us who can conquer and who will be conquered." He walked down the lines of students struggling with the exercise, straightening form and watching for people using their knees as a cheat. "My job is to make sure there's no weakness to expose."

Several students flopped to their backs, gasping for air and mopping the sweat off their faces.

"You know what waits for you in the woods?" McGregor warned.

"Perrin's ghost!" shouted a random voice.

Titters of laughter broke out among the students.

"Quiet! The lot of you!" McGregor boomed. "That's twenty more push-ups, and if I hear a grumble, I'll add ten more. The trials await you in the woods! It picks the weakest among you and stomps on you. Now start your push-ups."

The class went silent as those who had finished rolled back into position to start the exercise over.

McGregor led the students through different tumbles and directed them toward a small springboard next to the tumbling mat. The first student ran, bounced off the board, and rolled on the mat as directed.

Fritz whispered covertly to Marzi while waiting in line, "What is Perrin's ghost?"

She looked forward. "It's a school legend the upperclassmen tell the freshmen to scare them. They'll pick a younger student to haze during trials and then blame it on Perrin's ghost. Don't worry about it. You're too old."

"Don't worry about it?" It was the roly-poly boy from first period who had passed Faruk's note. "Perrin's ghost is real." He looked at Fritz with sincerity. "A student died in the woods, and he haunts anyone who goes out there."

Marzi scowled. "Edward was the freshman they picked to haze last year."

"Only I wasn't a freshman last year." He scowled. "I was a junior just like you all."

Faruk ran toward the vault, launched into the air, flipped, and landed in a perfect roll.

"Aye, that's good," McGregor exclaimed.

"What happened to him? The student that died, I mean," Fritz asked out of the corner of his mouth.

McGregor looked up, and Fritz hid his mouth by scratching his nose.

"Nothing! Because it didn't happen," Marzi said with a harsh whisper.

"It did too," Edward argued.

Marzi was three people away from the springboard.

"My brother was in school when it happened." Edward's eyes stared intensely behind his thick spectacles.

"Oy!" McGregor yelled, and the three stopped talking and stared forward.

Nicholaus vaulted, turned a flip, and landed with a perfect stance. He winked at Gelé as he walked off the mat.

Gelé rolled her eyes and shot him a coy glance. She vaulted into the air and flipped in reverse. She landed, went into a back roll, and launched into two back handsprings. As she walked off the mat, she held up her hands in a triumphant shrug at Nicholaus.

Two boys on either side poked him in the ribs, making rude comments and gestures about his manliness. Nicholaus pushed them away and flashed Gelé a cocky grin.

Gelé flipped her hair and walked to the back of the line.

Marzi was next. She did a simple flip, clean and graceful, and walked off the mat, her face stoic.

Fritz flipped off the vault and barely made the rotation. He landed and wind-milled his arms but stumbled backward on the mat.

"Tuck harder off the jump, Drosselmeyer," McGregor called.

Edward followed but missed the jump, caught his feet on the springboard platform, and landed chest first on the mat. He grunted, then rolled over, trying to catch his breath.

"Use your legs, Edward," McGregor yelled. "And tuck your chin."

"All of them," Nicholaus baited from the back of the line. He and his friends laughed as Edward crawled off the mat.

Up ahead, Andor, easily a foot taller than everyone else, clumsily jumped on the springboard in preparation for a vault. The wooden contraption snapped under his weight and an errant spring shot out across the mat.

McGregor reached up and smoothed his mustache with slow, deliberate strokes. His right eye twitched.

"Class is over," he announced.

Students immediately began chatting loudly.

"If you want me to show you the library, meet me in the lobby after you change," Marzi told Fritz, then turned and left.

Fritz promised to meet her there and started toward the boy's changing room.

Edward raced up and joined him.

"I'm Edward." He extended his hand.

"Nice to meet you. I'm Drosselmeyer." Fritz shook his hand.

"I'm the youngest in my family," Edward said. "I have three older brothers and all of them have attended St. Michael's."

"It's my first day here."

"Yeah, everyone knows," Edward said, then added, "We all want to know who your dad is."

"My dad?" Fritz asked as he opened his locker.

"Yeah. What nation are you from? Is your dad royalty or military?" Edward asked and began dressing.

"Oh ..." Fritz stammered. "I live with my uncle. My mom's brother."

Edward blinked but didn't say anything.

"I'm not actually sure what he does," Fritz responded truthfully.

"My dad is a duke and the ambassador from the Southern Kingdom. I live a few miles away in the embassy."

"My uncle lives ..." Fritz paused. "Somewhere close by. I live with him."

Edward checked to make sure no one was listening, then leaned in and whispered, "My oldest brother, Richard, was in the same class as Perrin. The story is true."

They picked up their bags, exited the locker room, and headed toward the main building across the lawn.

"Are you sure your brother wasn't just trying to scare you?"

"He was serious," Edward said. "Richard told me that …"

"Edward," Nicholaus spoke the boy's name in a slow, Slavic accent.

Both Edward and Fritz turned toward Nicholaus.

He was standing casually in a small circle of students. His two friends, Evgeny and Oleg, flanked him. Faruk, Gelé, and Vivienne completed the round. They all turned to look at Edward.

"You are the smartest one in gym," he called out. "We all …" he motioned in the air to include the whole school, "trust only in the mat to catch us when we fall, but you bring extra padding with you."

The students rewarded him with guffaws and slaps.

"Keep working, Edward," he continued. "Someday you will be an important part of the Southern Army. Perhaps a horse?"

His friends laughed, Vivienne giggled, and Gelé offered an uncomfortable smile. Faruk remained stone-faced.

Edward clenched his jaw. His face turned red, and he stormed away.

"What is the matter?" Nicholaus called after him.

Edward kept walking.

Nicholaus covered the territory between himself and Edward in a few, long strides. He spun Edward around. "I'm talking to you."

"Leave him alone," Fritz said through clenched teeth, eyes locked firmly on the ground.

Nicholaus stood full figure and puffed his chest out. "Or what?"

Fritz kept his gaze low and didn't respond.

"Or what?" Nicholaus repeated, voice tinged with anger.

Fritz caught the prince's eye briefly and looked away again.

Nicholaus's friends began to whisper, and the boy glanced from them to Fritz. His head shook as his rage grew, and he pulled his fist back for a strike, yelling, "Or what?"

Fritz had been struck so many times in the last week by Boroda that his mind stopped, and his body took over. He ducked under the swing, jumped in closer to the tall boy's frame, and delivered four swift punches from the lower abdomen all the way up to the rib cage.

Nicholaus grunted in successive bursts. He tried to breathe in fresh air to replace the lost supply, but his body didn't respond. He fell on the lawn and clawed the ground.

Evgeny and Oleg raced toward Fritz but McGregor's booming voice stopped them short. With a stern scowl, McGregor said, "I think we're done here."

Everyone looked at the large, bearded man whose arms were folded across his broad chest.

"Evgeny, Oleg, take Nicholaus to see the nurse. Probably nothing more than a bruised ego."

The boys helped the prince off the ground. "You're dead," he snarled at Fritz and Edward as he limped away.

"Are you satisfied, Drosselmeyer?" McGregor asked with a raised eyebrow.

Fritz nodded.

"I can't hear you, lad."

"Yes, sir," Fritz said.

"Good. Now get going, and if I ever catch you fighting again, it's the headmaster for both of you."

"Thanks for that," Edward said after they had left the field.

Fritz kept his head low and picked up his pace.

Edward adjusted his glasses. "You'd better be careful. I think Nicholaus meant what he said about killing you. He'll come after you and not even the school will stop him."

"Thanks. I think I can look out for myself," said Fritz.

Edward shook his head, "Even the adults don't mess with Nicholaus."

"How old are you?" Fritz asked suddenly.

Edward looked away, cheeks flushed. "Thirteen. I'm supposed to be in the eighth grade, but I skipped three grades when I was in elementary. Why do you ask?"

"I don't know." Fritz shrugged. "I thought smart kids would be the most popular in a school."

"It's not that helpful when people can just beat you up," Edward countered. "It's better to be strong."

Fritz didn't argue.

He patted Edward on the shoulder. "I have to meet Marzi in the library. See you tomorrow."

They parted ways, and Fritz jogged toward the library doors.

Marzi met him across from the librarian's desk and led him up to the third floor. They wove through a tangle of shelves to a corner where an arched door frame opened into a small room located in a turret.

The rounded walls had additional shelves built into the stone. Iron light fixtures, an old patinated mirror, and a long, Gothic, stained glass window lined the rough-hewn timber ribs.

"How was your first day?" Marzi asked.

"Fine ... I guess," Fritz said and sat on the couch. He stared up at the crossbeams of the ceiling and the dark void above.

"How are things going with Boroda?" she asked casually.

Fritz pulled some books and a pencil from his bag. "Good ... I guess."

"Is he better than your first wizard?" she asked again.

"My first?" Fritz asked, confused.

Marzi's eyes widened. "Boroda is your first wizard? You're really old to be new. Are you sure you haven't trained with anyone else?"

"I don't think I should be talking about it," Fritz stuttered.

Marzi waved him off.

"Everyone in The Order is extremely secretive." She brushed her hair back, and Fritz felt his pulse quicken.

"Yeah. I know. It's really, uh ..." Fritz trailed off as Marzi removed her jacket.

"I snapped when I was five," she said. "Hanja took me a few months later."

"Mm-hmm." Fritz tried to look away from her long neck and the silver dragon pendant just peeking out from her shirt.

"I don't remember anything about my childhood before Hanja," she continued. "I think the hardest part is not knowing who my family is." She adjusted her skirt to lay flat across her legs and set a book on her lap. "What's the hardest thing for you so far?"

Fritz looked away from her long legs, blushed, and rested both elbows on his knees. "I, um ... I almost got killed by an ape."

He groaned and clapped his hand over his mouth.

The playful smile on Marzi's mouth melted. A strand of hair fell loose, and she made no move to brush it back. She didn't move at all.

"Please don't tell anyone I said that!" Fritz begged. "I am so bad at keeping secrets. Please! Boroda will kill me. Please, promise me you won't tell."

Marzi spoke somberly. "I promise."

"Thank you," Fritz sighed. "I really shouldn't ..."

"Tell me about the ape," she commanded.

"What?" Fritz asked. "I probably shouldn't talk about that either."

"You've already started. Just tell me about it." Marzi gripped her book so tightly, her knuckles turned white.

Fritz sighed. "Ok. But do you promise …"

"Yes, I promise," she snapped. "Just tell me about the ape."

Fritz jumped at her outburst, then told her the story.

"Here's the weird thing," Fritz finished. "Boroda says that nobody knows where he lives. No one ever visits him."

Marzi looked confused. "Why is that weird? Nobody knows where Hanja and I live. Every wizard in The Order has several houses, and all of them are a secret. You have to have one place where you can relax and not worry about getting attacked."

Fritz laughed. "Well, apparently, Boroda's house wasn't it."

"Drosselmeyer, that's not funny," Marzi scolded.

Fritz shrank back.

"A wizard's house is the most closely guarded secret, second only to their name," she said. "When the wizards of The Order get attacked in their homes, it's a serious matter."

Fritz cocked his head. "Who said anything about wizards?" He accented the plural. "Did you get attacked?"

Marzi's skin flushed white.

"You DID, didn't you?" Fritz pointed his finger. "Come on," he said, guilting her, "I told you my story."

Marzi stood up and walked to the window, then paced to the opposite wall. "Can I trust you?"

A vein in Fritz's forehead pulsed visibly. "Yes!" he said.

"We got attacked, too."

Fritz gaped. "Are you serious?"

"Yes. It was a week ago. A Kano dragon completely burned the stables and killed most of our animals before Hanja and I could kill it. Hanja doesn't kill anything unless she has to," she explained. "Like your ape, Kano dragons are not violent unless provoked. They live with humans easily and prey mostly on rodents. The only reason one would attack a human would be if it were …" She stopped.

"If it were—under mind control?" Fritz asked.

Marzi nodded.

"Do you think the others have been attacked?" Fritz asked.

Marzi shrugged.

"Do you think we should warn them?"

"No!" Marzi said suddenly, then calmed. "No. Not yet, anyway. Hanja says not to trust any of them."

"Boroda says the same thing," Fritz added.

"Power makes people—even allies—do crazy things," Marzi said and sat back down on the couch.

"Isn't the point of us gathering in the garden while The Order meets to build trust?" Fritz asked her. "That game you all played with the flower and ice?"

Marzi shook her head. "No. Well, I mean, that game of adding to the spell is supposed to help us work together, but none of us use magic remotely close to what we're capable of.

"We don't want to show our real strength in case we ever ..." She stopped.

"In case we ever what?" Fritz prodded.

Marzi dodged the question. "Your move last time was brilliant. Even Faruk was impressed."

"Really?" Fritz waited for the punchline.

"Don't act surprised!" she shot back. "We were all trying to see what you were capable of, and you just threw mud. I mean, we all know the entire game is a charade. It was a genius move."

"Oh ... yeah ... I wondered if anyone caught that," Fritz covered.

Marzi stared up into the rafters. "Imagine what would happen if we actually did trust each other? Just think of all the good a group like The Order could do."

"Are they not already doing good? World peace is good, right?"

Marzi laughed, and the pellucid sound rang in Fritz's ears. "World peace. That's funny," she said. "The Order advises the world leaders to do what's best for The Order."

"So, I take it you're not a fan, then?"

"I am. Sort of," she quickly retracted. "I just wish it was less about how The Order can become powerful and wealthy and more about helping people with our magic."

"Like what, then? If world peace isn't good enough for you," Fritz teased.

Marzi lay back on the couch and threw her arms wide. "We could enchant statues with healing spells or have heated stones for the winter time or water purification spells. The possibilities are endless."

She sat up straight. "What are you smiling like that for?"

Fritz closed his mouth. "I'm not smiling."

Marzi looked up at the dim light coming through the windows. "It's getting late. We'd better go. See you tomorrow?"

Without realizing it, Fritz smiled.

"You're smiling weird again," she said. She picked up her jacket and bag. They said goodbye outside the school and walked away in opposite directions.

Fritz watched her round a corner and then skipped to the hedge. He traveled to the front door of Boroda's estate as he hummed his *Pickety Wickett* tune from the night before.

Boroda appeared in a roiling cloud of smoke. "Meet me in the training room. Now."

Fritz yelped in fright, hands raised, then traveled to the room.

"Your first day, Fritz! Your first day, and you've already made trouble," Boroda yelled as soon as he stepped from his misty cloud.

"What are you talking about?" Fritz asked.

Boroda spun to face him. "I'm talking about Nicholaus!"

"Who told?" Fritz demanded. "Mr. McGregor said …"

"Who told?! That's your first response?" Boroda roared.

"Nicholaus was being a jerk and picking on my friend for no reason," Fritz yelled back. "I was just sticking up for my friend."

Boroda thrust his hand out, and a spell slammed Fritz against the wall.

He gasped for breath, searching his memory for a counter spell to stop the crushing force.

"Nicholaus is the son of Czar Nicholaus, who happens to be my advisee!" Boroda said. "It is not your place to teach him a lesson. Do you understand me?"

Fritz couldn't breathe. His legs were dangling inches above the floor, and the pressure of Boroda's spell crushed down on his chest. "You're hurting me," he finally choked.

Boroda stopped pushing and stepped back. The rage softened to a mild annoyance. "From now on, leave Nicholaus to do as he pleases."

Fritz agreed, clutching his ribcage. *They can do whatever they want to you because you belong to them.*

"Go dress for training and meet me back here. We have work to do."

After three hours of combat, spells, and enchantments, they traveled to the kitchen and ate supper in chilly silence.

"Boroda?" Fritz broke the silence.

Boroda looked up from his plate.

"Are there such things as ghosts?"

"Why do you want to know that?"

Fritz shrugged. "Kids at school were talking about a ghost that haunts the woods. I'm just wondering if they actually exist."

"No."

"That makes me feel better." Fritz relaxed. "Several of the students are freaked out about Perrin's ghost."

The room darkened, and the ticking clock slowed and thudded loudly.

Boroda bared his teeth and slammed the table. The wood began to smoke under his red, glowing fists. "Don't ever say that name again!"

Fritz sat paralyzed with fear. He tried to nod, but his body wouldn't move.

The lights flashed back on, the clock ticked normally, and Boroda was gone.

He finally managed to whisper to the empty room, "Yes, sir."

# CHAPTER 8

Fritz lay in bed, carving a face into a wooden doll. His attempt at a smile resembled more of a snarl. He tossed the doll aside and, scooping up all the wood shavings, floated them to the trash bin in the corner of his room.

He yawned and stretched, then flinched from the soreness. It had been almost a month since Boroda had crushed him against the wall, but a few muscles in his ribcage still hurt.

Fritz eyed the large, wingback chair near the window, whispered a word, and the exact spell that Boroda had used sent the chair shooting across the room. He stopped it right before it hit the wall.

He'd traveled to his room that night, traced the spell from memory, and found it to be a much different kind of pushing spell. As he experimented with it, he realized that it pushed some but also co-opted gravitational pull to help. It took much less energy, and even though using it was like holding a ball against a wall with a broomstick handle, the amount you pushed increased the gravitational pull exponentially. In short, you could crush something, or someone, with very little energy.

Ever since that night, Fritz had practiced the spell on his own. He let the chair down and traveled to the library.

He grabbed *The Wizard's Compendium of Spells and Enchantments, Volume One* from the shelf, cursing whatever spell reshelved all the books each night, before settling into the window nook.

He flipped through the first three quarters of the book in his mind, making sure he could still visualize all the spells, and then set to work tracing the new spells. Around him, the scintillating wisps of magic tumbled in bilious clouds as he committed spell after spell to memory.

When the mantle clock chimed midnight, he set the book down and traveled back to his bedroom.

He pulled the covers up and was about to drift off when he noticed the doll's snarl. The shiny, glass eyes reflected the moonlight from the windows, creating an unsettling effect.

Fritz waved his finger, and the knee-high doll tumbled sideways and fell to the floor.

"Stupid doll," he mumbled and went to sleep.

"Today is the day you choose your subject for final juries," Ms. Wakimba announced.

The class groaned.

Marzi had a piece of paper on her desk with several options. Her hands were folded, and she sat upright, eyes fixed on Ms. Wakimba.

Fritz craned his neck to see which animal she'd picked.

Over the last month, they'd met every day in the library to study. Fritz had a harder time concentrating on the school subjects but managed to get some work finished.

He looked down at his own list. It was about as random a list as you could get. Twelve animals: one for each of the letters in his name. He'd chosen them by blindly pointing in an alphabetized book of zoology.

The previous afternoon he'd joked with Marzi, much to her horror, that he was going to make a list of animals that corresponded with the letters in his name and pick one at random when Ms. Wakimba asked for his selection.

"But you have to tell her class, order, family, genus, and species," she'd reminded him. "You can't memorize that for all twelve."

"Want to bet?" he asked, drumming his fingers together.

"You're on!" she fired back. "A dozen homemade cookies says you can't do it."

Fritz shook her outstretched hand. "I like chocolate chip," he said. Keeping her hand held firmly in his, he added, "No raisins."

Marzi began to respond but Fritz cut her off. "And I want them to be at least this big." He held up a circle formed by his thumbs and middle fingers.

Marzi folded her arms and partially suppressed a smile. "As soon as Marion sits down, I'll give you a number. That's your animal for final juries."

"Deal." Fritz clapped his textbook shut.

"Thank you, Marion," Ms. Wakimba said while scribbling in her notebook. Marion settled into his chair directly in front of Fritz and wiped his sweaty palms down his uniform pants. His neckline was glistening from nerves, and his sharp, beaked nose flared as he inhaled deep sighs of relief.

Fritz looked over at Marzi. She held up three fingers.

He looked down and counted. "D–R–O. O–Owl."

"Drosselmeyer?" Ms. Wakimba called.

Fritz closed his eyes and pictured the page in the library.

He stood and announced, "The barn owl."

"The barn owl? Would you care to be more specific?" She glanced up to make sure that he wasn't reading from any notes.

"Class: Aves. Order: Strigiformes. Family: Strigidae. Genus: Bubo. Species: B. Bubo."

"Thank you. You may have a seat."

He sat, then turned to Marzi, whose mouth gaped open, and held up his hands in a circle.

"This big!" he mouthed.

Her eyes narrowed, but the corners of her mouth turned upward.

"No raisins," Fritz mouthed again before he turned back around to face the front of the class.

Fritz lay sprawled on the small couch in the library turret. He made a moaning sound as he chewed.

"These are amazing!" he said to Marzi, who watched his feast of victory with annoyance and amusement.

"I'm glad you like them," she said, pouring on the sarcasm.

Fritz put the package on a table beside him and pulled out a tactics book. "I was hoping phys ed would just be exercising," he said. "Why are we reading about military tactics?"

"Chances are good that several of our classmates will engage each other in some kind of war," Marzi said flatly. She flipped a few pages in the same book.

"You're right, there," Fritz laughed as he began the chapter on battlefield formations. "I guess we want them to kill each other faster and more efficiently."

"I've been thinking about the attacks on our homes." Marzi suddenly closed her book with a pop.

"Yeah? Did you figure something out?"

"Maybe. What are the things you and I have in common?"

Fritz thought for a moment. "I don't know ... we're both wizards?"

"Yes, but that's probably the reason *why* we got attacked. We need to figure out *how* we got attacked so we can figure out *who* attacked us." She walked to the window and leaned against the stone pane. "How we got attacked is the tough part. You said no one knows where your house is, and Hanja told me the same thing."

She paused. "I was wrong about that. Sort of."

"Ok. Who knows where we live?" Fritz asked.

She began to pace. "There are people who know that we're wizards. That's not a huge secret. Not really. The Order is so diverse that we only have a few things in common. These things are so blatantly obvious that I overlooked them."

"Yeah, I can't believe you missed the totally obvious … things," Fritz joked.

"I'm serious! What is it that all the members of The Order have in common?" She waited for his response.

Fritz thought hard but gave up. "I don't know. Just tell me."

"Food!" she said.

"Food?" Fritz asked.

"We all eat food."

"I've seen the snacks you bring to school." Fritz wrinkled his nose. "We do not eat the same food."

"Of course not, but it all gets sent to the same place." She sat on the couch and poked the small table between them.

Fritz wrinkled his eyebrows. "Ok."

"I eat different food than you, as do Gelé, Faruk, and the rest. We probably all get our food from local markets, but we all have to store it."

"And we all have the same storage area." Fritz felt chillbumps rise on his arms. "But our storage rooms are locked. You can only get in if you know the right word."

Marzi bit her lip.

"And what about our uniforms?" Fritz asked before she could answer. "Do you get your uniform from the same shop as me?" He added, "That's another thing we have in common."

Marzi shook her head. "Only one shop makes the uniforms for St. Michael's, but I don't send my uniforms to storage."

"Oh," Fritz sagged. "What about furniture and items like that?"

"Hanja hasn't purchased furniture in years," Marzi said. "I think we just use the stuff her predecessors purchased." She grimaced. "They were serious hoarders."

"Tell me about it!" Fritz agreed, envisioning the endless piles of paraphernalia in Boroda's infinity room.

He stood and walked to the opposite side of the room. "So food seems to be the only thing we all consistently buy and send to the same storage area?"

"I can't think of anything else." Marzi shrugged.

"Let's say that's the connection," Fritz postulated. "That still doesn't explain how the animal got in the storage area to begin with or how it traveled to where we were.

"Correct me if I'm wrong, but you'd still have to know where you're going if you want to travel there, right? And an ape and a dragon have no will—only instinct."

"Yes," said Marzi, "you aren't wrong, but there is a place in every storage area where you can travel in an item that you can't see."

Fritz recalled the square area illuminated with a warm light. "Every storage area has that?"

"Yes. The infinity rooms were all built by the same wizard a long time ago," Marzi explained. "I've never been inside anyone else's, but I can imagine they're all pretty similar."

Fritz ran his fingers through his hair. "In that case, the animals wouldn't have to TRAVEL in ... They could have been TRAVELED in by one of the wizards."

Marzi nodded.

"I don't know." Fritz sat back down. "Why wouldn't the ape have appeared on the kitchen table with the rest of the food?"

"I don't know yet," Marzi said with exasperation. "I'm still trying to figure that out."

"It's a good start," Fritz said. "But Boroda doesn't use the unknown travel spot for food, and I was the one who traveled in my school uniforms. Those didn't come until after the attack anyway."

Marzi's body deflated, and she flopped back onto the couch.

"The only thing Boroda traveled in before the attack, that I'm aware of, was my apprentice uniform."

Marzi smiled and traced a vest on her shirt. "It was adorable."

Fritz ignored her. "He brought it to my room, and there was no ape. Just a moth."

"I hate insects," she muttered.

"Same," Fritz grumbled in agreement.

"I still think we're onto something with the storage, though." Marzi stood up. She began to pack her bag.

"I agree," Fritz said. "Maybe we could go there and check it out together sometime."

"Check it for what? What are we actually looking for? Footprints?"

"There might be a clue. You don't know!" Fritz flushed and hurried to pack his own books.

"That seems like quite a stretch," Marzi prodded.

"Fine!" Fritz snapped. "Then meet me for lunch."

Marzi stopped packing and stared, wide-eyed, at Fritz. Fritz froze.

"So we can talk about the attacks, I mean," he recovered.

Marzi continued to stare for several seconds. Her lips slowly curved into a coquettish smile, and she lowered her chin, now staring at Fritz from a sideways glance. "Sure. That would be fine."

Fritz's cheeks turned red. "How about this Saturday, say, noon?"

"Perfect." Marzi swung her bag over her shoulder. "See you this weekend."

"See you this weekend," Fritz said.

His heartbeat quickened.

"Fritz," Marzi said as she walked toward the door. "You're doing that stupid smile again."

He watched her leave then fell back onto the couch.

He *was* grinning, and he didn't care.

Fritz wiped sweat from his face and hung the fencing foils on the wall rack. His fencing lesson had been one of the best he'd had, with three strikes in his favor against Boroda.

Boroda had sweat stains under his arms and on his chest. He pushed several other weapons from the ground to their places on the wall.

"I've spoken with Czar Nicholaus about your encounter with his son," Boroda began.

"That was over a month ago!" said Fritz.

"Regardless. He mentioned it to me today and wants to speak with you directly."

"Do you know what he wants?"

"I imagine he wants you to apologize for your behavior."

"My behavior?" Fritz said. "Nicholaus has been picking on Edward since their freshman year. And not just Edward. A lot of kids."

"That isn't your concern." Boroda traveled the last weapon to the wall. "You are responsible for your actions. Not those of others."

"So we just stand by and let him bully other kids?" Fritz asked.

Boroda didn't respond.

"And why? Why does he get to treat people that way, but no one gets to treat him like that?" Fritz said. "I get it. Little people get stepped on all the time. I saw it in the orphanage every day. But one of the reasons I chose to be your apprentice was to stop people like Nicholaus. You said you'd train me to do that."

Boroda exhaled slowly, gathering his thoughts. "You aren't going to understand this, but I need you to trust me. Whatever the Czar asks you to do, I want you to do it."

Fritz crossed his arms.

"On a personal level, I agree with you. Young Nicholaus and his ilk should be held accountable for their actions, but we live in the real world where not all rules are applied equally."

Fritz began to protest, but Boroda held up a finger.

"So when the Czar asks you to apologize to his son, or whatever it is that he wants, you will do it with no questions asked. Am I clear?"

"I won't mean it."

"You don't have to."

"Fine. I'll apologize," Fritz said. "But I still think it's wrong."

"We will go there this Sunday. Wear your apprentice uniform."

"Yes, sir," Fritz said with an air of sarcasm. He traveled back to his room before Boroda could respond.

Later that night, Fritz worked on a few more pages of spells in the library, but he couldn't focus. After a long walk back to his room, he took out the leather-bound knife set from his dresser and carved mindlessly on his doll.

The smile still wasn't right, and now there were gashes in the doll's cheek from where he had cut too deeply. He threw the knife, and it stuck in the bedpost.

He pictured the anatomy book from the library shelf and traveled it to his bedroom. He studied the muscles in the face and even flexed his own facial muscles in a handheld mirror.

He threw down the book. "It's impossible to get this right!"

The doll stared at him blankly.

"I can't make the wood do what the muscles do, Doll." He curled his knees to his chest. "Wood doesn't stretch like muscle," he said, slapping his fists on the bed.

Fritz muttered a spell, and the wood shavings near the doll's feet slid up his body and reattached themselves to the toy's face. He climbed out of bed, angry and huffing. He traveled back to the library, snapped his fingers, and waited for his light to glow full power.

As he perused the shelves looking for a book on musculature, he ran his fingers across the spines, reading partial titles aloud as the rolling ladder slid across its track. "Markets. Martial. Melting. Mermaids. Mind control. Mining ..."

He stopped and rolled back a few inches.

"Mind control?" He pulled the small book from its spot and flipped through the pages. Several passages were underlined and a few had question marks drawn beside them.

He thumbed through the rest of the pages, and a note dropped from the back of the book. Fritz stopped it mid-flight and opened it.

The note was written in scrolling calligraphy.

*Why?*

*Plan?*

*Good or Bad?*

*Tell Boroda?*

*Tell R?*

The mantle clock struck midnight, causing Fritz to jump and almost fall off the ladder. He tucked the book and the note in his pocket and jumped from the rungs to the floor.

"Look what I found, Doll," he said to the toy before his smoky trail had vanished. "It's a book on mind control with a note inside." He showed the note to the inanimate figurine then studied it more carefully.

"Whoever wrote this knew Boroda," he explained to the wooden doll and tapped Boroda's name on the note. "They obviously had questions and wanted to tell

Boroda or R, whoever that is." He shrugged at the doll. "I don't know what the rest of it means. Maybe there are clues in the book."

He yawned, placed the book on his bedside table and went to sleep.

# CHAPTER 9

Marzi waved to Fritz from a small table in the back as soon as he stepped into the café. Her hair was pinned back with a plain clip, exposing her long neck and defined jaw.

Fritz wiped his palms on his pants and sat down.

"Sorry I'm late," he said. "I had an early training with Boroda."

She looked over his shoulder. The clock read noon on the dot.

"I got here early to read," she said and slid the book to the side of the table nearest the wall.

The waiter took their order then left.

"What's the plan?" Marzi asked.

"Well, I thought we could maybe go to the storage area and …" Fritz trailed off.

"You don't have a plan?" Marzi said, squinting at him.

"Honestly, I have no idea where to even start," Fritz confessed.

Marzi took the book she had been reading and opened it. "I was stuck, too, so I got *Clemmons Book of Logic and Deduction* and looked through it."

Fritz rubbed his neck. "I haven't gotten to that one yet."

"He said something in chapter three that stuck out to me." She read the passage to him: "'If you find that all possible options have been weighed and found wanting, it is then necessary to consider not the impossible, but the improbable. List them, no matter how bizarre they may seem. It is in this list that you will find the improbable morph into the probable or shed light on an avenue you hadn't thought to explore.'"

She put the book down.

"We agree that the storage areas are the best explanation for how they got to us, right? We've also established that it's impossible that an ape or a dragon could have traveled to our homes without us knowing, right?"

Fritz listened intently as he watched her pace.

"So, we have to find the improbable way they got to us." As she spoke, her pace quickened and her eyes sparkled. "I came up with a dozen crazy ideas that didn't make sense at all, but then I reread this and the word 'morph' popped out at me."

She looked at Fritz, waiting for him to share her excitement.

Fritz realized she'd stopped talking. "I'm still lost."

"Morph, Drosselmeyer. He said 'morph.'" She shook her hands. "What if the ape and dragon came to us, but we didn't recognize them because they didn't look like an ape or a dragon? What if they morphed?!"

"There's a spell for that?" Fritz asked.

"Spells can't be time delayed," Marzi explained. "You cast them, and they go into effect instantly. Well,

I mean, you can time the speed of a transformation spell, but …"

"So how did it happen?" Fritz interrupted.

"You told me that when Boroda handed you your apprentice garb, there was a moth," she said.

Fritz shrugged. "Sure. But we lived in the country. There were lots of moths and bugs. Especially at night when the house lights were on."

"Where did the moth go?" Marzi asked.

Fritz shrugged. "I don't know. But you aren't seriously saying that a moth could turn into a two-story-sized ape, are you?"

"I've never heard of it being done," Marzi admitted, "but that doesn't mean it isn't possible."

"Boroda looked at the spells on the ape. He probably would have caught a morphing spell," Fritz said.

The café owner set their plates down and left them to eat.

"Morphing isn't always a spell," Marzi explained. "It can also be an herbal reaction."

"What does that mean? Herbal?" Fritz shook his head.

"Herbal shops are usually run by hedge witches. They grow and harvest plants and make potions with them. They're more popular with lower-class wizards who don't have access to wizard-grade metal to store magic."

"Do you know a hedge witch we can ask?" Fritz asked.

"Hanja hates herbology. I think there's one around here that she uses when she has to, but I've never been. She's forbidden me from studying it."

"Boroda mentioned it to me but didn't give it much credence."

Marzi closed her eyes. "The few times I've heard Hanja mention her, I remember thinking it was a funny name, but I'm drawing a blank now."

Fritz brightened. "I bet Toby would know."

"Toby?"

"He's a local boy," Fritz said. "He delivers coal, so he knows just about every business in Anadorn."

Marzi grimaced. "It's not ideal, but it's something. Where's Toby?"

"I'll show you,"

Fritz paid for their meal, and they left the café.

Marzi took his arm and leaned on him, her teeth chattering. Fritz swallowed, trying not to trip. He forgot which direction the coal shop was at first then doubled back and led her there.

When Toby saw Fritz, his eyes lit up. He waved them over.

"Toby!" Fritz scolded. "Where is your coat? I thought you were going to buy one?"

"I did!" Toby said and coughed into his hand. "But Allison and her baby sister came down with the flu, and they only had a blanket, so I gave them my coat. I'm fine though."

He coughed again.

"You had enough silver for several coats," Fritz prodded. "What happened to that?"

Toby looked away. "Well, Mrs. Geddiston in number fourteen didn't have any heat at all, and she has holes in her wall you can see through, so I got her some coal and a blanket. Then there was Bill who stays near Millner's Alley, only he hadn't eaten in almost a week, so I got him some food and some shoes."

Marzi knelt down next to him. "When was the last time you ate?"

Toby looked at her suspiciously.

"This is Marzi," Fritz said. "She's my friend."

"Yesterday," Toby answered.

Marzi reached into her bag and pulled out a large sweet roll. "Here, have this."

Toby eyed it. "I don't want to take your food, ma'am."

Marzi looked surprised. "Well, I was just going to throw it away. I still can if you don't want it …"

Toby snatched the pastry from her hand and shoved the whole roll in his mouth.

"Toby, we need your help," Fritz said.

Toby looked up and sucked the sugar from his soot-stained fingers.

"We're looking for a shop that sells tea and plants and really odd things like roots," Marzi said. "It would probably smell really bad and have a funny-looking owner."

Toby thought for a moment. "Well, I don't deliver coal there, but Minerva Mooncup's is just across from

Mrs. Bolling's Hat Shop. It smells like a toilet sometimes, and Ms. Mooncup looks funny."

Marzi gasped. "Mooncup! That's it. Can you take us there?"

Toby glanced over at the coal shop. "I can't stay. I have more deliveries. Can you find your way back?"

Fritz assured him they could, and they set off.

Toby wound through alleys and streets, some that were so close together they had to walk single file. After quite a bit of walking, he pointed up a cobblestone street. "Second to the last shop there. The one with the purple awning."

Fritz gave him a couple silver coins. "Go buy a coat, Toby," he said. "And don't give it away."

Toby smiled and assured them he would get one. He ran back down the alley toward the coal shop.

Marzi looked somber.

"What's wrong?" Fritz asked.

She pointed in the direction Toby had disappeared. "That is. Why are we spending our time investigating who attacked one of our many houses when that boy is freezing because he gave his coat to someone who needed it more?"

Fritz didn't answer.

"These are the people I want to help with my magic." She dabbed at her eyes with her gloved hand. "I can wave my hand and make an entire banquet appear, but all I'm allowed to do is give him half a sticky bun."

Fritz began to say something but Marzi waved him off. "Sorry. Never mind me. Let's go see if Minerva is in."

As they neared the herbal shop, the stench made them both recoil.

"Watcher, have mercy! What is that smell?" Fritz asked.

"I don't know," Marzi said in a nasal tone. "But I understand why Hanja hates this practice."

They stepped into the shop. It was dimly lit and very damp. The smell of musty plants was thick enough to taste. Dried clumps of ferns hung from the ceiling and on the far wall. Several tables with boxes of glowing mushrooms cast an eerie glow on the rest of the room.

"May I help you?" an old, screechy voice asked.

Fritz and Marzi spun around.

Minerva Mooncup was about three-and-a-half feet tall, hunched over, and had a wild mop of matted hair sticking out from under a straw bonnet.

Neither Fritz nor Marzi spoke for a moment.

"S'alright." She waved. "I get this from all the first timers. Take your time. Gawk a little."

"No!" Marzi said, shocked. "It's not that. You just frightened us is all."

"Mm hmm," Minerva harrumphed. "I had to store my fang-toothed water snake somewhere while I cleaned his tank and forgot where I put him 'til I sat down on the can. *That's* frightening. Not this."

"We have a question about herbology," Fritz spluttered.

"And here I thought you was going to ask me about my cherry cobbler. Alright, what do you want to know?"

"We're looking for a morphing potion," Marzi said.

Minerva looked at them blankly then shook her head. "Do you want me to pick one for you?"

She flashed a coy smile at Fritz. "You'd make a handsome dog. *That* potion is on sale."

Fritz laughed nervously. "We don't know anything about them, so we're hoping you could tell us how they work."

Minerva wheezed loudly and moved her spindly arms in deliberate jabs. "Ah! Ok. Well, a morphing potion turns one thing into another for a certain amount of time."

"Not permanently then?" Marzi asked excitedly.

"If they was permanent, I'd look like the goddess of beauty and open my own skivvies shop on the main square."

"How long does a morph last?" Fritz asked.

"Depends on the strength of the blend. Nothing over a couple days, though." She looked them both up and down. "What kind of morph are you wanting?"

"We don't actually want one," Fritz told her. "We just want to see if certain ones are possible."

Minerva sighed. "In that case, I've got a snake to feed—and after what he saw the other day, I'll be surprised if he ever eats again."

"Please!" Marzi called out. "We'll pay you for your information."

A cloying smile spread over the hedge witch's face, and she bowed obsequiously. "At your service, my dear."

"Can someone turn an ape into a moth?" Fritz asked.

Minerva's warted face went ashen white, then red with anger. "Who are you? Who sent you?"

"Is it possible?" Fritz asked more forcefully.

"Get out of my shop!" she screamed, and the mushrooms darkened and began to hiss streams of spores into the air.

Minerva waved her hands and screeched. "You tell whoever you work for that if anyone sets foot in my shop again, I will feed them to my gilly worms!"

Minerva backed them out under the awning, and a small crowd of workers poked their heads out of the millinery shop across the narrow street.

"Like I told the other one, 'Madame Minerva Mooncup is discreet at all times and don't need threats to keep her quiet.' I'm not saying a word, an' it ain't because I'm scared!"

She slammed the door shut with a loud crack. A pot hanging from a wooden beam fell from its hook and shattered on the cobbles below.

Marzi tried to knock on the door, but Fritz pulled her away.

"Fritz, she might know who attacked us!" she protested.

"And I highly doubt she's going to tell us," Fritz said and hid his face from the group of workers. "It's safe to say the ape was morphed, and if I had to guess, your dragon was probably morphed, too."

Marzi quickened her pace. "I can't believe this. Someone altered animals and then morphed them to travel into our homes."

"Looks like it," Fritz said. "At least we know how they did it. We only have to figure out who and hope they tell us why."

They turned a corner and walked down a narrow passage.

Marzi looked around. "I'm going to go home. Let's talk on Monday."

"Ok, see you later," Fritz said.

Marzi disappeared in a cloud of red vapor.

Fritz grinned openly and watched her cloud disappear, running his fingers through the dissipating mist. He double-checked to make sure no one was watching, then traveled to his own room.

He twirled once in happy reverie and was about to flop on his bed when Boroda called to him from the mirror. "Get ready, Fritz. It's time to see the Czar."

# CHAPTER 10

Fritz stood in the spacious hall outside the Czar's office, unable to shake a sense of foreboding. The palace appeared to have once been a warm, inviting place. Floor-to-ceiling windows ran the length of the hall. Colorful tapestries and paintings hung on the walls opposite the windows. Gauzy curtains, pulled back and tied with gold tassels, draped limply from ornate, brass rods. Even with the curtains completely shut, the hallway wasn't too dark.

Now, Fritz noticed, the picture frames were lined with a layer of dust, and the windows were bolted shut. The plush furniture was shoved into a far corner and replacing it were bare, wooden benches that could better accommodate sword-wearing soldiers.

Boroda stood beside Fritz, his face cold and blank.

At length, two unseen sentries opened the door, and a deep, booming voice called out.

"Boroda."

Boroda entered the room with Fritz close behind.

"Your Highness. My apprentice, Drosselmeyer." He motioned with his hand, and Fritz stepped forward and bowed as Boroda had.

The Czar, a tall man with a barrel chest and thick black beard, was dressed in a rich red military costume, matching those of the guards who stood motionless on either side of his desk.

"Ah, yes. The boy who knocked my Nicholaus down."

Fritz swallowed.

The Czar motioned for Fritz to approach him. "I am surprised by your physique," he said, studying Fritz.

He walked in a circle, sizing up the teenager, then sat back down in his chair. "I was expecting someone bigger and more muscular."

Fritz concentrated on taking even, regulated breaths.

The Czar leaned back and placed his hands behind his head. "My boy is arrogant, mean, and weak. He deserved every last bit of what you gave him. Frankly, you taught him a lesson I wasn't able to. I feel as though I should thank you."

Fritz stared at the Czar as he felt his pulse slow.

"However," Czar Nicholaus continued, "you have also shamed my son and, by extension, me. This cannot go unpunished."

He stood, squaring his shoulders to Fritz.

"It is possible that you will one day serve my son in the same role as Boroda serves me."

Fritz tensed as the Czar walked behind him.

"The thought of serving someone so immature, selfish, and puerile as my son may seem unbearable. It would to me if I were in your position."

The Czar continued to circle Fritz. "In fact, I might be tempted to undermine his authority. If I did, I'd probably ally myself with some other noble's son. The Southern Kingdom, perhaps. I'm not accusing you of doing this; I'm only saying I'd be tempted to do that."

He looked down at Fritz. "Are you going to undermine my son's eventual authority, Drosselmeyer?"

Fritz shook his head slightly.

"I need an assurance from you, Drosselmeyer, that you will serve my son, or me—should, Watcher forbid, Boroda be killed …" He glanced at Boroda, who squinted in a soft grimace.

"I need to know," the Czar reiterated, "that I can count on your faithful service, both here as well as at school."

Fritz breathed harder but kept his face a chilly blank. He nodded at the Czar but kept his focus on a sizable cabinet against the far wall.

The Czar let out a low, booming laugh. "It has pride!" he called to Boroda and pointed at Fritz. "Good luck with this one."

He turned back to Fritz. "Drosselmeyer, I want you to meet a friend of mine." He nodded, and a soldier stationed behind Fritz opened a hallway door.

Slow, heavy footsteps accented by quick, light ones entered the room.

Czar Nicholaus dropped to his knees and held out his arms, and a warm smile crossed his face. "Alexei, come, give me a hug."

Fritz turned to greet the newcomer, and his breath caught. He started to move, but his body snapped rigid by an invisible force. Boroda caught his eye and shook his head almost imperceptibly.

Franz hopped up the stairs and hugged the Czar in a tight embrace. He was dressed in a colorful outfit similar to a Central Kingdom guard, with a wooden sword hanging at his waist.

Fritz felt tears burn the rims of his eyes.

"I got a new sword, Dyadya," Franz said. His green eyes sparkled. "Papa is teaching me how to use it but says I can't have a real one until I'm twelve." Franz unsheathed the wooden toy and demonstrated a lunge.

"Your Papa is very wise. It would be a shame to see you get injured from such a dangerous weapon," Czar Nicholaus said with grandfatherly warmth. He grabbed Franz around the waist and lifted him into a tight embrace.

He turned to Fritz. "Drosselmeyer, I would like to introduce you to my top official, General Pieter Andoyavich."

The general bowed.

"And his son, Alexei," the Czar continued with a slight edge. "Alexei, I would like to introduce you to Drosselmeyer."

Franz squirmed out of the Czar's arms and stepped halfway behind the noble's leg.

"No, Alexei, you must shake his hand. If you are to be a soldier in the Central Guard, you must act like one." The Czar pushed Franz forward.

Franz obeyed, and Fritz shook the small outstretched hand. Every fiber in Fritz's body wanted to wrap Franz in his arms and escape.

"Now, Alexei, I want you to go practice your sword fighting. I will come fight with you later." The Czar patted Franz's head then nodded to the General.

The General bowed, first to the Czar then to Boroda. He grabbed Franz's hand and walked him out of the room without speaking.

Czar Nicholaus returned to his desk. "Family is the most important thing we have, is it not?"

Tears ran down Fritz's cheeks.

"I would do anything for my family," the Czar continued. "I would risk my life for them." He lowered his voice. "I wouldn't hesitate to slay my closest friends and their families if it meant protecting my own."

He crossed slowly toward Fritz until his mouth was inches from his ear. "Am I clear, Drosselmeyer?"

Fritz bit his lip and nodded his head.

The Czar straightened and walked back to his desk. "Thank you, Boroda. That is all. I trust we will have no more issues at school—or elsewhere."

Boroda bowed. "I can assure you of it."

Czar Nicholaus didn't respond.

Boroda gripped Fritz's elbow and walked him quickly out of the room. No sooner had the door shut behind them than Boroda traveled them back to the foyer of his mansion.

"Get dressed and meet me in the training room," Boroda said without looking back.

"Why didn't you tell me?" Fritz yelled at him.

"Meet me in the training room," Boroda reiterated and disappeared.

Fritz didn't bother changing. He traveled directly to the training room, where he ripped off his cape and threw it on the ground.

"That was my brother!" he shouted into the mirror on the wall.

There was no response.

"How could you tell the Czar about my brother?" Fritz slammed his fist. The mirror tilted from the blow.

The resulting silence enraged Fritz. *They can do whatever they want to you because you belong to them.*

"I guess I shouldn't be surprised that you'd sacrifice my brother's life for your own advancement," Fritz spat. "From what I hear, that's pretty common with wizards."

Silence. Fritz bared his teeth. "Did you kill your last apprentice because the Czar commanded it or because you wanted to?"

Boroda exploded into the room in a fiery ball of magic. He hit Fritz with a powerful spell that knocked him off his feet.

Fritz caught himself against the wall and crouched.

Boroda ran at him, hands hurling a series of attacks.

Fritz traveled in a small statue from the garden and put it directly in front of Boroda's foot.

Boroda tripped and rolled. It was a graceful tumble; he popped up and whipped out a bolt of electricity.

Fritz blocked the bolt and felt his energy drain. He conjured up the spell Marzi had used in the garden, and a brilliant flash of light blazed in front of Boroda.

Boroda stumbled sideways.

Fritz threw a large beam of energy at Boroda's torso. The magic separated and flowed around him like a stream hitting a rock.

Boroda reached out and lashed Fritz's arms, pinning him.

Fritz reversed the spell.

Boroda stepped in close, striking him with his fist.

Fritz gasped in pain but blocked the next strike.

Boroda punched again.

Fritz used the momentum of the punch and threw Boroda against the wall.

The Life Bond spell cushioned the blow.

Boroda shot another spell.

Fritz blocked it, and his energy drained further. He was breathing hard and sweat streamed down his face.

Spell after spell hit Fritz's magical shield, and his blocking power faded.

Boroda wrapped Fritz's arms in a binding spell that Fritz couldn't unlock. He lifted Fritz in the air, the invisible coils constricting until Fritz's face began to turn red.

Fritz glared at him in defiance. His vision was blurring, and he couldn't breathe.

"If you ever speak of my apprentice again that way, I promise you will wish for death," Boroda whispered with an acid tone. He was panting, and his eyes were dark with rage.

Fritz struggled against the invisible bonds. The room was blurry and then blinked black.

Boroda released the spell, and Fritz fell to the floor. "Get dressed for training," he hissed.

Fritz clenched his fists.

The Czar had his brother.

Boroda had the Life Bond.

Fritz was Boroda's property.

He had no choice but to comply.

Fritz walked, not traveled, back to the training room. He was under no obligation to take the fastest route, and at the moment, he was in no mood to be amiable.

Having only walked the route once before, it took him longer than he'd planned to navigate the many hallways and staircases in the large mansion.

He paused outside the door, calming his temper before facing Boroda. As he reached for the knob, he heard Boroda raise his voice at someone.

Fritz opened the door slightly and peered in through the crack.

"If you didn't tell him, then who did?" Boroda said.

The mirror glowed and pulsed as the voice responded. "My wife doesn't even know the whole story, Boroda. Again, I have no idea how he found out."

"Drosselmeyer is furious with me." Boroda rubbed his eyes and ran his hands through his hair.

"Can you tell him?" the disembodied voice asked.

"He's not ready yet," Boroda replied with a heavy sigh.

"How soon until he is?"

"Not too much longer," Boroda answered. "He can memorize spells faster than anyone I've ever met. His instincts in a fight are spectacular." Boroda shook his head. "If I could stop losing my temper …"

The mirror continued to pulse. "This is only a small setback. I will continue to protect Alexei—with my life if I have to."

Fritz's eyes widened.

The General.

"I know you will," Boroda said. "Drosselmeyer will be here soon. I need to go. Find out who leaked the information about Alexei. If we have a mole, I want to know about it."

The mirror blinked off, and Boroda stepped back and began stretching.

Fritz leaned against the wall outside the door and tried to stop his head from spinning.

If Boroda hadn't revealed Franz's identity, then who had? *And why would they?* Fritz thought. *I'm hardly a threat to anyone.*

"Fritz!" Boroda yelled.

Fritz leapt up from the floor, heart pounding.

"Get down here, immediately!" Boroda yelled into the mirror.

Fritz traveled twenty feet into the training room. "Sorry I'm late."

Boroda softened and dropped his gaze. "Don't worry about it. Pick up a sword, and let's begin."

# CHAPTER 11

On Monday, when Fritz opened his locker, a large rat jumped out and bolted down the hall.

He yelped and leapt back.

Several girls screamed and jumped on tiptoes as the rodent ran past them.

Fritz saw Nicholaus at the end of the hall looking directly at him.

Nicholaus smiled and winked.

On Tuesday, when Fritz opened his bag to take out his textbook during first period, a rat scampered out and ran toward the doorway.

He yelled in surprise.

Ms. Wakimba spun deftly from the blackboard and demanded to know why. Her piercing stare and stony face tightened at his response.

"I'm sorry, I thought I saw … something," Fritz said.

Nicholaus was staring at him, a grin plastered on his face.

"Maybe the Headmaster should check your eyes," Ms. Wakimba threatened. She wrote him a warning and assigned extra work.

Nicholaus turned to him from the corner of the room and winked.

Fritz heard Vivienne giggle, so he turned to look at her. She and Gelé both waved at the young prince, and Gelé winked back at him.

On Wednesday, when Fritz sat down at the apprentice's lunch table, Gelé and Vivienne weren't there.

"What's up with them?" Fritz motioned to their usual seats.

"I guess Nicholaus likes pale blondes now," Faruk said with a shrug and motioned to Nicholaus's table.

Nicholaus had his arm draped over Gelé's shoulder while Vivienne chatted with Evgeny and Oleg.

Fritz opened his lunch pail; two small rats jumped out and scuttled toward Nicholaus's table.

Two girls carrying trays to their own table screamed. The room fell silent, and everyone looked their way.

The lunch monitor began weaving her way toward them.

"Nick!" Gelé punched the prince's arm playfully.

Vivienne picked up one of the rats and began petting it.

Nicholaus looked over at Fritz and winked again.

A vein in Fritz's temple began to pulse.

"You gonna let him get away with it?" Faruk asked.

"Faruk!" Marzi warned. "Don't encourage bad behavior."

"I'm just wondering what Drossie is going to do. Nothing more."

"I'm sure Drossie will keep a cool head," Marzi countered and looked at Fritz.

"They're just rats," Fritz said dismissively.

Andor made a few signs and Marzi shook her head, refusing to interpret.

Andor insisted and Marzi reluctantly shared his message. "Andor says that if you need help breaking his arms, he will be glad to hold back his friends."

Fritz signed, "Thank you."

Andor pointed at Fritz's apple.

"There are rat bites in it, Andor," Fritz mouthed.

Andor shrugged and snatched the apple.

"Will you be in the library today?" Marzi asked. "You haven't been coming this week."

Fritz mumbled an excuse, finished eating, and left without any further conversation.

On Thursday, during math, Fritz found a rat in his desk. It was a fat, black rat that barely moved when he opened the lid.

Fritz saw it and started.

He could see Nicholaus in his periphery. The dark-haired boy was looking in his direction. Fritz ignored him but with a red face and clenched jaw.

During the last class period, after a grueling round of calisthenics, McGregor addressed his panting class. "Tomorrow we begin to practice for the trials."

Some students groaned; others whispered excitedly.

"We'll be on two teams," he explained in a thick brogue. "Each team will have a flag planted somewhere on their side. Your job is to protect your flag and, if you can, take the other team's."

He stepped over Edward, who was still heaving from the workout. "I expect you to play fair. If you get shot, you leave the woods. Do you understand?"

The class moaned a lack-luster response.

"Dismissed!" he yelled.

Marzi caught up with Fritz. "Hey, I don't know what's going on with you right now, but I have some new thoughts about our discoveries last weekend. Can you come to the library today?"

"I can't. I have to, uh, train. Boroda is really being hard on me."

"Ok. Well, let's meet tomorrow?" Marzi asked.

"Sure," said Fritz. "Tomorrow is great."

"See you then." Marzi smiled and headed toward the girl's locker room.

Fritz walked into the other locker room and heard Edward whimpering.

"Give them back!" he demanded.

Fritz rounded the corner. Nicholaus held Edward's glasses above his head. Evgeny and Oleg stood next to him with arms folded. All three wore cruel grins.

"You have to take them, Squishy. Come on, be a man," Nicholaus sneered.

Evgeny and Oleg exchanged snickers.

Edward noticed Fritz and called out, "Drossie, tell him to give me my glasses back."

Nicholaus turned and smiled. "Oh, rats, guys. Look who showed up."

"Give him the glasses, Nicholaus," Fritz said and looked away.

Nicholaus folded the glasses in one hand. "No."

Fritz felt his pulse quicken.

Nicholaus squeezed his hand, and the glasses crunched under his grip.

"Hey!" Edward yelled. "Drossie, stop him!"

Nicholaus sneered. "Yeah, Drossie, stop me."

Fritz stood motionless.

Nicholaus backhanded Edward and the boy fell back, clutching his face.

The other boys in the locker room ran to see what the commotion was.

Nicholaus cocked his head. "You going to stop me, Drossie?"

Fritz gritted his teeth.

"That's what I thought," Nicholaus said. "Good boy," he whispered and turned, stepping on the glasses as he left the locker room.

Fritz knelt down by Edward and helped him up. "You ok?"

"No thanks to you!" Edward spat and yanked his arm free.

Fritz sighed, "Edward …"

Edward collected the fragments of his glasses without acknowledging Fritz.

Fritz felt his temper flare. "Why didn't you fight back?"

"He would have beaten me up!" said Edward.

"Well, I can't fight all your fights for you," said Fritz. "Maybe it is time to grow up and be a man."

Edward screwed up his face then ran out of the gym.

Fritz growled and punched a locker. He rubbed his eyes and walked after the boy.

"Edward, stop!" he called.

He caught up with the chubby boy and grabbed his shoulder.

Edward turned around, tears streaming down his face. "What?"

"I'm sorry. I shouldn't have said that," Fritz said. "Things are kind of rough right now and I … I just …" He threw up his hands. "There's no excuse. I'm sorry for saying that. Will you forgive me?" He extended his hand.

Edward considered the apology and accepted the gesture. His shoulders fell, and he huffed a long, belabored sigh. "I forgive you."

"Thanks," Fritz said. "And tomorrow, during trials, let's disappear in the woods and skip the whole thing."

"Deal. I'm pretty sure Nicholaus has already told his friends to save their ammo for me."

"Why does he dislike you so much?"

"My dad isn't just any duke or ambassador," Edward said. "He's next in line to rule the Southern Kingdom. Our King, my uncle, is sick and doesn't have any children."

Fritz let out a low whistle. "Wow."

"The Southern Kingdom is the biggest threat to the Central, and Nicholaus's dad …"

"I know who his dad is," said Fritz.

"Nicholaus is trying to humiliate me in the eventuality that my family begins to rule." Edward slumped his shoulders and reached up to adjust his absent glasses out of habit.

"Can't your dad do anything to stop the bullying?" Fritz asked.

Edward shook his head. "I'm the youngest of four boys."

Fritz looked confused.

"My oldest brother will be the King after my dad. Then my second, then my third ... I'm the last in line. No one cares about the last in line."

Fritz squeezed the despondent boy's shoulder. "I care about the last in line."

A genuine smile splayed across Edward's face. "Thanks, Drossie."

"I'm sorry for not sticking up for you," Fritz said again. "I can't explain it, but ..." He paused. "I have to be careful with Nicholaus."

"You don't have to explain it to me." Edward slumped his shoulders.

"It's ok," Edward said. "Maybe he'll leave me alone for awhile. I have to go." Edward stepped into a carriage, waved to Fritz, and was gone.

Fritz watched the carriage disappear around the corner. He walked to his hideaway in the hedges and traveled home.

He dressed, traveled to the training room, and began stretching. He and Boroda weren't supposed to meet for another two hours, but ever since he'd overheard Boroda and General Andoyavich's conversation, he purposed to do whatever it took to help keep Franz safe.

He began silently moving through the series of kicks and punches from his hand-to-hand combat training.

He envisioned Nicholaus and struck quickly.

He saw the Czar, surrounded by his guards, and hurried his attacks. He visualized the four guards advancing, and he brought them all down with a rapid succession of kicks and punches. Finally, he wiped the smug look off the Czar's face with a lethal heel kick to the head.

"I'd hate to be whoever that was," Boroda said from behind.

Fritz stood up and faced his teacher. His shirt was already sweat-stained, but he beckoned Boroda to the mat. "Let's hope it ends better for you than it did for them."

They sparred for an hour then finished the evening perfecting a generic but powerful blocking spell that would cover the most common magical strikes.

"If The Order is so powerful, and you're all friends, why do I have to spend so much time on defensive spells against other wizards?" Doubled over and panting, Fritz was nearly spent from magical exertion.

"I want you to be prepared for everything. Even the unimaginable," Boroda replied. He wiped off a blade with a rag and traveled it back to the rack.

"Do you trust The Order?" Fritz asked.

Boroda snickered and didn't respond. He handed him the rag. "Finish cleaning these."

Fritz obeyed. He smoothed the notches out of the blades and sharpened them on a stone. He finished wiping the blades down with oil and swiped the weapons through the open air.

"You want to threaten my brother?" he whispered to the imaginary Czar and stabbed the knives back into their slots. Once he was back in his room, he changed out of his sweaty clothes.

"Boroda doesn't trust The Order, Doll," he told the lopsided toy on his side table.

"If he can't trust them, how can I trust anyone to keep Franz from harm?"

"I am unsure, sir," Doll said mechanically.

"The answer is, I can't!" Fritz said.

He put on his shoes.

"I need to find out where that General lives so I can keep an eye on my brother."

Doll blinked and turned his head as Fritz walked over to his closet.

"Want to know how I'm going to find out where the General lives?" Fritz called to Doll.

Doll made no reply, and Fritz huffed in annoyance. He had enchanted Doll to respond to questions of ability but responses to questions about personal desires were tricky.

"Say 'Yes,' Doll," he commanded.

"Yes," Doll responded.

"Well, I'll tell you. I'm traveling to the Czar's palace to look for information."

# CHAPTER 12

Fritz didn't wait for a response from Doll. He adjusted his cap, spun around, and traveled to the hallway outside the Czar's office—a stun spell at the ready should he encounter anyone.

The hallway was empty, but he crept into a shadow just to make sure. He listened at the Czar's door for the sound of any occupants, but it was quiet. He traveled inside the room to the far corner where he would be the most hidden should a guard be present.

The office was, like the hall, empty.

Fritz crept over to the large desk and unlocked the drawers with a flick of his wrist. He shuffled through the papers but found nothing that listed the General's name or location.

He moved over to a cabinet and began to open the drawer, when he heard the door knob turn. Fritz dove behind the large piece of furniture before the Czar walked over to his desk and sat down.

Fritz started to picture his room but stopped; he couldn't risk traveling away and having the gust of smoke betray his presence. He squeezed back even tighter against the wall.

The Czar stood and walked to the center of the room. The hard surfaces of the space carried his voice with acute clarity.

"Welcome," he said to someone.

Fritz hadn't heard anyone else enter.

"Thank you," came the curt, formal reply.

Fritz froze.

That was Borya's voice.

He flattened against the cabinet, moving slowly to avoid any creaking floorboards. He peeked around the cabinet and nearly gasped out loud.

Borya stood with his back facing Fritz. Across from him was the Czar.

A figure, dressed in black, whose face was obscured by a tightly woven shroud, stood between them, his profile dark against the wooden interior of the room.

A lump on the third person's shoulder wiggled, then crawled to the other shoulder with a chittering squeak.

"A rat!" Fritz breathed and quickly tucked back out of sight.

"Duke Klazinsky is causing me trouble," the Czar said unceremoniously. "I'd like him gone."

"We had to come here just for that?" Borya droned.

"I think Boroda knows something is going on. I'm not going to chance using your magic mirror and having him discover our arrangement. Until I can be sure, all our meetings will be held in person," the Czar said authoritatively.

Fritz felt his pulse quicken.

"Do you no longer trust Boroda's loyalty?" Borya said with a hint of amusement.

"I'm sure you know he got another apprentice?" the Czar said.

"Yes," said Borya with a haughty laugh. "The Order gave him the mandate several months back. Looks as if he picked a blundering idiot just to spite us, but that's neither here nor there. What is it to you?"

Fritz scowled at the jab.

The Czar smiled. "Did you also know the apprentice has a brother?"

The black figure shrugged, causing the rat to lurch and scramble to the other shoulder.

"And how did you come by this information?" Borya asked.

The Czar tutted. "So, he didn't tell you?"

Borya tightened his grip on his staff.

The Czar straightened a medal on his chest. "Around the time he told me he would be absent to train his new apprentice, one of my Generals adopted a son. This general served under my brother so, naturally, I keep my eye on him," he said with a smug grin.

"The boy had blond hair and green eyes. Hard not to remember that combination—especially in the Central Kingdom where blond hair is such a rarity.

"The new apprentice had a tiff with my son at school, and when young Nicholaus mentioned that he wanted to gouge out his bright, green eyes with his thumbs, it made me curious, so I started asking around. Sure enough, the boys were adopted from an orphanage here in the Central Kingdom."

Borya stood very still. "Very interesting."

"The irony of it all is that they were both at Ivanov's."
The Czar laughed.

Borya stepped back. "You don't say?"

"I do say," the Czar quipped. "Which brings me to
my next request. I am having some boys shipped from
Ivanov's for my annual party. I guess the new apprentice
did some damage before he left, and Ivanov is terrified of
retribution. I told him you would accompany him in his
carriage."

Borya motioned to his protégé. "I can have …"

"No," the Czar interrupted. "I want him to be with
me. I don't know how much Boroda knows about my
parties and would rather have a fighter by my side should
he decide to cause trouble."

Borya scraped his staff on the floor. "I can assure
you, Czar, my skills are …"

"Rusty, Borya," the Czar snipped. "Your skills are
rusty, as are all the other wizards in your group. I will not
repeat my request again. I want you with Ivanov, and I
want the Black Wizard with me."

Borya said nothing, but the tip of his staff pulsed
lightly.

"Please take care of the Duke Klazinsky problem
soon, and then I will contact you again about the party."
The Czar dismissed the two with a wave of his hand.

Before they left, he called out, "Borya!"

Borya turned reluctantly, and Fritz scooted back, out
of view.

"Yes, Czar?" Borya hissed.

"Keep an eye on Boroda."

"Boroda will not be a problem for much longer, Czar," Borya sneered. Fritz heard the contempt drip from Borya's words and shivered.

Both wizards traveled out.

The Czar sat at his desk for a few minutes then exited.

Fritz traveled home and immediately began to pace.

"Should I tell Boroda?" he asked out loud.

"I am unsure, sir," Doll commented, turning its head toward Fritz.

"As soon as I tell him, he'll ask why I went." Fritz continued pacing as Doll's head followed his movements.

"Why did you go to the Czar's palace? The same Czar I told you to respect and whose idiot son I told you not to pick on?" Fritz mimicked Boroda's stern voice.

"I am unsure, sir," Doll answered the question.

Fritz paid no attention to Doll. "Because I don't trust you to keep my brother safe, Boroda. By the way, Borya is planning on doing something to you, but I don't know what. Also, he's throwing a party, and my old orphanage is involved but I don't know how or why. Oh, and I saw the Black Wizard … Yes, I know about the Black Wizard because I was eavesdropping on you when you were talking into the mirror about overthrowing The Order and the Czar. Also, he's going to kill someone named Klazinsky, but I don't even know if murder is a big deal to The Order, seeing as we apprentices are your chattel, and our families are little more than offal to you."

"What does the Black Wizard look like, Drosselmeyer?" He, again, mimicked Boroda's voice.

"Here, let me draw a picture of the Black Wizard for you. Yep, it's a person in black clothes. Hope that helps you find him, and I hope that you won't be mad at me and rip my skin off with some spell."

Fritz collapsed on the bed, slightly winded. He looked over at Doll, whose unblinking eyes turned in his direction.

"I can't tell him yet, Doll. I don't think he'd understand. I'll wait and tell him later." He curled up under his covers. "Is that right? Am I making the right choice?"

"I am unsure, sir," Doll replied.

"You and me, both, Doll," Fritz mumbled. "You and me both."

The students stood huddled on the school field near the woods. A heavy blanket of snow had fallen the night before, and an icy wind cut through their coats. Several students cried out from the gust, jumping up and down and rubbing their arms feverishly.

Gelé tucked her shoulder into Nicholaus's arm. Her blonde ponytail contrasted against his black jacket.

Vivienne stood between Evgeny and Oleg and con tinued to whisper while McGregor shouted rules and orders.

"If you see someone from the other side on your territory, stop them!" McGregor shouted.

Edward raised his hand. "How do we stop them?"

Oleg mimicked Edward's voice with a nasal whine and Edward looked down, blushing.

"Aye, it's a good question," McGregor said and pulled out a gun from under his coat. A nearby cluster of students gasped and fell silent.

McGregor pointed the gun at Andor and pulled the trigger.

Everyone screamed and ducked.

A blue cloud of smoke billowed around Andor, and he looked down at his chest, where a splotch of blue chalk dotted his coat.

"If you get shot, you're out," McGregor announced. "Each of you will have a gun and three shots. Use them wisely. First team to capture the opposing side's flag wins. If no one captures each other's flags, then the side with the most people still in the game wins."

He passed out the guns from a large chest as the class tromped by to the edge of the forest. Once the entire class had been armed with the appropriate colors for their particular team, McGregor raised a different gun into the air.

"You have half an hour." He pulled the trigger and the loud crack signaled the start of the game.

Students raced to the far edge of the woods to put themselves as far as possible from the opposite team and to hide their flag in as difficult a spot as they could find.

Fritz, Marzi, Edward, and Andor hurried back into the woods, out of sight from the rest of the class. Andor took the lead and, with his giant frame, cut a path through the snowy undergrowth. The others followed behind in his footprints. They had walked for several minutes when the woods opened up into a clearing.

In the middle of the clearing was a giant tree with sprawling branches hung low to the ground.

"Sweet! A tree!" Edward exclaimed and waddled past Andor.

He jumped up and grabbed the lowest branch but was unable to hoist himself any farther, so Andor lifted him up.

"Thanks," Edward said to Andor.

Marzi chuckled and walked around the perimeter of the tree. "This would be an excellent tree to duel in." She spoke too softly for Edward to overhear but loudly enough to catch Fritz's attention.

"How so?" Fritz asked her.

"The network of branches offers plenty of cover to intercept spells and many opportunities to change the direction of your attack with minimal movement," she explained.

"If The Order ever did get in a fight, who would win?" Fritz asked playfully.

Marzi thought for a moment. "It would be tough to tell. Sylvia, Glacinda, and Borya would probably be the first to die."

Fritz started. "Why's that?"

"They don't train anymore. They're lazy," Marzi answered bluntly.

"And the rest?" Fritz reached up and snapped off a twig.

"Eric fights a lot, but I think he would rely on brute strength too much. Andor's spells are very sloppy, but his hand-to-hand combat is very good."

"Does Hanja still train?" Fritz prodded.

Marzi smiled coyly at him. "That's none of your business."

Fritz laughed. "Fair enough."

"I heard about what happened in the boy's locker room," Marzi said, continuing to circle the tree.

Fritz grimaced.

"Did you get in trouble for hitting Nicholaus the last time?" she asked.

"Yeah, it was bad."

"I'm sorry," Marzi said softly.

"Thanks, but I'd rather not talk about it," Fritz said.

"Gelé is ingratiating herself with Nicholaus. I think she wants to take Boroda's spot in the Central Kingdom," Marzi said.

"She can have it. I won't stop her," Fritz mumbled.

Marzi raised her eyebrows. "You'd give up your position with the Czar? The Central Kingdom is the most powerful one by far. The Southern Kingdom is the next, and it's not even close."

Fritz turned to her. "I'm not even sure if I'm going to …" He was cut short by a small fleshy ball thudding into his shoulder. Instinctively, he grabbed it and threw it away from him.

It was a rat.

"Nicholaus!" he spat and swiveled around to find him.

The woods were empty.

"There's another one!" Marzi pointed to the ground.

A rat scampered on Fritz's foot, and he kicked it away.

Edward screamed and started to scurry down the tree. A rat jumped from the branches and landed on his back. He swatted at it, lost his grip, and fell. Andor caught him and set him on the ground.

More rats crawled over the snowy ground toward the group.

"What is this?" Marzi asked, kicking at a large brown one.

"Not sure," Fritz responded.

"Can we go?" Edward asked, hopping his way to the edge of the tree.

Fritz looked beyond the tree and his breath caught in his throat. The forest floor was churning as hundreds of rats raced in their direction.

"Run!" Fritz shouted, and they all launched into the woods, back toward the school.

The rats clawed through the forest floor after them. They ran deftly over the snowy patches and threaded the underbrush with ease.

The four students pushed through thorny patches and tree branches, driven faster by the hordes of rats closing in on them.

Edward screamed in pain and fell. A rat was hanging from his wrist, and several more were climbing over his baggy clothing toward his exposed neck. Blood trickled from his hand as the rodent clamped down.

Fritz blasted the rats off with a push of magic, then grabbed Edward's arm and yanked him forward.

The rats were almost on them. The frontrunners attacked, eyes red and glowing.

"There's the clearing!" Fritz shouted.

They turned and raced toward the open field.

The rats swirled like a tidal wave after them. The bushes shook with the hordes of rodents running beneath them. Snow fell from the branches as a battalion of rats took to the trees to chase their quarry.

Andor roared in pain and shook several off his back.

Edward was heaving, his plump body unable to keep pace. He stumbled on a small bush, but Fritz held him upright.

The rats overtook Fritz. They pounced, latching onto whatever they could sink their teeth into. Two large rats clawed up his coat toward his face.

Ignoring the burning in his side, Fritz ripped his coat off and tore through the trees toward the field.

They finally burst through the clearing. Several students with colored splotches of chalk on their coats looked at them with confused expressions as they exited the tree line and raced toward the center of the field.

When Fritz realized that they were no longer being pursued, he called to the group.

They slowed and turned to look at the thicket.

The rats stayed within the tree line. The roiling cloud of fur thinned as they retreated back into the woods.

Edward gasped for air.

"Did something scare you?" Nicholaus smirked.

He was standing a few feet away, a blue mark visible on his shoulder.

Gelé and Vivienne looked at Fritz with confused expressions but said nothing.

Fritz jumped up from the ground, intent on pummeling the smug prince, but Andor held him back.

"That's right. Let the ape stop you," Nicholaus said slowly.

McGregor fired his gun, signaling the end of class, and the other students trickled out of the woods. He looked around, counting students with his chin and, satisfied that all were present, blew his whistle to get everyone's attention. "Looks like the red team wins today."

The team members exchanged cheers, and everyone began talking at once.

"Turn in your guns here, and then you're dismissed!" McGregor boomed.

Later that afternoon, Andor, Marzi, and Fritz sat in the library turret room. Marzi dabbed Andor's bite marks with a cloth.

"What happened?" Marzi asked.

"I don't know, but it's been happening to me all week. This isn't natural. It has to be magic," Fritz mused.

"No one can do magic on school grounds," Marzi reminded him.

"We can't, or we're not allowed?" Fritz asked.

"Both," Marzi replied. "The Order put the enchantment on St. Michael's a long time ago. Not only can you NOT do magic here, but also, if you try, The Order will find out, and you can get removed. They take that very seriously."

"Does the enchantment include the woods?" Fritz asked as he paced.

"Yes," Marzi replied. "The entire forest is covered by the dome."

Andor began signing—too fast for Fritz to pick up—and Marzi watched with rapt attention. Her face paled.

"What?" Fritz asked anxiously.

"He said that two weeks ago, his house was attacked by a large bear. He said the bear had red eyes like the rats."

Marzi watched Andor carefully.

"He said this bear was also larger than the other bears in the woods near his house."

Andor quit signing, and Marzi looked at Fritz. "His axe did little damage to the bear—he had to hack at it many times to kill it."

"That's three of us," Fritz said shakily. "That we know of. Should … should we tell the others?"

"That's what I wanted to talk to you about," she replied.

Andor watched them talk and made a sign to Marzi. Marzi signed while she spoke.

"When we left Minerva Mooncup's shop last weekend, she told us that she would have been discreet whether she was threatened or not. She also told us to run and tell that to whomever we worked for. It sounded like someone threatened to hurt her if she told anyone what they bought."

Fritz looked at Marzi with a blank expression.

"She said, 'whoever you work FOR.' She knew we were apprentices and assumed that whoever bought the morphing blend sent us back to check on her."

Fritz's skin prickled. "Meaning the person who purchased the herbs had apprentices at their disposal."

Marzi pointed her finger at Fritz. "A wizard with an *apprentice* had to have bought the morphing blend from her."

"But that could have been any wizard," Fritz argued.

"Look at the whole picture, Drossie." She shook both hands, willing Fritz to understand.

Andor grunted and asked for an explanation of her last sign.

Marzi apologized to him for the meaningless gesture and continued. "Not many wizards are powerful enough to capture three large animals, let alone put all those enchantments on them after they're caught."

"So maybe they raised them."

"That would take a great deal of money," Marzi explained. "You're looking at an even smaller pool of wizards to choose from."

"Okay, so, we're looking for a powerful wizard with enough resources to capture or raise wild animals, enchant them, and purchase morphing herbs, and someone who knows how we access unknown objects in storage," Fritz said.

"If you look at wizards powerful enough to do all that, there are three. Mortin, Domicles, and Herrin. But I wouldn't call any of them wealthy, and they don't have apprentices. None of them know about our infinity storage rooms, that I'm aware of. They're eccentric and mostly stick to themselves." Marzi rubbed her hands.

"But that only leaves us with ..." Fritz trailed off.

"The Order," Marzi finished.

Fritz thought for a moment. "If we ever want to catch the guilty wizard, we can't tip them off with what we know."

Both Marzi and Andor agreed.

"We can't tell the others," Fritz resolved.

"Everything we know stays here," Marzi said.

Andor crossed the first two fingers of both hands.

Marzi did the same.

"What's that?" Fritz asked.

"It's a wizard's promise," Marzi informed him.

Fritz shrugged and copied them. "I guess I wizard promise too, then."

"How do the rats fit in with this?" Marzi asked.

"Let's save that for a different day," Fritz told her. "I have some ideas, but I want to check them out first."

"Ok. I guess I'll see you both next week?" Marzi stood up, waved to them both, and left.

Fritz and Andor followed her out, and they all walked to their prospective traveling locations and traveled home.

When Fritz tumbled into his room, he jumped on his bed and reached over to the bedside table to grab the worn book on mind control.

The note was still under the lamp, but the book was gone. The spell that reshelved books had taken the book from his room and put it back in the library.

"Watcher, curse your mother!" Fritz swore.

He decided to walk to the library to retrieve the book rather than travel. The stairs provided a good opportunity to work on his leg muscles and the old mansion was nothing if not interesting to explore.

Down the hallway, he heard Boroda's voice shout followed by the fleshy smack of a fist on furniture.

Fritz stopped at the top of the stairs then crept slowly toward Boroda's bedroom. He padded softly on the hallway rug and stopped outside Boroda's door.

"Watcher, curse that infernal coward!" Boroda shouted and hit another piece of furniture.

"Klazinsky didn't know much. We should still be safe, but we need to rethink our strategy," another voice said.

Fritz recognized General Andoyavich's low growl through the mirror. His heart stopped when he heard Klazinsky's name.

"Why the wife and children, too?" Boroda moaned.

"To send a message to the rest of us," Andoyavich said. "You must speak to the others in The Order. This is treason, plain and simple."

Guilt burned in Fritz's stomach. He could have saved Klazinsky if he'd been honest with Boroda, but he didn't expect the murder to happen so quickly.

"No!" Boroda shouted. "I have no backing in The Order. They would all side with Borya, and there is no way I can fight them all."

"Then at least find and kill the Black Wizard," Andoyavich shouted back.

"I can't trace him!" Boroda hit something again. "If I can't trace him, I can't find him. If I can't find him, I can't kill him."

"The Czar is planning another party." Andoyavich raised his voice. "The mines are bad enough for these boys but the parties …"

Boroda cut him off with a loud roar. "I know!"

There was silence, and Boroda spoke more calmly. "I know," he breathed out. "We have one shot to destroy The Order and the Czar. If we blow it, both of us are dead, and it won't help any of the children."

After a bit of silence, the muffled voice responded, "I understand. The others are getting nervous."

"The charms will be ready soon. I have a few more enchantments, and then I will send them out," Boroda replied, suddenly sounding very tired.

"Please hurry," Andoyavich pleaded. "Our window of success grows smaller. The Black Wizard is continuing to pick us off."

"I need to go train my apprentice," Boroda said abruptly.

"Is he ready?"

"Not yet. Soon, I hope."

Fritz heard heavy footsteps coming toward the door and traveled back to his room in a panic. He hoped his smoke trail was gone by the time Boroda exited.

Boroda said nothing about him being in the hallway that afternoon during training, so he figured he had eluded discovery.

In the days following, Fritz attacked his lessons with renewed vigor. He lifted heavier weights, scaled the hanging rope faster, fenced harder, and cast spells with more energy.

He wanted to know more about the festive party General Andoyavich referenced, as well as the mines. Fritz wasn't sure what boys had to do with any of it but suspected there were more forces at play than he knew.

For now, he needed to focus on his training, the animal attacks, and, if he had time, the mysterious note he had found in the library.

After training, he traveled to the library and found the mind control book back on the shelf where the reshelving spell had placed it.

Try as he may, he could not understand the book. Rather than show the spells needed to control someone, it described, in great detail, the psyche and mental responses to magical aggression. If it did list shapes required to use mind control, it left out the order in which to draw them or what direction they had to spin before casting.

Fritz fell asleep in the window nook reading the confusing passages. He was no closer to understanding the magic of mind control, and his thoughts kept drifting from the Black Wizard to Boroda's secret quest to destroy the group of wizards he was sworn to serve.

His one comfort was his master's commitment to the demise of Czar Nicholaus, the man who had threatened his brother.

He would assist in that endeavor at any cost.

# CHAPTER 13

"Have you heard from Edward?" Marzi asked Fritz. She was lying on the couch in the library turret, feet draped over the arm, science book open in her lap.

Andor glanced over at them from his spot on the rug, eyes locked on their lips.

Fritz looked up from his owl sketch and wrinkled his nose. "No."

Marzi sat up. "I didn't see him at all last week, either."

"I think what happened in the woods freaked him out. I don't blame him. It freaked me out, too," Fritz said.

"Have you made any headway on the rats?" she asked.

Andor motioned from his place on the floor, and Fritz apologized.

"Sorry," he signed. "I will ... try?"

He looked at Marzi, and she showed him the correct sign to use.

"I will try to ... sign ... when I talk," Fritz said.

Andor grinned.

"What's your hypothesis?" Marzi asked.

"Mind control," Fritz said and spelled the words out.

"Animals don't have a mind," Marzi quipped. "They only have instincts."

"Right," Fritz said, "but I'm reading this book I found, and it says that 'mind control' for animals has to do with shaping their instincts."

He put his picture down and brushed the charcoal off his hands. "Dogs like to sniff, right? That's their instinct. But you can shape that instinct to sniff one thing over another. So they'd sniff rabbits but not squirrels."

Marzi bit her lower lip. "But none of the animals that were sent to attack us hunt humans. Even Andor's bear will only attack a human if provoked."

"That's the advanced part of mind control on animals!" Fritz said excitedly, giving up on signing. "I don't understand it very well, and the book describes the spells instead of drawing them, so I haven't been successful in testing them ... But from what the book says, you can make a lion want to eat a cabbage instead of an antelope."

"That still wouldn't explain the rats," said Marzi. "None of the other students got attacked or said anything about seeing them. They were after us! And not just us ..." She motioned to herself, Fritz, and Andor. "They attacked Edward as well."

"Which means they were given specific targets. Not just 'attack the wizards,'" Fritz said.

"Whoever is controlling these animals is really good." Marzi shivered.

"And really dangerous," Fritz added.

"You should go see if Edward is ok," Marzi suggested as she stood to leave.

Fritz leaned back and stretched. "Ok. I'll go on Saturday or Sunday if I have time. Actually, wait. I don't know where he lives."

"I believe it's on Ambassador's Row," Marzi said while packing her bag. "Just travel around the outside of the forest until you see a large house with the Southern Kingdom's flag on it. Or you could ask Vivienne. The Southern Kingdom is Sylvia's territory. Maybe she's been there. I have to go. See you all on Monday." She waved goodbye and left the two boys alone.

Fritz and Andor talked a little while longer and then packed to leave. As they neared the second-floor landing, Fritz stopped Andor.

He signed, "I hear a noise."

Andor shrugged and kept walking.

"Stop! I mean it." Fritz motioned with sharp, punctuated movements. "It's Vivienne. She's crying."

Andor's face darkened and scanned the room, searching for Vivienne. Fritz followed the sound toward the back corner of the second floor.

"Stop it, Evgeny!" said Vivienne.

Evgeny whooped a high, quick exclamation of pleasure. His actions were being cheered on by several other guys.

Fritz and Andor quickened their pace, dodging bookshelves, carts, and end tables.

"I said stop! Get *off* me," Vivienne cried, her voice tense and desperate.

A loud slap, followed by a short, feminine scream, stopped Fritz. The assault was followed by a chorus of "oohs" by several others.

Peering through a small gap of books, Andor and Fritz could clearly make out the small assembly.

Nicholaus sat on a divan, arms draped around a wide-eyed Gelé. Evgeny had Vivienne pinned on a table with his body, but she held both of his hands by the wrists. Her shirt was crumpled, exposing her midriff.

A heap of liquor bottles cluttered the small table in front of the couch, most of them empty. The sour tang of alcohol permeated the air. Both Fritz and Andor could smell it from their hiding place several yards away.

"Evgeny, leave her alone," Gelé slurred. She turned to Nicholaus. "Tell him to stop."

Nicholaus shrugged but said nothing.

Gelé started to get up, but Nicholaus grabbed her waist and yanked her back down into the chair.

"Ow! Stop! You're hurting me," Vivienne cried out.

Evgeny grabbed both her wrists with one hand, wrenched his other hand free, and began to paw blindly at the bottom of her clothing.

Fritz breathed quickly. His anger flared, but he stayed still. Boroda was very clear about his boundaries where Nicholaus was concerned, but he never said anything about Evgeny or Oleg. They were fair game. He was about to sign something when Andor rushed past him, covering the distance in seconds.

He grabbed Evgeny by the collar and threw him so violently against a bookshelf, the giant oak furniture tottered. He grabbed the two closest boys, still stunned, and smashed them together like a pair of human cymbals. They crumpled in a heap on the floor.

Oleg ran at Andor, bottle in one hand, and threw a punch with his other, but Andor caught his fist and twisted it. The boy screamed, and Andor connected a right hook to his face. Oleg flipped over the chair and lay motionless on the floor in front of Nicholaus and Gelé.

Gelé tore away from Nicholaus and joined her sister behind Andor.

Fritz rounded the bookshelf, stepping over Evgeny's body. He put a hand on Andor.

"That's enough," he signed.

Andor nodded and then snarled at Nicholaus.

Nicholaus retreated unsteadily, buzzed from the alcohol, but with eyes wide open in fear of the hulking student standing over him.

Fritz smiled at him and winked. Nicholaus, drunk as he was, registered the insult but only curled his lip in retaliation.

Fritz motioned to Gelé and Vivienne, and they exited the library.

When they got outside, Vivienne hugged Andor tightly.

"Thank you!" she gushed.

Gelé lowered her head. "Thank you." She twisted her fingers, then stepped forward and hugged the large apprentice.

Andor, fully wrapped in the girl's embrace, gave Fritz a thumbs-up.

Vivienne looked at Fritz. "I'm sorry for not sticking up for you—you know, with the rats."

"Was that Nicholaus?" Fritz asked.

Gelé answered. "Yes it was, and I'm sorry, too."

Fritz shook his head, confused. "Is Nicholaus a wizard?"

The girls laughed.

"No," Vivienne said.

"Then how'd he do that? All the rats?"

"His dad is the Czar of the Central Kingdom," Vivienne explained. "He could probably pay Ms. Wakimba enough to put a rat in your bag."

Fritz chuckled. "That would probably take a lot of money."

Gelé held her sister but spoke to Fritz. "I promise you, the rats were not magical. Especially at school. He probably got one of his buddies to do it. They certainly had a good time laughing about it."

Fritz started to tell them about the woods, but then thought better of it. "I bet they make smarter choices after today."

Gelé and Vivienne looked doubtful but didn't contradict him.

They all said goodbye and traveled home.

After training with Boroda for several hours, Fritz collapsed into bed. Before he turned off the lights, he pulled out the note from his nightstand and read it again.

*Why?*

*Plan?*

*Good or Bad?*

*Tell Boroda?*

*Tell R?*

"About WHAT does he want to know and WHY, Doll?" Fritz asked.

The wooden toy turned its head and blinked. "I am unsure, sir."

Fritz shivered. "You are so creepy."

He studied the note more. *What plan? His own? Someone else's? Was it a good plan? Or was something else good or bad? Did he tell Boroda? Did he tell R? Who is R? Who is HE?*

Fritz shoved the note back in the stand. "Come on, Doll. Help me out. Who wrote this note?"

"I am unsure, sir." The doll blinked again, and Fritz sent it flying across the room with a little push.

"Creepy doll," he muttered and went to sleep.

Saturday trainings were the most grueling. They started with calisthenics then moved to weight training. Weapons came next and finally lunch. After lunch they practiced enchantments, then they ended with combat.

By the end of a Saturday training session, Fritz could barely crawl from his bath to his bed.

On Sunday, his day off, he decided to go visit Edward.

After traveling from bush to bush all the way around the perimeter of the forest, then walking two miles in the open, he finally found Edward's house.

It was a large, red brick townhouse with a Southern Kingdom flag waving proudly in the front yard. The gate was open, so Fritz walked to the door and rang the bell.

A maid opened the door and, after discovering whom he was looking for, informed him that the master was sick, and he would need to call later.

"Please, ma'am," Fritz asked politely. "Could you tell him Drossie is here?"

The maid curtsied politely and asked him to wait in the foyer while she relayed the message. A few minutes later, she ushered him up the stairs to Edward's room.

Edward was propped up on pillows, staring out the window in a very melodramatic fashion.

"Thank you, Annie," he said with a weak, breathy voice. "You may go."

She curtsied again and left.

He immediately sat up in bed and exclaimed energetically, "Hey, Drossie. Why are you here?"

"I wanted to check on you. Make sure you weren't dying. We've missed you at school."

Edward looked at the closed door and leaned forward. He whispered in a hushed, conspiratorial tone. "I can't go to school ever again. I can't go back into the woods."

"We've been several times since then and haven't seen any rats," Fritz assured him.

Edward shook his head. "I think the rats were a warning. I'm not going to chance it."

"A warning?" Fritz asked.

"Yes! From Perrin's ghost."

"It's just a story. There's no such thing ..."

Edward cut him off. "I have proof!"

He jumped from his bed and ran to his closet, climbed on a chair, and pulled a small box from the top shelf. From this box, he took out a stack of envelopes bound together by a ribbon. He tossed them to Fritz.

"I told you Perrin was a friend of my brother's," Edward said triumphantly. "Well, they were good friends. Maybe even best friends. They wrote to each other a lot, at any rate.

"I was bored last weekend, and it was too cold to go outside, so I decided to rummage through the attic. I found these tucked in the side pocket of a chest."

Fritz opened the letters and gasped. The calligraphy was unmistakably the same as the words on the note he'd found in Boroda's library.

Fritz scanned the first letter until he found the signature.

*Yours truly,*

*Perrin*

"See?!" Edward squeaked. "He's real, and he died in the woods. He haunts all the people that disturb him. He probably died under the tree I was climbing. I don't know how, but I do know I'm not going back. Ever."

"Edward," Fritz cut in. "Who knows about these letters?"

Edward shrugged his shoulders. "No one. Just me … and my brother, I suppose."

"It is really important that these stay a secret. Ok?"

"Ok." Edward cocked his head.

"Do you mind if I borrow these?"

"No, I guess. What do you want them for?"

"I want to see if the stories about this are true," Fritz said.

"Can I help?" Edward's eyes bulged behind his new glasses, and he leaned forward on his hands.

Fritz considered the offer for a moment. "Yes."

Edward bounced up and down, sending his pillows tumbling to the ground.

"I need to know how he died," Fritz said. "Everything—where it happened. When it happened. The circumstances surrounding it—everything. Can you find that out for me without raising suspicion?"

Edward's face lit up. "My brother is coming here sometime soon. Maybe I can ask him."

"Can you ask him without letting him know it's me that's interested?"

"Probably, but, I'm not sure why …"

"Good." Fritz stood up. "I have to go now. See you on Monday?"

"Sure," said Edward.

"Thanks, buddy," Fritz said as he gave Edward a chuck on the chin.

Annie saw him to the door. Once the door shut behind him, Fritz ran to the nearby shrub and traveled home.

The first period bell sounded right as Fritz plopped into his seat.

"Need to talk," Fritz signed to Marzi as he leaned over to open his bag. He twisted in his seat, pretending to stretch so he could sign the same thing to Andor, but Andor was absent.

"Please save the stretching for last period, Mr. Drosselmeyer," Ms. Wakimba barked. "And for the record, I see you communicating with Miss Pan." She glared at him over her spectacles.

Fritz spun around and opened his book.

Ms. Wakimba harrumphed and began to teach.

At lunch, Gelé and Vivienne put a delicately wrapped box on the table.

"Where's Andor?" Gelé asked.

"We have a gift for him." Vivienne giggled and pointed to the box.

"I don't know," Fritz said. "He wasn't in first period. He may have come in late."

"He wasn't in third period either," Faruk said.

Marzi sat down with her lunch and opened it in silence.

"Have you seen Andor?" Vivienne asked.

Marzi shook her head.

A girl at a nearby table stood up and pointed. "Look!" she said.

All heads turned.

Andor stood in the doorway. He was wearing a sweeping gown of orange and pink silk and a large-brimmed hat with tassels. His face was covered in white powder, his eyelids sparkled with dark blue makeup, and his lips were painted red.

The apprentices stood slowly, gaping.

The lunchroom erupted in laughter.

"What ... is ... happening?" Faruk asked.

Fritz rushed over to Andor, but Andor sashayed past him to the center of the room. He lifted the hoops of his voluminous gown to reveal frilly undergarments.

The lunch monitor was shrieking for everyone to be quiet, but her cries were drowned out by the students.

Andor began to dance wildly.

The excited students screamed and cheered.

Marzi and Fritz signed for him to stop, but he continued to whirl around in a frenzied dance.

Andor finally waved his gloved hand in a delicate fashion and sidled out of the room. A deluge of students swept out into the hallway to watch him go. He moved in giant stag leaps down the hall and disappeared around the corner.

Fritz and Marzi bolted after him, followed closely by Faruk, Gelé, and Vivienne.

When they rounded the corner, Andor lay face down on the floor, his hoops splayed over his head, bright red bloomers gleaming next to the white under-fabric of the dress.

"Andor!" Marzi cried and began to untie the back of the dress.

"That was humiliating," Nicholaus said, and the group spun around at the sound of his voice.

Nicholaus, followed closely by his bandaged entourage, walked by the apprentices without uttering a word. He stopped next to Andor, looked down, smirked, then left.

"Jerk," Vivienne muttered.

"Andor!" Marzi called and turned him over.

He opened his eyes, sat up, and signed, "What?"

"Why are you wearing a dress?" Marzi signed back.

Andor looked down, then up, face full of confusion.

"I don't know," he responded.

"What's the last thing you remember?" Faruk asked, and Marzi translated.

"School. Put bag in locker. Went to gym," Andor motioned.

He stood up, and the top of the dress fell, leaving his chest bare. He covered his pectorals with one arm in mock embarrassment and signed to Marzi. "You tease. Shame."

Marzi translated, and the group laughed.

"That dress doesn't look half bad on you," said Gelé.

Andor struck a pose.

Faruk and Fritz grabbed Andor by the arm and pulled him away from the girls.

"Come on, you giant ginger," Faruk joked.

"You are one hot mama!" Vivienne catcalled while Fritz translated her message, shaking his head the whole time.

Andor's locker was open. His school uniform was missing, but his gym clothes were still there.

"Put on these until we can find your uniform," Fritz signed.

Andor stripped out of the dress and laid each piece neatly on the bench. He pulled on his gym clothes, and the trio began searching the locker room for Andor's school uniform.

They searched the cubbies, showers, and storage rooms but came up empty. They crossed the hall into the girls' locker room and checked all the same spaces.

When they opened the washroom, they saw Andor's clothes lying in a heap, and bottles of makeup, face powder, and women's clothing strewn across the floor.

"Well, this is where it happened," Faruk said.

Fritz studied the scene. "Yes, but how?"

"I don't know," Faruk replied. "Normally I'd say someone used a mind control spell on him but, well …" He waved his hand in the air.

"We're at school," Fritz filled in.

"We're at school," Faruk punctuated.

Fritz thought for a moment. "What happens if someone uses magic on school property?"

"One, you can't," Faruk reminded him. "And two, you get roasted by The Order for even trying. And by roasted, I mean removed. And by removed, I mean killed."

Fritz shook his head in disbelief. "You're absolutely sure no one could tamper with the spells here?"

"Positive." Faruk dumped a tray of white face powder in the trash. "I guess you could try," he said, "but the magic they used was really old. It doesn't look like the magic we use now."

Fritz sighed and let it go. "Ok. Thanks. I appreciate it."

"Appreciate what?" Faruk asked.

"Answering my questions," Fritz said. "Boroda never answers any of my questions."

"No?" Faruk said and stopped sweeping the mess. "What's he like? He's the most secretive wizard in The Order, and that's saying a lot when you remember that we have Hanja."

Fritz laughed loudly. "He's mean!" he said, wiping his eyes.

"No!" Faruk challenged. "I don't see that in him."

Fritz nodded his head in big, slow bobs. He lowered his voice and looked around. "He has broken so many of my bones during our training sessions, I'm beginning to get used to the feeling."

Faruk raised his eyebrows. "Does he heal you afterward?"

"Yes," Fritz said. "Or he stands over me while I do it. Always nitpicking. 'You haven't cleared the muscle. Did you connect the inner ring first?'" He mimicked Boroda's deadpan directions.

Faruk burst out laughing. "That sounds just like him."

"What's Borya like?" Fritz asked. "Does he do stuff like that?"

Faruk sobered up slightly and chewed the corner of his lip. "Boroda heals your bones. Take it from me, he's one of the nice ones."

He loosened his tie, unbuttoned his shirt and exposed his collarbone. An irregular knob stuck up from under his olive skin.

Fritz winced. "Did Borya do that?"

"I was eight when it happened," Faruk said. "I was late to training and then couldn't get the hang of a certain spell. He broke my collarbone with his staff."

"I had no idea wizards were this ... cruel," Fritz murmured.

"None of us did." Faruk straightened his clothing. "We never talk about it."

Fritz sat down on a bench. "That's what Marzi says. I don't understand it. We're all supposed to be a team. I think we should all be able to trust each other and talk about, you know, stuff."

Faruk grinned. "You and Marzi, huh?"

Fritz blushed. "No. It's not like that."

"Why not?" Faruk prodded. "She's gorgeous."

"Very," Fritz agreed.

"I couldn't get three sentences out of her, and I hear you guys have been spending every afternoon together." Faruk sat next to Fritz and nudged him playfully. "You guys are talking, right? Or is there more than just 'talking' going on?"

Fritz's blush turned crimson. "No! We're talking … like, actually talking."

"Still, that's impressive," Faruk complimented. "From what I hear, Hanja values privacy and deals very harshly with any breach. If Marzi is chancing Hanja's wrath to spend time with you, she must really like you."

They were interrupted by a yelp behind them.

A freshman girl, gym bag in hand, stood in the doorway.

"Sorry!" Fritz and Faruk apologized profusely and dragged Andor through the crowd of girls.

"Andor, are you ok?" Vivienne asked when the boys were safely outside the girls' locker room. "What happened to you?"

Andor looked back at the throng of half-dressed women he'd just passed and responded to Vivienne with a big smile and a thumbs-up.

Vivienne and Gelé both followed his gaze.

Gelé rolled her eyes, and Vivienne slapped his arm in mock retribution.

"Boys." She shook her head, giggled, then walked with him to his next class.

# CHAPTER 14

Even with his ability to remember spells, Fritz found himself struggling for the right defensive counterspell when sparring with Boroda. His attacks were blocked with relative ease while his own protective spells—and energy—were drained in minutes. Boroda, in rare form, praised him for his variety of counterattacks. "It's impressive, but if you run out of energy, it won't matter."

Fritz grimaced as his broken wrist reset. "I thought that's why we train—to get stronger." His tone was pointed and barbed.

"Yes, but you vary your attacks and defenses so often, you aren't matching the power of the block with the strength of the blow. You're wasting energy," Boroda explained. "A little girl with a dagger can kill a wizard if he's unprepared."

Fritz clenched his teeth.

Boroda had stopped telling him to control his temper. He just shook his head as Fritz lashed out in anger, then waited patiently as Fritz healed a broken bone, bloody gash, or pulled muscle.

Fritz's wrist snapped back into place, and the warmth of healing washed over him.

Boroda held out his hand to Fritz to help him up off the floor. "I think training is over for today."

Fritz looked at him surprised. "Why? We still have over an hour."

"I think I've been pushing you too hard lately," Boroda confessed.

"I don't mind it. Training makes me better."

"Ok. Then your choice of training to fill out the hour. What do you want to learn about?"

Fritz thought for a moment before he said, "Celestines."

Boroda raised an eyebrow. "Any reason?"

"No reason in particular." Fritz lied. "I've heard about them, and I'm curious is all."

Boroda studied him for a moment. "I don't believe you. Tell me the truth. Why do you want to learn about Celestines?"

"Will you tell me the truth back?" Fritz asked.

"I will."

"Promise?" Fritz held up the wizard's promise sign.

Boroda returned the sign.

"How did you know to come to the orphanage?" Fritz asked. "I know Borya has a Celestine, and that's how he knew when I snapped. I know he told you, but you have to know a place to travel there, right?"

Boroda smirked.

"Faruk told me that the Celestine has different alarms for when a wizard snaps or tries to do magic at school," Fritz said.

"I can tell you how," Boroda said after a small hesitation. "I can even show you, but I will need your solemn word that not one bit of what I show you will ever be spoken to anyone."

"I promise."

Boroda opened his arm and swirled it around Fritz. In an instant, they were floating in an inky blackness. There was neither wind, cold, nor warmth. It was still. Completely still. Lights floated around in coruscating strands, highlighting the deepening wrinkles in Boroda's hardened face.

A pinpoint of light, brighter than the rest, started to grow in circumference, and Fritz realized it was headed toward them, or they were headed toward it. Direction had no bearing in this deep space.

Boroda held out his hands, pulling the object in his direction.

It was clear, like water, yet solid, like glass. Inside, a light pulsed but without a source. Boroda floated to the other side of the glowing orb so that it hung between them.

"Is this the Celestine?"

"This is *a* Celestine." Boroda punctuated the article.

"Borya's Celestine is an older, more inferior magic than this, and as far as Borya knows, his is the only Celestine in existence."

Fritz smiled. "Really? Awesome." He felt a swelling in his chest—a familial pride that Boroda had, in some way, outsmarted Borya. Fritz looked at Boroda, wondering if his own father had been as smart and powerful as he. There was no way to know, so he shook the thought from his head.

Boroda stared into the orb. "Borya refuses to let any other wizard near his Celestine. Researching this one was very difficult and required personal ... sacrifice."

"Didn't he show his Celestine to you when I snapped?" Fritz asked.

"No," Boroda replied. "Borya didn't know you existed until I told him I had chosen an apprentice."

"Wait." Fritz waved his hands. "If you didn't learn about my snap from Borya, what did you tell the others about how you found me?"

"I told them I discovered you from gossiping townsfolk." He spoke softly, and his voice shook. "It's not the first time I've told them that."

Fritz felt his heart beat faster.

"It's true that most wizards get their apprentices through the recommendation of the Chief Wizard, but there is no rule prohibiting you from choosing your own if you discover someone."

Boroda waved his hand over the Celestine, and small puffs of clouds like tiny explosions appeared under the surface.

"From descriptions I found in ancient texts, Borya's Celestine looks like this." Boroda pointed to each puff. "This puff would alert me that someone snapped in the Polaris province of the Northern Kingdom. I would have to travel there and ask around until I found a child with magic."

Fritz whistled. "That would take forever."

"Correct," Boroda said. "Which is one of the reasons I spent several years making this."

"How does yours work?" Fritz asked.

Boroda closed his eyes, and the orb flashed. "I'll show you what I saw the night you snapped."

The light in the Celestine faded, and then Fritz saw the orphanage. He was in the hallway outside the box. Dolph was pounding on the door.

The box exploded and the stocky man flew back, out of sight. Fritz staggered out of the box, and the Celestine followed his path into the room. Ivanov came into view and then shot back into the bookshelf and crumpled out of view.

The Celestine went dark, then pulsed with light again.

"My Celestine can show me any place in the world I wish to go. I can travel there even if I've never physically been before."

"Does this one alert you every time someone snaps?" Fritz asked.

"No," Boroda replied. "That is not its purpose."

"Why did you make it?"

"I had my reasons," Boroda said.

"Can I make one?"

"Globe magic is a lifetime pursuit. I gave up many years of my life making this," Boroda said with an exhausted breath.

"What is globe magic?" Fritz briefly took his eyes off the Celestine.

"Globe magic is creating a world within the confines of a globe. Infinite space, yet contained. Only the ones outside the globe can see the limits."

"And why did you make one?"

Boroda studied Fritz with a look of reticence. "I used to work for a different Czar."

Fritz frowned. "None of the other Kingdoms have Czars. Just Kings, Queens, Emperors …"

"I've always been with the Central Kingdom, but it was previously ruled by a different Czar. Czar Pieter— Czar Nicholaus' brother."

"I've never heard of him," Fritz admitted.

"No one your age has. It is forbidden to speak of him," Boroda said. "He was a very good man who ruled his people justly. He died … The circumstances were very suspicious, to say the least."

"Was he killed?" Fritz prodded.

"No one knows." Boroda shrugged. "It was my job to protect him, and I failed. When Czar Nicholaus began ruling, the nobles who had served under his brother began dying as well. Many were made to look like accidents, but it was obvious to anyone with half a brain that they were murdered."

"Did you ever find out who killed them?" Fritz pictured the Black Wizard standing near Borya. His arms prickled.

"No," Boroda answered. "It is one of the reasons I spent so much time creating this."

Boroda pushed the Celestine away into the infinite darkness. Fritz watched it shrink in the distance.

"The Czar is a very wealthy man," Boroda said. "Most of his wealth comes from the mines in the Central Mountains."

"We heard about those," Fritz said. "We used to tell new orphans that if they didn't behave, they'd get sent there and fed to a troll."

Boroda grimaced. "There is a seemingly endless supply of precious metals and gems, but the rock is very difficult to cut through. There are natural tunnels that make the metals and gems more accessible, but an average-sized man can't fit in there. A small boy, however …" His voice trailed off.

Fritz went pale.

"A small boy can fit with relative ease." Boroda ground his teeth. "By the time I discovered they were using child labor in the mines, Czar Nicholaus was already addicted to the wealth and beyond my council. I began to look for allies to help, but the Czar is an arrogant, paranoid man who will kill at a whim, so looking for help within the Czar's ranks is a slow, dangerous process."

"Can you stop him?"

Boroda paused.

"I am trying, but there are many forces at work that prevent me from just killing him."

"Like what?" Fritz demanded more harshly than he'd intended.

Boroda ignored the tone. "Every leader of the Five Kingdoms has a Life Bond, of sorts, with their wizard."

Fritz was stunned.

"It's not as restrictive as the one we share, but it's similar," Boroda explained.

"Also, there's the question of succession, as well as The Order's response to unsanctioned regicide," he added.

"So, you built the Celestine to figure out where the Czar was getting his slave labor from?" Fritz said, confused.

Boroda laughed softly. "No. I could have figured that out on my own, though I do watch the orphanages regularly."

He looked at Fritz warmly. "That is how I found you. I've been monitoring Ivanov's for quite some time and happened to be watching the night you snapped."

Fritz gasped at the sudden realization that the other boys at Ivanov's were not adopted but carted off to the mines. He clutched his stomach and wished he was on solid ground. "Why did you build the Celestine, then?"

Boroda paused, deep in thought. He finally faced Fritz and spoke in a calm, resolved manner. "I built it for the eventual war I will wage on the Czar."

Fritz inhaled slowly, swallowing halfway through the breath. "Boroda, I have to confess something."

Boroda looked at him. The light of the Celestine was growing dim, and the blue pallor of this world darkened his features.

"I traveled to the Czar's palace to figure out where my brother lives," Fritz began. "I only wanted to keep an eye on him after the meeting with the Czar. I nearly got caught, but I overheard the Czar talking to Borya and another wizard about killing someone named Klazinsky."

Boroda flinched.

"The Czar ordered the Black Wizard to kill him and also to be his protection at an upcoming party."

Boroda's eyes flashed with anger. "Why didn't you tell me this immediately?"

"I thought you'd be mad at me for going there," Fritz stammered. "I'm sorry. I should have said something."

"You're positive it was Borya?" Boroda gripped Fritz's arms tightly.

Fritz nodded.

"Tell me the whole story. Leave nothing out," Boroda commanded.

Fritz told him the story and included every detail, from his hiding place to the rat perched on the Black Wizard's shoulder. When he finished recounting the ordeal, Boroda said nothing.

They continued to glide through the air until they touched down on a hard floor; the blackness faded away, and the training room appeared in its place.

"Never speak of this to anyone," Boroda said and disappeared in a flash.

Without hesitation, Fritz traveled to his room.

As he dressed for bed, he thought about all the boys at the orphanage who had been "adopted." He felt sure they were sent to work in the mines and wondered if any still remained alive.

He pushed the dark thoughts from his mind and traveled to the library. He needed to clear his head. He gathered the books he'd been studying and muttered about the cleaning spell that reshelved them every night.

Next, he traveled in his wooden doll and sat it beside him in the window nook.

"Hello, Drosselmeyer," it said flatly, the rubber vocal folds vibrating with help from an enchanted brass ring around its waist.

"Hello, Doll," he responded. "Ready to test more spells tonight?"

"Yes, Drosselmeyer," Doll responded.

Fritz leaned back, opened a book on physical transformation and laid it next to the book on anatomy. He began tweaking the facial patterns of his doll.

"Smile," he commanded, and the doll responded but with an unnerving effect.

"Yikes!" Fritz recoiled. "It's your eyes. Why aren't they squinting?"

"I am unsure, sir," Doll responded mechanically.

Fritz turned to the section on eyes and read until sleep forced his own eyelids shut.

He dreamed about eyes that night, but not the penciled drawings in the anatomy books. He dreamed about Marzi's eyes. Deep pools of brown that sparkled with the warmth of a thousand suns every time she smiled.

Her eyes turned dark and slowly faded into the sad, searching eyes of the boys he'd known in the orphanage.

They were trapped underground and reached out for him. He tried to grab their outstretched hands but couldn't grasp them.

The mountain cave opened, the narrow gaps turning into teeth. The boys screamed as the newly formed, stony troll ground them in its maw.

Fritz jolted awake, sweaty and shivering. He dressed and sat in his chair by the fireplace until it was time for breakfast.

Boroda was absent, so he traveled in his own food and left the dishes on the table.

When he stepped out from the secret hedge near the school, the sunlight peeked through the clouds like a pleasant surprise. He basked in the warmth and thought of Marzi's eyes from his dream last night. He meandered toward the school, soaking in every ray of warmth.

# CHAPTER 15

That Monday, Fritz arrived first. He settled down, pulled out his books, and started on his first assignment when Marzi rushed in.

She emptied her bag frantically and pulled out a box. She slid it to Fritz and beamed. "Try it!"

Fritz opened the lid, cautiously at first, then tossed it back and grabbed a cookie from the stack.

"Did you lose another bet?" he asked and bit off a large chunk.

"What do you think?" Marzi asked.

"It's very chewy," Fritz said. "But it's still good. What flavor?"

"I invented them after I made your cookies," she said excitedly. "I've had to work in secret, so it's taken me a bit longer than I wanted, but I'm almost there."

"Almost where?" Fritz swallowed and took another bite. "I think you should know by now that I'm not great at reading your mind, so unless you like our game of twenty-one questions, you should just tell me."

Marzi ignored him. "I felt horrible about leaving Toby with just a sweet roll. It's hardly filling and has no nutritional value. Ever since then, I've been working on a recipe that will keep someone full for up to a week."

Fritz stopped chewing and looked down at his half-eaten cookie.

"I finally worked out the spell, and it hinges on enchanting iron and adding it to the recipe." She put a vial of powder on the table. "We need iron anyway, so why not piggyback on it and use it to hold an enchantment?"

Fritz set his cookie down. He was feeling much fuller.

"Full is good, but you can still die from lack of nutrition," he added.

"I know." She frowned. "And there is no enchanted substitute for nutrition."

"So how did you solve it?" Fritz pushed his homework back and shifted uncomfortably. His stomach felt like it was going to pop.

"I want to go back to Minerva Mooncup's and see if she has any herbal blends that I can add to this to make it nutritionally effective for a week."

"No!" Fritz said with unexpected force. "We are not going back there."

"Come on, Drossie," she begged. "It's for a good cause. Besides, if we go back there to buy something, maybe she'll tell us some information."

"Or maybe she'll stay true to her promise and feed us to her gilly worms."

"Do you have a better plan for helping the starving children?" she fired at him.

"No," he shot back.

"Then my idea is best."

"Except for the part where she kills us."

"We're wizards, Drossie. She's just a hedge witch. If we get in any trouble, we can travel out of there."

Fritz scowled.

"Think of all the kids we can help," Marzi said. "You can figure out how to get them all coats, and I can make sure they're full and properly nourished."

"Why do I have to get them coats?" Fritz complained.

"Because I've already figured out the food ... mostly. Are you going to come with me or not?"

Fritz growled and slammed his book shut. "Fine! I'll go, but the minute she starts yelling and those mushrooms do that glowing thing, we travel out of there, got it?"

"Got it." Marzi smiled.

Fritz formed the wizard's promise in a silent but forceful question.

Marzi returned the promise and, without warning, hugged Fritz tightly around the neck. "Thank you so much."

He stuttered a quick, "No problem," and quickly slid his book bag over his lap.

"How do I keep the kids warm, Doll?" Fritz asked the toy that evening.

"I am unsure, sir," Doll replied.

"I wish I could just buy coats, but not everyone wears the same size," he mused. "And who has that many coats?"

"I am unsure, sir."

He opened a book labeled *Practical Spells and Enchantments for the Busy Wizard*. He'd found the book while researching mind control, and the cartoon illustrations of a smiling housewife creating various spells and enchantments had caught his eye. The book had a section in the back of patterns to make clothing, and Fritz wondered how to manufacture the number of coats needed to clothe all the beggar children in Anadorn.

Fritz found a spell in the book to keep children warm by enchanting a brass button and sewing it on an undergarment in case the child lost their coat.

"I guess I could make them all shirts, but they'd have to be different sizes." Fritz fell back on the cushioned pillows in his library nook. He stretched out his finger and traced Doll's outline absentmindedly. "What has buttons but doesn't need to be worn?"

Doll rotated his head. "I."

Fritz waited for Doll to finish his statement. He sat up and made sure the enchantment was still working.

"Doll, what has buttons but doesn't need to be worn?" he asked again.

Doll blinked. "I."

"I … am …" Fritz coached the toy through the scripted response, checking the spell for a glitch. "I am … unsure." He finished and reiterated the question.

"What has buttons but doesn't need to be worn?"

"I," Doll answered again and blinked.

Fritz bolted upright. "Doll, you're a genius."

Doll had no learned response for that.

"Dolls!" Fritz said and jumped up from the seat. "I can make a doll for each child and enchant the buttons to keep them warm. One size fits all, and if you don't want to carry a doll, you can put it in your pocket."

He danced around the room, singing "Pickety Wickett sailed over the sea to find a rare gift for Rosamund Lee."

He stopped dancing long enough to put an enchantment on Doll that would make him tap his feet in time to the music, then continued to jump around the library. When the clock struck midnight, he saw his books disappear from his window nook and materialize back into their slots.

He hurled an epitaph at the cleaning spell, just for good measure, and traveled back to his room for the night.

Fritz shared the good news with Marzi before first period.

She shushed him and glanced around. "Stop saying 'enchant' so loudly."

Fritz grimaced. "Sorry. I'm going to … sew the buttons?"

"Tell me in the library," Marzi said and turned toward the classroom. Her long hair whipped out as she spun, and Fritz watched it fall back into place.

He trotted to catch up with her.

During lunch, Edward approached the apprentice's table. "Drossie, may I speak with you?"

"Sure." He followed Edward into the hall.

"I just found out my brother is going to be here this weekend. We're going to have a State's Dinner for all the Southerners next week. Mom said I can invite someone," he said. "I figured I'd ask you."

"Thank you. Tell your mom I accept." Fritz clapped his hand on Edward's shoulder.

Edward gave him the date and time to be there.

"What have you found out from your brother so far?" Fritz asked him.

"Nothing." Edward dropped his head. "I don't know how to find out."

"That's ok," Fritz said through clenched teeth. He figured it was better to keep Edward in the dark anyway. "If you can make the introduction, I can try to get some information."

Edward promised he would and even shook hands on it. They parted and Fritz sat back down at the table.

"What's going on with Edward?" Faruk asked casually.

"Nothing," Fritz replied.

"Southern Kingdom, huh, Drossie? Central Kingdom not enough?" Vivienne said, just loud enough for the table to hear.

Gelé slapped Vivienne's hand. "Shh."

Andor grinned and glanced back and forth, confused.

"Giving up on Central Kingdom already?" Faruk asked and winked.

"Faruk!" Marzi warned. "You shouldn't talk about this in the open."

"It's just us," Vivienne cut in. "No one can hear us."

"Marzi's right," said Gelé. "Save it for the garden."

"Speaking of which," said Vivienne, "full moon is in a couple days, and I'm getting a new dress!"

"I'm getting a new one, too!" said Gelé.

"What?!" Vivienne nearly shrieked. "What does it look like?"

"It's so beautiful. It's made of a metal weave with blue gems," her twin said. "The tailor said he will have it finished tomorrow. I can't wait!"

"What happens at the full moon?" Fritz asked.

"That's when our 'aunts and uncles' meet," Faruk hinted with an obvious wink.

"Ah!" Fritz said, suddenly understanding.

They continued to chat until the bell rang then left for their classes.

That afternoon in the library, Marzi finished her work shortly ahead of Fritz and began making plans for the next day.

"Let's go to Minerva's tomorrow right after school. I hope it won't take longer than two hours, so I don't have to tell Hanja where I've been."

"Same," Fritz agreed. He traced the bone structure of the barn owl's wings on some paper and checked his work. Satisfied, he folded it up and put it in his bag.

"If I can get the herbs I need, I'll bake the food Thursday and Friday night and then we can meet on Sunday to distribute them." She picked up her bag from the floor. "Can you have the dolls ready by then?"

"I will," Fritz said. "I think there might even be loose buttons in our storage. Wouldn't be surprised. Everything else in the world is stored in there."

Marzi stood up. "Thank you so much for helping me do this. It really means a lot to me."

Fritz joined her. "Glad to help."

She stood on her toes and kissed him on the cheek. She walked ahead, and Fritz stood there, frozen. She turned to see what was wrong.

"Seriously, Drossie. You have to stop smiling like that."

Fritz dropped from the bar where he'd been doing pull-ups and walked in a circle, waiting for the burning in his muscles to subside.

"Do we have any buttons in storage?" Fritz asked.

Boroda frowned. "Probably. Why?"

"I would like to use them for an experiment," Fritz said.

"What kind of buttons?"

"Brass would be ideal."

"Let's see." Boroda disappeared in a cloud of smoke. Fritz hurried after him.

When he stepped into the hallway of Anadorn Market, Boroda had just finished unlocking the door. They walked down several aisles, searching for the accessories.

Bolts of cloth lay stacked in neat piles. The material was thick, yet very soft to the touch. Several packages of batten sat nearby, and a few shelves down, near some ornate masquerade costumes, was a trunk filled to the brim with buttons of every conceivable shape and size.

"Will these do?" Boroda asked.

"Yes!" Fritz exclaimed. He ran his palms over the buttons and let them cascade through his fingers.

"Good. I have a meeting to attend. I will stop by the shop and have them deliver some needles and thread."

"Oh! Thank you," Fritz said, then looked around. "I can't believe we don't have any up here."

"We may, but it would be a tragic case of both literally and figuratively looking for a needle in a haystack. You are welcome to use any of it you want." Boroda motioned to the trunks of buttons.

"I've been called away to an emergency meeting. Enjoy your evening, and we will continue training tomorrow." He bowed slightly and disappeared.

Fritz memorized the locations of everything and traveled back to his room. He traveled in the cloth, buttons, and batten, and while he waited for needle and thread, sought out a pattern for a doll.

*Practical Spells and Enchantments for the Busy Wizard* had several patterns. Most were too difficult and too time consuming for Fritz, but one pattern in the *Crafts to Teach Your Children* chapter was extremely simple.

As Fritz began cutting it out with scissors, he saw some small print on the bottom of the page, below the picture of the doll.

*Note. See page 317

Fritz flipped over to the page.

*If pressed for time, follow the spell below to enchant your scissors to cut for you. Also works with garden shears.

Fritz laid the material out as instructed and cast the enchantment.

The scissors took off clipping at an alarming speed.

He waved his hand, and some needles and several spools of thread from the square patch of light in the storage area materialized on his desk. He threaded the needle and flipped through the book in search of another practical spell.

"There it is!" Fritz exclaimed.

*In a pinch, you will find your children's toys to be an excellent substitute for servants. If they possess the proper joints for the work they are given, they can perform repetitive tasks with alarming accuracy.*

*Once enchanted with this spell, you must demonstrate the task, then let them copy your movements. Remember, they will copy it exactly as you demonstrated, so keep your tasks neat and tidy.*

Fritz cast the enchantment on Doll, and the toy turned its head and watched without blinking.

Fritz sewed a doll, applied the buttons, and stuffed it.

Doll grabbed the material cut by the enchanted scissors and copied Fritz's moves. He finished the stitching, snipped the thread, and started again on another doll.

As he watched Doll sew, Fritz let his mind wander over his life the past few months, from the orphanage up to the moment Marzi kissed his cheek. He reached up and felt the spot where her lips had touched him. Fritz blushed at the memory and hoped she would do it again. A stuffed doll landed at his feet, interrupting his reverie. Doll was already on his tenth toy and didn't need any supervision.

Fritz stretched out on his bed to relax while Doll finished his work. He pulled out the stack of letters Edward had given him and shuffled through them.

Perrin and Richard, Edward's oldest brother, were very good friends. Many of the notes joked about childish adventures in caves and finding pirate treasure. In one letter, Perrin complained about his boredom and the absence of his Uncle Boroda.

Fritz dropped the letters and slapped his own forehead. "Watcher! How could I be so stupid?!" His heart beat quickly. "Perrin was Boroda's apprentice."

He stared at the letters in his lap.

"It makes sense," he yelled to Doll. "Boroda had an apprentice that died in the woods, so he'd obviously be touchy about it. That's why he got so angry at me when I brought up Perrin's ghost."

Fritz picked up the letters and read some more. The last letter made his pulse quicken again.

> *My dearest friend Richard,*
>
> *Please forgive the appended nature of my letter, but there is a matter of utmost urgency I need to speak with you about. To lessen the shock of our discourse, I feel I must prepare you slightly in advance.*
>
> *We have been best friends since the day we met, and there has been no secret I've kept from you—save one. I only tell it to you now because the exigent circumstances require both your help and your knowledge of my past.*
>
> *I am confident you will treat this letter and what I have to tell you with discretion.*
>
> *Yours truly,*
> *Perrin*

"What did you want to tell Richard?" Fritz asked, tapping the letter in time with the clicking scissors.

The scissors ticked steadily, eating up the material and spitting out doll-shaped blanks. Then the ticking grew uneven—almost like scratching.

Fritz looked up to see what the matter was, but the scissors were still cutting and Doll was still sewing accurately.

The scratching turned to scuttling, and he sat up and looked around.

The noise grew louder.

The hairs on his arms stood up.

The noise was now coming from the hallway outside his room.

Fritz held up his right hand and a sword materialized. His left closed around several small blades perfectly balanced for throwing.

The scraping stopped, and several huffs of breath blew dust from the floor under his bedroom door. The sniffing stopped, and then the door exploded open.

A large rat, the size of a dog, flew into the room, eyes red and trained on Fritz. A haze of magical runes spun wildly around the creature.

Fritz struck the rat with his sword, and it shrieked in pain. Its tail whipped to strike Fritz's head.

He ducked and severed the appendage with a swipe.

More scuttling, then two more rats ran into the room.

Fritz threw four knives, one for each eye, and the rats fell to the floor, dead. He raised his hand and the sword vanished, replaced by a large axe. He buried the axe firmly into the squirming rat that lay at his feet.

He turned around to see another rat hurtling at him from behind. It landed on him and sank its teeth into his shoulder.

Screaming, he blasted the rat away from him. Bits of his shirt hung from the jagged teeth. It merely grunted as it slammed against the wall and then scurried back toward him.

Three more entered the room.

Fritz was light-headed from pain. But before the rats could charge him, he traveled to the training room. He rolled to a stand and checked his shoulder. A soft pop alerted him as another rat leapt from a swirling cloud of magic followed by a wave of rats.

Fritz jumped into the air, traveled in a spear, and hurled it at the closest rat, pinning it to the ground.

The rat tried to claw the lance free but just spun on the floor, leaving a bloody circle under its body.

Fritz threw a fireball, and the rat stopped moving. He aimed fireballs at the other rats, but they were pouring in through the portal too quickly. One bad throw, and he might burn down the house.

He traveled in spears until they formed a cage around him, each one skewering a squealing rat. But the angry horde of rodents were not deterred and immediately began scaling the shafts.

Fritz breathed heavily, then climbed on top of a table and shot a beam of ice, enclosing several animals in a block. The rest charged him, and soon he was running out of the room. He jumped back to dodge a smaller, lithe rat who had made its way through the wall of spears.

He traveled to the kitchen, landing on the large, sturdy table.

The rats followed.

Fritz flipped over to a counter and began hurling knives. Several rats fell, while others scrambled toward him with blades and handles sticking out of their bodies.

Two rats latched onto his arm. He growled and melted them with a burst of heat.

Fritz felt his energy drain further. He pushed the rats back and held them behind an invisible wall. His power weakened against the strain of their collective pushing.

*If you run out of energy, it won't matter*, Fritz heard Boroda's warning. *A little girl with a dagger can kill a wizard if he's unprepared.*

Fritz wiped the sweat from his eyes, searching desperately in his mind for a way out. The rats would follow him wherever he traveled, so running was not an option. His breath came in heavy gulps as his spell weakened under the rat's persistent pushing.

Rats at school. Rats in the woods. Rats on the Black Wizard.

He didn't want to die by rats.

He refused to die by rats.

Anger welled up in his stomach. The apprentice's charm around his neck began to glow hot. Someone was trying to kill him.

He reached out with his mind and grabbed the throat of a large rat with two knives sticking out of its back and yanked. Even though he was several feet away from the animal, he felt the delicate bones crumple, and the rat fell to the floor with a satisfying thump. Blood poured from its mouth.

Fritz's green eyes flashed silver, and he smiled before lunging off the wall and charging the rats.

He traveled from one corner of the room to another, crushing throats, snapping spines, and ripping organs from rodent bodies. He fell into a rhythm of traveling, crushing, breaking, and burning.

The rats roiled, their angry masses trying to follow his travel paths, but as they trickled from one portal, he crushed them and traveled again. The seething mass was shrieking frantically, unsure of where their quarry was.

The numbers dwindled until there was one rat left. Fritz pinned it to the floor and studied the magic runes swirling around it.

It was a complex network of spells unlike anything he'd ever seen. A few of the shapes were unknown. He made a mental note and planned to ask Boroda what they did.

Once he was satisfied with his examination of the rat, Fritz snapped all of its legs, savoring the rodent's shrieks of pain. He worked his way through the rat's body, cracking bone after bone until he ended with a twist of the spine so violent that the rat's body lay half facing the floor and half facing the ceiling.

He began to quiver and realized his strength was gone, and the adrenaline was fading fast. He searched his charm, but it was empty. He gasped heavily and stumbled toward the mirror on the far wall. He called out Boroda's name and sank to the floor, unconscious.

# CHAPTER 16

Fritz's eyelids fluttered open.

He was in his bed. Beside him on a tray was a cup of the liquid Boroda usually forced him to drink when he spent all his energy. Doll was standing still; a large pile of toys lay around him.

Fritz sat up and rubbed his shoulder—it was clean except for the raised scars left from the rat's teeth.

Boroda appeared and sat down in a chair. "How are you feeling?"

Fritz squinted at the sunlight streaming in. "Like someone hit me on the head. How long have I been out?"

"Just the night." Boroda handed him the mug of tea. "And other than fatiguing your magical energy, you are otherwise ok." He checked Fritz's shoulder. "Looks like you healed well."

He began checking other injuries. "Would you care to tell me what happened?"

"I don't know exactly," Fritz said. He narrated the happenings as best he could and when he had finished, he sat silently, waiting for Boroda to respond.

Boroda didn't reply. He stared into the distance, brow creased in thought.

"I saw some magic symbols I'd never seen before," Fritz added. He traced the symbols in the air with his finger. The warped helix made of spinning squares popped and fizzed.

Boroda shook his head. "This is a spell that would take most people months to memorize."

Fritz didn't react. "What does it do? I don't recognize the blending of these two shapes."

"The spell enables you to follow someone when they travel," Boroda explained. "There is a momentary lag when our portals remain open, leaving just enough time for another wizard to travel through. This is why we double check our surroundings before traveling."

"So, the rats were enchanted to follow me?" Fritz asked then took a long gulp of the tea.

"Yes," Boroda said. "The rats were pierced with small bits of metal, and this spell was attached to them. Whoever sent them didn't mean for you to survive the attack."

Fritz shifted uneasily.

Boroda put his fingers to his head. "And were it not for my last-minute, emergency meeting, I would have been here to help you fight them. It's either an unfortunate coincidence or suspiciously convenient."

"Meeting? With whom?" Fritz set his mug down and hugged his knees.

"Borya," Boroda said curtly.

"Borya!" Fritz asked. "Why would Borya attack members of The Order?"

Boroda's head snapped up. "Members?"

Fritz grimaced.

"Fritz, what do you mean, 'Members of The Order'?" Boroda demanded, remaining calm.

Fritz sighed. "Marzi and I figured out how we were getting attacked."

"You told Marzi?" Boroda erupted. "This was supposed to remain a secret. Our lives, Fritz, are supposed to remain a secret."

"I know. I'm sorry," Fritz said. "It slipped out one day, and then she told me that she and Hanja had been attacked, too. Then we found out that Andor and Eric were attacked …"

Boroda was shaking his head. "That doesn't make sense. That doesn't … Hanja? Eric?"

Fritz twisted his bedsheets. "Am I in trouble?"

Boroda was lost in thought, so Fritz scooted to the side of the bed. "I should get ready for school."

Boroda spoke softly but faced away from Fritz. "I will write you a note excusing your tardiness to school." He vanished from the room as Fritz rushed to pull on his uniform.

He walked slowly from the hedge to the front steps, his muscles tight and his vision blurry. He saw the purple dome of protective spells and nearly walked into it with his magic vision on.

He blinked it off and walked into school.

Mrs. Fairchild studied the note Boroda had scrawled hastily on a torn piece of paper. She called Peabody to come verify the note's authenticity.

Peabody studied the note and Fritz carefully. "I hope this family emergency won't disturb your concentration."

"No, sir," Fritz responded.

He tapped Mrs. Fairchild's desk with the note. "Give him a pass and mark him tardy."

Mrs. Fairchild smiled at Peabody, her bright red lips parted, and she obeyed.

Fritz grabbed his tardy note and hurried from the office. He didn't like Headmaster Peabody or Mrs. Fairchild and was glad to be gone.

Edward caught Fritz as he left the office.

"Why are you late?" he panted as he slung a heavy pack over his shoulder.

"My uncle thought I needed more sleep," Fritz said.

"Ms. Wakimba is furious you skipped her class. It was your turn to present today," Edward said.

Fritz stopped and groaned. "My owl project. I forgot all about it."

"We all wondered if that was why you skipped," Edward said quietly.

"No ... but I'm glad I did now."

"Better hope she doesn't fail you just for making her mad," Edward warned. "She nearly failed my second brother for talking during another student's presentation."

"Thanks for the heads-up," Fritz said. "See you at gym?"

"Sure." Edward winced, and they both ran to their next period.

Fritz dreaded the conversation with the apprentices at lunch. They would see right through his story, but they might understand his need for secrecy. He hoped they wouldn't pry.

He picked up his tray of food and set it down on the table. Everyone sat quietly and didn't acknowledge him.

"Is everything ok?" he asked, eyeing each person. He stopped at Gelé.

Her hair, usually pulled back, was hanging loosely over half her face. "Nice hair, Gelé. I like the new look."

He glanced at Marzi, and she gave him a fierce glare and put her finger up to her mouth.

Fritz responded with a confused frown.

Vivienne sniffed and wiped her eyes.

"You ok, Viv?" Fritz asked, and Marzi cleared her throat loudly. He looked at her, and she shook her head at him.

Gelé reached over instinctively to her sister and when she did, Fritz saw the dark purple splotches.

He looked closer and saw her bruised cheekbone covered with hair and makeup. Her lip was swollen and scabbed.

"Gelé!" Fritz said. "What happened?!"

"Nothing!" Gelé said.

"It's not nothing," Vivienne said.

"I can't," Gelé said softly to her sister.

"It happens to us all, Vivienne," Faruk said. "I've seen plenty of bruises and cuts on you over the years."

Gelé shook her head. "It wasn't Glacinda ... this time."

Andor, Fritz, and Marzi exchanged glances.

Vivienne melted into tears and took her sister's hand. "Tell me what happened!"

Gelé just shook her head.

Andor signed, "Time to break the rules?"

Fritz and Marzi gave each other a knowing glance.

"You were attacked, too?" Fritz asked bluntly.

Gelé froze.

Marzi rose from the table. "Everyone, come to the library."

No one questioned her command. They followed her to the library and up the stairs into the tiny alcove.

Fritz sat directly across from Gelé. "You got attacked last night, didn't you?"

Her chest heaved and tears welled up in her eyes.

"What animal was it?" Marzi asked.

"A bear!" she mouthed.

Andor waved excitedly.

"That's what attacked Andor," Marzi filled in. "I was attacked by a dragon and Fritz got attacked by an ape."

"You all have to promise that you won't tell anyone about this!" Gelé cried.

They each held up the wizard's promise.

"We were attacked by a polar bear," Gelé filled in. "Only not like any of the ones we normally see. This one was huge and completely mad. Spells had very little effect on it. It took us hours to kill it." She wiped her face as Vivienne wrapped her in a hug.

"Glacinda nearly died trying to kill it," she continued. "I was so exhausted after fighting that I was barely conscious. Glacinda was too weak to cast healing spells. She made me take a healing potion and, as you can see, it's taking awhile."

Faruk whistled low. "Is the bear local? Had you seen it before?"

"No!" Gelé exclaimed with fresh vim. "I know all the animals near us. This was not one of them. There were spells and enchantments on this bear, and we're not even sure how it got in the castle. We keep everything shut up tight. No one knows where we live—we don't even have servants."

"They're traveling in from storage," Fritz announced.

"What?" Gelé asked.

"Marzi and I figured out that they are being put in the 'unseen delivery' section and then traveled in on the back of whatever we get from there," Fritz explained.

"I traveled in my new dress, but I didn't see a bear," Gelé interjected.

"That's because whoever is sending them is using a morphing blend from Minerva Mooncup," Marzi told them.

"The hedge witch?" Vivienne said. "She's so sweet. Why would she do that?"

"Whoever asked for the blend threatened her. She nearly killed us when we asked her about it," Fritz said.

"Gilly worms?" Vivienne asked with a slight spark in her eye.

"Yep," said Fritz.

"Who would do this?" Gelé said and started crying again.

"Whoever is doing it isn't messing around," Fritz said. "Marzi, Andor, and I were attacked by a horde of rats in the woods a few weeks ago on the first day of trials. There were thousands of them, and they were all attacking us."

Everyone gasped.

"We couldn't outrun them. I had to blast a large rat off Edward. We barely made it out of the woods alive."

"Wait …" Vivienne sat back, "you blasted a rat off Edward here at school?"

"In the woods," Fritz clarified.

"Drossie, how could you do magic on school property?"

Fritz shrugged. "I mean … I don't know. I just … did?"

"Maybe the woods aren't under the dome," Gelé suggested.

"The dome covers everything," Faruk countered. "Believe me, I've checked."

"Maybe Edward just shook it off," Marzi proffered and squirmed in her seat. "Drosselmeyer obviously didn't do magic on school property. There are enchantments, and he would have been punished by The Order."

"The Order should hear about the attacks," Faruk spoke up. "We should tell them."

"No!" Four voices responded in unison.

Andor accented his reply with three emphatic "no" signs.

Gelé clenched her fist and glared at Faruk. "If Glacinda finds out I told you all anything, I'm done. She will remove me in an instant."

Faruk threw up his hands. "Ok. Ok. I won't say anything. I promise."

The bell rang, and they all jumped. They chuckled at their reaction to the sound, and the atmosphere lightened.

"Time for class," Faruk said and walked out the door.

Marzi and Fritz stayed behind.

When the others had exited, Marzi asked, "Are you still on for tonight?"

"Yes. I'll meet you here after school."

"Minerva has to give us some answers," Marzi said, resolute.

"When we talk to her," said Fritz, "Let's begin with 'pretty please' and go from there."

Marzi laughed. She turned to leave but Fritz didn't follow. "Are you coming?"

"I have some things I have to look into," he said. "I'll meet you here after class."

She left, and Fritz waited a few minutes before exiting the school. He crossed the road and hurried around the corner so he wouldn't be seen by any teachers. He blinked on his magic vision.

The school was enveloped in a dazzling, rounded dome. The shapes were innumerable and so beautiful it nearly took his breath away. He approached the dome and looked at the patterns closely.

Fritz walked the perimeter, careful not to touch it for fear of setting off a warning. As he approached the far side of the school wall, he stopped and squinted.

The enchantments formed floating, latitudinal strips, or rings of repeated magical glyphs. Each ring turned counter to the one above and below it in a slow, steady rotation. The ring closest to the ground was the largest, and each ring closer to the sky got progressively smaller, forming a tight, dome-shaped wall of enchantment.

He craned to see as high up the dome as possible, and every ring of glyphs he saw repeated the same pattern.

He bit his lip, deep in thought.

"How far up do you go?" he wondered aloud.

Satisfied for the present, he blinked off his magic vision and sauntered to class.

# CHAPTER 17

Fritz and Marzi crossed their fingers and traveled to the alleyway near Minerva Mooncup's shop. No one was present when they stepped from their misty shrouds. They glanced around, but all the shutters in the alleyway were closed to keep out the cold winter air.

As they walked toward the alleyway entrance, Fritz told Marzi about the attack the night before.

"What?!" she exclaimed.

"I think Nicholaus is behind all of this," he told her. "He has to be. The rat connection is too much of a coincidence to be anyone else."

"Nicholaus isn't a wizard," Marzi said.

"But with his dad's money and connections, he probably has access to wizards."

"Yeah … to Boroda," said Marzi. "Unless you want to accuse your own master of the attacks, I'd suggest keeping your gaze wider than Nicholaus. I get it—he's a jerk—but I don't think he's that smart."

They walked up to the shop, and Marzi took a deep breath deeply to calm her nerves.

They entered the shop, and the familiar, dank smells once again accosted their olfactories.

"Let's get this over with quickly," said Fritz.

The beaded curtain swished and out stepped a tall, thin woman with straight blonde hair wearing a circlet of flowers woven into the thin copper bands on her head.

"May I help you?" she asked. Her dress was made of a delicate material that swished with every movement she made.

"We were looking for Minerva Mooncup," Marzi said.

With a coquettish grin, the lady asked in a breathy voice, "I'm afraid Minerva isn't in. I'm Finuala. How may *I* help you?"

Fritz eyed the gauzy material wrapped around her body in delicate folds.

He swallowed. "We were looking for an herb blend with one week's nutrition."

Finuala caught his gaze and raised an eyebrow flirtatiously. "Of course. Is there anything else you want?"

Fritz blushed.

"I was also looking for some morphing herbs," Marzi said.

Finuala glanced at her dismissively then addressed Fritz. "I'm afraid those potions are beyond my ability. You would need to see Minerva for that."

She glided behind the front counter. "Is there anything else?"

"No, thank you," Marzi said, her voice laced with annoyance.

"The potion will take an hour to make." Finuala made eye contact with Fritz. "Please wait."

She slid through the beaded curtain.

Fritz followed her exit, craning his neck.

Marzi punched his shoulder. "Hey! Pay attention."

"I am!" Fritz said, rubbing his arm.

"If Minerva isn't here, how are we going to find out about the morphing potions?"

"I don't know," Fritz snapped back.

"Look around the shop and see if you can find anything that might give us a clue," Marzi said, scowling.

They began to walk around the little shop, looking at the assorted bottles and bags of mixed herbs and oddly colored liquids.

Fritz approached the mushroom table warily. There were hand printed cards stuck in the dirt explaining the benefits of each variety.

He picked one up.

*Funghi Wartius: health giving. One mushroom feeds one person for one day.*

"That's odd," he said. There was a pile of mushrooms already cut lying in a heap near the edge.

"What is?" Marzi asked from a few aisles over.

"Here's a mushroom that will feed a person for a day," Fritz said. "You should just get a whole bunch of these."

Marzi walked over and looked around. She knelt down and examined several packages below the mushrooms.

"Look at this!" she exclaimed.

She held up a large glass container filled with a mixture of dried herbs. A note was taped to the top.

*Nutritional Blend: One tablespoon, brewed = one day of eating.*

"You think Finuala knows this is here?" Fritz asked. "She's probably in the back making the same thing. I should go back there and tell her."

Marzi frowned. "Something doesn't feel right."

Fritz grabbed the glass jar. "I'll go ask her."

Marzi snatched the jar back. "*I'll* go ask her."

"Fine." Fritz yanked the jar away. "You ask her, and I'll hold the jar."

Marzi shot him a dirty look and strode quickly toward the front counter.

They walked through the curtain and into a room stacked floor to ceiling with dried plants. Finuala wasn't there, so they walked past the plants to another room separated by a beaded curtain.

There was a crunching noise coming from the far corner.

"Maybe she's chopping dried herbs?" Fritz whispered.

Marzi shoved him forward.

The crunching was coming from a large chest.

Fritz opened the chest, and Marzi shrieked and jumped back.

Inside the chest, a mass of worms churned over each other, hungrily chomping on their meal. Sticking out of the wormy mound was the unmistakable half-eaten face of Minerva Mooncup.

Fritz let the lid fall back with a loud slap. "Watcher, help us!"

Marzi grimaced. "Gilly worms."

They crept back the way they had come, glancing around for any signs of danger.

"Where is Finuala?" Fritz whispered.

"I don't know, but it's safe to assume she's not a friend," Marzi said.

She traveled away the jar of mushrooms, still in her arms, and closed her hand around a katana with a worn leather grip and a razor sharp blade. Both she and Fritz prepared defensive spells and held them at the ready in their hands.

With eyes peeled, they inched forward toward the door, making slow, smooth movements.

Fritz heard the beaded curtain rattle in a small breeze as the floorboards creaked under their feet. Behind him, the crunching sound of the gilly worms grew louder and became more sporadic. The chewing sounds melted into the unmistakable sound of tiny claws scuttling. The hair on Fritz's neck stood straight up.

"Rats!" he warned.

Seconds later, a deluge of the rodents poured into the room.

Marzi aimed her spell, and several rats turned to dust.

Fritz scorched several, but they advanced too quickly for him to kill.

Fritz and Marzi leapt up on a table, firing spell after spell. The rats continued to pour in, clawing up the table. Fritz kicked two back and crushed them midair with a clap.

Marzi screamed and knocked one from her leg. Blood trickled from the wound.

With a sweep of his hand, Fritz threw a spell at the advancing horde. The rats tumbled back as if hit by an invisible ocean wave.

"Let's get out of here!" shouted Marzi.

Fritz held her back. "No! They will travel with us!"

"There are too many, Drossie!" she screamed. "We can't fight them alone."

She now held two katanas and hacked at the rats as they climbed the table.

Rats were beginning to climb the walls and cross the ceiling.

One dropped on Fritz. He threw it to the floor and crushed it. He pushed hard against the stick roof, and it exploded in a shower of wood bits. The rats left behind leapt at them from the edges of the new hole above them.

Fritz looked over at the chest in the corner.

"Gilly worms!" he shouted to Marzi.

They both reached out and pulled against the wooden planks of the chest. The front panel exploded and thousands of worms spilled to the floor. A nearby rat squealed as the worms crawled over it and began tearing into its flesh.

Marzi continued hacking away at the rats with her swords as Fritz traveled piles of the worms, sprinkling them over the rodents.

The rats rushed the table, driven mad by dark enchantments and carnivorous worms chewing at their flesh. Even with the worms weighing them down, the swarms of rats continued to advance.

Sweat was streaming down Marzi's face as she blasted away rat after rat. The reserves in her charm were perilously low, and her stance faltered from fatigue.

Fritz had a sword in one hand and a ball of fire in the other. He could feel his energy, already low, slipping away. The sounds dulled, overtaken by the blood pumping in his ears.

Inside his chest, a familiar rage boiled. It felt the same as when he was locked in the box at Ivanov's, but this was not the time to reminisce or analyze the sensation. His green eyes sparked silver pops of energy.

With a yell, he jumped high in the air and, when he landed, slammed his fist on the table. A shock wave spread out, knocking the rats off the table and momentarily confusing them. He reached out, and several nearby plants shot out tendrils and wrapped themselves around the table. Vines snaked across the floor, wrapping around furniture and shelves.

The rats, unphased by the vines, continued to rush toward the table. They scaled the twisting plants with ease and scrabbled to the tabletop.

Marzi stared at Fritz in wonderment as vine after vine covered the floor.

A rat jumped onto the table; Marzi cut it in half and kicked it to the floor. Another rat with a gilly worm hanging off its back crested the edge and charged.

"Drossie!" Marzi called out and sliced two rats mid-air. "Whatever you're doing, do it fast. There are too many for me to fight alone."

He held up his hand and squeezed it into a fist. Thorns sprang from the network of vines, and an instant later, the squeaking stopped.

Fritz felt the electricity race through his body. His eyes buzzed with every pulse. He grabbed Marzi around the waist, pulled her close, and kissed her.

Several seconds later, she pushed away.

The buzz of energy drained from Fritz, and his eyes faded back into an emerald green. He stared at Marzi and stuttered. "I'm … sorry. I didn't mean to …"

She stared at him in bewilderment. "I'm leaving."

She disappeared, leaving him alone with a room full of dead rats and crunching gilly worms.

Fritz dropped to the table. His head was swimming. He traveled back to his room and, gasping for breath, fell on his bed. His vision faded, blinked, then went dark.

# CHAPTER 18

Marzi ignored Fritz all day Thursday.

On Friday, she purposefully let herself get shot during trials so she could exit the woods and sit alone.

Friday after school, Fritz finally caught up with her.

"Hey! Are we still on for tomorrow morning?"

"Yes," she said. "Why wouldn't we be?"

"It's a bit chilly outside and pretty cold inside as well," Fritz said. "Listen, I'm sorry for what happened," he began, but she cut him off.

"You apologized already."

Fritz furrowed his eyebrows. "Is there … is there a problem, then?"

"No. See you tomorrow morning." Marzi stormed away.

Faruk walked up behind Fritz. "What's wrong with her?"

Fritz shook his head. "I honestly don't know."

"Is she mad at you?" he pried. "Wait … are you guys … are you a thing?" He rubbed the tips of his fingers together in a kissing motion.

Fritz grabbed Faruk's wrist to stop the gesture and glanced around, making sure no one was watching. Satisfied that no students had seen the exchange, Fritz faced Faruk and tried to sound indifferent. "No! We're not."

Faruk studied him. "I think you're lying." He broke into a wide smile. "Watcher! You are lying. You guys are a thing! You're thing-ing, aren't you?"

"We're not thing-ing," Fritz said. "We just kissed, and that's it."

Faruk's jaw fell open. "Oh, wow! Dude! If The Order ever finds out about this, you will get skinned alive!"

Fritz leaned in and whispered. "What are you talking about? Is there a rule against ... thing-ing?"

Faruk chortled. "Um, no official rules, but The Order frowns on coalitions."

"But we're not a coalition," Fritz argued. "We're not even a couple. I don't think, anyway."

"Hey. Your secret is safe with me," Faruk backed away. "But if I were you, I'd end this thing-ing. Fast."

He backed away until he ran into a student. He apologized and kept going. As he exited the school, he turned to Fritz at intervals to mouth the word "fast."

Fritz traveled home and got dressed for training. He kicked the large pile of dolls lying on his floor.

"Why are women so confusing?!" he shouted.

"I am unsure, sir," Doll said. Some stray threads were hanging off his head.

Fritz swatted the toy. "Shut up."

He traveled to the training room and stretched while he waited for Boroda.

During their training on weapons, Fritz continued to miss easy shots.

"Focus!" Boroda jabbed with the end of a wooden staff.

Fritz blocked it but put too much weight on his front leg.

Boroda twisted in the air and struck Fritz on the back of the head with his staff. Blood oozed out of the gash.

Fritz ignored the wound and struck out again, but Boroda waved his hand, and both weapons disappeared.

"Sit down. Let me take care of that."

Fritz obeyed.

"You seem distracted. What's happening?" Boroda asked.

Fritz bit his cheek. "I'm just having some problems at school."

Boroda wiped Fritz's head and neck with a rag and water. "With whom?"

"Not Nicholaus," Fritz assured him, and the wizard's shoulders relaxed.

"Then whom?" Boroda said.

Fritz breathed out slowly. "Would it be ok if I didn't tell you right now? There's a lot going on, and I'm trying to figure some things out."

Boroda waved his hand over the gash, and it began to close. "Of course. I will respect your privacy, as long as it doesn't compromise mine." He stepped away.

Fritz stood up and traveled in the weapons again.

Boroda attacked, and Fritz countered the blow. They continued sparring for an hour before calling it quits.

"Someone else in The Order got attacked," Fritz said while stretching after the workout.

Boroda didn't react. "Who?"

"I promised not to tell, but I thought you should know."

Boroda's face clouded over.

"Marzi and I also got attacked by rats today after school."

Boroda looked up. "Perhaps I didn't make myself clear where Marzi is concerned."

Fritz interrupted. "We were following up on our lead on Minerva Mooncup!"

"Minerva ..." Boroda stopped. "What has she got to do with this?"

Fritz backed away a tiny step. "I tried to tell you a couple nights ago. Marzi and I figured out how the animals made it to our homes."

Boroda waited, and Fritz continued. "They're being traveled in through the unseen section of our storage."

"How do you know this?" Boroda asked.

"It's the only place all of the wizards have in common that's linked directly to our homes."

Boroda shook his head. "I think I would have noticed an ape."

"But would you have noticed a moth or a fly?" Fritz asked.

Boroda froze.

"We figured out that the animals were being traveled in but only after being morphed into another animal.

We went to Minerva Mooncup's shop to ask her if it was possible, but she thought we were working for whoever had hired her to make the morphing blend. She threatened to feed us to her gilly worms if we came back."

Boroda chuckled. "Gilly worms."

"Marzi and I traveled back today to get …" Fritz paused. He didn't want to tell Boroda what he and Marzi had planned. "Information," he said, breaking the pause quickly, "when we discovered that Minerva had been killed. When we were looking around, we got attacked by rats. There was this girl, Finuala, who was working the shop, but she disappeared. Marzi thinks she was the one who killed Minerva."

"I doubt Finuala was actually Finuala," Boroda said.

"What do you mean?" Fritz asked.

Boroda stood up and turned in a circle. His clothing stretched, his hair grew, and his body shrank. When he faced Fritz again, he was a stunning brunette with blue eyes, dark red lips, and sensuous curves.

Fritz gaped.

"I'm Katie," the woman said. Her voice was soft and feminine. She turned and was, once again, Boroda.

"Wizards usually have several human personas to use as a disguise," he explained. "Finuala could have been anyone."

Fritz shook his head. "That's not the only thing."

Boroda raised his eyes. "There's more?"

"When I was fighting the rats, I was wiped out. I had no energy left and was about to pass out. Then I had this burning in my chest. My vision was both hazy and clear. I don't know how to describe it any better than that, but I made magic happen that I don't know the spells for. My apprentice charm had no energy stored, but I still killed all those rats."

Fritz paused to take a breath, and Boroda studied him carefully.

"It felt like when I snapped," Fritz finally admitted.

Boroda stood and helped Fritz to his feet. "Thank you for telling me. I am glad you are safe, but ..." He searched the room. "This relationship with Marzi needs to end."

Fritz lowered his head.

"I can't explain everything right now ..."

"Then when?" Fritz exploded. "You keep saying I'm not ready, but I've fought off enchanted animals, trained every day for months—I've even gained the trust of the apprentices. When will YOU trust me?"

Boroda let the air clear. "After that little tirade, longer than I thought."

He vanished from the room, and Fritz threw a spear at the wall. The weapon wobbled in the wooden panel. Once it was still, Fritz returned it to its rack, repaired the gash in the wall, then traveled to his room.

He wanted to be in the school library with Marzi. He enjoyed the seclusion of their little room. There was no magic or spells to worry about there. He laughed to himself. How strange that he felt the most free to love inside the restrictive confines of St. Michael's.

The thought triggered his memory of the dome surrounding the school. He washed quickly, changed clothes, and traveled to his own library. After a half hour of searching the shelves, he finally found a book that satisfied his curiosity.

*Ancient Magic: A Study by Artenimus Forge*

He skimmed the large book quickly, looking for any reference to domes. When he found it, he read carefully.

*Ancient magic was built on the concept of a globe or sphere. Every enchanted object was concealed in a sphere (for full coverage) or dome (for half coverage) of magic.*

*While this practice of Globing or Doming items was faster, it proved to be less efficient and, therefore, was dropped for the modern practice of attaching an enchantment directly to the object being enchanted.*

*The main reason for its ineffectiveness was the use of Capstone Glyphs. The Capstone Glyph (see picture opposite page) is a glyph placed at the top of the sphere or dome that holds all the accompanying spells used in the enchantment together. Once this capstone is removed, one may alter the enchantment as they wish or destroy it altogether.*

Fritz continued reading until the clock chimed midnight. He tossed the book in the air on the twelfth chime, and it vanished and materialized back in its place on the shelf. For good measure, he shook his fist and cursed the reshelving spell.

He traveled back to his room and climbed in bed. Tomorrow, he and Marzi were going to give food and enchanted warming dolls to the poor kids in Anadorn. Normally, the prospect of spending time with her would make him too happy to sleep, but now, it made his stomach ache.

He thought about their kiss and what Faruk had said about The Order's reaction. He had no desire to make trouble with The Order and even less desire to cause any for Marzi.

He pictured her smile, her laugh. He felt her lips on his. Fritz punched the bed.

If he had a relationship with Marzi, it would be only a matter of time before The Order found out, and they would both suffer. Perhaps get removed.

He wasn't positive what would happen to the two of them, but he would put nothing past The Order if they felt their power was being threatened.

He decided to tell Marzi that he could no longer spend time with her. He would, though, wait until after they had distributed their food and toys.

Fritz covered his head with his pillow and rolled over in his bed. As much as it hurt to give up his time with Marzi, he had to do it for both their sakes. Another piece of him sacrificed on the altar of safety.

The Order had taken his brother and now the girl he loved.

As with the Czar, he had no choice.

He was their property.

.

# CHAPTER 19

Toby greeted Fritz and Marzi with a hug, leaving sooty handprints on their clothing. He was wearing a new coat, already covered in a thin layer of coal dust.

"Hey Toby!" Fritz said. "We need your help."

"With what?" he asked.

"Marzi and I have a bag of toys and food, and we want to pass them out to the kids here in Anadorn," Fritz explained.

His eyes grew wide. "For free? Like Christmas?"

Fritz laughed. "Almost exactly like Christmas."

"Can you show us where they are?" Marzi asked.

Toby thought a minute. "Let's start in Milner's Alley."

For the next three hours, Toby darted from house to house, with Fritz and Marzi in tow.

The older children accepted the food and dolls with caution. The younger children latched on without a moment's hesitation. Many of them were more excited about the toy than the food.

When they took hold of the dolls and felt the warmth envelop them, every child, young and old, hugged them tighter and sighed.

Marzi ran out of food before Fritz had emptied his room of toys.

Fritz carried a leather bag large enough to conceal his whole arm. He traveled in a doll from the large pile in his room and presented it to a waiting child.

As the day progressed, Fritz developed a flare for pulling the doll out, making it do flips in the air, and finally coming to rest in the expectant child's arms. A crowd of children and adults gathered around to watch the tricks and applauded loudly when he balanced a doll in each hand and on his head. Fritz bowed, passed the dolls out, and motioned to Marzi, who only bowed her head.

Marzi stood by, watching politely, but her expression was never more than amused congeniality.

When the last doll had been handed out, Fritz and Marzi waved goodbye to Toby, who hugged them and raced off to join a group of boys.

Marzi turned to leave, but Fritz stopped her.

"We need to talk," he said.

She turned and folded her arms.

"I understand my mistake. I crossed a line, and I'm sorry," he began. "We are part of a group that requires us to be emotionally independent and ..." He struggled for the next words.

Marzi's face was immovable.

"I like you, Marzi."

Her eyes widened.

"I like you a lot and ... and every minute I spend with you, I like you more. But thinking we could ever be anything more than friends, given our situation, is ludicrous and potentially dangerous for us both."

She dropped her arms. Her mouth opened slightly.

Fritz felt tears sting his eyes. "I think it's best if we don't see each other outside of school anymore."

Marzi bit her lip. A tear rolled down her cheek. She clamped her mouth shut, and her face scrunched into a scowl.

"Fine," she said.

Fritz waited for her to say something else but she just glared at him.

Marzi turned and vanished.

Fritz didn't bother to see if anyone was watching. He stepped from the alley into his room, a dark cloud of smoke dissipating behind him.

That evening, after getting coached on formal attire and etiquette from Boroda, Fritz stood outside the Southern Kingdom's embassy, dressed in a stiff tuxedo.

A servant met him at the door and led him to the drawing room. It was filled with lavishly dressed women in flowing skirts. Each woman had jewels hanging from her neck, ears, and hair. The men wore black formal attire with medals and bars signifying political and military rank pinned to their jackets. Servants milled around with trays of food and drinks held high, waiting for guests to avail themselves of the delicacies.

Edward met him just inside the door of the drawing room. "I am so glad you're here. The adults are talking about taxes and codes and land and—ugh. I was about to fake an illness just to leave."

"Have you gotten to talk to your brother yet?" Fritz asked.

"No. He's been busy the whole time," Edward confessed. "Everyone wants to talk to him."

"I need to get him alone," Fritz reminded him.

Edward frowned pensively. "After dinner, everyone will move to the den or the patio. We can try to get him then."

"Ok," Fritz said. "But he has to be alone. I need to know what he knows about Perrin."

"And how we can escape his ghost during final examinations," Edward added with a serious tone.

After an interminably long dinner, dessert, and official toasts, the company wandered to various rooms to talk, smoke, or enjoy coffee.

Edward pulled Fritz over to a corner where several men were arguing.

"Richard!" he called out and, when ignored, yelled again louder.

The tall, slender man with his back to them turned. "Not now, Edward."

"I wanted to introduce you to my friend," Edward began, but Richard was already in a full-voiced argument with the other men again. Edward tugged on his arm and Richard turned around, red faced. "Can you talk to my friend …"

"No, Edward, I'm busy," he said again, but before he turned back, Fritz grasped his hand in a tight handshake.

Richard started and stared at Fritz. "It's good to meet you," Richard said pointedly and tried to yank his hand away.

"And you," Fritz added. "I was wondering if we could go somewhere quiet to talk?"

"I'm afraid it will have to wait. I am otherwise engaged." Richard motioned to the group of men who hadn't seemed to notice his absence.

Fritz didn't release his grip. "My Uncle Boroda sends you his greetings."

Richard froze. He motioned with his head, and he, Fritz, and Edward left the room and walked down the hall to a large, unoccupied sitting room.

Richard shut the door and turned to face Fritz. "Who are you, and what is this about?"

"My name is Drosselmeyer, and it's about Perrin." The words spilled out and Fritz swallowed, trying to calm his thumping heart.

Richard stiffened. "What about him?"

"I need to ask you some questions about him."

Richard's face flashed with anger, but he recovered and replied in a soft, nonchalant tone. "Why do you think I would know anything about him?"

"I thought you were ..." Edward jumped in but Fritz stopped him with his hand.

He reached into his jacket pocket and pulled out the stack of letters and handed them to him.

Richard breathed in. He turned to his younger brother and barked, "Edward, leave us."

Edward protested but when his older brother snapped his fingers, he deflated and obeyed with reluctance.

"Where did you get these?" Richard demanded.

"From Edward," Fritz answered. "He assured me he didn't read them."

"What business are these of yours?" He held the stack of letters out.

"I have questions about his death." Fritz spoke in a calm, even manner, trying to diffuse Richard's agitation.

"Why not ask your uncle?" Richard asked, his annoyance growing.

"My uncle has forbidden any discussion regarding Perrin," Fritz explained. "You're the only person I know of who might be able to clarify some questions I have about him and his death."

"His body was found in the woods. That's what the papers said, and that's all I know of it," Richard spat.

"The nature of your letters suggests that you were good friends. I find it hard to believe that's all you know of it."

"Again, Master Drosselmeyer, I don't see how my friendships, be it with your cousin or not, are any of your business."

"Because, sir," Fritz said, "I suspect foul play. I found a note from Perrin in a book in my uncle's library before I even read your letters. He was researching something sensitive, the repercussions of which are still relevant and potentially dangerous to me and people I love."

Fritz slid Perrin's note across the table. He sat up, trying to match Richard's posture and regal air of authority.

Richard picked it up, read it, then slid it back to Fritz. "What was he researching?"

"That is extremely sensitive," Fritz confided. "I will tell you if it means reciprocity of information, but I need your word that you will be discrete."

Richard studied Fritz, then, after a look of satisfaction, nodded his agreement. "And likewise, you must promise on the Watcher and your eternal soul that what I say here does not leave this room."

Fritz agreed.

Richard moved farther away from the door, sat down, and motioned for Fritz to do the same.

"Perrin and I were best friends. We met at St. Michael's as children, and it was as if we were from the same womb. Though I was never allowed to visit his home—something of an oddity, your uncle is—Perrin was a constant resident here at the embassy.

"We spent most of our childhood exploring the woods behind my estate. They are a large wood filled with many adventures for two boys at play. In fact, if you go far enough into them, you will come to the fields behind St. Michael's.

"One day, while at play, we found a cave. It was well hidden by brush, and you had to approach it from a very overgrown side of the hill to even see the entrance. It immediately became our fortress. Over the years, it was many things—a pirate's cove, a rowdy pub, a magical entrance to a mystical world of elves and fairies …"

Richard looked away and spoke as if in a dream. "As we grew older, our affection for each other … grew and the cave was used for … other purposes.

"Because of my family's position and my expected service to the crown, the nature of our friendship had to remain a secret, or the shame that would befall my name and prospects would doom me and my family to ruin.

"The cave was, ironically, the only place where I could be myself and also live in a fantasy." He paused to catch his composure.

"The letters you read were written during the summer of my last year at St. Michael's. I spent that summer in the capital city of Thalmin, in the king's court. It was a busy summer of meeting people and being introduced in influential circles.

"I'm afraid that my replies to Perrin weren't as numerous as his letters to me. I hid these letters in my trunk and sent it back at the end of my time in Thalmin, only to be forgotten—until now, obviously."

He inhaled deeply and slowly released the breath. "However, his last letter to me spoke of something he had discovered that was quite sinister. It also referenced a secret he had to tell me but one that had to be delivered in person.

"On this same trip, I was betrothed to the woman who is now my wife. It was a political match, of course, but that's the way things work, and Perrin and I were very open with each other about the limitations of our friendship.

"I came home, fully committed to honoring my duty to king and country, and convinced myself that I would be as distant from him as I could.

"When he asked to meet at the cave, I had every intention of telling him no—that my position and career were at stake, and a friendship like ours could not continue for fear of discovery.

"I went to the cave with the sole purpose of telling him exactly that, but when I saw him waiting for me in our sanctum, my passion got the better of me. Before he could relay any information, we were ... otherwise engaged in activity that was not conducive to talking."

Richard lowered his voice. The crackling fire nearby washed him in a warm light. "It was during the middle of this ... meeting ... that I was struck from behind on the head, and when I regained consciousness, Perrin was dead."

The pounding in his chest reverberated in his ears, but Fritz sat motionless.

"I was terrified. I panicked because I didn't know how to explain his death or our presence in the cave. The truth would have meant ruination for me and a final black mark on his honor.

"I can still see him clutching my jacket, eyes blank, staring at nothing."

Richard cradled his forehead in his hands, not bothering to hide the quaking in his voice. "I dressed him and carried him to the edge of the field near St. Michael's. Then I went back to my house. McGregor found him the next day, and I pretended to be shocked just like everyone else."

Richard wiped his eyes. "And that is all I know."

"Were there any wounds or defensive marks on him?" Fritz asked delicately.

"None," Richard replied. "Whoever killed him hadn't left a mark or broken a single bone."

Tears streamed freely down the noble's cheeks. "I still think about him all the time. It's why I still keep these letters and my jacket. They are all I have left of him."

Fritz allowed Richard time to compose himself.

Richard straightened and cleared his voice. "I've told you my story. Would you give me the same satisfaction?"

"Perrin was a wizard. And so am I." He berated himself for the inelegant delivery and wiped his sweaty palms on his pants, trying to gain composure.

Richard stared, and after seeing that Fritz wasn't joking, he smirked. "Surely, you think me a fool."

Fritz considered a moment. He waved his arms and instantly, both he and Richard were sitting in the Anadorn Fountain Plaza.

The winter chill hit them and Richard jolted upright, spinning several times. "What is this? What have you done?"

"Something only a wizard can do," Fritz responded calmly.

Richard sank back into the library chair, dazed.

Fritz waved his hand and a tea cart appeared in the snow. He lifted the cup without moving a muscle and poured tea from a hovering teapot. He floated the saucer to Richard.

"Do you believe me now, or do I need to prove myself further?"

Richard shook his head. "No. No, I believe you. I am fully convinced."

Fritz waved his hand, and they were back in the library with only a dissolving cloud as proof they'd ever left.

"Revealing a wizard's identity is one of the biggest signs of trust any wizard can give. I believe that was part of the secret Perrin was going to tell you that day."

"Why didn't he tell me before?" Richard was breathing heavily.

"We belong to a powerful alliance of wizards. There are dire consequences for sharing this information unnecessarily," Fritz explained.

"Did this alliance find out that he was going to tell me? Did they have him killed?" Richard asked.

"I don't know for sure," Fritz said. "The note I gave you came from a book in my uncle's library."

"A large leather book about glyphs or some nonsense?"

Fritz cocked his head. "No, but I know the book you're talking about." He waved his hand and held out *Ancient Magic* for Richard to see. "This one?"

"Yes. I teased him about it that night. Told him he needed to read real books."

"What did you do with the book?"

"I don't know. It was probably left behind in the cave. He didn't have it when I ..." He swallowed and wiped away fresh tears.

"When you discovered he was dead?" Fritz finished.

Richard clenched his jaw.

"Was he acting strangely or any differently the night you were with him?"

"Not particularly. Why?"

"The book where I found his note—it deals with mind control."

Richard recoiled, and Fritz continued. "It's a very convoluted type of magic and frowned on by most wizards. I thought that, perhaps, Perrin was being controlled by someone or discovered someone else's plot to use mind control."

Richard shook his head. "He was as wonderful as he had always been. Naki was not given to extreme shifts in mood."

"Naki?" Fritz asked.

"Oh, it was a nickname I occasionally called him. A shortened form of his surname, 'Adrionakis.' He was very embarrassed by the name and made me promise never to tell anyone. I only used it when we were alone."

Fritz frowned. "I was unaware he had a surname. No matter—you would know if his personality was altered in any way."

"It was not. That I can assure you with the highest confidence."

Fritz stood. "That is all I have to share." He hedged, then asked, "Would you tell me how to get to the cave? I'd like to see if there are any clues."

"It's been over a decade," Richard said skeptically.

"There are certain clues that may not dull with time. Things to which your eyes are not privy," Fritz reminded him.

Richard acquiesced with a nod and explained how to find the cave. They shook hands again and exited the room.

Edward leapt up from the floor in the hallway. "Finally!"

Richard shook Fritz's hand, said goodbye, and excused himself.

Edward turned to Fritz. "Did you find anything out?"

Fritz walked quickly down the hallway in the opposite direction Richard had gone. "Maybe. I have to look into something."

Edward brightened. "What? Can I help?"

"I need to leave, but I need to go through your garden without being seen by the other guests," Fritz said.

Edward thought for a moment and pointed back toward the room they'd just exited. "There's a window back there that opens to the side of the garden."

"Thanks, Edward. You're the best."

Fritz shook his hand and dashed back to the room. He slipped out through the window and crouched behind the tall shrubs just outside the ledge. He stayed low until he was safely out of sight and in the woods.

Hiking through the brush was difficult in his formal clothing. He ripped off his jacket in frustration, stripped off the stiff clothing, and sent them back to his room. He traveled in appropriate attire for tromping through scrub brush and set off at a quicker pace through the woods.

After half an hour of searching in the dark, he found the cave. Even without the summer foliage as camouflage, the cave entrance was well hidden and difficult to find. He wound his way down the hill where the path spiraled like a conch into a small cave.

He snapped his fingers and the ball of light he used in the library appeared above him. He adjusted the spell, and the light brightened enough to illuminate the space around him.

The floor was rock, ground smooth by years of erosion. Sand covered most of the ground, with weeds growing beyond the entrance to the cavern. The walls were patinated in a greenish-brown moss.

He blinked on his magic sight. The air was clear. No spells or enchantments. The run through the woods had made him warm, so he took off his coat and walked through the cave.

"Come on, Perrin," he mumbled. "Give me something."

Fritz played through the evening in his mind. Perrin had been interrupted and was in a very vulnerable position. His first instinct was to grab Richard's coat and cover up. If he figured he was about to die, that was his only chance to leave a clue.

He glanced down at his hand where his jacket hung loosely. The brass buttons glinted in the overhead light.

Fritz shivered from the damp air in the cave and walked out into the forest. He waved his hand over one of the buttons and repeated the warming spell he'd placed on the children's toys.

He stopped mid-spell.

Richard's jacket.

Perrin was holding Richard's jacket.

Fritz whirled around. He had to get back to Edward's, fast.

A twig snapped, and Fritz instinctively raised a blocking spell.

The bolt of magic hit him, and even with the magic shield in place, knocked him to the ground.

In a panic, he traveled to the top of a nearby tree to see who was attacking him.

The attacker followed through Fritz's traveling portal and batted him from the tree with a powerful backhand.

Fritz crashed through several branches before he slowed his descent. The impact on the ground knocked the breath out of him, but he rolled to his back and shot a blast of magic at his assailant.

The Black Wizard dodged the blast and stared at Fritz, awaiting his next move. The dark eyes glinted with fiendish glee from underneath the black cloak.

Fritz didn't move, so the Black Wizard hurled a spell at him.

Fritz dodged, spun, and instead of a spell, flashed a blazing white light.

The Black Wizard yelled and, with eyes shielded, traveled to Fritz and swung for his face.

Fritz ducked and punched the figure in rapid succession in the stomach.

The assailant doubled over and flew back into a tree. The Wizard sent a volley of magic spells, but Fritz dispatched each one and returned fire.

The Black Wizard leapt close and landed a punch.

Fritz grunted and blocked the next punch.

The Black Wizard kicked, and Fritz moved just enough to take a glancing blow—but not fast enough to escape the backhand.

Fritz fell back.

The Black Wizard rushed at him, a long dagger now poised to strike.

Fritz jumped at the shrouded attacker, closing the distance and making it difficult to put any power behind a stab.

Fritz felt the knife slice through the outside of his arm as he wrapped his arms around his assailant. He hurled his attacker at a nearby tree, aided by the pushing spell he had learned during his first weeks with Boroda.

Fritz spun off a different tree as the Black Wizard quickly regained balance, having hit the tree with a cushioning spell. Fritz then delivered a powerful chest kick.

The Black Wizard grunted, spun quickly, and caught Fritz in the side of the head with a heel.

Fritz crashed to the ground and rolled over quickly. His vision was blurry, but he could make out the shadowy assailant leaping into the air, feet raised for a fatal stomp.

Fritz rolled away, and the attacker smashed into the ground.

The Black Wizard attacked with a push of energy.

Fritz flew back but kicked his legs up, landing horizontally in a crouch on the side of a tree. He pushed off the tree with a rage-filled yell and, shortly before impact, traveled several feet behind the figure. Before the Black Wizard could turn around, Fritz had grabbed the hooded figure in a magical pull. He flung his enemy at a large oak.

The Black Wizard struggled to stand and shakily lifted a hand. Before Fritz could react, a rat was on his shoulder, sinking its teeth into his neck.

Fritz gritted his teeth and threw the rat against the tree with so much force that the rodent burst open.

Fritz faced his foe. His eyes turned silvery green, and his body buzzed with energy.

The Black Wizard attacked with deadly speed, but Fritz saw each strike as if it were happening in slow motion. He deflected two punches, twisted out of the way of a knee, and struck back with both palms.

The attack hit the Black Wizard in the face, and the satisfying pop of the nose echoed above the sound of crunching leaves.

Fritz jumped up, spun around, and kicked the Black Wizard in the chest, sending the figure sliding several feet in the damp earth.

Fritz landed, ready for another attack, but the figure waved its arms and disappeared in a cloud of smoke.

Fritz was tempted to follow, but he had more pressing issues. He traveled to the side of Edward's house, opened the window he'd escaped from, and raced down the hallway toward the sound of laughter.

Edward saw him before he entered the drawing room. "Hey, you're back!" His face contorted. "Why are you dressed like that? Why are you bleeding?"

Fritz glanced down at his arm. The blood was beginning to clot. He would take care of it later. He ignored it and pulled Edward away from the party.

"Edward. Show me the trunk where you found the letters."

Edward looked askance at Fritz. "Why?"

Fritz stepped in close and whispered, "I don't have time to explain. Show it to me."

Edward waved in surrender and pointed toward the hallway. "Ok. Sorry. Follow me."

They climbed up to the attic, and Edward led him through piles of crates to the trunk. "This is all my brother's stuff," he explained.

Fritz threw open the chest and blinked on his magic vision. He dug through the contents frantically until his fingers closed on a sturdy piece of material. He yanked it into the open.

"It's my brother's jacket," Edward said, unimpressed.

Fritz studied the buttons.

At first he saw nothing, then a sparkling halo faded into view. Fritz fed it energy, willing the message to strengthen.

"Are you ok?" Edward asked. "You're staring at the jacket pretty hard."

Fritz ignored him.

The magic strengthened, and Fritz dropped the coat when he saw the shape Perrin had drawn.

Perrin's last message was "O."

"That doesn't make sense," Fritz muttered.

"What doesn't make sense?" Edward pried and examined the coat as well.

Fritz collapsed on an old armchair, ignoring the plumes of dust. "It's a useless shape, isn't it?"

Edward held the coat aloft, straining his eyes in the dim light. "What are you talking about, Drossie? Are you ok? You're still bleeding."

Fritz stood on wobbly legs, his energy running dangerously low. "I need to go, Edward. Please don't tell anyone about this."

"I won't," the boy assured him and offered his arm.

They both left the attic and exited the house through the front door. Fritz stumbled out the gate and as soon as he rounded the tall hedges, he disappeared in a puff of smoke.

# CHAPTER 20

"Time to go." Boroda's voice boomed from the mirror.

Fritz took a deep breath and checked the clock on the wall. It was evening. He looked around in a confused stupor. He had slept all day.

"We leave for The Order meeting in ten minutes," Boroda said, and Fritz's clock clicked louder.

Fritz ran to the mirror. "Boroda! We need to talk!"

Boroda's face appeared, floating in a green haze. "About what?"

"I was attacked last night," he said.

"Attacked by what? By rats?" This time Boroda spoke from behind him in his room, and Fritz spun around with a yell. Boroda handed Fritz his apprentice uniform shirt.

"By the Black Wizard," Fritz said. "But the Black Wizard did use a rat to attack me."

"Hmm," said Boroda. "Interesting. What were you doing when you got attacked?"

Fritz caught his breath. "I was walking in the woods." It was half true. He jumped into his pants and tucked the shirt in. "We fought with both magic and hand-to-hand combat, and I beat him."

"Do you suspect the Black Wizard is the one who sent the rats here?" Boroda said, ignoring the brag.

"And at Minerva's," Fritz said, his excitement building. "I think everything is connected. The attacks on me and your plan to overthrow The Order ..."

Fritz froze, his tie halfway finished.

Boroda's eyes narrowed. "What do you know of my plans?"

Fritz began to stutter.

Boroda stood up, and the lights dimmed.

"Tell me what you know!" he demanded.

"I overheard you talking to the General," Fritz confessed. "I know you're planning on taking them down along with the Czar."

He backed away from Boroda, flinching.

Boroda appeared calm, but his eyes were icy. "I will meet you at the glen of trees where The Order meets."

He disappeared, and Fritz slumped to the floor. He yelled in frustration and slammed his elbows into the dresser. When the clock registered two minutes until the meeting, he stood up, grabbed his hat and cape, still dirty from his forest excursion, and traveled to the glen.

Other wizards popped into view.

Borya called the meeting to order and then dismissed the apprentices.

Fritz stepped from his traveling mist and blinked at the bright, cloudless blue sky. He walked past the meticulously trimmed hedges to the pavilion. Once underneath the awning, he took off his cape and hat and flopped onto the couch.

The others sat in their places, all amusing themselves. Marzi read a book, focusing her attention on its pages.

"Is Glacinda going to tell them about the attack?" Vivienne asked. She made a seed sprout and pulled tendrils from the stem in rapid succession.

"No," Gelé said, then added, "I don't think we should talk about it."

"Who's going to know?" Vivienne asked. "Does The Order listen to us here?"

"The garden is a safe space." Faruk flicked a tiny fireball at Vivienne's flower.

"In that case, I doubt she will tell them," said Gelé. She sat upright in her chair, no magic on display.

"Why?" Vivienne demanded.

"The Order is already on edge," Gelé asserted, and everyone looked her way. "Think about it. No other group of wizards would dare attack The Order. They would be obliterated."

"What are you saying?" Faruk eyed her suspiciously.

"I'm saying ..." she started to say, then paused, sweeping the pavilion with her eyes. "I'm saying that we should entertain the possibility ..." She hesitated.

"That it's someone in The Order," Fritz finished for her. Silence.

Andor signed an expletive.

"That's a very bold statement," Faruk said in a low tone.

"It's the only explanation that makes sense," Gelé said.

"It's not like any of us are in on it," Vivienne quipped. "Sylvia is away all the time. She could be planning this, and I'd have no idea."

"You and Faruk are the only ones who haven't been attacked yet, now that you mention it," Marzi said, eyes still on her book.

"I think we should probably change the subject," Faruk said in a serious tone. "If we start accusing each other's masters of treason, things could go south very quickly."

"For once, I agree with you," Marzi added and closed her book.

Gelé scowled.

"Let's explore the garden," Faruk suggested, breaking up the tension.

"We've tried." Vivienne slumped dramatically in her chair. "We've gone miles and miles and—nothing. It goes on forever."

Fritz stood up and stretched. "I'll explore it with you. What could it hurt?"

He looked over at Marzi.

She picked up her book and flipped it open, purposefully obscuring his face from her view.

"Might be nice to get away." Fritz walked out of the pavilion.

"Awesome!" Faruk said. "I'll go this way." He pointed to his left.

"I'll go that way," Fritz countered.

Andor took straight ahead.

"The girls are going to wait here," Vivienne said, gesturing to the pavilion.

"Girls," Faruk chided, then disappeared in a puff of smoke. Andor followed.

Fritz looked at the farthest point and traveled. He landed on a hedge and rolled off, yelping in pain. "Stupid thorns."

He healed the scratches with a quick spell then traveled again. This time, he pushed against the ground, wobbling on the unsteady point of the spell, hovering long enough to step to the right of the hedge onto the gravel-lined path.

The distant horizon was still just as far away. The glassy blue sky and warm sunlight enveloped everything in a comforting glow. The pavilion was nowhere to be seen—hundreds of miles away at this point.

Fritz pushed off the ground, balancing the trajectory of the spell better but feeling his strength begin to wane as he forced himself higher. He landed again and took a few steps, an idea burning in his mind.

He began to spin, his cape flaring out. As he spun, he drew symbols for a spell. A rune for wind, a few lines to give it shape, another set of sparkling characters to add direction. Dust began to swirl around him in a vortex, picking up speed and power.

Fritz felt his feet lift slowly off the ground. He found his center of balance, adjusted the spell, and shot into the air with a powerful gust of wind underneath him. His hair blew flat against his head. He closed his eyes and stretched out his arms, enjoying the sensation of weight-lessness. He let out a loud whoop and changed directions, soaring back toward the pavilion.

He stopped, looked down, and let out a low whistle. The vast expanse of green hedge rows lay in a complex maze.

He blinked. It wasn't a maze. It was *shapes*. He soared higher into the air until he could see miles of hedges below his feet.

The hedges made shapes, and they were shapes he'd seen before. There was the cube, the helix, the swirl—it was an exact replica of the dome that protected the school.

His heart beat faster, and he scanned the verdant patterns below him. He leaned forward and flew toward the pavilion, taking in the shapes as he went.

The pavilion sat in the dead center of a circle where all the hedges converged. He flew a giant circle around the pavilion to confirm his suspicions.

The hedges formed spells and, like the dome magic of old, terminated at the top with the pavilion. The capstone spell was the wooden structure they'd been relaxing under.

The trellises formed a circle made of dashes, as the lines were interrupted by the entryway into the sunken pavilion.

He floated to the ground and walked back to where the girls sat talking.

"Hey Drossie. That was fast," Vivienne called out when she saw him.

"I reached the end," he joked, sprawling on his couch to take a nap until Faruk and Andor returned. He dozed off for a while, recouping the strength he'd expended on his flight.

Faruk and Andor arrived within minutes of each other. Andor had scratches all over his arms, and his axe had small notches in the blade. Faruk wiped a small bead of sweat from his forehead and almost immediately began launching tiny fireballs at Vivienne's topiary.

The tone sounded, and everyone got up to leave.

Before he left, Gelé called out to Fritz. "Drossie, are you sure about how the attacks happened?"

"I am," Fritz responded. "It's probably best not to travel anything in until we figure out what to do."

"When will that be?" Faruk asked.

"Very soon, I hope." He waved goodbye and disappeared in a whiff of smoke.

Boroda was waiting in Fritz's bedroom when he stepped from the cloud. His face looked old and worn. There were dark circles under his eyes, and the lines in his forehead creased with a mixture of pain and sadness. "Did you attempt to do magic at school?"

Fritz went white.

Boroda pulled at his hair. "Fritz!" Nearly sobbing, he called louder, "Fritz!"

"Please, hear me out," Fritz begged softly.

"It doesn't matter." Boroda looked up. His eyes were red. "The Order has commanded me to remove you."

Fritz grabbed the poster of his bed and gripped tightly. "Remove?! What does that mean?" Fritz knew what it meant but couldn't wrap his mind around it.

"It means that once I remove you from The Order, any member or their apprentice can kill you, no questions asked and without repercussions."

"Will they come after me?"

Boroda squeezed the sides of his head. "If they fear you will reveal secrets about The Order."

"Boroda, you have to listen to me," Fritz reached out toward the wizard. "Something's not right."

Boroda kept his head cradled.

Fritz spoke urgently. "Yes. I performed magic at school. I'm sorry; I wasn't thinking. I was getting attacked, and my friends were getting attacked, and I used a spell—one spell—to help us escape. I was doing it to help save the other apprentices."

Boroda sat still, then slowly lifted his head. His brow was still creased but with question, not sadness. "Did you say that you *performed* magic?"

"Yes, but …"

Boroda interrupted him. "Just so I understand you correctly, you are saying that you actually cast a spell while on school grounds?"

Fritz nodded.

"Tell me the story," he commanded. "Leave nothing out."

Fritz told him about the rats at school, about Nicholaus, and about Andor's stunt as a woman in a large skirt.

"At first, I thought Nicholaus just had friends plant the rats on me, but there was no way he could plant that many in the forest. After the attacks here, at Minerva's, and in the woods with the Black Wizard, I think the Black Wizard may actually be working for Prince Nicholaus. Not the Czar. No matter what, the enchantments placed on the school grounds no longer work."

Boroda sat still.

"I cast that spell over a month ago," Fritz finished. "I didn't even realize I had used magic until a couple days ago when the apprentices had an emergency meeting to discuss Gelé getting attacked."

"I wondered why Glacinda stayed in her chair tonight," Boroda mused.

Fritz gritted his teeth and chastised himself for giving up his secret so easily.

Boroda didn't stop to ponder the new information but walked over to the fireplace, sat in the chair, and studied the blaze.

Fritz joined him. "Are you still angry with me?"

Boroda waved him off. "Something isn't right. But … I can't put my finger on it."

"If the Black Wizard is the one sending the rats," said Fritz, putting the pieces together, "then the Black Wizard must be a student at St. Michael's."

"If the spells are no longer working, then he'd be able to practice magic and not even the apprentices would know." Boroda squinted, and the flames on the logs grew larger.

"Are there any other wizards who attend St. Michael's?" Fritz asked.

Boroda shook his head. "Just the apprentices."

"Then the Black Wizard must be one of us." Fritz felt his heart thump strongly. "Anyone can change shape and size. You said so."

"The Black Wizard has been killing for over a decade now," Boroda said, squeezing his eyes shut. "The only apprentice who's still around now would have been five or six for the first kill."

Fritz stared at Boroda intently. "You said a girl with a knife can kill a wizard if he's sloppy."

Boroda looked at him.

"Could a small wizard kill a human if he's being mind controlled?"

Boroda recoiled. "Mind controlled? Where in Watcher's name are you getting that?"

Fritz folded his hands and looked away.

"There's something else I need to tell you," Fritz said. "But I need you to promise you won't get mad."

Boroda set his jaw. "I'm beginning to tire of hearing 'something else I need to tell you,' Fritz. If you have any secrets left, I would appreciate knowing them now before other people get killed."

Fritz exhaled nervously. "I also investigated your last apprentice, Perrin."

Boroda's face clouded.

"Several months ago, I found a note he'd written stuck in a book on mind control in the library. It looked like he had discovered something suspicious and that he wasn't sure who to tell." Fritz traveled in the note and handed it to Boroda.

Boroda looked at it, and tears welled up in his eyes. He cradled the note in his hands.

"I didn't even know who wrote the note until later when Edward showed me some letters written by Perrin to his oldest brother, Richard. That's when I learned who wrote this note and made the connection that Perrin, the famous ghost at school, was your apprentice.

"The note looked ominous to me, so I dug further. Yesterday, I questioned Richard about Perrin's death and, while I am not at liberty to give you all the details, I learned that Perrin was killed while he was investigating the questions written on that note."

Fritz watched Boroda from the corner of his eye. He was staring forward, unresponsive.

Fritz continued, "When Perrin was killed, he was carrying a book with him, but it wasn't the book I found the note in. It was an entirely different book."

"There was no book on his body," Boroda rasped suddenly.

Fritz closed his eyes. "Perrin was killed outside of school grounds. His body was carried, post mortem, to where it was discovered."

"What?" Boroda hissed suddenly.

"At midnight," Fritz said. "All the books that have been taken out of your library travel back to their spots unless they're being actively used. The book he had was transported back at midnight as part of the cleaning spell. There was no way of knowing he ever had it."

Fritz lowered his voice. "The two books he was reading were about mind control and ancient magic."

Boroda began to cry. His moans grew into sobs. "I should have listened. I should have listened."

Fritz spoke louder and faster, trying to keep Boroda's attention. "Before he died, he had time to leave one final message; I think it's a clue but I can't figure it out. It was a magical symbol attached to the brass button of a jacket. It was the circle symbol."

Fritz drew it in the air. "Does this mean anything to you?"

Boroda whispered Perrin's name and rocked in his chair.

"Boroda?" Fritz asked tenderly. "Can you think of a connection between those two books and the symbol 'O'?"

"Perrin!" Boroda sobbed inconsolably.

"The Black Wizard attacked me when I was investigating Perrin's death. I think it's connected somehow with the death of your generals and whatever Borya has planned," Fritz continued.

Boroda didn't respond. His shoulders were quaking and his hands muffled the guttural sobs.

"Boroda?" Fritz asked shakily.

Boroda stood up. His eyes were glassy, and his body sagged.

"Where are you going?" Fritz called after him. "Please, Boroda, don't."

But the grieving wizard stepped into a plume of thick, black smoke.

Fritz stripped out of his uniform and left it on the floor. He crawled into bed and pressed his face into his pillow.

"Why is this happening?!" he cried out.

"I am unsure, sir." Doll turned his head to look at Fritz.

Fritz grabbed the wooden toy and held it against his chest.

"Doll, I think you're my only friend left."

# CHAPTER 21

Fritz shoved several books from his bag into his locker. He grabbed some paper and pencils then swung his locker shut. It made a sharp rap, and a small group of freshman girls jumped and looked over at him.

"Drossie!" Vivienne said. "Has Marzi found you yet?"

"No," he growled and pushed past her.

Vivienne threw her hands up. "What's wrong with you?"

Fritz rounded the corner and walked into Faruk and Gelé. They both looked at him in surprise.

"Hey, man," Faruk said. "Did Marzi talk to you yet?"

"Yeah, what did she say?" Gelé asked.

"I haven't talked to her," Fritz said and sidestepped them. He stormed into his first period class.

Nicholaus sat in his regular seat near the door. He grinned and winked as Fritz walked past.

Fritz briefly considered breaking every bone in the prince's body but decided against it.

"Drosselmeyer," Ms. Wakimba said his name slowly, ire dripping from her voice. "I am looking forward to your report today."

She flashed a sardonic smile.

"Yes ma'am," Fritz replied.

Andor lumbered into the room and looked around. Nicholaus made some faces, but Andor ignored him and clomped over to Fritz.

He signed frantically, "Marzi is in the library. She needs to talk to you."

"No," Fritz responded with a flick of his thumb and first two fingers.

"She's hurt," Andor said. His face was creased with concern.

Fritz didn't hesitate. He bolted from his chair, ignoring the confused stares of his classmates.

Ms. Wakimba called after him. "Where are you going, Mr. Drosselmeyer? Drosselmeyer!"

Her calls faded as Fritz raced down the hallway toward the library. When he crested the stairs, his pulse was at full pump. He ran to the small turret room where he found Marzi sitting on the couch.

She looked up at him with red, bloodshot eyes. Her arm was wrapped in a sling, and he could see several bruises poking out just beyond the neckline of her shirt.

"What happened?!" Fritz demanded and ran to her side.

Marzi wiped her eyes.

"Did Hanja do this to you?" Fritz said, pointing at her arm.

Marzi sniffed and looked away.

"Why?" He sat next to her on the couch.

Marzi shifted and winced.

Fritz looked down. Her knee was swollen.

"Why didn't you heal these?" Fritz asked her.

"Hanja said I had to leave them or it would be double next time." Marzi's shoulders quivered.

"That's not right," Fritz hissed and balled his fist.

"There's something else," Marzi said. "Something I need to tell you."

Fritz took her good hand in his.

Marzi gently pulled her hand away and looked at Fritz. "When you first joined The Order, Hanja told me to get you to like me. I was supposed to find out as much as I could about you and Boroda and report back to her."

"Ok … everyone was trying to do that," Fritz said.

"That's why I brought you up to this room and pretended to be your friend. Then, we started investigating the attacks, and it was the first time I ever enjoyed being around someone.

"I tried to tell myself that it was just an act; you couldn't really be this nice. I tried so hard to only pretend to like you."

She sniffled. "Then you kissed me, and I knew I couldn't do it anymore. I couldn't spy on you for Hanja."

She lowered her head. "I told her that I couldn't do it. I said you were too tight-lipped, and she threatened to hurt me badly if I didn't get her some information.

"Then you ended our relationship … or whatever that was, and when I told Hanja, she lost it. She waited until The Order meeting was over and then … " Marzi motioned to her arm.

Fritz gritted his teeth.

"I wanted to apologize for my actions."

Fritz shook his head. "You don't need to apologize to me."

"I do!" Marzi cried. "I used you. You were so nice and decent and honest, and I was so wrong and petty and foolish. I'm so sorry."

Fritz stared into her eyes.

She trembled. "Boroda needs to know that Hanja is working with Borya to unseat him."

"What?" Fritz asked, confused.

"It's been happening for years now. Hanja doesn't know how much I overhear her when they're talking. Borya wants Boroda out and has promised Hanja his position in The Order if she can get him any information about how to get rid of him. That's why I had to spy on you."

Fritz tried to control his breathing.

"I also want you to know that Hanja told me to get more information, or this 'will look like a small training accident.' I'm going to tell her no, Drossie. I won't betray someone I …"

"My real name is Fritz," he interrupted.

Marzi started.

"My parents died when I was very young, and I grew up in an orphanage just outside the capital of the Central Kingdom."

"Fritz, stop!" Marzi choked through the tears.

"What else does she want to know?"

"It doesn't matter," Marzi began to sob. "I'm not telling her."

"You have to." Fritz squeezed her hand. Marzi squeezed back then pulled away.

She raised her voice. "If she knows this information, she will own you."

Fritz locked eyes with her. "It's a small price to pay if it helps protect someone I love."

Marzi returned his stare, fists clenched. "It's no use telling me because I won't betray someone I love."

They both froze.

Fritz leaned in and kissed her.

Marzi wrapped her uninjured hand around his head and held him tightly.

Fritz pulled away and tenderly ran his fingers through her hair.

Marzi laughed.

"What?" he asked.

"You're doing that stupid smile again," she said. She kissed him just to get rid of it.

Fritz walked Marzi outside the school. She didn't question him until he helped her sit down behind the hedges opposite the road in front of the school.

"Why are we here?" she asked.

Fritz's eyes began to spark, and he pulled up a healing spell. Before she could protest, he reset her arm. He turned to her knee, and she gasped as the swelling dissipated, and the joint mended.

"Hanja is going to be furious," she said.

"Then you fight back," Fritz replied.

Marzi laughed and stood up. "A whole lot of good it will do. She has the Life Bond to protect her."

"Then I'll fight her," Fritz volunteered.

Marzi blushed. "She's an excellent warrior."

"I have a better reason to win," Fritz said and pulled Marzi into another kiss.

They heard the bell ring from across the road and Marzi pulled Fritz by the hand.

"Come on. I don't want to be late for my next class."

"You go ahead," Fritz told her. He didn't let go. "I have to take care of some things."

She slowly let his hand drop. He watched her until she had disappeared behind the doors, then he ran, full speed, to his secret hedge and traveled back to the mansion.

Fritz shouted for Boroda as soon as he returned home.

Boroda didn't answer.

Fritz continued to yell. He traveled to the kitchen, the library, the den, but Boroda was nowhere.

He grabbed a hand mirror on a nearby table and concentrated on the glass. It wavered, the patina deepened, and a corner of Boroda's face came into view.

Tucked under Boroda's chin, in a full embrace, was the top of an ice skate. The jagged lettering "PA" was unmistakable.

Fritz turned and traveled to the pond shack where Franz had last worn that skate. The snow had melted.

Now green buds popped out on the trees and bushes. The cottage was still in ruins, large chunks of wall were missing, and bits of furniture could be seen through the gaps.

"Boroda!" Fritz shouted and opened the shack door.

Boroda jerked his head around. His eyes were glazed, and he registered no surprise at Fritz's appearance. Near him lay several empty liquor bottles.

"Boroda! You're in danger. We're both in danger," Fritz said.

Boroda slung a bottle lazily, and it dropped to the floor and shattered. "It doesn't matter anymore."

"I don't know what is wrong with you right now, but you need to snap out of this." Fritz slapped Boroda's cheeks.

Boroda tried to shoo him away and grabbed an empty bottle. It began to fill with a clear liquid.

Fritz took the partially full bottle from Boroda's hand and let it fall to the floor. "Borya is conspiring with Hanja to unseat you from The Order."

Boroda stared at him and tried to point an accusing finger at Fritz, but the skate he held slipped from his hand and fell to the floor. He leaned back on the bench, mumbling.

"Please, Boroda," Fritz begged. "I really need your help!"

Another voice, low and distressed, also called out. "Boroda! Boroda! Where are you? I'm under attack. I need your help."

Fritz whirled around, but no one was there.

"Please, Boroda! They have my boy. There are wizards here."

Fritz grabbed the hand mirror from the ground where it had fallen. He saw the floating head of General Andoyavich staring back at him, eyes wide with terror.

"What's going on?" Fritz asked.

"Drosselmeyer?" the General asked. "Where is Boroda? Get him quickly."

"He's not available. Are you getting attacked by the Black Wizard?"

"No. It's some other wizards and men from the Czar's army. They just showed up here. They're attacking my men. They're burning my house. They've taken Alexei …" He paused. "They've taken Franz."

Fritz's eyes flashed silver green. "Where did they take him?"

The General glanced behind him.

Fritz could make out flames in the background, and the mirror began to cloud over with smoke.

"I was watching Ivanov for Boroda. The Czar must have found out. My cover is blown. Tell him to come immediately," the General said.

He raised a sword over his head, and Fritz saw him block a blow, then plunge the weapon into the chest of a soldier.

The mirror went blank.

Fritz shook Boroda, yelling his name, but the wizard had passed out. He tugged at the sides of his hair and let out a long, angry growl.

Fritz stopped to think. If the General was watching Ivanov, then he must live close to the orphanage.

Fritz squatted on the floor and jumped. Smoke trailed him as he leapt from the fishing shack floor over the iron gates of Ivanov's Home for Orphaned Boys.

He sprinted up the front steps and blasted the door off its hinges. The fetid smells of the rotting building hit him and memories came flooding back in lonely, terrifying waves.

He raced down the hallway and up the stairs to the second floor. He paused at the top and looked around.

"Hey! What d'you think you're doing?" Dolph was still dressed in his undershorts and pointed at him with a partial bottle of vodka.

Fritz snarled, "Dolph."

"Who's that? I told you little pissants to leave me alone. Get back to work."

Fritz shot out a blast of magic.

Dolph flew backward and landed on the floor with a loud grunt. He rolled over to his belly and cried out, "It's you!"

"Yes, Dolph. It's me. I need to find out where General Andoyavich lives. Where is he?"

"Listen, I'm sorry. I should've never hurt you." He crawled forward on hands and knees.

"Tell me where the General lives or where Ivanov is right now," Fritz responded, ignoring Dolph.

"I'm so sorry. I am so, so … " As Dolph neared Fritz, he suddenly jumped forward into a tackle. "Got you!" he yelled.

Fritz fell to the ground, confused.

Dolph raised his fist and brought it down hard.

Fritz stopped the blow inches from his face with a pushing spell.

Dolph grunted with exertion, trying desperately to finish the swing.

Fritz waved his other hand, and Dolph was yanked off of him and into the wall opposite Fritz. Boroda's special spell began to slowly squeeze the air from his lungs.

Dolph gasped. His legs dangled above the floor, and he clawed at his throat.

Fritz held him against the wall. "Where did Ivanov take Franz?"

"I don't know where your brother is," Dolph croaked.

"Wrong answer, Dolph," Fritz growled. He rotated his hand, and Dolph's foot twisted, and the bone popped.

Dolph screamed in pain. "I'm telling the truth. I don't know!"

Fritz applied pressure to the other foot, now soaked with the drunken man's urine.

Dolph roared as his other foot twisted and cracked.

"Ivanov knows," Dolph cried out, saliva seeping from his mouth and nose. "He left two days ago for the Czar's party."

"Where is the party, Dolph?" Fritz snarled. "I don't have time for this."

Fritz twisted Dolph's arm until the shoulder popped out of joint.

Dolph screamed again. Every move sent jolts of pain through his body.

"I don't know. There's a letter from the Czar on his desk. It will tell you!" Dolph sobbed.

Fritz let him drop to the floor, then raced up the stairs to the office. The memories made him woozy, but he shook them from his mind and rummaged through the papers on the desk.

He finally found a letter with the Czar's wax seal stamped into the paper. After many sentences of impossibly scrolling calligraphy inviting the possessor of this letter to a party, it finally announced where it was to be held.

*Alexander Palace.*

*Alexander Palace?* He didn't know where that was. As he stood up to leave, he heard the click of a gun being cocked.

Dolph was lying on the ground, his legs bent at odd angles, his gun pointed at Fritz. His mouth was twisted into a deranged smile. His yellow teeth bared in a self-conceited grin. "I win, you freak."

Fritz knocked the gun from his hand with a flick of his wrist; it fired and the bullet hit the wall behind him.

Fritz felt his green eyes pop with familiar electricity. He lifted Dolph from the floor.

The large man struggled against his invisible bonds. "No! I didn't mean it!" he wailed.

"All those years of beating weak, defenseless kids," Fritz said, shaking his head. "The bones broken ..."

Dolph's arm snapped.

"The indignities suffered."

The other arm bent at the forearm.

Fritz stepped close to Dolph.

"And now, the last thing you will ever feel is the utter hopelessness we all felt at your hand."

Dolph was shaking with rage and pain, but his cries were stifled. His shirt gaped open in front and Fritz's small, gold medallion peeked from behind the soiled material.

Fritz yanked the charm from the large man and leaned in closer so his face was next to Dolph's.

He whispered, "This is for Nurse Galina."

Dolph flew back. His body bent in half from the momentum. He hit the wall and every bone shattered from the force. Blood leaked out of his mouth, nose, and ears. His face was frozen in terror, an exact replica of the faces of so many boys from years past.

Fritz looked out the windows into the main work area below Ivanov's office. The boys were folding laundry, ironing, and stitching seams. A few boys looked back and forth from the office to their work, curious about the gunfire but not wanting to incur the wrath of Dolph.

Fritz waved his hand, and the clothes vanished. The boys shrieked and looked around in surprise. Fritz closed his eyes, and the tables began filling with hot, steaming dishes of food. He traveled in the largest pieces of meat and the biggest loaves of bread he could think of. Charred vegetables, creamy potatoes, and several gigantic cakes appeared where the clothes once sat.

The boys stared in astonishment. Then, as if on cue, they rushed the table and began eating the food before it disappeared.

Fritz eyed his family heirloom briefly before pocketing the trinket. There was no time to waste on sentimentality. He traveled out to the black iron gates and, summoning the pent-up rage of a lifetime, twisted them open. One gate ripped free of its hinges and crumpled to the ground with a deafening clang.

Before the boys could run to the door to investigate the sound, he traveled back to the fishing shack.

"Boroda! Boroda, wake up!" He slapped Boroda's face and called to him.

The wizard groaned.

"I need to know where Alexander Palace is."

The wizard rolled his head and squinted. He held out his hand and tapped a finger on a glass fishbowl.

Fritz shook his head. "Boroda, you need to sober up. General Andoyavich needs your help. I need your help. Please, my brother is in danger."

Boroda shook his head and tapped the bowl again, then turned his head and vomited.

Fritz looked at the bowl.

Boroda kept his finger on it even as he turned over and began to snore heavily.

Fritz shot up.

"The Celestine."

He glanced down at Boroda. "Thank you."

Fritz closed his eyes and when he opened them, he was floating in the clear, black sky filled with stars. In front of him, the Celestine pulsed with ivory light.

He touched the glassy sphere and, with a desperate quake in his voice, whispered, "Show me Alexander Palace."

The inky blackness melted away as the stone walls and forest of Alexander Palace replaced it. He studied the structure, and his green eyes sparked with silver electricity.

"Hold on, Franz. I'm coming."

# CHAPTER 22

Though not as big as the Czar's main residence in the capital, Alexander Palace was no less imposing with its sheer walls, solid oak gate, and posted sentries.

Fritz stood just inside the dense forest that circled the perimeter walls. He studied the armed guards walking in concentric circles, crafting a plan to get beyond them. The Celestine hadn't shown him inside the courtyard. Even if it had, anyone who saw him suddenly appear in a flash of smoke would raise the alarm, so he would no longer have the element of surprise.

He swept over the woods for anything he could use to camouflage himself. After several minutes, nothing had presented itself as useful. He looked again at the guards, wondering if he could defeat them all without depleting his strength. Once inside, he had no idea what he would face.

Above him, a bird of prey screeched and swooped down. It emerged from the forest floor with a small creature in its talons and flew off to its nest.

Fritz thought momentarily about his failed exam with Ms. Wakimba. He'd worked hard on his project and then, when it was time to present, the grade was no longer important.

His world had changed so quickly, and things like grades and classes all seemed so trivial now.

Suddenly, it dawned on him how he was going to get past the guards.

He ran over his fact sheet on the barn owl in his mind. He knew its muscle structure, its bone density, and wing length. He knew how much it weighed and the shape of the lenses in its eyes.

He paced the forest floor and pictured the creature. As he paced, his body shrank and his arms extended. His clothing sagged from his shoulders and finally dropped from his truncated body.

He lifted off into the air, flapping his long wings and letting out a loud screech. He flew over the woods, amazed at the clarity of vision his new eyes gave him. Small creatures scurried to hide. He watched with precision as their tiny bodies scrambled across the ground.

The guards below paid him no attention.

He glided over the courtyard in search of a landing place where he could safely turn back into a human. He circled the palace and found a central rooftop hidden from view and landed there, flopping forward on the flat surface.

His feathers shortened and melted into skin. He stood up on his own legs and stretched his arms.

The early spring air felt chilly against his naked body, so he crouched below the ledge of the rooftop to escape the icy draft. He traveled his clothes in from the woods, yanking them on as he explored the terrain.

He found a half-rotted door covered in moss and kicked it open. The dust and smell of molding junk long-forgotten assaulted his nose. He coughed and turned away. He took a deep breath of fresh air, ran through the splintered frame, and wound his way through the attic until he found the upper hallways.

The distant sounds of laughter drew his attention to the floors below.

After descending a large staircase, he rounded a corner into a grand hall where groups of men stood laughing and drinking among tables laden with food. Servants bustled in and out with drinks.

Fritz saw boys intermingled with the men, bruises visible on some of their faces and arms. Every one of them stared at the floor with limp shoulders and listless expressions. Their eyes were dark, soulless pits. The joy and sparkle of youth was gone, ripped from them and replaced with this forsaken reality.

Guards with swords hanging at their sides and pistols strapped to their hips stood at intervals, surveying the degenerate behavior.

At the front of the room, overseeing the festivities from the center position of a long table, sat the Czar.

Behind him, just within earshot, stood Ivanov. His spidery fingers clasped together, his hungry eyes scanning the debauchery. He licked his lips as he watched his wards being dragged from group to group.

Fritz had always told Franz to be happy for the boys who got "adopted." He'd painted a picture of happy families and full tables. Now, he surveyed the final fate of the adopted boys.

How wrong he'd been.

They were fodder for these disgusting creatures. Sent to a secluded location to service every whim of their vile captors with absolutely no way to defend themselves.

The room full of nobles who let it happen—even encouraging the behavior—laughed raucously while the lives and souls of these boys were exploited for their pleasure.

Why did no one stand up to challenge this?

Were there no soldiers with a conscience who would use their swords to protect the innocent?

Fritz looked around at the participants. Everyone in the room was guilty, either by action or complicity. They abused or let the abuse continue when it was in their power to act.

Fritz stood at the door, unnoticed. As he scanned the room, tears stung his eyes.

The reality of this world hit him, and his knees almost buckled: The weak would suffer at the hands of the powerful, but the powerful would never be held accountable. It was the tragic state of their existence.

These boys didn't have a brother to stick up for them.

They didn't have a wizard to take up their cause and keep the wolves at bay.

They didn't have a champion to break their chains and tell their captors, "No."

That had to change.

"No more!" he whispered aloud.

He strode into the room, his green eyes flashing with a brilliant silver light. His hands charged with a blinding ball of magic.

All activity stopped, and the men—guards included—looked at him with confused expressions.

"Fritz!" the Czar called out expectantly.

"You have me confused with someone else," Fritz growled. "Fritz is gone. I'm Drosselmeyer—and this party is over."

A nearby guard leapt up, sword drawn, and Fritz shot a bolt of lightning through the man's chest. The stunned guard looked down at the fist-sized hole and coughed. He dropped his sword and crumpled to the floor.

The other men in the room began to run.

The large doors at the back of the room slammed shut at the sweep of Fritz's hand. He traveled in seeds, and snaked vines along the wall, interweaving them through the handles and hinges, locking everyone inside.

Fritz soared into the air and shot a bolt of magic into two men. Their eyes burst from the heat. The boys who had been wrapped in their arms ran screaming for the corner of the room.

Three guards charged him with swords drawn, and he yanked the swords from their hands, swung the blades around his body in a fast arc, and skewered the soldiers to the wall.

Fritz crushed the windpipe of a man cowering behind a teenage boy. The boy turned and smashed his elbow into his captor's nose and raced over to the far corner with the other boys.

He leapt and rolled, switching between magic and combat to conserve his strength. His charm was still empty from the fight with the Black Wizard, but the drain of magic, if present, wasn't registering. His strength welled up in angry pools of seemingly endless churning energy.

The piles of soldiers lay strewn about the room, quickly defeated. The limp, crooked bodies of the nobles dotted the room. Some on the floor, folded in unnatural formations, others pinned to the wall by spears and swords.

Five nobles remained alive, all pressed together in the front of the room near Ivanov. Three held knives at the throats of boys and shouted threats of violence. The childless nobles promised wealth and other untold glories if they were allowed to live.

"Stop this!" the Czar boomed from behind the men. The small huddle parted. The Czar stepped forward from among them and fixed his dark eyes on Fritz.

"Where is my brother?!" Fritz demanded.

The Czar ignored his question and flashed a triumphant grin. "Feeling tired yet, Drosselmeyer?"

In response, Fritz blasted him with a spell that should have thrown him into the air or knocked him unconscious, but the regent stood upright, shaken from the force but unharmed.

Fritz blinked his magic sight on and saw a network of protective enchantments around him. Before he could decipher them, a black-robed figure materialized next to the Czar.

"Get me out of here!" the Czar ordered and grabbed the Black Wizard's shoulder.

The Black Wizard turned and squared off with Fritz.

"Take me away from here," the Czar commanded with more volume and a tighter grip.

The shadowy figure stared at Fritz, eyes filled with hatred. He crouched low, ready to spring, but the Czar yelled at him.

"I said take me away. Now!" He shook the wizard with both hands, and they disappeared in a puff of smoke.

Fritz yelled and threw a blast of magic at the spot where they had been standing. It left a crater in the wall.

He walked slowly toward the remaining five men, now whimpering. Ivanov stood in the middle, eerily calm for someone in his predicament.

The first noble began screaming, but it turned into a gurgle as all his capillaries burst and the blood drained into his lungs.

The boy in his clutches pulled away as the remaining boys shook off their captors and ran. Frozen with terror, the men watched their fellow noble writhe on the floor.

Fritz inched closer.

The second noble yelped and let out a blood-curdling scream until his skin melted away and the red-hot sludge of his organs spilled out.

Fritz took a few more steps.

The third noble barely had time to gasp before his head snapped and twisted toward the back wall.

The fourth man fell to his knees, begging for mercy.

Fritz looked at him with disgust. He lifted the man into the air and then slammed him down on the stone floor. His bones crunched and blood began to pool around him.

The fifth noble tried to run, but his body stopped mid stride, straightened, and began to slowly extend. Ligaments popped and tendons stretched until the magical pull extended beyond its capability to hold the skeleton together

Fritz faced Ivanov. "Where is my brother?"

Ivanov smiled. "The Black Wizard said you'd be coming."

Fritz sent out a blast that knocked the tapestries off the wall, but Ivanov didn't move.

Fritz looked confused.

Ivanov lifted up his hand. A silver bracelet around his wrist flashed with a spell blocking enchantment.

The old man stepped down from the dais and walked cautiously around Fritz. "Fritz," he said with an air of intrigue. "I always thought you were special."

Fritz kept his eyes on Ivanov. "Where is Franz?" he asked again.

Ivanov licked his lips. "They wouldn't let me have him. Borya said no."

"What does Borya have to do with this?" Fritz demanded.

Ivanov lifted up his bracelet. "He gave me this. Said it would protect me against magical attacks."

"Why would Borya protect a pervert like you?" Fritz spat. "These parties aren't his style."

Ivanov wheezed. "You are just as stupid as you've always been. Sure, you could hold your own with Dolph, but he always beat you eventually because you couldn't see his end game."

"What is Borya's end game?" Fritz asked.

Ivanov laughed out loud. "These parties are only a halfway point for the boys. A little *initiation* into their true purpose."

He began breathing heavily, sucking air in-between his teeth. "Your brother was supposed to be here for this party, but Borya said no. Franz was supposed to be mine. That was our deal, but Borya said …"

Fritz punched fast and hard.

It landed solidly on the side of the old man's head.

Ivanov tumbled to the floor and retreated from Fritz's steady advance. He held out the bracelet, shaking it. "No! No! Stay back!"

"It will only stop my magical attacks," Fritz said. He held out his hand and a sword appeared. He swung the sword in a practice circle.

"I gave you a home. You can't do this!" Ivanov screamed at him and stumbled over the body of a noble. He bumped up against the wall and stood up, hands clasped in front of him. "Please! Have a heart!"

Fritz raised his eyebrows. "A heart?"

"Yes, sir." Ivanov whimpered and tried to pat Fritz's shoulder. His tongue continued to flick over his dry, cracked lips. Ivanov bowed his head repeatedly, the obsequious gesture making his stringy hair flop back and forth.

"You and Franz were always my favorite … "

Fritz's hand shot out so fast, silver streaks of magic popped and flashed behind it. His pointed fingers ripped through Ivanov's chest, cracking the ribs and disappearing into the cavity. He closed his hand around Ivanov's heart and yanked his hand back.

Ivanov registered it all for the next ten seconds. He saw his heart pump and then quiver to a stop. He saw his own blood trickle from his mouth onto Fritz's sleeve. He stared into Fritz's silvery-green eyes.

His own hand was clasping Fritz's arm. The silver bracelet flashed in the room's light, and he slumped forward.

Fritz let the body fall, wiped the blood and gore from his sleeve, and turned to the boys huddled in the corner. "Get dressed," he said. "We're leaving."

Fritz traveled them back to the main room of the orphanage, where they were greeted with tables full of food and boys wolfing down as much of it as possible. The boys from the party raced into the fray to partake. The other boys hugged their friends, and the cries of jubilation rang through the dingy room.

Fritz traveled back to the fishing shack where Boroda lay listless on the ground. He pulled the wizard to his feet, amid protestations, and traveled him back to the mansion. He half carried, half dragged him to his bed and laid him down on the mattress.

Boroda traveled in another bottle of alcohol, and Fritz boiled the liquid before it reached his lips, making it undrinkable. The older man gave up and slumped back into his bed, no longer resisting.

Fritz undressed Boroda to put on his bed clothes and startled at the scars covering Boroda's chest and torso. There was so much about his master he didn't know and so much he wanted to find out, but not now. He had to find Franz and make sure he was safe.

"Boroda, I really need you," Fritz whispered.

Boroda was asleep and lost in a dream. The only intelligible word Fritz could understand was, "Perrin."

Fritz sat down by Boroda's bed and cupped his face in his hands. "I can't fight the Czar on my own," Fritz told the unconscious man. "He has my brother. I'm running out of time."

Fritz sighed heavily, fatigue from his fight beginning to set in. He leaned on the nightstand next to Boroda's bed.

Inside the stand, something clicked unevenly. It was a faint tick but the lilting cadence caught Fritz's attention.

He opened the door and saw the crudely built clock from the country manor.

The initials "PA" were etched into the side.

Below it, face down, was a picture frame.

Fritz turned it over.

It was a faded picture of a beautiful woman standing near a shoreline on a sunny beach. Her gauzy dress wrapped loosely around her figure. Her long hair draped past her tall, slender neck, and her lips parted in a laugh. She gazed beyond the edge of the photograph, a look of love and contentment on her face.

"Who is this?" Fritz asked the sleeping wizard.

Boroda was no longer thrashing around in his bed.

Fritz had never stopped to think that Boroda might have ever been in love or even been married. He had never seemed the type for such sentimentality. He wondered what happened to the woman in the photograph.

He turned the frame over again and noticed some writing in the lower corner. He held it up to the waning sunlight coming through the bedroom window.

*To my true love, Pickety Wickett.*

—Rosamund Lee

Fritz nearly dropped the frame.

Rosamund was a real person, just like Drosselmeyer.

If Boroda's current state had something to do with the characters in the nonsensical poem, perhaps the person in this picture could help.

He took the photograph and stepped back through a misty cloud into the inky blackness he'd visited only hours ago. He struggled against the fatigue setting in and stretched out his hand, beckoning to the ivory point of light in the distance.

The Celestine moved toward him.

Touching the globe, he commanded, "Show me this woman."

The orb did not respond.

He tried again. "Show me where this woman is!"

Nothing.

Frustrated, he glanced down at the picture and chewed his lip in thought. "Where was this taken?"

The Celestine pulsed.

Fritz peered into the ball.

Waves lapped on a sandy shore. A small village, now unobstructed by the woman's body, jutted into frame.

Fritz vanished from the Celestine and landed on a small, shell-strewn street that led down a hill to a tiny village with cottages dotting the shoreline.

As Fritz walked through the small village, people looked at him cautiously. A few retreated into their houses and shut their doors. He saw a small store with an old man smoking a pipe, sitting on a well-worn canvas chair.

He crossed to the old man and greeted him with a polite, yet weary salutation.

"I am looking for the woman in this photograph."

"What is your business with her?" he asked in a relaxed, yet guarded, manner.

"It's personal but urgent. Can you help me?"

The man looked him up and down, ground out his cigarette, and called to his wife.

The plump woman stepped out of the shop before he finished calling her name.

"She likes to listen in on my business," he told Fritz with a loud whisper.

He handed the picture to his wife. "My wife is the nosiest person on the island."

"We're on an island?" Fritz mused.

"Of course!" the man waved his hands. "Did you ride a horse here? No. You took a boat." The man muttered something while his wife studied the photograph.

"Do you know her?" Fritz asked.

"Sure. We know everyone on the island," the man said.

Fritz felt his patience wane and fought to keep his voice cordial. "Please, tell me where I can find her. It's important!"

The husband and wife whispered to each other, then the wife stood up, smiled sweetly and motioned to her shop. "Do you like anything here? Would you like to buy something?"

Fritz sighed. Exasperated, he stuck his hand in his pocket and traveled in a handful of gold coins from the chest in storage. He threw the money on the ground in front of the shop owner. With a snarl, he demanded, "Tell me where she is."

Their eyes bulged at the sight of the gold.

The wife pointed to a small path and began picking up the money from the dirt.

Fritz trudged down the path in the direction the shop owner's wife had shown him. The late afternoon sun and briny gusts of wind nicked away at his fatigue, and he quickened his steps.

The island was a large, rounded mountain jutting out of the ocean with the little town carved into the western shore. His current path ran up the mountain and twisted around a stony outcropping before it climbed up a steep wall toward the northern edge.

Set back into a sloped clearing was a quaint, stone cottage painted white. A short wall no taller than a chair encompassed a sandy courtyard. Several native trees sprouted from the bricked entrance and a few trees grew through the roof of the cottage. Outside the front door, strands of shells hung from strings and clinked in the ocean breeze.

Fritz knocked on the door, and a slender woman with long salt and pepper hair answered. She was, undoubtedly, the woman from the photo. Older now, but every bit as beautiful.

"What do you want?" she asked curtly.

"I'm a friend of Boroda's. Are you Rosamund Lee?" Fritz asked.

She sighed and stepped aside. "Come in."

Fritz entered and bowed.

"Who are you?"

"My name is Fritz."

She extended her hand. "I'm Cora."

"Oh," Fritz said, dazed. "I'm sorry. I thought your name was … "

"What do you want?"

"I need your help," Fritz told her. "My brother's life is in danger, and the only person that can help me save him is Boroda. He learned some news about the death of his former apprentice, and now I'm scared he might be drinking himself to death. I found your picture in the drawer of his bedside table and thought that maybe he'd listen to you."

Cora sat back in her chair and studied Fritz carefully. "What makes you think he would want to hear from me? I haven't talked to him since he told me about the death of my child."

"Your child?" Fritz held his breath.

Cora straightened. "Perrin was my child."

Fritz gasped. "I am so sorry. I didn't know."

She looked away, fighting her emotions. "Boroda was never able to get past the death of Perrin," she said harshly. "He will not forgive himself. It has consumed him."

She stood up and walked over to an open window that looked over the ocean. "Give him time, Fritz. He will come back to you." Cora turned around and rested her elbows on the sill. "At least, that is what I still hope for."

Fritz joined her at the window.

"He is grieving the death of his son. Neither you nor I can shorten that process for him," Cora continued.

Fritz gasped, as the hair on his arms stood up. "Perrin was Boroda's son?!"

Cora smiled. "Yes."

"That means you're his …" Fritz's head was spinning.

"Wife?" Cora asked with a wry laugh. "Of a sort."

"But Perrin called him 'uncle,' like I do," Fritz said.

Cora shrugged and stared out over the ocean. The sun was setting and the light bathed the little house in an orange wash. "Boroda and I were married when I was very young. He was still an apprentice, and I was a naive island girl. We were deliriously happy.

"We dreamed of having a family, and Boroda believed he could be both a wizard in The Order and a husband. He found out before too long that those choices were mutually exclusive.

"Boroda promised he would leave The Order. He said we could choose new names and move somewhere no one would find us. We teased each other with pet names.

"I called him Pickety Wickett. It's from a children's story we tell here on the island about a useless man who was always getting into trouble.

"He called me Rosamund Lee after an aunt he had that was extremely fat and rude."

Fritz filled in the last link. "And Perrin was Drosselmeyer?"

Cora nodded. "We tried for several years to have children. We had almost given up when I finally got pregnant. Perrin was born, and on the day of his birth, Boroda told me that there was a magical bird called a Drosselmeyer whose song was so beautiful, it would make even the saddest person smile." She turned her face away from Fritz. "Boroda told me that the song of the Drosselmeyer bird could never hope to compare to the sound of our son's laughter."

"So what happened?" Fritz asked, still spinning from the revelations.

Cora shrugged. "Our son 'snapped,' as he called it. Practiced magic. Lifted a rock with his mind and threw it into Boroda's lap.

"By this time, Boroda was a full-fledged member in The Order himself. He told me that The Order now knew of Perrin's existence but not his lineage.

"If our son was to remain safe, he would need to come with him to live and train as a wizard in The Order. He assured me he would keep him safe and would bring him back as often as he could.

"They did visit me often, at first.

"Then Boroda, without telling me why, said he was going to destroy The Order and that it wasn't safe for Perrin to visit me. He had to build something that would require all his time and energy, and he constantly feared that the other wizards would find out about me and use me to get to him."

She laughed a short, single outburst laced with hurt and disdain.

"I saw him a few years later but it wasn't to tell me that he had destroyed The Order. It was to tell me that my boy was dead. He blamed himself. He said I would be in danger if he stuck around, promised to come back to me as soon as he could, and that was the last time I ever saw him."

Cora's hair fluttered in the salty ocean breeze, and the setting sun began to dip below the horizon. "Tell me, Fritz. Other than a photo, what makes you think that man loves anyone but himself?"

"Perrin's death is directly tied to The Order," Fritz said with urgency. "Boroda has spent the last decade planning a war against a group of powerful wizards as well as the leader of the most powerful kingdom in the world. He has given up everything he loves to devote himself to this cause." Fritz stared into the setting sun. "The only people I would do that for are the ones I love very, very much."

Cora remained stone-faced.

"When Boroda gave me my wizard name," Fritz continued, "he could have chosen any name in the world, but he picked a name that he would have to say day after day for a long time. A name that would live on, long after he was gone."

Fritz turned to face Cora. "He named me Drosselmeyer."

Cora stared blankly at the water. After several minutes, she straightened and faced Fritz. "Take me to him."

Fritz didn't wait another moment. He grabbed her wrist and in seconds, they were in Boroda's room.

Cora was unfazed by the trip. She saw Boroda and ran to his bed. "Wake up, my love. Someone needs your help."

Boroda stirred. His skin was clammy and gray. He slowly opened his eyes and tried to sit up. His voice was weak. "Cora?"

"Yes, Boroda. It's me." She leaned in and kissed him gently on the forehead.

"How did you get here?"

"It was your new Drosselmeyer. He found me."

Boroda looked at Fritz and pain creased his eyes. He reached out his hand, and Fritz took it.

Fritz kneeled next to Cora. "Boroda, the Czar has Franz. I think the other members of The Order are helping Borya. They attacked General Andoyavich—I don't know if he made it. The Black Wizard is guarding the Czar now and …" His emotions bubbled. "And I need your help. I don't think I can fight them on my own."

Boroda breathed short, heavy breaths. He struggled to a seated position. "You will need more than just me."

Fritz traveled in a mug of tea and gave the rancid smelling liquid to Boroda. The simple act of magic made his head spin as the energy seeped from him.

Boroda sipped it and grimaced. He began to set the mug down, but Fritz lifted it toward his lips, forcing him to gulp more of the acrid brew. Slowly, his skin turned from ashen white to his normal pallor.

Boroda reached for a hand mirror and searched for Andoyavich.

The General appeared after a few seconds. His background was nondescript, and he spoke cautiously into the mirror. When he saw that it was Boroda, he berated him for being absent, then updated him on the events.

"It wasn't the Black Wizard. These new wizards weren't in masks. One had flowers in her hair, and the other was larger than any man I've ever seen."

"Eric and Sylvia," Boroda spat.

"They killed my men, and they took my Alexei," Andoyavich choked. "I'm in hiding, but I can't stay here forever. Glasinov is the only other one that answered my call. He was attacked by a woman wizard. He said she was ruthless and bore the sign of a dragon."

"Hanja," Fritz whispered.

"I'm sorry for my absence," Boroda apologized. "Stay where you are. Perhaps all is not lost."

The General saluted, and the mirror blinked off.

Boroda looked at Fritz and swung his legs out to the floor.

"It's time to destroy The Order," Boroda said.

Fritz squared his shoulders and set his jaw like his master's. "Tell me what to do."

# CHAPTER 23

Fritz jogged up the steps to St. Michael's, past the school office, and down the hall. It was lunchtime, and the noises and smells of the cafeteria wafted through the air.

Fritz rounded the corner and ran into Nicholaus.

Both boys yelped in surprise. Oleg and Evgeny stood close by, bandages still wrapped around healing limbs from their encounter with Andor. Just behind them were two men Fritz had never seen. They were expressionless, muscular, and wore tight-fitting clothes with no insignia.

Fritz moved around Nicholaus, but the young prince stopped him with an arm.

"You hit me," he grunted.

"Not on purpose," Fritz retorted. "Excuse me."

"No!" Nicholaus pushed Fritz back with both hands. "Apologize."

Fritz slowly hissed, "I don't have time for this, Nicholaus."

Nicholaus nodded, and the two men behind Oleg and Evgeny bolted forward, grabbed Fritz by both arms, and dragged him backward into a classroom opposite the hallway. It happened so fast that Fritz didn't even struggle.

The two bodyguards threw Fritz to the floor and stepped aside to let Nicholaus walk between them.

Oleg and Evgeny followed. Oleg turned to shut the door.

"You don't want to shut the door," Fritz called to Oleg as he stood up and brushed himself off. He glanced up at the clock. Still a half hour before lunch would end.

Oleg paused, and Nicholaus raised an eyebrow. "Why?"

"The doors are very thick and soundproof," Fritz said. "No one will hear the screams."

The prince smiled, his teeth on full display. "That is what I am counting on. It will be silent—like the library—or like Andor's head." He nodded to Oleg, and the boy shut the door. The solid wood thudded as it closed.

Nicholaus didn't say anything, but his smile stayed plastered across his face. He moved to the side, and his two bodyguards walked forward, the unspoken command crystal clear.

Fritz watched the leader. He was shorter but had larger muscles. His fist was already clenched. The second guard circled around behind Fritz, keeping a row of desks between them. Fritz took a slow, deliberate step toward the main guard.

*The longer a fist has to travel, the more power it has*, Boroda had told Fritz. *Everyone expects you to run away. Do the unexpected.*

The first guard punched, and Fritz leapt in close to the smaller man. The punch only had inches of travel time, so it felt like a tap on his stomach. He followed through with a head butt, and the guard launched back.

Fritz rolled backward onto the floor as the second guard's fist swung over his head. He completed the roll and jumped into the air, driving his knee into the guard's ribcage. He heard a pop, and the guard yelled out and retreated, tripping over a row of desks in the process.

The first guard struck at Fritz's head.

*The head is a very small target*, Boroda had told him, *but, nine times out of ten, people aim to punch there. A small fist has only a few inches in which to inflict maximum damage. Move your head a few inches, and the punch becomes impotent.*

Fritz cocked his head a little to the left and felt the air stir his hair as the guard's fist whizzed by his ear. He countered with a spear held to the guard's throat. The short man coughed. Then his eyes grew wide as he tried to breathe through a paralyzed larynx.

Fritz spun and elbowed the man's jaw. The man crumpled to the floor.

The second guard had regained his footing and charged. Fritz lowered his body and used the taller man's forward momentum to throw him over his back and onto the floor, keeping a tight grip on the guard's wrist. Fritz ignored the screams from the guard and kicked his face as he dragged him by his wrist onto his stomach. In a swift movement, Fritz spun in a circle around the man's prone body, keeping his hand clamped firmly, until he heard the snap of bones.

The guard screamed so loudly, Fritz wondered if anyone outside the doors could hear it. He dropped to the floor and slammed his fist into the back of the guard's neck, and the screaming stopped as the man lost consciousness.

Fritz rose from the floor to look for Nicholaus, who had moved behind Oleg and Evgeny. He found them cowering by the wall. Evgeny grabbed for the door handle, but Fritz locked it with the twitch of an eyebrow. He walked toward the boys with resolute steps until he was a foot away from them.

Without warning, Fritz punched Oleg and Evgeny in such rapid succession that neither had a chance to flinch. They fell to the floor and only Nicholaus remained upright.

"If you touch me, my father will …"

But the threat was never completed.

Fritz jumped, spun, and kicked Nicholaus in the chest. The prince flew back into the wall. The thunk of his cranium hitting the stone wall was hollow but decisive, and Nicholaus lay motionless on the floor.

Fritz exited the room, closed the door behind him, walked up to the apprentice's lunch table, and stood behind the chair he usually occupied.

The group looked up at him with gasps of amazement mixed with horror.

"What are you doing here?" Vivienne blurted.

"I need your help," he said.

"We could get in a lot of trouble for even talking to you," Gelé whispered. "You got removed!"

"Please! It's extremely important. Just come to the library," Fritz begged.

The small group looked at each other, silently searching for consensus.

"I'll come," Marzi said and stood up.

"Count me in, Drossie," Faruk added and stood.

Andor stood and raised his two thumbs.

Gelé and Vivienne acquiesced.

They all left the lunchroom, walked to the library, and ascended the stairs to the small turret on the third floor for the second time in a week.

Everyone sat, except Fritz. He faced them all.

"First off, I know that one of you reported me for using magic on school property last month, and I want you to know I don't care about that. I'm not trying to get back in The Order."

"We didn't tell," Vivienne said. "The Celestine alerts Borya."

Fritz shook his head. He held up his hand, and a ball of light appeared.

The apprentices gasped and, in a jumbled mix of exclamations, warned him to stop and asked what he was doing.

Fritz extinguished the light, and the group hushed. "The enchantments here at school haven't worked in a long time. I don't know how long, but it's been a while since anyone's been alerted."

The apprentices exchanged confused looks.

"The Order is fighting each other right now, and we're the ones getting caught in the middle of their war."

"What are you talking about?" Marzi asked.

"I don't know all the details, but there are some power grabs going on, and my brother is caught in the middle of it. The Czar has him and could try to use him as a bargaining chip to tip the scales in his favor."

"Your brother?" Faruk asked.

"My real name is Fritz. I'm an orphan from the Central Kingdom. I have a younger brother named Franz."

The entire group, except Marzi, sat slack-jawed.

"My younger brother was sent to live with a wealthy family when I was chosen by Boroda.

"Because of this squabble our masters are involved in, his life has been put in jeopardy. I need to rescue him, but it's too much for me to do alone."

"I am sorry, Drossie ... or Fritz," Vivienne said sincerely. "I really am. But if we help you, we could get removed, too."

"I know," Fritz said, "and it's wrong of me to ask you ... but—" His voice cracked. "My brother is all I have left."

"Where is he?" Marzi asked with trepidation.

"At the Czar's palace."

"The Czar's ... for the love of Watcher, Drossie. You can't go there!" Vivienne shrieked.

"You'll be killed," Gelé cut in.

"The wizards are sanctioned to kill you on sight as it is," Faruk said. "Walking in there would be suicide."

340

"Maybe not," Fritz replied. "I've been there before. I think I can sneak in there, find Franz, and get out."

"Then what do you need us for?" Gelé asked.

"There's a new wizard that's protecting the Czar," Fritz said. "He's known as the Black Wizard. He's an assassin and, I think, the one responsible for sending the enchanted animals to kill us."

Fritz looked at his friends eagerly. "If he shows up, I don't think I can fight him and all the guards. He's good but not better than all of us together. I need your help to distract him long enough for me to escape with my brother."

Vivienne raised her hand. "Are you absolutely positive this Black Wizard is responsible for the animal attacks?"

"As positive as I can be," said Fritz. "He fought me recently and used some of the same magic techniques as our animal attackers. It links him with a lot of the underhanded activity toward us."

"Toward us ... and The Order, right?" Vivienne pressed.

Fritz stammered. "Y–yes. I guess so."

"So if we attack him, it's revenge, right?" she asked.

"You could say that, yes," said Fritz.

Vivienne stood up and announced. "Technically, I'm not helping you. I'm seeking revenge on the Watcher-forsaken mole rat that hurt my sister."

Gelé shot up. "You mess with my friends, you mess with me. I'm in."

"I'm in." Marzi stood.

Andor waved his hand, signaling his intent to join.

Faruk stood up. "Let's do this."

"This is dangerous," Fritz warned. "I can't promise that any of you will make it out alive."

Marzi chortled. "Probably a better chance than training with our wizards."

The group chuckled.

Fritz held his hand out, and they all joined in the huddle. "Thank you all for helping me. Meet me here after school, and let's go fight some bad guys."

The apprentices dissolved the huddle and left the library for their next class.

Marzi stayed behind. "Drossie ... Fritz." She blushed and looked away. "I hope you can get your brother. I'm sorry you had to go through all of this just because some adults couldn't behave."

Fritz took her hands in his. "If I hadn't gone through this, I'd have never met you."

She blushed.

"I don't know if I will ever see you again after today," he confessed. "If this goes well, my brother and I will have to hide from The Order for the rest of our lives."

Marzi bit her lower lip and glanced up at him.

"No matter how today ends up, I want you to know that I love you with all my heart." Fritz leaned in, placed his hand against the back of her neck, and kissed her hard.

Marzi yielded to his embrace. She wrapped her arms around him and pulled him closer.

The two began to float in the air on a spell neither one cast. They stayed in each other's arms until the next bell rang.

After she left, Fritz walked over to the small mirror in the room and spoke into it. "Boroda!"

The mirror blinked and Boroda's face hovered. His hair appeared disheveled.

"Yes?" he asked. He sounded distracted.

"They're all in. We're going to the Czar's palace after school. I didn't tell them about The Order's involvement, like you said, so I guess the apprentices are clueless," Fritz told the floating image.

"Good," Boroda mumbled, obviously disinterested. "That's ... really good."

A slender hand snaked around his chin and pulled him out of the frame. There were some muttered voices, and then Boroda appeared again in the mirror.

"I will get you all the defense spells and enchantments ..." The hand appeared again. "Very soon," he said, his speech rushed. Then, the mirror blinked off.

Fritz snickered and lay down on the library couch to focus on storing energy in his charm.

Once satisfied with his charm's reserves, he traveled to the mansion and called to Boroda from the large foyer mirror. Boroda met him in the lobby, shirt still untucked.

Boroda filled the remaining space in Fritz's charm with the collection of defense spells he had been working on for General Andoyavich, plus a few extras—for good measure. Fritz double-checked a duplication spell under Boroda's guidance, and, once assured of its accuracy, traveled back to the library.

# CHAPTER 24

Fritz spent the remainder of the afternoon examining the complex symbols in the defense spell Boroda had given him. He made a copy of the spell. To the duplicate, he added an almost imperceptible change to the swirling runes. In less than an hour, this particular bundle of spells would be useless, leaving the wearer void of any protection.

This one was for the traitor.

The apprentices trickled into the room one after another. The air buzzed with energy.

"What's the plan, Drossie?" Faruk asked.

"I'm taking us to the Czar's office," he explained. "Unfortunately, it's the only place in his castle I've been. He should be at dinner soon. Hopefully, we can sneak in and out without being noticed."

"Before we go, though," he said and lifted his charm. "I have something for you."

Fritz drew out a collection of protective spells and held it in the palm of his hand. He tossed the glowing bundle to Faruk and pulled another from his medallion. Faruk studied the spells, whistled low, and packed the collection into his own charm.

Fritz pulled another bundle of spells out and cloned it. He floated a copy of the original spell to each of the apprentices. "Woah, Drossie. Where'd you learn that trick?" Vivian asked, packing it neatly into her charm.

Fritz addressed the group, leaving Vivian's question hanging. "I don't expect The Order to be there, but if they show up, this bundle of spells should hold off any attack long enough to escape. They'll probably figure out a work-around pretty fast. If it comes to a fight, counterattack as quickly as possible before they have a chance to adjust."

Marzi grimaced and shook her head as she tried stuffing the spells into her charm.

"It's too full," she announced. She pulled several spells from her charm, and the glowing lines dissolved into the air. She attached the spell bundle, and it dissolved into the metal.

The others followed suit, except for Andor, who tried using brute force to shove the bundle into his charm.

Gelé motioned to him. "You'll have to get rid of something."

With a look of immense sadness, Andor began unpacking his charm like a child forced to throw out toys. He tossed small spells into the air at the beginning but paused when he held a large, twisting swirl of runes. He hesitated and looked back at his charm reluctantly.

Marzi patted his arm. "It's ok, Andor. You can get rid of it. We can all learn sign language without it."

Gelé approached him and placed her delicate hand on his shoulder. Andor stared in wondrous disbelief at her gesture.

"I will learn sign language," she mouthed, "if you will teach me."

The red-haired giant released the spell like a bird from a cage and watched it sparkle and fizzle into the space up above. He packed Fritz's spells into his charm and signed "finished" to the group.

"Let's go," Fritz said and closed his eyes. A swirl of mist surrounded them and when it dissipated, they had arrived in the large, wooden chamber in the Czar's palace.

"We don't have much time," Fritz said. "The hallway is this way."

Faruk stopped him. "Just in case there's fighting, I think we should be in battle gear."

Faruk stepped away from them and spread out his arms. His school clothes began to warp and twist until he was left with a black leather jerkin, a black eye mask, and a curved scimitar. His medallion, a series of sharp boxes and angles, gleamed against the jerkin.

Gelé's school outfit transformed into a gleaming silver gown. Spires of ice jutted from the top of her head like a tiara of translucent stalagmites. She gripped the handle of a long, transparent sword. Resting against her skin, her pendant—a delicate swirl of silver—glistened blue in the reflection of her dress.

"Let's go already," Vivienne said. Her short, green dress hung in leafy patterns. Flowering vines that snaked together to hold her hair up also formed her umbrageous mask. A short dagger adorned one hip. On the other, she wore a small leather pouch. Her medallion looked like a wild tangle of circles and lines. Small gems punctuated the charm at random places.

Marzi wore a red fitted tunic studded with metal spikes. Two swords crisscrossed her back. Her charm—a jagged swirl of silver resembling a dragon—hung at her neck, secured by a black choker. "Andor and I will neutralize any guards that are outside."

She signed to Andor to follow her. His charm, a simple weave, flopped loosely from a leather strand over his leather vest. He pulled a large club from his belt and motioned for Marzi to lead the way.

"Where's your battle outfit?" Vivienne asked Fritz.

"I don't have one," he said.

"Of course you do. It's passed down from previous generations of apprentices," Faruk said. "It's in your charm."

Fritz fingered the small pendant at his neck. He closed his eyes and willed his battle gear on. He felt his clothes writhe on his body. His hand closed around a wooden staff.

He opened his eyes to inspect his new attire. His hooded coat hung mid-calf, the rich scarlet vest offset by gold ropes cinched, creating a tailored fit. The material stretched and twisted as if it were part of his skin. Fritz punched the air, testing the range of movement. He flexed and grinned at the cloak's response to his bicep.

"Are you ready to go or do you want to primp some more?" Marzi teased.

Fritz turned his attention to the group. "When we find the Czar, I'll grab him and find out where my brother is. You fight off the Black Wizard—if he shows up. When I'm safely away, you all travel to safety."

They agreed and started a careful path over the squeaky floor boards toward the door, but Fritz stopped them again with a harsh whisper. "And remember, the Black Wizard can follow you when you travel, so have a spell ready when you get to where you're going."

The apprentices quietly assured him they would and continued to creep toward the exit.

"Also …" Fritz whispered again, and the apprentices whirled to glare at him, annoyance clearly visible on their faces. "Be safe."

"Are you finished?" Vivienne asked. "Or do you have something else to say?"

Fritz cleared his throat and looked away from their stares. "No. I'm finished. We can go."

Marzi stepped outside the door.

Two guards were on duty, both leaning against the wall. When Marzi stepped into the hallway, they barely had time to register her presence.

She moved with fast, precise strikes. A single kick to the first guard dropped him to his knees, and a rigid hand to the throat paralyzed his vocal cords. She smashed his head against the wall with a hook kick, and he fell to the floor.

The second guard only squeaked the beginning of a yell before Andor's backhand sent him reeling across the hallway into the wall, cracking the plaster and leaving a large indentation.

The group moved down the hallway in ghostly silence. Fritz turned down a passageway, but it was a dead end. They returned the way they came and tried a different path.

"Sorry," Fritz whispered. "I've only ever been to the office."

Andor signed something, and Fritz brightened.

"Andor says he smells food in that direction."

The apprentices chuckled and followed Fritz quietly down the hall.

A servant stepped from a doorway in front of them and, when she saw them, gasped. She inhaled to scream, but Fritz reached out and shut off her airway. She clawed at her throat, trying to breathe, then slumped over. He released her windpipe and floated her gently to the floor.

Faruk motioned to a large set of double doors.

"This is it," Faruk said and lit up his sword.

"When we go in, I'll grab the Czar and travel out. If the Black Wizard shows up, you keep him busy until I have my brother. Got it?" Fritz reiterated the plan.

"Got it, Drossie," Vivienne said, annoyed.

"I'll sneak in and locate the Czar ..." Fritz began, when Faruk blasted the doors open.

The Czar sat at a table on the wall opposite the doors, and between him, at more modest tables, sat the elite guards and soldiers sworn to protect him with their lives. The room immediately fell quiet.

Paul Thompson

"Welcome, Drosselmeyer," the Czar said with a smug grin. "I feel like I'm saying that to you a lot these days."

"Was he expecting you?" Marzi tightened her grip on her sword.

"I expect you're looking for your brother," the Czar said with a chuckle. "He's fine. For now …"

Fritz shot out a blast of magic toward the head table. The magic stopped short and rebounded against a protection spell. The force of the blast knocked several guests over, but the Czar sat motionless—eyes locked on Fritz.

"Guards," the Czar called out. "Get them."

The guards erupted in shouts and charged the small group.

Andor swung at some oncoming guards, and two of them went hurtling back over the crowd like small bags of sand.

Gelé yelled and sent a circle of icy spikes that hemmed in a small group of soldiers. They stopped moving for fear of being pierced, and she wrapped them in ice up to their elbows.

Vivienne opened her pouch and threw seeds at three soldiers coming at her with swords drawn. Vines erupted from the seeds, twisting around their arms and feet. The soldiers thudded to the floor, kicking and flailing against the bonds. The vines latched onto the pillars and climbed toward the ceiling, yanking the unsuspecting soldiers into the air.

Faruk blocked a sword with his own blade and shot out a blast of magic. His attacker fell to the ground, unconscious.

Fritz charged toward the head table, dodging guards and yanking guns from hands, and throwing both the guns and the guards across the room.

The Czar sat motionless, a sneer plastered across his face.

"More guards are coming," Marzi shouted. "Viv. Shut the door."

Vivienne flipped over a charging guard and threw seeds at the door. Roots exploded from the pod and in seconds, a sapling sprouted and grew into a large tree directly in front of the door. She lifted her hands and a tight cluster of trees sprang up on either side of the massive tree, all the way to the edge of the room.

Gelé dodged a sword, twisted around another soldier, and iced his feet to the floor. She continued the arc of ice up his back, freezing his arms and sword in a striking pose. He looked confused and yelled for help. Gelé covered the lower portion of his mouth with a sheet of ice.

Gelé then backed four soldiers into a corner and raised her hands as a thick ring of ice surrounded them and shot up above their heads.

Despite a small cut on his arm from a landed blow, Andor continued to battle five men at once. The men hung from his feet and back, trying desperately to trip the large apprentice.

Andor twisted and launched one of the men on his back into the wall. He kicked the others from his feet and punched the floor, his fist encased in a flaming ball of magic. A shockwave tossed them into the air, and he grabbed them all in an invisible grasp and slammed them into the floor.

The blast knocked Fritz off balance, allowing his attacker to jab at him with a knife. It stuck in his side, and he grimaced.

Fritz broke the man's arm and headbutted the screaming soldier. He tossed the knife aside, healed his cut as best he could, and advanced to the table.

Only a few men remained. They gathered at the head table, ready to protect their Czar to the death.

Vivienne joined the apprentices as they lined up to face the shrinking force. She took out a single seed and tossed it on the floor.

The men yelped and a few swung their swords in random arcs.

Vivienne shook her head. "It's just a seed."

They eyed her and tightened their formation.

"I'm just kidding," she admitted and flared her fingers out. Vines shot out from the seed like cobras striking. They wrapped the small group of men in tight coils and squeezed until the writhing bodies went limp.

"Be on the lookout for the Black Wizard," Fritz whispered to the team.

The group circled up, backs to each other, spells at the ready.

"Where is my brother?" Fritz asked the Czar.

The Czar smirked. "Touch one hair on my body, and you'll never see him again."

Fritz returned the threat. "If I find one scratch on him, I will make sure the story of your death terrifies people for centuries."

The Czar leaned his head back and laughed. "Ooh, what a fantastic deal. How could I not take you up on that?"

He held up his hand. A silver bracelet hung loosely on his wrist. "Do you really think a little apprentice like yourself can challenge the Czar of the Central Kingdom and win? I've paid too much money to be left defenseless. Try your best." He chuckled, a low, rumbling sound full of conceit, and stood. "And for your impertinence …" He motioned to the wreckage and bodies. "I'm going to cut off one of your brother's hands right before I kill you."

"I believe Borya gave Ivanov a similar charm," Fritz said.

The Czar looked blankly at Fritz, unimpressed.

"I got to have a really good look at it after I killed him," Fritz said calmly but pointedly. "The problem with powerful people like you is that you never have enough. You keep taking what's not yours until little people like me have nothing left to lose."

Fritz's eyes began to turn a darker shade of green. The spinning glyphs around the Czar's body pulsed with a deep, powerful magic.

"Tyrants like you will continue to oppress the rest of us because you have an army to protect you from assault and The Order to ward off attacks from other wizards. But we, the *little apprentices* as you called us, have worth, dignity, agency, and humanity.

"You only fight for power. We fight for survival.

"And now, I understand a little bit more how this world works. Tyrants will always subjugate weaker people until someone stands up and says, 'No.'"

The enchantment on the Czar's bracelet appeared in a perfect replica above Fritz's hand. He reversed the protective spell, snapped his fingers, and the protection on the charm vanished.

The Czar, unaware of the now useless jewelry adorning his arm, snapped his fingers back. "And I suppose you think you're the one to stand up to the most powerful person in the ... "

Fritz lifted the Czar into the air, cutting him off mid-sentence. "Tell me where my brother is."

The Czar yelled out in fright and began to turn red and purple as the air was squeezed from his lungs.

"Conserve your strength, Drossie," Gelé warned.

"Where is my brother?!" Fritz yelled again and squeezed a bit more.

"In the dungeon!" The Czar coughed and a splatter of blood fell over his chin.

Fritz let him drop to the ground. "Vivienne, will you bind him?"

A vine twisted around his body, hoisted him off the floor, and lashed him to a chair.

"You have no idea the pain I will cause you," the Czar said through bloodstained teeth.

Vivienne flicked her hand, and tiny thorns sprouted from the vine. The Czar gasped and then cursed them with hisses.

"Breathe shallow breaths," Vivienne told him. "It will hurt less."

A cloud of smoke billowed from behind them, and Borya stepped into the room, followed by four members of The Order.

# CHAPTER 25

"Let him go!" Borya commanded.

The apprentices spun around. Five of the members of The Order stood in a single file line, weapons at the ready.

Fritz felt the hair on his neck rise.

The apprentices wilted and stepped closer together.

"Not until I get my brother," Fritz shouted back.

"Faruk!" Borya shouted at his apprentice. "Go home. Leave now, and I will say nothing of your actions here tonight."

Faruk lowered his sword, looked at the group, and shook his head. "Sorry, guys."

"It's ok, Faruk," Gelé said.

Faruk disappeared with a puff.

"Boroda will not be a member of The Order much longer," Borya announced for all to hear. He looked at Fritz. "He will soon be sentenced to death, as you are now."

The head wizard took a step forward, and The Order followed him, struggling to keep their shoulders slightly ahead of the wizard next to them. "Leave now, and I will rethink your punishment. Stay, and I will …"

"Did you know about the boys?" Fritz interrupted.

Borya halted.

"Is the rest of The Order going to stand by while you profit off of human trafficking?"

The wizards exchanged furtive glances.

"The Order does not answer to you or ..." Borya interjected but was cut off again.

"And do they know you've been keeping a secret wizard in your employ to kill for the Czar? That you've been plotting to take over everything—the Central Kingdom, the Southern, the Northern ... even The Order?"

Glacinda lowered her weapon slightly and looked at Borya accusingly.

Borya laughed defensively. "You have no proof." He raised his hand, sparked with a spell.

Fritz waved his hand, and the limp body of Ivanov appeared in front of The Order.

Everyone jumped back.

"Meet Ivanov," Fritz told him. "He was the Headmaster of my orphanage and a special guest at the Czar's soiree."

Fritz spoke loudly enough so the four wizards flanking Borya could hear. "I was in the office the night Borya and the Czar told the Black Wizard to kill Klazinsky. I also heard your plan to remove Boroda."

"Interesting story, Drosselmeyer, but this goes far deeper than you could ever imagine. I assure you, my relationship with the Czar is completely professional and does not violate the rules and regulations ... "

"Vivienne, will you release the Czar?" Fritz said over his shoulder.

Vivienne flicked her wrist and the vines uncurled.

"Borya, you treacherous goat, get me out of here!" the Czar screamed.

Borya offered nothing but a blank stare.

The Czar held out his hands to the old wizard. "Travel me away, now."

The wizard didn't budge. He squinted, calculating his next move.

"I did not pay you all that money to …"

Borya cut the Czar off with a flick of his hand, launching him backward, where he landed unconscious on the floor.

"The balance of power is sacrosanct with the mission of The Order," Fritz announced. "I am calling on The Order to detain Borya to be tried in the wizard's court for crimes subversive to The Order's sworn duty."

"Go home, Drosselmeyer," Hanja said dismissively. "Unless you crave death, go home."

"He's not going to give you the position," Fritz taunted. "He promised it to Glacinda, too." It was a gamble. Sylvia had attacked General Andoyavich for Borya and Hanja, and by Marzi's report, was already plotting Boroda's demise. No reason to think Glacinda wasn't involved as well.

Hanja shot Glacinda a heated glare.

"Is that true?" Sylvia shrieked. "Borya, is that true?"

Borya kept his gaze on Fritz.

"You promised to give ME the medallion!" Sylvia was livid.

"You're giving HER the medallion?" Hanja faced Borya, and her swords smoldered.

"Shut your mouth! All of you!" Borya roared and the room vibrated with the force of his shout.

"Drosselmeyer is obviously trying to play us against each other," Borya said to the other wizards. "And I would be willing to bet Boroda is behind all this."

"The deal was: Sylvia got the medallion and I got control of half the Central Kingdom," Eric growled through gritted teeth.

"But which medallion?" Fritz called to Eric. "When Borya sent that bear to your house, he may have had a different ending in mind."

Glacinda gasped and pointed at Borya. "A bear?! Did you attack me as well?"

"That's probably where Hanja was going to get her medallion," Fritz added, watching with growing satisfaction as The Order turned their angry glares on each other.

Glacinda snarled. "We all know what Hanja would do to climb the ladders."

Hanja swung the tip of her sword toward Glacinda.

Borya clenched his fist tighter, and the light in the room dimmed in response.

"I said, 'Enough.'" His voice rumbled low and vibrated the air around them.

"This is ridiculous." Glacinda swished her skirt. "Gelé," she called out. "Go home, now."

Gelé gripped her sword with both hands and tossed her head back. "No."

"Vivienne!" Sylvia's shrill tone cut in. "Be a good girl, and let's go."

Vivienne didn't budge.

Eric signed to Andor, "Go home."

Andor motioned back, "No. With my friends."

"Marzi!" Hanja's tone dripped with venom. "Leave them. We will deal with your actions later."

"Glacinda, is it true what Drosselmeyer said? About the boys? Did you know about that?" Gelé asked.

Glacinda sneered in disgust. "Of course not. I deal with matters of national importance. Not some trivial orphanage."

"They were boys, Hanja!" Marzi said. "They were young boys! Defenseless children!"

"I knew nothing about it." Hanja reached for Marzi's arm.

"But you do now," Marzi said and yanked her arm free.

"All of you do!" Fritz called out. "The Order is now responsible for this information. Remove Borya for his crimes and retain your honor or ignore it and seal your complicity."

"This has gone on long enough," Borya growled. He turned to the other wizards. "Is this what the mighty wizards of The Order have come to? Allowing your apprentices to stand there and defy you? Are you really this weak?"

"Don't tell us how to train our apprentices," Hanja spat at Borya.

"I call an emergency meeting of The Order," Glacinda's eyes were narrow and her tone sharp and bitter. "We will discuss your future in The Order."

"Who died and made you leader?" Sylvia screeched back.

Glacinda rolled her eyes and walked over to Gelé. "We're going home." She grabbed Gelé by the arm.

"No!" Vivienne's voice rang out, and Glacinda stopped, taken aback.

"I'm sorry?"

Vivienne breathed heavily through gritted teeth. "You will regret the day you ever touched my sister."

A vine shot from Vivienne's hand and hit Glacinda in the gut.

Glacinda grunted and sailed backward, her staff still standing upright next to Gelé.

"Vivienne!" Sylvia yelled in shock and horror. She waved her hand, and the vine vanished under a counterspell. She reared her hand to strike Vivienne but a spire of ice shot through her arm. Blood spurted from the wound, and she whimpered in surprise and pain.

Hanja reached out for Marzi, but Fritz jumped in front of her, grabbed Hanja with both arms, and traveled to the small café he and Boroda had visited in the Southern Kingdom. He struck the stunned and confused

Hanja with the heel of his palm and traveled back to the room as she reeled back over the counter.

As soon as Fritz appeared back into the room, Borya raised his staff and fired at him.

Fritz raised his hand, and the beam hit an invisible wall and dissolved.

Borya looked confused. "But you're an apprentice. You can't stop that spell."

"They can if they have the right counterspell," Boroda said as he appeared behind the stunned wizard.

Borya spun around, and Boroda punched him with a powerful uppercut. He flew up in the air and landed several feet away with a thud.

Boroda shouted, "I don't need to remind any of you that the Life Bond only applies to your own wizard!"

The apprentices regrouped, backs to each other in a small ring.

"So, is this it?" Gelé asked, out of breath. "Are we doing this? Are we fighting each other's wizards?"

Vivienne spoke first. "I will if you will."

"As will I," said Marzi.

Andor looked side to side, searching his friend's faces for an explanation.

Marzi signed to him, and he lowered into a fighting stance.

Glacinda struggled to her feet as a broken spire regrew on her icy crown.

Sylvia, wound freshly healed, joined her.

Eric lifted his hammer and signed to Andor, "Your death will not be honorable." Then he charged, yelling as he ran.

The other wizards joined him.

Marzi whipped knives at Eric, grabbing the endless supply from behind her back and flicking the blades with deadly speed.

Eric blocked knife after knife and kept charging.

At the same time, Sylvia ran at the group, vines snaking from her body, but slipped on a slick patch of newly formed ice. She tumbled forward, her plump body bouncing on the ground.

Glacinda sent an icy-tipped spear hurtling at Vivienne's head, but Gelé raised a second ice wall and stopped the lance midair. Vines sprouted and lashed at her as Vivienne choreographed their movements.

At the front of the room, Borya exchanged blows with Boroda. Each blow boomed and shook the room.

Unlike Borya, Boroda was in fighting shape. He easily dodged the blows and spells hurled at him and returned his own attack with a ferocious energy.

From the back, Marzi pointed her hand at a small chunk of ice. It flashed with a blinding light, spinning in Eric's direction.

He covered his eyes, and Marzi spun low and kicked at his legs, her foot glowing with a reinforcement spell.

Eric tripped but rolled out of the way and shot at Marzi.

She blocked the spell but the force still toppled her backward.

Fritz sliced into Eric with a fiery beam of heat.

Eric spun, hand clutching his side, and fired back at Fritz. The protection spell deflected the attack but wavered under the force of it.

Fritz sprouted a vine and wrapped it around Eric's feet.

The giant wizard sliced the vine with a swipe, and Fritz ducked closer and kicked.

Eric barely registered the attack and struck at Fritz.

Fritz blocked the blow with a spell. He felt sweat beads form on his brow. He had to conserve energy.

Hanja appeared and flew through the air at Marzi, her own two swords drawn.

Inches before she plunged her weapons into Marzi's chest, Andor appeared in a brown puff of smoke and Hanja's swords sank deep into the fleshy sides of his waist.

Hanja, unable to stop her trajectory, plowed full body into his chest. She looked at the large apprentice, stunned.

Andor ignored the weapons sticking from his sides and punched Hanja full in the face.

Hanja reeled back, tripped over a fallen soldier and hit the floor. Shaking, she rose, then fell to a knee, struggling to regain balance.

Marzi pulled the swords from Andor and began to heal his wounds.

Sylvia and Glacinda exchanged blows with Gelé and Vivienne. The two girls struggled to hold off the more experienced wizards.

Gelé screamed as an icy dart pierced her shoulder.

Andor raced to the side of the room and swung at Glacinda.

Glacinda raised a column of ice in front of him, but Andor's punch knocked through the pillar and a large chunk hit the petite wizard in the chest. She toppled backward with a croak.

Nearby, Borya missed Boroda's chest with a spell but clipped his arm.

Boroda snarled and blasted Borya backward with a counterattack.

The older wizard sprang up and charged Boroda, screaming with rage.

Boroda smiled. *A calm wizard always wins.* He raised his hand, and a column of rock shot from the floor, catching Borya under the chin, knocking him off his feet.

Boroda followed up with a volley of spells, and Borya frantically fended them off with ever-decreasing accuracy.

On the other side of the room, Sylvia lassoed Gelé with a vine, and tiny thorns sprouted from the stems into her shoulders and arms. Gelé struggled against the barbed trammel, but her screams of pain only made Sylvia cackle louder.

Fritz looked up from where he had rolled out of the way of Eric's hammer. "Marzi, take Eric!"

Both Marzi and Andor jumped in to face the enraged giant head-on.

Fritz reached out, sprouted a vine, and wrapped it around Sylvia's neck.

Sylvia ignored the vine, assuming her Life Bond would protect her.

Fritz tightened his grasp to constrict the vine, and Sylvia released her hold on Gelé.

Gelé fell to the floor in a squat and shot darts of ice into Sylvia's hands and feet, pinning her to the plant.

Glacinda glanced over at her impaled comrade, and Vivienne, bleeding from a gash in her cheek, shot a volley of thorns into her.

Glacinda shrieked as the darts injected their poison into her. She writhed in agony, a torrent of healing spells swirling around her.

Fritz turned back to help Marzi but Hanja stood right behind him, her hand already posed to strike.

Hanja hit Fritz on the cheek.

He fell back from the blow but rolled to a fighter's pose to meet her. He blocked her strikes, but they kept coming faster and faster.

She spun and kicked him.

He turned and caught it on the hip.

Hanja fumbled slightly, and Fritz took advantage.

Ignoring the pain, he stepped in close to Hanja and open-hand slapped her.

Hanja looked startled and struck at him.

Fritz dodged the strike and slapped her other cheek.

She tried to kick, but Fritz spun in and slapped her face twice.

Hanja pulled out two gleaming daggers and attempted to ram them into Fritz's chest.

Fritz spun his arms in a circle, deflecting both blades, and followed through with a headbutt.

Hanja's face was swollen from Andor's blow, and she dropped the daggers, reeling in pain. A vine wrapped around her waist from behind and yanked her back. Vivienne, flanked by Gelé, stood over her, holding the base of the plant in her hand. Hanja severed the vine with the swipe of a sword, but Gelé launched a chunk of ice, and it clipped the hilt of her weapon, flipping it out of her hand.

"Drossie!" Marzi yelled out.

Eric had her pinned against the wall with one hand. He raised his other hand and a large, serrated knife materialized. Eric yelled and plunged the knife downward.

Fritz yelled out in fright and anger and managed to erect a wall of ice just in time to catch Eric's knife.

The muscular wizard twisted his wrist and the ice surrounding it shattered. His other hand still held Marzi fast, but the ice wall had grown around it and weakened his grip.

Marzi squirmed with renewed intensity.

Andor raced to Marzi's rescue and punched Eric from behind, but the Life Bond responded with glowing shields.

Eric caught Andor in the solar plexus with his heel, and the apprentice doubled over. He dropped Marzi and raised his foot to stomp Andor.

Marzi jumped, both feet glowing, and struck Eric's back.

He lurched forward and tripped over the gasping Andor and fell to the floor.

Fritz shot a bolt of lightning at the prostrate wizard, and he arched in agony as the electricity burned his skin.

At the back of the room, Boroda continued to strike at Borya.

One of Borya's arms hung limply as blood leaked from his nose and mouth.

Borya tried to punch Boroda, but he was too slow. Boroda blocked the flaccid jab and elbowed him in the face.

Borya tottered backward, spent. He raised a simple dagger and ran at Boroda, voice raw from screaming.

Boroda lifted a stone tile and flicked it at Borya.

Borya blocked it but stumbled to all fours.

Without warning, Andor raced past Fritz with a yell, drew his leg up mid stride, and kicked Borya in the gut.

Borya sailed upward, slammed into a pillar, and fell to the floor. The old wizard twitched but made no effort to regain his footing.

Andor raised both fists, ready to smash the downed wizard, but Boroda stopped him. He motioned to the medallion and mouthed, "Do not kill."

Andor obeyed but still kicked the unconscious wizard with his heel.

By this time, Eric had risen and was locked in battle with Fritz.

Marzi joined him.

Eric blocked them but with increasing anxiety growing on his face. He returned his own spells, but the apprentices countered them with the complex spells stored in their charms.

At the front of the room, Hanja, who had cut herself free from the vine, kicked Gelé and sent her flying over a table.

Gelé didn't move.

Vivienne screamed and punched at Hanja.

Hanja slapped her fist away with ease and grabbed Vivienne by the throat. "You pathetic little flower," she said, sweat beading up on her forehead.

Vivienne choked and writhed in Hanja's grasp. Blood streamed from her nose, staining her mouth and teeth red. A seed fell, unseen, from her hand. She struggled to hold on to consciousness.

"Flowers always look weaker than they are," she choked in slow sputters. "That's what makes us strong."

Hanja laughed. "Well, then, you mighty flower, better luck in the afterlife."

Hanja drew back her own sword, the tip pointed at Vivienne's gut.

Vivienne looked over Hanja's shoulder, and a smile flickered over her lips.

Hanja whirled around, but it was too late. The Venus fly trap that had silently sprouted behind her snapped with wicked speed and engulfed her entire body.

Hanja cried out and lashed wildly with her sword. She flailed and thrashed, trying to escape, but the thick, viscous fluid inside the plant slowed her progress. Hanja began to shake and foam from her mouth as the digestive juices paralyzed her. She hung halfway out of the overgrown trap, eyes frozen open in terror.

Vivienne slumped to the floor, and Andor rushed to her side.

Eric caught Marzi with a left hook, and she hit a pillar and crumpled.

Fritz yelled out Marzi's name.

Eric laughed cruelly. "I got your girl, Drosselmeyer." He twirled his hammer in a taunting fashion and set off at a run toward Fritz.

Fritz saw blood trickle from Marzi's nose, and his eyes turned completely silver.

Fritz cast Boroda's time spell, and the activity in the room slowed to a crawl.

Fritz studied the protective shield of magic surrounding Eric. He traced the spells as quickly as he could. His charm ran out of energy, and he felt a pull on his own strength. He calmed his breathing and concentrated on the shield's magic.

Eric inched forward, his hammer beginning its slow descent.

Fritz calmly connected the spell fragments, reversed them, and cast it at Eric.

Time returned to normal speed.

Eric barreled forward, realizing an instant too late that his shield was down.

Fritz spun, and with a deafening roar, punched Eric with a white-hot fist of magic. Eric's body rocketed into the air.

Fritz reached up, his vision blurring from spent energy. He lashed a spell around him and smashed the giant's body into the floor.

The stones cracked and cratered around Eric. His arms twisted at odd angles, his open eyes glassed over, and his breath gurgled in short, painful spasms.

The room went quiet.

Fritz fell to the floor, trying to suck in as much air as he could.

Off to the side, Andor cradled Marzi in his arms. She groaned in pain.

In the front of the room, Gelé and Vivienne leaned against the same pillar, their hands weakly wrapped in an affectionate hold.

Boroda rushed to Fritz and checked him for injuries.

"He didn't show," Fritz said to Boroda and coughed. "The Black Wizard didn't show."

Boroda chuckled and began to wave his hands over Fritz's chest. "What is that saying about the best laid plans?"

Fritz struggled to stay upright. "I was hoping we could end this today. I really wanted you to get revenge for Perrin."

Boroda quieted him. "There's still time. Let's just enjoy this victory."

Fritz started to laugh but cut it short, wincing at the pain. He surveyed the wreckage and chaos around them. "Yeah, I really did great here, didn't I?"

"I suppose we could have done worse." Boroda began to heal several wounds on Fritz.

The Order was broken and unconscious. The apprentices were injured and spent, but alive. Soldiers still struggled against icy prisons and viney tethers. The Czar moaned in the distance and lolled his head around.

Boroda gripped Fritz by the shoulders and stared into his dark, green eyes. "Even if I never get revenge for Perrin, I am still proud to call you Drosselmeyer."

A glowing, blue blade poked through Boroda's chest. He stared at it for a moment and slumped forward.

Fritz screamed and caught him as he fell. Boroda's skin turned ashen, and his eyes glazed over.

"Don't worry, Drosselmeyer," the Black Wizard said, his billowing cloud of smoke still dissolving. He sheathed his sword and skipped back toward the head table. "I didn't kill him. I can't have you getting your medallion before me. He's paralyzed forever, but he's not dead."

# CHAPTER 26

"Take off your mask, Faruk," Fritz said through clenched teeth. "I know it's you."

The Black Wizard waved his hand, and the mask vanished. Faruk smiled at them, eyes wild with excitement.

The apprentices stared at their comrade in stunned silence.

Andor tried to jump up, but Faruk pinned him to the ground. Andor struggled against the spell, but his strength gave out. He lay panting on the floor.

Faruk sneered at Fritz. "How long have you known, Drossie?"

"I had a pretty good idea when you attacked me in the woods," Fritz said, staring at a new swirl of magic around Boroda, the paralysis caused by a spell he'd never seen before. No physical wounds, outside of the ones Borya had inflicted, were visible. Fritz cradled his master, ignoring the older wizard's gasps of pain. His long, black cape, now stained with blood, draped over Fritz's arms.

"Really? I'm impressed," Faruk scoffed. A rat appeared and scurried across his shoulder.

"The rats gave you away," Fritz said calmly. "At first, I assumed the rats were a calling card from Nicholaus but when you, as the Black Wizard, used them against me in the woods, well, that's when I realized how connected everything was ... the death of Perrin ... the animal attacks on The Order … the attempt at Minerva Mooncup's."

Marzi winced and moaned. Andor struggled to grab her hand, but Faruk tightened his grip.

Fritz stared at Faruk, willing his face to remain stolid. "I thought the animal attacks were Borya's doing, but when Marzi told me he and Hanja were allies, I realized the attack on her didn't make sense. It had to be another player with his own agenda."

The Czar stood up shakily and reached for Faruk. "Get me out of here."

Faruk opened his hand, and the Czar slammed heavily in a chair. Ropes slithered up his legs and twisted around his wrists and ankles.

"I'm sorry, my liege," Faruk giggled maniacally. "We still have some unfinished business."

"Was Borya responsible for Perrin?" Fritz asked.

Faruk sat down cross-legged on the table. "You really want to go back that far?" He rolled his eyes and swung his feet out in a crazed, childish kick. "Ok. I guess since you'll all be dead soon, it won't hurt.

"This all started years ago with Borya. I was a six-year-old boy when General Nicholaus approached the old goat and told him he wanted to be the Czar." Faruk twirled his finger at the tethered leader. "In exchange for an act of regicide, he would reward him with a lot of money. Of course, Borya didn't want to chance being found out, so, in true Borya fashion, he made me do it."

"You?!" Vivienne gasped. "You were just a kid."

"Yeah!" Faruk laughed. "A little kid that no one would suspect. But, I couldn't figure out how to do it. The death spell was way too complicated for a six-year-old, so Borya used mind control."

Faruk tilted his head to look at Fritz. "That first kill was a sloppy combination of magic and mind controlled combat that nearly killed me; but, what doesn't kill you ..." he trailed off. "Anyway." He snapped back to the present. "The new Czar Nicholaus was so impressed, he offered Borya a lot of money to use me for similar activities.

"Borya kept experimenting with mind control, except the spells weren't written that clearly, and they hurt when he tried them ... terrible, excruciating pain! Also, I wasn't lying about Borya being mean. He actually broke my collarbone—when I was six—for not memorizing complex spells." He burst out laughing.

"The mind control and the training hurt so badly that by eight, I was doing the killing on my own." He looked at the shocked reactions of the apprentices. "As a kid! I know, right? Messed up! But you know, after a while, killing kind of grows on you."

Gelé shook her head. "Faruk, I am so sorry. I had no idea."

"Well ... after Borya made me kill the old Czar, I felt so guilty, I tried to run away. Borya was always at the school in those days, so I ran into the woods and ended up near a little creek. That's where Perrin found me—his fellow apprentice—a little six-year-old boy, crying by the creek behind the fields.

"He saw my broken collarbone and healed me. I started crying and confessing and accidentally told him that I was being mind controlled to do bad things. I was terrified Borya would catch me, so I traveled back home."

Faruk stared off into space. "Perrin was very nice to me. But Borya saw my healed collarbone, broke it again to find out who healed it, and I spilled the beans about telling Perrin what I'd done to the Czar.

"The next time I saw Perrin in the garden, he began asking me questions about Borya's mind control. I didn't realize it at the time, but he'd seen me travel home from the creek on school property. That must have tipped him off about the old enchantments not working anymore. He also asked some of the older apprentices about the school magic while we were in the garden."

Faruk crossed his chest. "I promise, I was going to keep all of that a secret, but Borya could tell I was hiding something and … well … you all know Borya. He's not one to leave loose ends lying around. He convinced me to tell him everything. And so, he learned that Perrin knew about his wicked schemes."

Faruk scowled in the direction of his injured master and wrapped his arms around his knees, the memory still raw in his mind. "And after he broke several of my fingers, he followed Perrin to the woods one night and killed him."

Faruk swung his head in a long, exaggerated arc to where Boroda and Fritz sat, huddled on the floor. "Sorry about that, Boroda." He brightened suddenly. "Anyone want to kill Borya? I won't stop you, and nobody here would blame you."

"Why did Borya disable the school's enchantments?" Fritz asked.

"Beats me." Faruk shrugged. Then he burst out in erratic laughter. "Get it? Beats ... me? Because Borya beats ...?"

He cut the joke short and let out a long, contented sigh, then leaned back and tucked his knees under his chin. "I was a smart kid, though. I listened and paid attention. That's how I found out his plan to double cross the Czar and take the Central Kingdom for himself. He also had plans to kill everyone in The Order."

"Borya was going to destroy The Order?" Vivienne asked, confused.

"Not *destroy*," Faruk corrected. "*Kill*. He was obsessed with something called 'The Divine Convergence.' Oh Watcher, if I have to hear another drunken tirade about that ..." He giggled. "After he's dead, I guess I won't."

Faruk began rocking back and forth. "As I grew, I could no longer count on my status as a child to protect me, so I became the person you all call," he stood and bowed with a flourish of his wrist, "the Black Wizard."

Faruk looked around the room with a wild stare. "Because I wear all black and I am—wait for it ... a ... wizard!" He shook his head and rolled his eyes.

"So, this whole time, I was doing all the work. I did all the killing, plus I kept my grades up at school—and I got sick of it. I decided to turn Borya's plan against him and, who knows, maybe take command of the Central Kingdom for myself, or at least cause a little chaos and screw things up for Borya.

"When I learned about morphing blends, I just knew I was onto something, so I experimented ... a lot. I wasn't really sure what to do with it until I traveled in some clothes from storage, and there was a moth in my new clothing.

"Sound familiar?" He cackled. "That's how I got the idea to travel in morphed animals. I only needed the right timing to attack everyone and cause a little fight among family."

He sat back down on the table, grabbed a small piece of cheese from a nearby plate and popped it into his mouth. "And that brings us nearly to the present!"

Faruk clapped his hands. "I was just going along, murdering people occasionally, trying to keep Borya off my back, when I met our dear schoolmate, Prince Nicholaus, and the plan practically plopped into my lap."

The Czar struggled against his ropes. Faruk sauntered over to the bound regent and squeezed his cheeks.

"Nicholaus was too perfect! He was conceited, self-conscious, and dumb as a brick. So, I decided to learn mind control."

Faruk began listing off steps on his fingers. "I was going to foil Borya's plan by causing a war in The Order. I was going to put Nicholaus under a mind control spell. I was going to kill the current Czar—a beautiful irony, if you ask me—then that would leave me as the actual ruler of the Central Kingdom."

"You've been studying mind control all this time?" Marzi asked weakly.

"Since the eighth grade. It was a humble beginning—bugs and spiders—but I quickly graduated to mice and rats." The rat on his shoulder responded with a squeak and scurried down his arm. He held it in his hand and scratched the rodent's belly. "Rats are my favorite. They're opportunistic little scavengers."

He sat up and pointed at Fritz. "*You* were the wild card," he said at a volume so loud that everyone jumped. "When you knocked Nicholaus down at school, I knew you were on a different level.

"But when the Czar told me and Borya who you were and that you had a brother, I knew I had a winning strategy to end it all. I didn't know you were eavesdropping. That was rude."

"And what strategy was that?" Fritz asked flatly, but every last bit of his attention was focused on his hands. He traced the paralyzing spell from memory with movements so small they were barely noticeable. Only a few shapes left, and he could cast the counterspell.

Faruk smiled in fiendish glee. "Powerful people are so predictable, aren't they? I told Nicholaus that I was a wizard and wanted to help him take over the throne."

Faruk looked at the Czar again. "I swear, your son sold you out for the price of potatoes, basically. You really did a bang-up job raising him."

He turned to the apprentices again. "All he wanted, at first, was for me to humiliate Drossie. So I started with the rats at school and ended with the attack in the woods—just to prove my mettle, you understand.

"Nicholaus was impressed and agreed to let me 'serve him.' He got a little ahead of himself when his boys started getting handsy with my girls here, and that's when Andor beat them senseless." Faruk feigned a bow to the constrained giant.

Andor was still pinned to the ground and completely unaware of anything being said. He craned his neck to see Faruk's lips, but the spell held him too tightly.

"Nicholaus complained and wanted Andor humiliated, too. He threatened to call our arrangement off if I didn't come through. I figured Andor was only mentally two steps above a trout, so I mind controlled him—maybe you all remember?" Faruk twirled his finger, and a bright dress spun its way around Andor's body.

Andor stared at the dress, confused. He reignited his struggle, but Faruk tightened his grip, and Andor scratched the stone tiles, struggling for breath.

Faruk's eyes darkened. "In the meantime, Drossie, I was trying to figure out how powerful you were. Our first encounter in the garden made it obvious that you had no clue about magic, but you were too old to have recently snapped.

"I occasionally listened to your conversations through the mirror in the school library, and when I heard you tell Marzi you were going to Edward's house,

I got a little nervous. I followed you that night and saw you talking with Richard. Then, when you ran to the cave in the woods, the very cave where Borya had killed Perrin, I knew you were also very close to discovering the long-buried secret and potentially ruining my years of planning."

He tipped an imaginary hat to Fritz. "You won that fight fair and square."

"The rat was a mistake on my part—I see that now. But in the end, I learned a lot about you, too, so the fractured jaw was worth it." Faruk began to swing his legs again. "I was also impressed when you figured out the Minerva Mooncup connection. I had been visiting her for years, not as Faruk—but as the apprentice Finuala."

He winked at Fritz. "She's hot, right?"

Fritz could only shake his head. "You're insane."

"When I discovered the right morphing blend, Minerva wanted to sell it, but I threatened her with an excruciating death if she ever told anyone about it. A bit much, I know, but I was excited. Then, after you found her, and I heard you and Marzi planning a return trip, I had to kill her. She knew too much."

The rat, who had perched on his shoulder again, stood and shrieked.

"I have to say, Drosselmeyer, you do have the Watcher's luck about you. You survived my ape and my super rat invasion—I'd been breeding those guys for a long time—and you survived the attack at Minerva's the second time …"

He walked over to the Czar and kicked him with his toe. "Then this idiot gets all insecure, kidnaps your brother to control you and stop his generals from throwing a coup, and throws a party."

The Czar cried out, more from fear than pain.

"And when you crashed that party, Drossie …" Faruk whistled and punctuated his words. "You. Crashed. It. Hard. I've killed a lot of people and consider myself pretty good at it, but your artistry …" He thumped his chest with his fist in a show of admiration and respect.

He sighed a loud, long sigh. "Your insane infatuation with your family, though, nearly cost me power and a LOT of money."

Fritz laughed. "All of this for power and money? That's it?"

"You say that as if power and money aren't everything," Faruk said, hopping back up on the table and swinging his legs in uneven arcs. "I'm finished with being hurt, Drossie. I'm done being controlled by others. I'm tired of being treated like a rat—always serving at the whim of people with more wealth and power than me. I've carried this curse long enough, and I think it's time for the nobility to feel the agony of what I've had to endure."

He stopped swinging his legs. His visage hardened, and his eyes gleamed. "When I have all the medallions, I will make sure that every noble and his family feel my torment. I will be king, not of rats, but of the world, and all will writhe at my feet."

The rat on his shoulder squeaked on cue and scampered to the table.

Fritz shook his head. "How many people will you kill to accomplish your vision?"

"How many have you killed to accomplish yours?" Faruk shot back.

"I was protecting my brother," Fritz snapped.

"And I'm protecting myself." Faruk stood slowly to his feet. "I don't have a brother. I'm all I have."

"You had us." Fritz motioned to the nearly catatonic apprentices.

Faruk shook his head. "The Order poisoned us like they poison everything. We're expendable to them. They knew it, and we knew it. No sense getting close to someone who could be dead the next day for disobeying an order."

Fritz breathed deeply and kept his mouth shut.

"For a moment earlier today, I wondered if we could be a team …" Faruk's voice trailed off, and he stared into space. "But it was foolish to think so. We aren't family. We will never be family."

He paused, then a wide, wild grin spread across his face. "Speaking of family." He lifted the Czar from his chair and held him, suspended in the air. "Nicholaus sends his love, and before you get all mad about your son selling you out and letting me kill you, don't worry—I'm going to kill him, too."

The Czar struggled, eyes wide with terror.

"And that thing you have about boys ... ugh." Faruk shivered. "You deserve this." He slowly moved his hands apart.

The Czar shook violently, screaming like a mad man, as his skin ripped down the middle of his body and pulled away from his bones. Pieces of muscle and tendon clung to the fascia, and Faruk dropped the Czar's body into the pool of his own blood.

Gelé cried, and Vivienne held her.

Faruk turned to the apprentices and Boroda. "Now for you all. And don't worry, because you are my friends, I'll make your deaths quick, and then I'll kill your wizards ..."

He stared into the air like he was figuring an arithmetic problem. "And I think that means all the medallions are mine ..." He pondered then shrugged. "We'll see. First things first. Let's kill Borya."

Fritz jumped up and threw a beam of magic at Faruk.

Faruk blocked the attack as if he were batting away a fly, hit Fritz with a powerful wall of magic, and knocked him back into the pillar.

Fritz groaned, and his vision blurred. He tried to roll over, but Boroda tapped a finger.

"Not yet, Drosselmeyer. Wait," Boroda whispered, lips barely moving.

"Storing up your energy while I prattled on!" Faruk yelled. "Smart thinking, Drossie. This is why the other apprentices followed you into battle." He swept his hand, and Franz appeared in his arms.

Franz glanced around, frightened by the sudden change of setting, dropped the toy sword in his hand, and tried to pull away.

Faruk wrenched his arm and pressed the tip of a knife to the little boy's neck.

"The memory spells on this little boy are amazing." Faruk lowered his cheek next to Franz's, grinning at the boy's attempts to pull away. "A fighter, too, just like his brother."

"Tell me what you want, Faruk," Fritz begged. "Do what you want to me, but don't hurt him."

Faruk looked at Fritz, no mirth left. "Kill Borya."

Fritz stayed still.

Faruk pressed the knife tip right below Franz's ear. A small trickle of blood ran down his neck, and he began to cry.

"Ok!" Fritz yelled. "I'll do it!" He looked down at Boroda, who nodded once.

Fritz turned to look at the barely conscious wizard lying at the back of the room. He lifted the head of The Order from the floor. Borya cried out in agony as his broken body shifted. Fritz closed his eyes, thrust his arm at Borya, and a sword launched from a dead guard's hand. It punctured the wizard's chest.

Borya began to shake, his body pinned to a pillar, his feet dangling inches off the floor.

Staring at Fritz, Borya fought to take a final breath. "The Divine Convergence will destroy you all."

His head fell forward, and he died.

The medallion around Borya's neck began to glow. Beams of light shot out from the charm, and it vaporized.

The same beams reappeared around Faruk's neck. His back arched, pulled upward by an unseen force. The knife in his hand dropped to the floor.

As soon as the blade left his neck, Franz ran from the floating body and hid behind a pillar across from Fritz.

Andor sat up, free from his restraints, then froze when he saw Faruk bathed in light and wearing Borya's medallion.

Faruk opened his eyes and looked at his hands. He flexed them and looked at Fritz with an evil glint. "Well, Drosselmeyer, looks like I'll be king after all."

"King of the rats," Fritz spat.

He jumped out from behind the pillar, but Faruk was faster and more powerful now. Before Fritz had raised his hand, Faruk conjured a spell and lifted him from the floor.

Fritz hung in space, powerless to resist.

"Goodbye, old friend," Faruk whispered with a surprising air of authenticity. He reeled back and cast the spell formed in his hand.

Boroda sprang from the ground, shielding Fritz from the deathly blast. The spell hit him in the chest and knocked him back.

Fritz pulled him behind a pillar and hugged his mentor tightly. "Why did you do that?"

Boroda curled his hand around Fritz's neck and whispered a single word: "Time."

His heart stopped, and his body went completely limp.

"No!" Faruk yelled. "No. No. NO."

Marzi jumped from the floor and hurled a spell at Faruk.

Vivienne screamed, and vines shot from a handful of seeds she'd thrown, wrapping themselves around Faruk's body.

Streaks of ice laden with spikes raced down the vines at breathtaking speed as Gelé's screams joined her sister's.

The icy spires glowed white with deadly magic. Marzi poured every last ounce of fury into the shards.

Andor jumped from the floor several feet into the air. He raised his club above his head, ready to deliver a powerful blow.

Faruk blasted the entire group back with a single yell.

Gelé, Vivienne, and Marzi toppled to the floor, both from the blast and from exhaustion.

Knocked from the air by the shock wave, Andor crashed to the ground. He rolled to a stop as his dress tangled around his legs. Sweat and fresh blood poured from his wounds.

Fritz emerged from behind a column, Boroda's medallion blazing brightly around his neck.

He leaned over and whispered in Franz's ear, "Tell her we're ready."

Franz looked confused but agreed, then disappeared in a puff of smoke as Fritz traveled him away.

Far away, in Boroda's bedroom, Cora sat in a chair, staring at a fixed place on the wall ahead.

Franz appeared in a puff of smoke. He jerked his head around, ready to dodge whatever this new setting threw at him.

Cora sat up in surprise. She saw Franz's green eyes staring back at her in confusion.

"Are they ready?" Cora asked him.

Franz nodded.

Cora removed a cloth from her lap and held up the Celestine.

Faruk grabbed his sword, now flaming blue, and attacked Fritz. He swung, but Fritz sidestepped and counterpunched in the same move.

Faruk regained his footing and swung again.

Fritz blocked the sword with his staff, twirled it, and threw it from Faruk's grasp.

Faruk spun, and his sword suddenly shot from a cloud of smoke at Fritz.

Fritz spun sideways, but the sword sliced into his arm down to the bone. He backed behind a pillar, gasping with pain, and tried to concentrate on a healing spell.

Faruk raced toward Fritz, sword blazing and rats materializing behind him as he ran.

Marzi rose to her feet, her face wan from exertion. She sprinted unsteadily toward the fight. Faruk was about to round the pillar where Fritz was healing the gash in his arm. She leapt forward and stuck two knives in Faruk's back.

Faruk yelled out and pushed against her with a quick spell. Marzi landed on top of Andor and moaned.

Faruk tore the knives from his back and stretched both hands out toward the apprentices. "How about a taste of my childhood?"

He reached out and forcefully took hold of their minds.

They all shrieked in pain and writhed on the floor.

Fritz's hands shook as he tried to mend his arm but his concentration faltered. He could hear his friends screaming in agony. Faruk was, for the moment, distracted. Fritz tapped into his new medallion, and strength surged through his body.

Faruk dropped one arm and a long whip, glowing silver with heat, melted from his hand and coiled on the floor under him.

"Drosselmeyer, your friends need you," he taunted.

Fritz stopped his healing spell and, gut boiling with rage, stepped out to face Faruk.

Faruk lashed out with lightning speed, and the whip struck Fritz in the face. The vision in his right eye went blank. The smell of burning flesh filled his nostrils. Fluid from his punctured eye ran down his cheek. Another crack of the whip, and his back flared with pain. He flailed his hands, his staff stuck into a nearby column, and he clawed at his face, trying to regain sight.

The apprentices were stiff, frozen to the ground in Faruk's control.

"Come out and play, Drossie!" Faruk screeched.

He twisted one hand, and the apprentices all cried in renewed agony.

Fritz pushed the pain from his mind and calmed his breathing. Boroda's body lay nearby, face set in a placid smile. The final word was still frozen on his lips: "Time."

It was time.

Fritz rose and stepped out from behind the pillar. Blood ran from his eye, and the skin around the wound was charred black. He held his head high in willful defiance.

Faruk whooped and coiled the whip back for a final strike, but Fritz vanished in a silvery puff of smoke.

Faruk's whip cracked through empty air as he ran for the melting cloud, desperate to catch it before it disappeared completely.

Fritz landed in the library turret room and rolled to a stand. He turned toward where he'd just traveled, lifted his hands, and the Celestine appeared, still warm from Cora's lap.

The portal he'd traveled through re-opened. Fritz gathered the entirety of his magical reserves, raised the spell already in his mind, and whispered, "Time."

The cloud rolled to a stop.

Faruk—body suspended half in the library and half in the Czar's palace—pointed his snarling visage toward Fritz.

Fritz held up the Celestine and traced a shape on the surface of the globe: O.

It was Perrin's final message. The key to unlocking globe magic.

The Celestine pulsed, and Fritz threw it at Faruk. He canceled the time spell, and life snapped back to regular speed.

Faruk, whip in hand, tore through the portal directly in the path of the Celestine. The glass ball melted open, still a sphere but ready to accept whatever touched it next. It enveloped Faruk, pulling him into its interior.

The sneer on Faruk's face quickly turned to panic as he realized his loss of control. He whipped around and reached out to grab hold of something to stop his descent into the globe.

Books and furniture flew around the room in a wild cyclone as Faruk scrambled desperately for a handhold. He reached out and a roiling cloud of smoke opened into a ring. On the other side of the churning circle, the small group of apprentices lay motionless on the floor, still firmly under Faruk's control.

Faruk turned briefly to Fritz, his eyes flashing with pure hatred. He yanked the apprentices to him, then stopped fighting the Celestine's pull.

In a blur of color faster than a breath, Gelé, Vivienne, Andor, and Marzi were whisked through the portal and deep into the interior of the Celestine.

In the aftermath of the chaos, the room fell silent.

The "O" on the Celestine continued to burn until its lines fractured, leaving a dashed circle behind. Then it sealed shut and returned to the perfectly smooth globe it had been only a minute before.

Fritz's world went black, and he fell to the floor.

"Welcome, Drosselmeyer," a female voice said behind him.

He looked around, clutching the Celestine tightly in his arms. The library had faded away, and he was now hovering in a bright void. There was no sky or ground—just light.

A beautiful woman clothed in golden robes hovered near him. Her hair hung freely around her face, and her blue eyes sparkled against her dark brown skin.

"Where am I?" Fritz asked, his voice echoing in the bright abyss.

"You are in the realm between worlds," the lady answered.

"What does that mean?"

"It means you are now responsible for a world you've created. You belong to the Guild of Watchers," she explained.

"I need to get my friends out of this globe. Can you tell me how to do that?" Fritz held out the Celestine.

The woman frowned. "To do that is not an easy task."

"I will do anything." He searched her face. "Please. The girl I love is trapped inside."

The woman took the Celestine and looked into it. After a few moments, she handed it back to Fritz. "They will remain in there as they were out here until they are set free."

"Under Faruk's control?" Fritz asked, his voice tinged with anger.

The lady nodded.

"How do I set them free?" Fritz begged.

"One who is magic must enter the globe and kill the one who holds the others in his control. Then, those who have the will to choose may leave the globe with your permission."

Fritz traced an "O" on the Celestine, but the rune would not appear. The broken "O" that sealed the globe faded, leaving a blank surface on the Celestine.

"Tell me how to enter the globe," Fritz demanded. "I need to get in there *now*."

The lady let out a beautiful, musical laugh. "If you enter your own world, you will be trapped, and then no one can escape. You must send another."

"All I have to do is send another wizard into the Celestine to kill Faruk, and the others can come back?"

The woman bowed slightly. She breathed out, and sweet-scented air wafted past Fritz. "Goodbye, Drosselmeyer, High Wizard of The Order."

Fritz closed his eyes, breathed in deeply, and when he opened them, he was in the library.

Liquid from his eye oozed down his cheek as blood from the wound in his arm soaked through his uniform.

The couch where he and Marzi had spent so many hours together lay in a splintered heap against the wall.

Fritz traveled back to the mansion, collapsing on the floor of Boroda's room.

Franz sat huddled in the corner, staring wide-eyed at the new stranger.

Cora looked past Fritz, waiting for Boroda to appear. When she saw the medallion around his neck, she flung her arms around him and sobbed on his shoulder. Fritz buckled under the weight, and he felt the heaviness of the day press down on his chest. He held Cora as tightly as he could. The three of them remained in Boroda's room until the solitary clock on the wall chimed the top of the hour.

Fritz traveled in Boroda's body and laid him on the bed. He put his arm around Franz and led him out of the room. He would grieve his master's death later, but this was Cora's time to mourn her husband.

Under Boroda's memory spell, Franz could remember nothing of his life with Fritz, so this bloodied wizard before him was but a stranger. After helping Fritz wrap bandages around his head, Franz ran off the room and searched for a place to hide until his father, General Andoyavitch, could come to collect him. He felt no imminent threat in the mansion; still, he longed for his own mother's loving embrace.

Franz finally found a spare bedroom and curled up in a chair. He could hear Cora's muffled sobs echoing down the hallway. Her long, heartbroken wails made his skin prickle. He clutched his knees tightly to his chest, burying his head in the chair cushions to drown out the noise.

Fritz collapsed onto his bed. His body ached from wounds he was too weak to heal, his throat hoarse from crying.

His bandaged eye had been damaged beyond repair. He didn't know enough about the eye to heal it, and by the time he learned, not even magic had the ability to quicken dead, scarred flesh. He would have to wear a patch.

Perhaps tomorrow, if his strength allowed, he would check on the other wizards. His body ached with fatigue, and the mere thought of moving from his bed made his muscles tense.

He would also have to find and train an apprentice to fight Faruk. He took off his apprentice charm and held it in his hands. It was a toy compared to the medallions The Order wore—it was a toy compared to the medallion Faruk wore. Whoever fought him would have to be well-trained.

*A little girl with a dagger can kill a wizard if he's unprepared.*

Boroda's words gave him small comfort.

"Where am I going to find another wizard who can fight?" Fritz's voice quivered as the last bit of strength drained away. His body and spirit drifted into the healing embrace of sleep.

Doll, alert to his creator's voice, turned his head and answered, "I."

## THE END

# ACKNOWLEDGMENTS

A special thanks …

To Kevyn Robertson for teaching me about ballet during our many musical theater adventures together.

To Kathy Chamberlain for letting me play Drosselmeyer and ask all the questions.

To Katie Martin for translating my directions from ballet to musical theater.

To Al Gallo for being an awesome brother on stage.

To Toby Mattingly for playing my apprentice. You were a HUGE inspiration.

To Betty Lipscomb for watching my dog C.K. and so much more.

To Ashley Boyd for reading the first part of the book and then listening to me blather ad infinitum about the story.

To Benjamin Hannah for reading my manuscript and discussing time travel at length over chips and salsa.

To Sandra Nichols and *Snug on the Square* for keeping my coffee cup full.

To Darci Wantiez for introducing me to my editors.

To Lori Lynn and her editorial team (Mary Rembert, Clare Fernández, Ollie Cunningham, and Natalie Brandon): Without your editorial wizardry, my little book would never have made it.

To Shanda Trofe for your beautiful design choices. Without your guidance, this book would be printed in comic sans.

# BACKSTORY

In 2019, the Chamberlain School of Ballet in Plano, TX, asked me to dance (and later "move on cue" when they saw me "dance") in their Christmas production of *The Nutcracker* at the Eisemann Center. I played Uncle Drosselmeyer and, having never seen the ballet, had many questions about my character.

While preparing for the role, I searched for any clues as to why Drosselmeyer would send his niece, Clara, into another world to battle a rodent king. None of the instructors or bunheads had any clue, and when I asked the prima donna (NYC ballet) about it, all she told me was, "Get out. I'm changing."

Not to be dismayed, I decided to write my own backstory to *The Nutcracker*, and my hope is that for years to come, every actor/dancer who is tasked with playing the enigmatic character Drosselmeyer will have a new source from which to draw inspiration and motivation.

# ABOUT THE AUTHOR

Paul Thompson is an award-winning, internationally performed composer for theater and film. The youngest of five children, Paul often escaped familial hazing with a good hiding spot and a great book. After earning two black belts and getting his own apartment, he got involved in local and professional theater without fear of wedgies from his older siblings. Paul is the CEO of House of El Music and currently lives in McKinney, Texas, with his moderately well-behaved beagle, C.K.